Soul Shot Skirmisher

Soul Shot Skirmisher

Book 2: Dragons and Debauchery

Cullen Spurr

Published by Level Up in the United Kingdom in 2025

Cover illustration by Sippakorn Upama

ISBN: 978-1-83919-599-0

www.levelup.pub

Koda (2018-2025)

Writing these books won't feel the same without you batting my hands off the keyboard every five minutes for a stroke. You hit the level cap and ascended way too young. I miss you....

Panda Vision (Recapping The Story So Far)

"Hi everyone and welcome to Panda Vison! The only talk show where your host is both a Panda and a sage daemon.

"With me tonight is the hardheaded and overly jacked silver-ranked adventurer, Sally!" Panda said as he lounged back on his plush armchair.

The audience clapped vigorously as Panda gestured off to the side of the stage. Sally, a large catonid woman, walked on stage looking rather uncomfortable before taking a tenuous seat opposite Panda.

"So, Sally," he continued before she had time to say anything. "Fancy helping me recap Kaleb's journey for our lovely audience here?"

"Not really, and since when did you host a talk show…in fact, what is a talk show?" Sally replied in a confused and agitated manner. "Where the hell am I Furball?"

Sally pulled her oversized black sword from her inventory and glared menacingly at the live studio audience.

"Sorry folks, it looks like we're having technical difficulties with our guest here." Panda announced in a jerking tone as he dodged out of the way of a stray catonid fist. "In the meantime, please enjoy this short video recap."

1

Two large red curtains closed, blocking a fleeing Panda from view. A projector shone onto the curtain from somewhere and the following clip played, narrated by a familiar and soothing voice.

Previously on Soul Shot Skirmisher:

Kaleb woke up naked in a palm tree jungle. He wasn't expecting this, having fallen asleep in the cab of his truck the night before.

A system message explained that he had been isekai'd to another world called Celestia and that he had a new tattoo on his back which was part of a cosmic treasure map.

Kaleb adventured through the jungle killing stag monsters, cultists and getting a series of snarky and often passive aggressive system messages along the way.

After being captured by a group of cultists our hero managed to break free but in doing so, he accidentally killed an outworlder named Brad and adsorbed his map piece.

Soon after this he met a strange god named Chrysus who seemed to have a vested interest in getting Kaleb to work for him, but Kaleb is an atheist, so he declined much to the god's dismay.

Kaleb then summoned a demon, which actually turned out to be a daemon, named Panda and the two of them escaped the cultists and found their way to Havar.

In Havar, Kaleb joined the Adventure Society, met people of difference races, finally got some clothes, and embarked on a series of three quests which he had to complete in order to take the exam to become a fully-fledged adventurer.

The first quest had him team up with a muscle-bound catonid named Sally. The trio ventured to a little-known island and murdered their way into the Goblin King Coronation ceremony.

The self-proclaimed *charismatic* Panda convinced the goblins that he and his team were foreign goblins who had travelled there to take part in the tournament. Somehow the ruse worked and Sally managed to convince the goblins to allow her to take part in a battle royale.

She nearly won this battle but was defeated until Kaleb ruined the tournament and breached the safe zone rules by killing the other competitor. As you can imagine, this mightily pissed off the enraged crowd who chased Kaleb through the mountain whilst he fled with an unconscious, and very heavy, catonid on his back.

Kaleb fought valiantly at the literal edge of a cliff until Director Lucas swooped in at the last second, saving the trio and taking them back to Havar.

In his next quest Kaleb wandered the local sewers, killing all the slime who lived there including taking on a slime queen and just about surviving. In the process he was stuck with a weird communist torch which made other economic groups dislike him and he once again lost his clothes.

His meditation techniques were coming on nicely by this point as well, a little too nicely if you ask the system. Through meditation, Kaleb managed to forcibly increase his stamina and was warned that if he tried this again he would die. He learnt a lesson that even the youngest Celestians know: never piss off the system.

He was also invited to take part in a tournament to decide who would be Chrysus' next high priest, an offer he promptly declined.

Having raised enough money for his dream armour, by murdering slimes, Kaleb returned to an armourer who he had made a deal with and collected his prize.

Soon after he embarked on the last of his three quests which took him to another island where he met a dryad child in an abandoned village which seemed to have popped up out of nowhere. The dryad led him into a tower where a strange magic activated and he found himself in the middle of The Orcish Inquisition where he was forced to watch the young dryad and her mother be brutally murdered by a callous orc.

Seeing such a tragedy, and with his pregnant wife never far from his mind, Kaleb had a bit of a mental breakdown and unlocked a strange and powerful soul attack which he used to torture and tear apart the orcish aggressor.

In his mind, he couldn't distinguish between the dryad and his own family who were likely still back on Earth.

Director Lucas and another God named Diako were watching this incident and it seemed like Diako was happy with the development. This odd god has been pulling some kind of strings behind the scenes, probably, it wasn't always clear…but *something* was definitely going on there.

Upon returning to the Adventure Society, Kaleb was promptly told that his examination would start immediately and that is where we find ourselves at the beginning of this story. The beginning of the Adventure Society examination.

"There was also some stuff with a samurai in the desert and an assassin named Jack but that's really all we've got time for folks." Panda said sticking his head between a pair of closed red curtains. "I hope you enjoy the rest of the show!" He wailed before being promptly yanked back behind the curtains. Sally could be heard rampaging as Panda Vision faded out to the sound of vases being broken.

Chapter 1
It's Your Funeral

"The other participants are waiting in meeting room C," Lucy explained. "The exam won't start for twenty minutes, but please make sure you arrive early. It's down the hall." She smiled at me in her typical, friendly manner.

I attempted to return her smile but it came out as more of a grimace as I sighed and left the reception. Meeting room C was probably near the room where I'd first met Sally.

That felt like so long ago.

I couldn't believe I'd have to take the exam straight away. I'd only just gotten back from my last quest on the island where the fort had appeared. I hadn't even slept yet!

I needed sleep, a resupply of food, water, and more potions. I wasn't prepared at all.

Just focus on one thing at a time. I thought, remembering my mother's wise words from when I was a child.

When the world seems too much to handle. Just focus on one thing at a time.

So that's exactly what I did. I left the reception and crossed the foyer towards the hallway on the far side.

Panda jumped down from the reception desk to follow me.

"That was a bit sudden," he complained. "We didn't even have time to buy me some new reading material."

"Your books are probably the *least* important things we didn't have time to buy," I replied irritably.

We entered the corridor and a few doors down I saw the sign for meeting room C. It was one of those typical glass office rooms you'd see inside any modern office building back on Earth.

It had a floor-to-ceiling window with a glass door next to it. Through the window, I could make out a few people sitting around the oval table in the middle.

I took a breath and opened the door.

There were four people already there. They all turned to look at me with expectant gazes. That expectancy soon fell away though, as they realised I wasn't the examiner.

I awkwardly manoeuvred around the group and took the only available seat, next to a nervous-looking girl.

"Where am I gonna sit?" Panda complained loudly.

"Just sit on the table like you normally do," I replied.

He shrugged and began trying to climb onto the table. His short, furry legs kicked out behind him as he scrambled onto it.

The girl next to me giggled and put her hand to her mouth. She was a human with teal hair and a round, anime-like face. She was wearing a white robe that hung majestically down her slender body.

"Get that filthy familiar off the table." A slight, brunet man across the table from me scoffed indignantly. "Don't you have any manners?"

"Oh, I'm sorry, who the fuck are you exactly?" I replied irritably. He'd picked a bad time to speak to me like that. I was still reeling from my last quest, and I was stressed from the sudden realisation that I'd have to jump straight into the adventurer exam without a break.

In short, it was a bad time to fuck with me.

A vein seemed to pop out of the man's temple—if you could even call him a man, he looked young—as he stared back at me with venom in his eyes.

"I am Jake Millicent, heir to the Millicent line. You ought to be careful how you speak to me, peasant." He announced, spittle flying from his lips, and I noticed the two other men in the room shrink back slightly. One of them sighed and the other closed his eyes in the way a person does when they have a stress headache.

I, however, had no idea who this little prick was and I had no intention of backing down to some jumped-up pipsqueak who thought he was all that.

Also, did he just call me a peasant? I didn't know we were in an episode of Blackadder.

"Yeah, sorry mate but I've never heard of you. Though I'm pretty sure Millicent is a girl's name," I said, crossing my arms and leaning back in my chair with a scowl taking up permanent residence on my face.

Both Panda and the girl next to me laughed. Though she tried to hide it with her hand, whereas Panda very openly laughed and even pointed at Jake as he did so. It was pretty childish, but oddly satisfying to watch.

Jake's face began to turn a deep scarlet colour as he stared at me with uncomprehending eyes.

"You jest. There is no way that *any* adventurer in Havar hasn't heard of the Millicent family." He bit back, clenching his fists on the table and leaning forward. "I'll have you know that we are a proud adventuring family, we are nobility. If you apologise now I won't tell my father about this insult."

I turned to Panda with a confused expression.

"I thought Havar was socialist," I said quietly. "Nobles and socialism don't mix."

"I don't think *your* socialism is the same as *their* socialism," he said, obviously trying hard not to out me as an outworlder.

"Are you ignoring me?" Jake asked incredulously and I turned back towards him.

"Ok listen," I said, taking a breath. "Maybe I was a little rude, but I'm not having the best day. That being said, I'm not going to apologise to some wannabe noble whose first threat is to tell their daddy on me. I thought we were here for an adventurer exam, not a playground contest of *my dad's better than yours*," I replied, trying to calm myself with a deep breath that definitely came out as a sigh.

I wasn't in the wrong here. This dickweed had been rude to me first. But I still didn't want the aggro, especially when I didn't understand the politics of this world—even if this guy was an entitled douche.

"Your common is showing," Jake replied, lifting his chin up and quite literally looking down his nose at me. "You wouldn't be so quick to dismiss me if you knew who my father was."

I sighed and placed my hand to my temple. This guy was the absolute worst.

"My father this, my father that, is that all you can say? Talk about daddy issues. Maybe you should try fighting your own battles instead of relying on something as ridiculous as your family name. Just a suggestion," I said into my hand as I shook my head, a sharp pain stabbing me from behind my forehead.

"You underestimate me, peasant," Jake said, standing up suddenly and slamming his hands on the table. "I have no problem with fighting my own battles, I was just trying to be more diplomatic about this. I'd hoped you'd be intelligent enough to understand the disparity between nobility and commoners…I guess not."

He drew a longsword from his inventory and pointed it at me. A thin smirk appeared on his lips, condescension ruminating in his beady eyes.

I looked up at him and lifted a single eyebrow.

"Panda, what do the Adventure Society rules say about fighting among members?" I asked monotonously.

I was sick of this guy. I'd happily put him in his place, but I didn't want to lose my membership either. Also, I was a bit worried about the acidic nature of my powers.

I'd never fought someone who I probably could kill, without killing them. I didn't want to kill this guy; I wanted him to shut the hell up and back off.

"I think the rules state that duelling is ok," he said, scratching the back of his head absently.

"Your pet is right," Jake said, placing his foot on the table and leaning forward in an embarrassing pose. "Duels are allowed by the rules of the Society. Do you accept?"

I stood up and felt a smile begin to tug on my lips.

"It's your funeral," I said, summoning my bow.

Jake stared at me for a moment and then tipped his head back and laughed. The two other guys in the room joined in, laughing as well. One of them even slapped the table. It was all a little over the top in my opinion.

"You're an archer?" He said, struggling to breathe through his intense laughter. "All that tough guy talk…and you're only an archer?" He laughed, lowering his sword as his face contorted.

His two friends laughed along with him. The girl who was sat next to me, on the other hand, didn't show any sign of emotion at all.

It was a little creepy. Something about her bothered me, but at least she wasn't joining in with the three stooges.

"Hey kid, do me a favour and shoot this little prick, in his little prick," Panda said, pulling out his bamboo pipe and lighting it up.

I was almost certain that this was a no-smoking area, but it didn't matter right now. I nocked an arrow and began charging my *Soul Shot*.

"Um…Kaleb. Isn't that overkill?" Panda said, immediately changing his tone as he recognised what I was doing.

I ignored him. I knew what I was doing. Besides, I only charged it a *little* bit.

Jake looked up at me, his laughter stopping abruptly. His eyes focused and locked onto me like pinpricks as his sword began to glow.

"Call it, Reggie," he said, not taking his eyes off me.

The guy who had been laughing so hard he'd slapped the table looked up, still giggling slightly.

He was a thick-set, stout man with closely cropped hair and a small scar on his lip. He stood up and lifted a single arm in the air.

"Ok," he began in a soothingly baritone voice. "When I drop my arm, the duel begins. A winner will be decided when one of you either can't fight anymore or surrenders."

I nodded, still keeping my gaze firmly rooted on Jake. I would end this farcical duel in a second. The little prick would never challenge me again.

I mean, who looks at a panda climbing onto a table and gets annoyed? Absolute sociopaths, that's who.

Jake nodded too, still staring at me as his sword began to glow brighter. It reminded me of the attack Sally had used in her fight during the goblin king coronation quest.

Though it was a far cry from anything as powerful as she could do. She was a silver-ranked catonid bodybuilder. Whereas Jake was a skinny rich kid with an inferiority complex.

"That's a big sword," I said slowly. "You trying to compensate?"

The vein on his forehead grew larger, I was worried it might pop and spray rich-kid goop all over me. His face turned a deeper shade of scarlet and he gritted his teeth.

"Reggie, start the damned match already." He snarled as his sword shone even brighter. "I need to put this peasant in his place."

Reggie nodded at us both and threw his arm down.

Jake charged forward, screaming for some reason, and I released my arrow. It soared across the room, impacting him in an instant.

The arrow tore through his sword hand and smashed through the glass wall at the back of the room. The glass shattered and everyone jumped in unison.

It seemed that they had all underestimated me.

Jake's sword fell to the table with a loud clank. The glow he'd put into it vanished instantly and it went back to its former, dull appearance.

He looked down at his hand in shock. His face went pale as he registered what had happened.

His hand was lying on the table near his sword and pumps of blood shot out of his bubbling wrist like they were on a timer dictated by his heartbeat.

"My hand…" He whimpered, looking between his wrist and his severed hand in disbelief. "What happened to my hand?"

Everyone in the room looked at me as I dismissed my bow and sat back down in the chair like nothing had happened.

Reggie and the other guy stared at me with open mouths and even the girl next to me looked shocked.

The door burst open and something that looked like a *WWE* wrestler in a cat cosplay burst into the room.

"What the fuck is going on in here!" She snarled, slamming the tip of her oversized, black blade into the floor, and slicing the carpet.

7

"Hi, Sally!" Panda said, waving with his free hand as smoke curled and twisted in the air around him.

Sally ignored him, marching further into the room. The two guys and the girl next to me all shrank back into their seats as, what I could only assume was, her magic pressure forced them down.

I couldn't sense it, having no mana myself, but I could tell that was what was happening. She was a force to be reckoned with at the best of times, but especially when she was mad.

She looked at the shattered glass and then at Jake who was still whimpering and looking between his severed hand and his bleeding wrist.

Then her dark blue eyes landed on me and I felt a tingle in my soul. It was only slight, but I could feel it. Was this what mana sense did? Was Sally trying to exert her ferocious mana pressure on *me*?

My *Usurper* skill prevented people from being able to force me into submission with their monarch-based soul manipulation skills. I wasn't sure if what Sally was doing counted as that, but either way it wasn't going to work on me.

"Kaleb, explain," she said.

"He challenged me to a duel so I *disarmed* him," I replied, struggling to keep in the laughter as the rest of the room stared at me with horrified expressions.

Chapter 2
Panda-napped

"Disarmed him?" Sally said slowly. "Well you didn't do a very good job, did you? He only lost his hand."

"That was a bit of an *off-hand* jibe," I replied, struggling not to laugh.

Sally looked at me with a stern expression as Jake continued whimpering as his wrist bled and bubbled.

"Stop whining, you're supposed to be an adventurer!" She snapped at him.

She picked up her oversized sword and channelled mana into it until it glowed, much like Jake's had before our duel. Except Sally's sword glowed like an inferno, I could feel the heat radiate as it threatened to give me sunburn.

She grabbed his arm roughly and pressed his severed wrist to the blade. He screamed bloody murder as it sizzled and the smell of burnt flesh filled the room. It was repulsive.

"Wow," Panda remarked as we watched. "That sword really comes in *handy*."

She turned to him with a stiff look. Her gaze was terrifying. She was obviously quite upset with our conduct so far.

"Stop!" She growled. "I can't handle these awful puns anymore."

I couldn't hold it in anymore, so many puns. It was too much. The floodgates opened and I burst into laughter. Panda seemed to feel the same way as he held his stomach, laughing with the kind of grimace that only came from the extreme abdominal contractions caused by a giggling fit.

The kind that wasn't funny anymore but you couldn't stop. The kind that physically hurt as your stomach muscles tensed up over and over.

The rest of the room looked at us in abject horror as we giggled like schoolchildren. All the while, Jake sobbed in the corner, nursing his sizzling, cauterised wound.

The pain must have been excruciating. I noticed that his wound wasn't bubbling anymore though so Sally's *first aid* must have stopped my acid from working as well.

Sally ignored us and picked up Jake's hand. She passed it to him without so much as a hint of being affected by the act of holding a severed hand.

"Take this. If you get to a healer fast enough they'll be able to reattach it." She sighed and rubbed her temple with her free hand. "If not, you'll have to wait a few days for the system to grow it back."

Wait, the system grows back limbs? I thought, furrowing my brow. Of course that made sense. I'd taken some nasty hits over the last few months since I'd arrived in Celestia.

I'd taken damage that would have easily killed a normal person back on Earth. Hell, I'd even had an arrow shot through my jugular.

If the system could heal that with potions, meditation, or sleep, then it could probably heal anything short of death. Still, though, the idea of a person's hand growing back was a weird one.

I wonder if it works like it did in Deadpool where it grows back as a baby hand first? I thought, feeling the tug of a smile on my lips at the imagery.

Jake took the hand with his uninjured one and nudged his sword, bringing it back into his inventory. He nursed his severed wrist against his chest, looking truly pitiful.

"What about the exam?" he said slowly as if he was torn between fixing his injury and becoming a full adventurer.

"You'll have to take the next one," Sally said sharply, and he looked at her with wide, glossy eyes.

His expression hardened after a moment and he glared at me. The vein in his forehead reappeared and his eyes shot venomous daggers at me as he clenched his teeth.

"You'll regret this…" He stopped, likely realising he didn't know my name.

"It's Kaleb," I said.

"You'll regret this Kaleb," he continued as if his threat wasn't significantly blunted by his blunder. "My father will be hearing about this."

"Yes, I'm sure he'll be furious that his noble son started a duel with a commoner and lost," I replied, an edge of snickering in my tone. "It must bring great shame to the great Milicent family to lose to a simple peasant like me."

He locked eyes with me for a moment and then left the room in a huff. He didn't say anything else.

Contact (Sally) would like to chat with you.
Do you accept?
Y/N

I jumped slightly in my seat as the sudden notification appeared on my HUD. It'd been so long since I'd accepted Sally onto my contacts list, that I'd completely forgotten I had one.

Right back when we first set off for the goblin king coronation quest she'd shaken my hand, adding herself to my contacts.

She did it to share the quest with me, but she was still my only contact. I'd never actually used the chat feature before.

I mentally asserted yes.

Sally: Gonads, I don't know how that happened but I can't be seen giving you favour. Stop getting into fucking duels!

Kaleb: Sorry Sally. He was asking for it though, and he challenged me, not the other way around.

Sally: He's a noble. They're like that. My advice is to try and ignore them, they can be a real pain to deal with.

Contact (Sally) has ended the chat.

Using the chat feature was intuitive. I just thought out a message, which transferred in writing onto my HUD, and then I mentally asserted that I wanted to send it.

I felt a little sour as I read Sally's messages though. This duel wasn't my fault. The last one…well I *was* under the influence of berry-infused smoke that made me act like a frat guy.

This time though, it was definitely the other guy's fault. I wasn't sure what to make of her advice about trying to ignore nobles. I mean, I didn't want anything to do with them if they were all going to be like Jake Milicent.

Still, though, I wasn't just going to sit back and take shit from someone just because of their title. The local culture might say otherwise, but I'm from Yorkshire and we don't take shit from anyone. Let alone those who can't back up their words.

After Jake left the room, Sally took his seat and sat at the head of the table. She sighed loudly and rubbed her temples with her hands. As she creased her arms to do this, her steroid-test biceps flexed menacingly and the three other examinees shrank back even further into their chairs.

I couldn't feel it myself, but I guessed she released some of her mana again – or aura, or whatever it was they called it.

"Right," she said slowly before looking up at us. "My name is Sally. I'm a silver-ranked adventurer and I've been tasked with overseeing this examination…Unfortunately," she finished, shooting me a look which I smiled at.

She took a few moments to compose herself and then leaned back in her chair, placing her feet on the table. She plucked a cigar out of her inventory and lit it with the tip of her oversized, black sword.

Then, she took a deep drag, tipped her head back, and let out a sweet-smelling puff of thick smoke.

I hope she's not taking that smoke back. You're just supposed to hold cigar smoke in your mouth. Taking it back is a one-way ticket to lung cancer city. I thought as I watched her inhale the black cloud.

Panda joined Sally in lighting up, once again puffing on his bamboo pipe. He sat cross-legged to the side of me, on the table.

I noticed my sleeve twitch and I turned towards the girl who was sitting next to me. Her cheeks were slightly red as her hand tugged gently on the sleeve of my armour.

"Hey," she said quickly, in a whisper. "Can I stroke your panda?"

I looked at her for a moment in disbelief. I wasn't exactly sure what I was expecting her to say but it definitely wasn't that.

I felt myself blink a few times as I looked at her big anime eyes. I couldn't say no to a face like that.

"Yeah, go ahead," I whispered back.

Her round face lit up as sparkles danced in her eyes and a cute, but kinda evil, smile formed on her lips.

Without warning, she reached out from behind and grabbed Panda under his arms like a plushie toy. She pulled him into her chest and began squeezing him like he was a teddy bear.

"Oh wow, he's so warm and fluffy," she gasped.

"What the…" Panda said as he was suddenly yanked from the table and into the clutches of a stranger. "Kaleb help! I'm being Panda-napped." He squealed, looking at me with a panicked expression as he struggled to comprehend what was happening.

"Pandas are an endangered species, manhandling me is a crime!" He yelled at Bell, who simply hugged him tighter, childish delight shining in her big eyes.

"Panda shut the fuck up," Sally said, lifting her foot and slamming it back down onto the table. "Jeez, I'm a god damned adventurer, not a babysitter. Lucas is gonna pay for this gig." She muttered to herself before taking another drag.

Reggie and the other guy looked awkwardly between us and Sally. I could tell that they didn't have a clue what was going on.

Panda stopped shouting but he did continue to look at me with pleading eyes as the girl nuzzled him like a plushie. I fought the urge to laugh and instead returned a barely contained smile.

"Alright class, listen up," Sally said, seeming to have gathered her thoughts finally. "In a minute we're going to leave the city to take on an exam quest as a group. The Director has given you a doozy of an exam quest. I don't think I've ever seen one quite like this before."

She chuckled to herself as her eyes glazed slightly. I was sure she was reading a quest notification as she spoke.

"I'll have to add you all to my contacts to share the details." She sighed, removing her legs from the table, and leaning forward.

She stretched both of her hands out towards the two guys closest to her who tentatively shook with her. She grinned as she squeezed their hands and both experienced simultaneous pain; it was obvious by the mirrored grimaces on their faces.

Poor guys. I thought, *she did that to me too on my first quest.*

Then, she stood up and skirted the table, moving towards the girl next to me. The girl was so immersed in her toy panda that she barely noticed Sally until she was practically on top of her.

"If you hug him any tighter he might explode," Sally said as she reached the girl.

The girl looked up at her and her eyes widened, if that was possible, as she stared at the towering, hulking catonid before her.

She relaxed her grip on Panda slightly and took Sally's outstretched hand.

"What's your name, kid?" Sally asked with suspicious politeness.

"It's Bell, ma'am," she replied awkwardly.

"Well, Bell. I'm glad you like animals," Sally replied with an evil glint in her eyes. "Because if you wanna pass this exam, you're gonna have to kill one. We're going dragon hunting."

Chapter 3
How To Slay Your Dragon

The whole room was silent as we all turned to face the grinning lunatic who stood next to Bell.

She looked around at us with a ferocious determination in her eyes and a giddy smile on her face. Her silver, cat ears wiggled slightly and I could see her suppressing her tail which obviously wanted to wag.

"A dragon?" I said finally, in disbelief.

She focused on me and brushed her shining, silver hair out of her eyes. They glinted with the depths of the dark blue ocean. It was quite off-putting.

"See for yourselves," she said cheerily.

Contact (Sally) wants to share a quest with you.
Do you accept?
Y/N

New Quest!
How To Slay Your Dragon

There have been reports of a dragon nesting at the top of the big mountain in the middle of the island. The Havar local government have tasked the Adventure Society to handle the issue.

Remember when you first got here? I told you there would be dragons.

Objectives:
Find the dragon's lair 0/1
Kill the dragon 0/1

Reward: X1 *item upgrade token, adventurer rank-up*

***Speak to the Adventure Society to claim your reward.
Reward payable upon the successful completion of the
above objectives****

Well, shit. I thought as I read through the quest. Thinking, back, the system had mentioned dragons when I first arrived on the island.

I distinctly remembered it saying as much in the opening announcement. It was the same announcement that mentioned the map tattoos and hunters—though I hadn't seen any of those yet unless the cultists counted.

More importantly, I was now convinced that the system added different parts to notifications for different people. There was no way it would reference something as personal to me as *first arriving here,* in a quest that multiple people were given.

I felt like that information was somehow important, though I didn't know why. I'd already discovered that the system had a personality, even if it was a shitty one, during my sewer quest.

It had gotten upset that I'd burnt *Stalin's Stylish Socks* when I used them to create a torch to explore the boss room.

Everything about the system seemed weird to me. Though nobody else seemed to think so. It must have just been because I was an outsider. How could a natural phenomenon that had never existed on earth, not feel weird to an outworlder like me?

"Miss Sally," Reggie spoke up, looking up at Sally with fearful eyes. "I don't mean to question your methods, but why is a group of temp adventurers being sent to kill a dragon? That sounds like something I'd expect someone like…well, like you, to be asked to do."

He had a point.

I didn't know how powerful dragons were in Celestia, but if they were anything like the creatures of legend back home then we'd need to send a team of powerhouses to kill it.

Yet, instead, the Adventure Society was sending a bunch of phase two rookies. It didn't add up. There was no way this could be as simple as the oversights and lack of information that Director Lucas had mentioned to me before.

This felt like some sort of test.

It is a test you bellend. It's the adventurer exam. My thoughts chided. I was right, this was an exam. Though dragon hunting still felt a little extreme.

"Adventure Society intelligence believes the dragon will be around the level 50 mark," Sally answered, still grinning wildly. "So, it will probably be a phase three, but a weak one. That fact is the reason why I'm to accompany you.

"We'll be taking on monsters as we work our way there so I can score you on teamwork, solo work, and tactical prowess. Once we get to the dragon's lair we'll do some scouting and you can devise a strategy. In other words, if you fuck up, I'll be there to help."

The whole room sighed with relief at that last part, myself included. I'd seen Sally fight before and her power was no joke. If she was watching our backs and the dragon really was only a level 50, we'd be relatively safe.

"Don't sigh like that!" she continued, looking around the room with an admonishing gaze. "Adventuring is *never* safe. I'm not some kind of safety blanket for you bunch of sorry fucks. I fully expect you to kill the thing yourselves and I won't be jumping in unless you seriously mess up. For the record, that means someone will probably die before I save your asses. So you'd better not need saving in the first place."

The collective mood in the room dampened again. No one wanted to be the guy who died so Sally would rescue the rest.

I wasn't certain about facing a level 50 dragon solo, but I was at level 34 now so I was confident I could pull my weight in a team of phase two adventurers—hopefully.

I absently pulled up my stat sheet for a moment. I hadn't checked my progress properly since before my last quest.

Status Sheet:

Name: Kaleb Akabane
Race: Outworlder
Class: Apex Predator (unique)
Adventurer Rank: Temp
Level: 34
Map Pieces 2/10,000
HP: 386/336 (386)
Stamina: 348/317 (348)

Strength: 289 (317)
Agility: 124 (142)
Perception: 120
Vitality: 256 (306)
Intelligence: 56

Personal Skills: *Speak English Damnit!, Eat Anything, Minor Poison Resistance, Usurper (unique), Health Sense (common)*

Class Skills (Passive): *Newly Qualified Bowman (0.3%), Dagger (lvl 10), Novice Apex Skirmisher, Acid Dhampir Dagger, Acid Arrows, Environmental Hazzard*
Active Skills: *Perception of the Apex Predator (rare), Soul Shot (ancient)*
Blessing: *Blessing of Wealth*
Familiars: *Panda (Daemon)*
Titles: Audacious Soul Expander
Admission: Pentagram [Right hand (Morningstar Hotel and Spa)]

Ah, is there any better feeling than numbers going up? I wondered as I looked through my stats. My HP and stamina were looking pretty good. However, it made me wonder how much Sally had invested into those stats at level 91.

I wondered if they were over 1000. That would be damn impressive. A person would be practically unkillable with 1000 HP.

Maybe at that point, I'd be strong enough to protect my wife and child if I found a way to bring them into this world.

When I'd first arrived in Celestia, my wife had been pregnant. Nearly two months had passed since I'd arrived. It stood to reason that she'd given birth by now…and I'd missed it.

My heart hurt as I thought about them. It was hard to deal with that when I knew nothing about how to reunite with them again. For all I knew they thought I was dead, or worse…that I ran away.

I'd never do that. I grew up without a father and I'd be damned if I did that to my own child. No fucking way. For now, the only thing I could do was focus on gaining power and increasing my stats.

I needed to be strong enough to protect them…of course, I also needed power to get them here. If the system could do it then so could I…hopefully…maybe.

Gaining power. That was my goal. The only thing that mattered to me in this world. So, I guess, in order to meet that goal, I was about to go out and slay me a dragon.

"Right," Sally said, slamming her fist on the table in front of Panda, Bell, and me. "Enough gawking. Let's get going. This dragon ain't gonna kill itself."

Reggie and the other guy sitting at the bottom of the table gawked at her bravado. Neither of them looked particularly happy as they got up from the table and followed Sally out of the room with slumped shoulders.

"Hey, toots. You gonna let me down yet or what?" Panda said, scrabbling to get out of Bell's tight grasp.

"Oh," she replied as if he'd woken her from a daze. "Sorry Mr Panda, you're just so fluffy. I could hug you…" She leaned in closer and whispered in his ear, "*Forever.*"

Who was this girl? Something about her put me on edge, yet at the same time she had such a disarming personality. She seemed pretty young, though it was hard to tell in this world.

She wore long, white robes, so it stood to reason that she was probably a healer. At least, that was the impression I got. Someone who loves pandas and seemed so…innocent, was probably a healer.

I'd complained a lot about my lack of mana since I'd arrived here, but honestly, I couldn't think of anything worse than being a healer. It definitely wasn't for me.

Healers needed teams. Healers couldn't fight.If I was a healer, I had no doubt I'd have died already. Probably on the first day.

Though I guess non-outworlders wouldn't have that problem. She'd probably completed her three quests with the help of a team. Either that, or she'd taken fetch quests and saving cats from tree quests.

I hoped she wasn't going to be a liability on this dragon-slaying quest. Having someone to patch up my wounds would be useful, but probably not as useful as having an OP wizard shooting fireballs or something.

After all, in Celestia, it wasn't that hard to heal. You just had to survive the encounter.

"Come on," I said, scooting around the edge of the table. "Let's go."

Bell let go of Panda and he scurried away from her like a frightened bunny rabbit. She looked a little sad as she watched him go, but quickly stood up and followed us out of the room.

I lifted Panda over the glass from the window I'd shattered. I wouldn't want him to cut his paws or anything. Then the three of us trotted after Sally and the others.

We caught them in the foyer and Sally glanced back at us with that typical battle junkie look in her eyes. I'd seen it plenty of times before on my last quest with her.

"So, Gonads, I heard you soloed a slime queen not long after we parted. That's impressive for a noob," she said, patting me on the shoulder so hard I thought I was going to sink into the floor.

"Yeah, it ate all my hair in the process though," I replied meekly, trying not to show the pain in my shoulder. Her *light* pat had lost me two HP. She was too strong for her own good.

"Is that why you're wearing that creepy hood?" she replied. "I figured you fancied yourself an edge lord or something."

"It's just part of my armour. I honestly forgot I had it up," I said, taking it off with my hand.

Sally looked at me a moment and stopped dead in her tracks. The others stopped as well and turned to look at her.

She stared at me for a moment and then burst out laughing. She had a strong, bellowing laugh as she tilted backwards and wiped a tear from her eye.

"Holy shit Gonads, you do not suit short hair at all." She laughed, struggling for breath. "Why is your head shaped like that?"

"Shaped like what!?" I replied, hurriedly feeling my skull. It felt perfectly normal to me.

"It is shaped a little weirdly," Bell said from beside me and I looked at her with shocked eyes. "It's not a bad thing though. It suits you," she hurriedly added.

Like that was going to help. She may as well have said: *Oh yeah Kaleb, you're an ugly bastard, but it suits you.* Yeah thanks so much for that Bell, it's nice of you to say.

This was Sally's fault. I turned back to her with a death glare which was apparently the wrong way to handle the situation because she laughed even harder.

I could feel my cheeks go red, there was only one solution.

I activated my armour's full set bonus and turned invisible. I could only do it once a day, and it didn't last very long because the length was determined by my intelligence stat.

However, it was worth it. As I used the valuable second or so that it gave me to storm out the door.

"Hey, where did Gonads go?" I heard Sally say from behind me.

23

Chapter 4
It's Always Sunny in Havar

I walked out of the door with a smug expression on my face as my invisibility faded. I didn't get much time out of it, but I learned something valuable.

If I could fool Sally, even if only momentarily, then even as pathetically weak as the ability was right now. It could still be useful. I may have wasted it for the day, but it was worth it.

Less than a moment later she spotted me and led the rest of the examinees in my direction.

"When did you get a stealth skill, Gonads?" she asked as she fell in step with me and led us towards...wherever we were going.

"It's part of my armour's abilities," I replied. "It's not very useful yet though."

"If you ever make it to the continent you'll find armour that's better than even my skills," she said quietly. "It's fierce over there though, much more dangerous than in Havar. And I don't just mean 'cause the monsters are stronger."

The continent. I'd heard people talk about it before. Supposedly it was a higher-tier place filled with high-level monsters and adventurers to match.

Director Lucas' father lived there, or so he'd said. I wondered what kind of man he was. Lucas once told me that he'd been exiled from his family. A man powerful enough to do that to a gold-rank adventurer must be a sight to behold.

Sally led us towards the interior gate, past *Taylor's Tailor,* the first store I'd ever entered in the city. I hadn't been inland since I'd arrived in Havar.

Every quest I'd been on was either on a smaller island off the coast or under the city itself. Outside of the cultist compound and the area of palm tree jungle, I'd arrived in, I didn't know anything about the island itself.

I didn't even know its name.

Apparently, there were other towns and villages dotted about somewhere, but Havar was the only city. I wondered what they were like.

Havar had a high population of lycanids, catonids and humans, with small minority groups of other races dotted around. I wondered if that was the same for the rest of the island. I wondered what other races even existed in this world.

As we crossed the bridge leading out of Havar, I caught the back of a huge, armoured lycanid. He turned as we approached and moved aside as he caught Sally's visage.

"Your transport is waiting for you up ahead Miss Sally," he said curtly in a husky growl.

She nodded her thanks and we continued onwards. Panda was waddling close to me, idly smoking his bamboo pipe as we went.

He was going to be so pissed if we had to spend a long time in the transport. He didn't have any books to read and worse, he'd be in close proximity to Bell who would no doubt pester him.

We rounded a corner near the bridge and Sally halted the group in front of our transport. It was an open-backed truck in olive green with a symbol on the hood.

The symbol was made up of the letters A and S where the S hung from the middle, horizontal bar of the A. It was obviously an Adventure Society symbol, but not one I'd seen before.

"Right, pile in crew," Sally said as she stood on the step which led into the cab of the truck. "I'm driving and we have quite a bit of distance to cover. Don't worry though, I'm sure there will be chances for you to…*stretch your legs.*" She finished with evil undertones as she winked at me.

Reggie and the other guy climbed aboard first, though they looked disheartened. I think they were friends with that Milicent guy who'd started a fight with me.

They probably weren't too happy about having to work with a guy they'd openly laughed at not long ago. Especially when that same guy shot their friend's hand off.

A strong part of me wanted to do my own thing and let them fend for themselves but Sally had already said that she was grading us on teamwork so I'd have to let that childish notion go.

I needed to pass this exam.

Bell climbed up into the back of the truck and I lifted Panda into the truck bed behind her. The truck's rear had curved metal beams which decorated the back. On the back of the cab itself was a retracted, material canopy which looked like it could be pulled over the beams if needed.

It was nice to know we had rain protection, though so far the weather in this place had always been sunny.

"It's always sunny in Havar," I mumbled to myself as I climbed in. It reminded me of a TV show I used to watch with my wife on an evening after work.

I took my seat on the uncomfortable wooden bench, leaving my right leg to loll off the back of the truck. It reminded me of a WW2 troop transport and also looked eerily similar to the one I'd stolen to escape the cultist compound.

I wondered if all the land vehicles in Havar were just old versions of our own, with magic fuel sources. On the sea they had pirate ships and yachts alike, so maybe somewhere someone had a *Ferrari*.

That'd certainly be something, a magic *Ferrari*.

The truck trundled into life, as I imagined Sally slipping on the mana-sucking armband that powered these things, and we set off.

The truck bounced uncomfortably down the main road out of Havar and we passed by the barn that Panda and I had stayed the night in on our way there.

I wondered if the little girl who was living in the farmhouse was doing ok. However, that thought didn't last long as I realised we were heading straight towards the palm tree jungle and I groaned internally.

"Stupid steroid test cat," Panda muttered under his breath.

I looked towards him, I'd been looking ponderously out at the road and had almost forgotten I wasn't alone.

"What's wrong mate," I asked, pulling my leg inside the truck, and turning towards him.

"I don't have any new books to read," he said exasperatedly. "I'm a sage and I need my books to increase my sagely wisdom."

"You're a sage?" Bell asked, looking towards him in wonder.

Panda ignored her and looked away, folding his stubby little arms. He usually loved female attention, maybe it was the squeezing that had soured him towards her.

"He's a daemon," I answered in his stead.

"Isn't that just old-timey speak for demon?" she asked.

"That's what I said when I summoned him!"

"Mistakes like that are exactly why you should be grateful that you did summon me, kid." Panda huffed, still refusing to look at Bell, or even acknowledge her existence by the looks of it.

I ignored him and continued talking to the girl.

"Bell, that's your name right?" I asked, I knew it was because I'd been sitting next to her when she introduced herself to Sally, but it seemed like an easy way to keep the conversation going.

"Yup, but my enemies call me *The Destroyer*," she replied with a slight smile. "And if I heard Sally right, your name's Gonads right? I've got to say, that's a pretty weird name. I don't know what it means here but it's definitely not a person's name where I come from."

Panda chuckled and began to turn towards Bell before catching himself and quickly turning back around. He quite literally had his back to her as he stared out of the rear of the truck.

"No…" I replied with a sigh. "That's just what Sally calls me. My name is Kaleb."

"You shouldn't lie about your name Gonads," Panda said loudly.

I shot him a look but he was still facing away from Bell so I doubt he saw me.

"You're not from around here then?" I asked Bell, brushing past Panda's comment.

"No, I'm from…somewhere pretty far away," she said wistfully. "I really like it here though, it's a lot more exciting than where I come from."

"I'm not from Havar either," I replied.

The truck hit something and I bounced painfully on the bench. I looked around, annoyed, and realised we were fully submersed in the palm tree jungle now. The shade was a welcome touch but the bumpy ride got even worse.

I made a quick mental apology to my ass, then looked back towards Bell.

Her teal-coloured hair was wafting in the breeze. I couldn't believe that people who looked like anime characters existed in this world. Funny coloured hair, a round face and large eyes. They were the hallmark of anime girls.

Just as I had that thought the truck rolled to a halt.

That was fast. I thought. We'd barely been driving for twenty minutes.

"Everybody out," Sally announced, pulling herself out of the window and banging on the roof of the truck cab.

We all complied, piling out of the truck, and moving around the front to join her.

"I told you we'd be stretching our legs frequently," she said menacingly as she gestured towards a large...*thing* that was blocking the road. "Let's do some solo battles to start with. Bell, you're up."

I looked at the thing that was blocking the road and I couldn't make heads or tails of it. It was a large, grey ball. It looked like a boulder, apart from that its body moved up and down ever so slightly.

That was it, there were no eyes, teeth, legs, arms, nothing. I focused on it and the notification popped up.

You have discovered a new monster:
Dhur

The *Dhur* is a type of earth elemental, common to dry, arid climates. It's just a big magic rock, there's not much more to say really.
They're quite tough to kill but they don't usually attack unprovoked.

In fact, I'd say you'd have to be quite bold to attack this boulder. Though I guess after your run-in with the *Slime Queen* you're already bald enough. Ah, wordplay. How I have missed you.

"You can do better than that," I said, raising my head to the sky with a smirk on my face.

"Who are you talking to?" Sally asked with a furrowed brow.

I looked down to see the other examinees staring at me like I was tapped in the head. I felt my cheeks redden as I hastily muttered: "No one."

It definitely came across as a little sheepish as Bell smiled at me and then walked towards the dhur.

"Wait Bell, you're a healer, aren't you? Isn't it dangerous to take that thing on alone?" I called after her worriedly.

She looked back at me with a confused expression and opened her mouth but Sally muted her with a raised palm.

"Shut it Gonads, just sit back and watch," she said with a knowing smile.

She nodded to Bell who shrugged and continued walking towards the large, grey boulder monster. It was at least three times her height.

Sally obviously knew something that I didn't, but I had no idea what that something was.

Bell strolled up to the thing calmly without drawing a weapon.

Is she a DnD monk? I wondered. *There's no way she's gonna pull some karate shit and chop the thing in two with her hands is there?* However, as I thought about it, I realised how awesome that would be.

I just couldn't see it though. She was a cute, anime-looking girl in a white robe. If that didn't scream healer, I didn't know what else did.

She walked a little closer until she was about twenty feet or so away from it, then looked back towards the group.

"You might wanna move back," she said in her sweet, innocent tone.

Then something changed.

Her face contorted into an evil grin and her eyes deadened. Suddenly that sweet little girl was nowhere to be seen. In her place was a woman with the face of a psychopath.

I knew that look. Sally had it too. There was no mistaking it.

Bell…was a battle junkie.

"It's fireball time, motherfucker!" she yelled.

Chapter 5
It's Acid, It Melts Things

I watched in awe as Bell approached the rock and her cute, innocent face contorted into that of a psychotic battle junkie.

She raised her hand towards the dhur and grinned maliciously as she shouted: "Fireball!"

A magnificent ball of red and orange flame burst from her hand and shot into the dhur's body. I didn't even know that massive rocks *could* catch fire, but apparently they can.

The fireball spell kicked off some insane heat. It felt like I was standing next to an inferno. The heat was so hot it was painful to stand near it and I wasn't even that close.

It must have been agonising for the poor dhur she threw it at.

The flames sputtered and licked at the palm trees surrounding the dhur. I watched, frozen to my spot as the closest trees burst into flame.

Within seconds those flames began to spread and Reggie jumped backwards in panic. He was a stumpy, but well-built, dude. Not the type you'd expect to have a weak constitution. Though I guess they say never judge a book by its cover for a reason.

He was right to panic though. In this arid climate, a forest fire could be deadly.

Whilst the trees continued to burn, the dhur's fire went out and it began rolling slowly towards Bell. She grinned and fired three more fireballs in quick succession.

They did nothing.

The fireballs bounced off the living boulder as it spun towards her. It was like watching a Zamboni trying to crush a person. It moved so damn slowly.

Bell stood firm though, firing even more useless fireballs at the thing. She cackled like a witch as she went. I couldn't see her eyes from where I was stood but I imagined them glowing with psychotic joy.

"Hey, Bell!" I shouted, unable to stand and watch any longer. "Try a water spell, rocks are weak to water...I think."

She halted her barrage of fireballs and turned back to me for a moment. Her evil, battle junkie face had switched back to one of innocence in an instant.

"I don't know any water spells," she called sweetly.

"Ok...what spells do you know?" I shouted back.

"Fireball."

I stared at her and the world seemed to stop as I blinked a few times, dumbfounded.

"You *only* know fireball?" I said slowly.

"Yeah, why would I need anything else? Fireball is awesome." She smiled sweetly and then turned back around and fired off a few more ineffective fireballs at the dhur.

The dhur kept rolling towards her. Honestly, it was probably the least dangerous thing in the immediate vicinity.

The palm trees were much worse.

The fire was spreading, jumping from tree to tree like a monkey swinging through a cluster of...well...trees. The clearing was a blazing inferno and it felt like my skin might melt off my body at any moment.

I looked to Sally for some sort of guidance. However, she watched Bell silently with her arms folded. She obviously had no intention of helping.

Stupid steroid-test cat. I thought, doing my best Panda impression in my mind.

"Fuck this. I'm going in there," I said, angrily barging past Reggie and his friend as they watched the inferno with slack jaws.

A fat lot of use these two clowns are. I thought scathingly.

I walked into the clearing with clenched fists and summoned my bow. I half expected Sally to stop me but she just stood there, leaning against the truck with folded arms and a flat expression.

I lifted my bow, nocked an arrow, and channelled *Soul Shot* the skill was quickly becoming my go-to move. *Soul Shot* allowed me to channel the energy of my soul into a single arrow, boosting its power dramatically.

Soul Shot (ancient)

Due to a complete lack of mana, you've realised the potential of the soul earlier than most. You have gained a deeper understanding of the soul through meditation. As demonstrated already, you have unlocked the potential to infuse the power of your soul into certain attacks.
Who'd have ever thought meditation would be so useful? Next, you'll be unlocking a skill for virtue-signalling monsters to death.

The amount of power used is directly proportional to the amount of stamina you've chosen to assign to the shot.

I charged the shot and my arrow was enveloped in an acid-green glow. It wasn't lost on me that my soul's colour was reflective of my class's main skill.

I felt my arm ache as the power reached its climax and I fired the arrow into the side of the boulder.

The arrow created a backblast of force as it exited my bow, almost blowing me off my feet and forcing a startled Bell to dodge to the side.

It embedded itself into the boulder in an instant and as it continued its slow roll towards us, it suddenly stopped.

The arrow that had gotten lodged in it was acting as a block to the sphere's rolling ability. Or at least it did for about 0.3 seconds before the arrow shaft broke and the dhur continued onwards.

Well, shit.

On the upside, the tiny hole where the arrow had pierced was glowing a sickly green colour and small veins were growing from it.

Acid *should* affect pretty much anything. I mean it's acid. It melts things. Why should a big living rock be any different right?

I fired off another arrow, without using *Soul Shot* this time and it chipped the dhur slightly. A minuscule green tinge was left as the arrow dropped to the ground.

Perfect! That means I just need to keep firing until the acid melts it.

"Hey!" Bell shouted from beside me. "Get your own rock monster! This one is mine."

She almost sounded pouty, like a child whose parents refused to buy them a new toy. I stared back incredulously.

"I don't think you *can* kill this thing on your own," I said back after a long second of staring at her in disbelief. "It's a fucking rock and you shoot fire. Not exactly a match made in heaven."

She scoffed at me, looking slightly offended and then fired off another barrage of fireballs at the dhur which was still slowly advancing towards us.

I shrugged and charged another arrow with *Soul Shot*. I fired it to the same effect as the last one. The boulder was starting to chip slightly, which I took as a good sign. I had to take a few steps backwards though as it had finally gotten close enough to us to potentially do something.

As I slowly retreated, I continued firing a mixture of normal arrows and *Soul Shot* arrows until my stamina was practically depleted. Then I swigged a quick stamina potion and fired some more.

Then the dhur stopped. Bell and I ceased fire and watched it carefully. Was it over? Had we won?

No, no, definitely not that. I thought as the large boulder started to glow.

An earthy, yet ethereal, glow enveloped its body as the ground started to shake. I tensed up as a supreme amount of pressure started emanating from its cold, rock body.

A grating sound came from its spherical shape and bits of rock began to separate. Two, piercing brown eyes opened in the middle. They looked between Bell, who had sparks in her hands, and me, who had a bow. Those eyes did not look happy.

The grating sound continued and a large mouth appeared in the area where I'd fired my first arrow. It stretched the full width of the dhur, its teeth were all molars, perfect for grinding up prey like us.

It opened its mouth and began a rhythmic chomping which sounded like rocks smashing together, and then it continued its pursuit.

I fired an arrow into its mouth and it chomped straight through it, it wasn't slowed in the slightest. It was a rocky *Pacman* that had just eaten a power pellet, and we were blue ghosts.

"Kill it!" Bell shouted, sparking flames into her hands like *The Human Torch*. "Kill it with fire!"

She began blasting fireballs again to no effect. They did seem to buffer it slightly though as it continued rolling towards us, chomping every time its new mouth completed a revolution.

I continued firing arrows at it, aiming for its eyes when I could. It was a weird evolutionary trait: having a face but moving by rolling. I almost felt bad for Rock *Pacman* as it slowly moved towards us.

Eventually, we retreated back to the truck and the dhur was beginning to chip quite badly, but it still didn't stop its advance. More worryingly, thanks to *Smokey The Bear* and her fireballs, we were surrounded by an out-of-control forest fire.

I heard a scream and looked behind me to see a blazing loconut falling from a tree. It hit the floor and smashed open as blood and guts spilt out into the clearing.

The smell was vile.

Burning organs are not good for the nose, let me tell you.

We needed to put the fires out, but I had no way of doing it myself. As I kept firing, I had a brain wave and shouted behind me to Reggie and his friend whose name I hadn't learned yet.

"Oi, Reggie!" I shouted. "Do either of you two know any water magic?"

"I don't," Reggie replied in his deep, romance audiobook narrator voice. "But Jamie does."

I had to assume that Jamie was the other guy and not some rando Reggie knew back in Havar. Surely even he wasn't that stupid.

"Yeah, I know a little bit, not much though." A timid voice said from behind me.

"That's better than nothing. Try to put the tree fires out and maybe blast some water at this fucking rock will ya?" I shouted back.

I shouldn't have to tell these bozos to help out. They're supposed to be adventurers, aren't they? I thought scathingly as I fired off another shot.

Bell continued firing an excessive number of fireballs at the dhur. Honestly. Her mana count must have been insane.

Her face scared me as she fought. She had a huge ear-to-ear grin but it didn't reach her eyes. They burned with a sadistic joy. It was unnerving, but not as unnerving as her rendition of *Disco Inferno* which she sang enthusiastically as she fired.

I fired another arrow into the dhur which was looking bad now. Its outer layer was cracking badly. It was starting to look like the potholes on the street by my house – which is to say, it was starting to look like the potholes on *every* street across all of England.

Our country had a shit tonne of potholes.

I charged a miniature *Soul Shot* for my last arrow, aiming carefully for its eyes for the hundredth time that fight. I hadn't managed to hit it yet since it kept rolling, but I was sure that the eyes were the weak spot.

My stamina was whittled down to almost nothing and I wouldn't be able to fire another shot. I barely managed to put extra power into the shot as I fired. At the same time, Bell shot another fireball.

They both hit at pretty much the same time and through some combined force, luck or just the slow trundle of whittling down an enemy's health, the dhur cracked in two and fell apart.

"Thank god for that," I sighed, leaning back slightly, and dismissing my bow.

I couldn't have fired another shot. My stamina was all but depleted. I felt tired all of a sudden but I turned to Bell anyway.

"Who *only* learns fireball?" I asked incredulously, placing my hands on my hips.

"Why would I need anything else?" she asked innocently, raising a finger to just below her lips. All signs of the battle junkie psycho had completely vanished.

"Oh, I don't know…because fire doesn't solve all problems?" I exclaimed. "Did you never play *Pokémon* growing up? Even kids learn that fire beats grass, grass beats water and water beats fire. It's super fucking basic."

Of course, we were fighting a rock monster, but Charizard would have a hard time against Graveler in the game.

"Of course I did!" She said back in a slightly raised, but somehow still sweet, voice. "I chose *Charmander* and I made it so strong it could beat all the others, regardless of their type. Why would I raise a team of six mediocre *Pokémon* when I could raise *one* super strong one."

I opened my mouth to argue back but then my brain ticked over for a moment and I stared at her open-mouthed.

She looked like she wanted to continue as well, but then she did the same thing and I shit you not, we both pointed at each other, at exactly the same time, with open mouths.

We were one person shy of that *Spider-man* meme on the internet.

I didn't know what to say. I couldn't say anything with Reggie and Jamie still around. This girl was from my world. She was one of the players.

I had so many questions.

"Will you two stop flirting in gibberish and help us?!" Panda shouted from near the truck.

I turned towards his voice, broken out of my momentary haze, and opened my mouth even wider – if that was possible.

A burning palm tree cracked and fell towards the truck, and everyone stood near it.

Chapter 6
Earth, Gravel, and Slime

The cracked palm tree branch burned wildly as it separated from the rest of the tree and plummeted towards the truck. The world seemed to slow down around me.

Panda, Reggie, and Jamie looked up in awe. Jamie was shooting water from his hands and it seemed to be helping slightly, but the overall inferno was simply too much for him to handle alone.

Reggie and Panda stood nearby, looking skyward towards the falling branch and their doom. Sally, however, still leant against the truck with her arms crossed and a flat expression.

I resummoned my bow and aimed at the falling branch. Though my stamina was so low, I doubted I could fire off a single shot. To make matters worse, at my best guess, I'd need a *Soul Shot* to do the job. Anything less than that and the branch wouldn't break into small enough pieces to mitigate the damage.

I felt something brush my shoulder and I turned just in time to see Bell. She walked calmly past me, there was no sign of her battle mode on her face. She looked...calm.

She raised her hand towards the falling branch and I felt all the blood rush from my face as I realised what she was about to do.

"No, don't!" I shouted.

But it was already happening. She shot a magnificent fireball spell from her palm which rocketed towards the branch. The heat seared my cheek as it rushed past me.

The fireball was a cacophony of swirling reds and oranges, and death, lots of death.

It felt...*powerful.*

I wasn't sure why. I had no mana of my own, which left me blind to magic in almost all cases. But for some reason, in that moment, I could feel the raw power of her spell.

I saw Panda's eyes go wide with horror as he realised what she'd done. He must have had the same thought as me. Her fireballs were much more dangerous than the branch was

In all likelihood, all it would do was burn the others to a crisp and wreck the truck.

The fireball whizzed through the air, rotating, and burning with more intensity as it went. Then it hit the branch.

To my amazement, the branch exploded into tiny splinters of burning wood and the fireball blasted into the sky before dissipating.

Panda and I sighed in relief at almost the exact same time. Reggie and Jamie had never even known how close they were to death by fireball.

Time sped back up again as Bell turned to me with a smile and her hands clasped behind her back.

"Haven't you ever heard the phrase: fight fire with fire?" She asked.

"I don't think *that's* what it means..." I began but changed my tone halfway. "Thank you."

She smiled and walked back towards the truck, her pristine white robe flapping in the wind.

I looked back around the clearing and the fire was raging wildly. More and more loconuts dropped from trees in a flaming harmony of death screams and splattered organs. It was super gross.

We needed to quell the flames somehow before the entire jungle was engulfed. I looked to Jamie but his paltry water magic was barely better than a child's water pistol.

Seriously. How is the guy an adventurer? I thought as Jamie determinedly shot flaccid spurts of water onto the tree closest to him.

I couldn't fault him for his effort, but honestly, the guy was weak as shit.

I needed to think of another way to quell the flames. None of my skills were useful in this situation, but there had to be another way. I desperately searched through my inventory and found something.

If my life were a cartoon, a little lightbulb would have appeared over the top of my head.

I pulled out a vial of slime condensate and rushed to the nearest tree. I threw the condensate as high up the tree as I could and it shattered against the top branches, putting a serious dent into the flames on the leaves up there.

Perfect.

I had over 10,000 vials of slime condensate from my quest in the sewers. Every slime I'd killed had dropped one, and I'd gone full murder hobo on those little fuckers.

I quickly ejected all 10,000 of the vials and in less than a second the entire clearing was filled with them. The pile was so tall it dwarfed me and honestly, I was lucky they didn't crush me when I took them all out of my inventory at once.

"I don't think it's the right time to be reorganising your inventory, kid," Panda called from behind me.

I turned around to see both Panda and Reggie staring at me with furrowed brows.

"Reggie, by any chance can you use wind magic?" I asked hopefully.

"No…I'm a healer," he replied half-heartedly.

He's a healer? I thought. *So the girl in the white robe is a fire mage and the stocky, stout dude is a healer. Talk about refusing to conform to stereotypes.*

Reggie's lack of wind mana put a slight dampener on my plan, but I still had one more option.

With a sigh, I looked towards Bell who was zealously cheering on Jamie and his flaccid water pistol-like magic.

"Bell, I need a fireball," I called reluctantly, cupping my hands around my mouth.

She turned suddenly with a huge, creepy grin on her face.

"Can you shoot it at the base of these vials? I need them to explode outwards towards the trees," I said, moving towards her as Panda and Reggie retreated past me with wide eyes.

She answered with a simple nod and held out her hands before her. It was the same thing she did when she first attacked the boulder and I really hoped that it wouldn't be overkill.

I only needed her to blast the slime condensate at the trees. I didn't need her to incinerate them before they could do their work.

After a moment she fired a tiny, pinprick of a fireball which disappeared into the ground near the slime condensate.

"Well that was anticlimat," Panda began.

He was immediately interrupted as the earth below the vials exploded upward like an erupting volcano. The ground shook violently as earth and vials alike shot into the air.

I looked up in awe, which was a huge mistake.

Earth, gravel, and slime rained down on us like a tropical storm and I was drenched from head to toe in the nasty goop that was created by the three things mixing together.

Also, it hurt because gravel is nasty…and I got some in my mouth.

I rubbed the slime condensate out of my eyes and spat out the gravel dirt. It tasted gross, like Frenching a vegan.

After a few moments of rubbing, I could finally see again. I looked up and saw the carnage.

The fires were put out so yay us, we stopped the forest fire from decimating the local ecosystem. However, in place of the clearing now sat a deep crater surrounded by blackened trees and loconut corpses.

It was definitely a win though…kinda.

I looked towards Sally who was still leaning against the truck with her arms folded. There wasn't a spec of dirt, slime, or gravel on her. I had no idea how she'd avoided the sudden rainstorm but I'd have to put it down to silver-rank fuckery for now.

I had more important things to think about: like how we were going to get the truck past the new crater and how long it would be until I could take a shower.

"…And boom goes the dynamite!" Bell said, spinning towards us with a happy smile on her face.

She was covered in slime and dirt, just like I was. Her teal hair now looked more like the underside of a layer of teal icing on a chocolate cake. She didn't seem bothered though.

Panda on the other hand looked mortified as he desperately tried to ring slime condensate out of his fur.

"At least it's not water, this time," I said, casually patting him on the head.

"How many times do I have to tell you that pandas are not aquatic mammals, kid?" he replied sourly. "You're quickly becoming my least favourite human."

"You sound like my parents," I replied, moving past him to Jamie, who was still shooting little spurts of water from his hands.

I clapped my hand on his shoulder and he looked at me with stoner eyes and an uncomprehending face.

"You can stop now mate, it's over," I said gently.

"Did I do it?" he asked dazedly. "Did I put out the fire?"

I looked at him for a moment. He looked exhausted and possibly in shock.

"Yeah, you sure did buddy. You can go rest up in the truck now if you want to," I replied, squeezing his shoulder slightly as I gestured with my free hand towards the back of the vehicle.

He staggered away from me with a slight smile.

"He used up nearly all of his mana trying to put out that tree," Sally said.

I turned to the sound of her voice to see her step towards us, arms still folded. Reggie and Bell winced at her words, I, however, had no idea why that was wince-worthy. I'd used up literally *all* of my stamina before and I was ok after a bit of meditation.

"Is that bad?" I asked dumbly.

Reggie and Bell both looked at me with raised eyebrows like I was an idiot or something.

"Yes, Gonads," Sally replied in a condescending tone which I absolutely did not appreciate. "If a person uses up most or all of their mana they suffer from something called mana brain.

"As I'm sure you know, mana is governed by the intelligence stat. So if you use it all up then the processing power in your brain stops working properly. Nobody really knows why, but it is a constant problem for mages."

I nodded at her as she spoke. I guess it explained why he seemed so brain-dead. I'd put it down to shock, but apparently not.

"Have you seriously never used up most of your mana before dude?" Reggie asked, clapping me on the shoulder and chuckling.

When did he get so friendly?

"I don't have any mana," I replied frankly.

"Yeah, I know you're not a mage or anything," he replied. "I watched you fight, but don't you use mana to make your arrows glow?"

"No, I mean I literally don't have *any* mana. Zero, nada, none," I said. "As for how I make my arrows glow...it's a trade secret." I winked and ducked out from under his hand which was still on my shoulder.

He looked at me for a moment with uncomprehending eyes, and then it hit him.

"What!? You don't have any mana, like at all, like as in it's not even a stat for you?"

"Yup."

"I didn't even know that was possible," he yelled.

"Neither did I," Sally butted in. "But Gonads here is a bit of a special case. Anyway, how are you bozos going to get my truck past this giant hole you've made?"

I looked towards the huge crater in the ground. It really was something, impressive even. Though I had no clue how to get the truck past it.

Maybe if we cut down some of the trees around it we could circumvent the crater entirely. With no wind magic among us, it was all I could think of. Well, that or building a bridge with the palm tree wood but that would probably take a while and I was no structural engineer.

"I could shoot it across with a fireball?" Bell said innocently.

46

In unison, Sally, Reggie, Panda, and I all yelled, "No!"

Chapter 7
Fireball Wizard

I reached into my inventory and pulled out three rusted goblin axes. It was the only thing I could think of. We needed to find a way to get the truck past the huge crater Bell had created and the only way forward that I could see was to cut down some trees near it and drive around.

I'd looted the goblin weapons after nearly dying on a cliff during my first-ever Adventure Society quest: *The Goblin King Coronation*. Literally, thousands of goblins had swarmed me like a herd of zombies and I fought them off...mostly. I *may* have had some life-saving help from Director Lucas towards the end.

I pulled out the three axes and handed one to Reggie and one to Bell, keeping one for myself. I had to assume that Jamie was down for the count on account of his mana brain issue. Panda was too busy ringing slime condensate out of his fur to help, or at least that's what he said...yup that was the reason, and definitely not because he's a damn tiny panda who is useless at physical tasks.

"OK guys, if we're going to get the truck past this ditch we'll need to cut out a road around it," I began. "I think if we cut two trees deep all the way around one side of the hole we should be able to drive around without risking falling in."

The other two nodded and we began work clearing the trees. It wasn't too difficult, to be honest. With increased stat skills and the trees being burned partly to ash already, we moved at a much faster pace than a normal human could.

And, speaking of normal humans, it occurred to me that all the examinees in our little cohort were human. There wasn't a single lycanid or catonid, excluding Sally but she was the examiner so she didn't count.

Both of those races were more numerous in Havar, so it struck me as being a little odd. It's surprising what random thoughts come into your head when you're chopping trees.

I had to take a break after felling the first one to refill my stamina coil. I'd used up most of my stamina already by fighting the dhur, and chopping wood was hard work.

I dropped into a meditative pose, with my index finger and thumb touching in a circular shape, and dived into my soul view.

My health rope seemed to be doing pretty well. It extended through my extremities, into my limbs and all around me. It was a thick, healthy, crimson rope.

That was how I interacted with my HP and stamina stats in my soul view. I had to visualise them as something tangible so I could mould and strengthen them.

However, as I learnt after defeating the slime queen, I couldn't strengthen them too much or the system would get mad.

I switched views and checked on my stamina coil. It was emitting a weak yellow glow. I expected as much.

My coil started in my core itself and it swirled out from there to my muscles. It looked a bit like a curly straw, especially when I pumped fresh energy into it, which was exactly what I was about to do.

I breathed in deeply and visualised the oxygen which filled my lungs as a white, neutral energy. I then focused on guiding that energy into the core of my stamina coil. From there it would naturally take a ride on the curly straw slide and refill my stamina.

Once I was done, I woke myself from the meditative trance and rubbed my eyes. The forest was bright compared to the backs of my eyelids and it took me a moment to get used to the change.

I looked around and realised that most of the trees were gone. Had I really meditated for that long? Maybe Bell and Reggie were really fast lumberjacks.

I stood up and saw them dealing with the last few trees. I almost went over to help, but they hadn't cleared any of the stumps yet and that needed doing before we could drive through.

I noticed that they'd dumped the felled trees into the pit itself. I wasn't so sure that was a good idea since they were tall and it almost gave the ditch the appearance of being a funny-looking bush. Still, I had stumps to clear so I let it slip my mind for now.

I didn't really know how to remove tree stumps, but I figured with my enhanced strength I could find a way. I smashed the axe into the earth immediately next to the closest stump and worked on pushing it underneath the stump itself.

Then I pushed the handle down as a lever and it…snapped. I was hoping the stump would pop right out of the ground but I guess it's not that easy.

Sally snickered from her perch, leaning against the hood of the truck, and I scowled at her.

"Kaleb, you don't need to do that." The friendly voice of Bell chimed from across the newly cleared patch. "I can just burn them out."

"No more forest fires! I don't have any more slime condensate," I chided back.

"I won't start any fires." She jogged towards me and then bent down and whispered: "For now." Then she touched the stump of the tree with the tip of her index finger. "Fireball." She whispered.

A tiny, pinball-sized fireball moved slowly from her finger and pushed into the centre of the stump which smouldered slightly, then the roots began to singe. After a moment they disintegrated and all that was left was a blackened stump with nothing anchoring it to the ground.

Bell picked it up and tossed it over her shoulder into the pit.

"See." She smiled. "I told you; fireball is the only spell you need. It's the Swiss army knife of spells…"

"How come you have so many types of fireballs, but no other spells," I asked her, following behind as she got rid of the stumps one by one.

"It's my class." She giggled. "I'm a *Fireball Wizard*."

"I thought they called them mages around here," I replied.

"They do, but my that's my class name. When I picked it the system made some bad joke about an old British band called *The Who*, but the class itself is perfect."

I was a little worried about the naivety she was showing by sharing so much about her powers with me. I'd tried to play my class close to my chest since I'd gotten it. I didn't know what anyone else's class was either now that I thought about it.

The conversation also reminded me that Bell was an outworlder too. I really needed to talk to her about that properly when we could get a moment of privacy.

Bell looked up at me when I didn't reply after a few seconds and continued the conversation by herself.

"What kind of class did you pick? I saw your green arrows; might I assume the system made a *Green Arrow* joke when you picked it?" She giggled. "Is that why you're wearing that superhero costume?"

51

"No, it just told me it thought I was going to become a stealth archer. The system insults me as much as it makes jokes," I replied. "And it's not a superhero costume!"

The joke is on the system though. I thought. *Once I get my stats high enough to properly use my armour, I will be a stealth archer.*

I chuckled to myself and Bell pulled a funny face at me.

Thinking about my class, I pulled it up on my HUD and had a quick read-through.

Apex Predator (unique)

Well, would you look at that, your fighting style has been so varied so far I've had to create an entirely new class for you. Before you start feeling too special I've already had to do this for over 500 of the 10,000 players brought here.
So far you've used a bow, a dagger, a vat of acid and a truck to slaughter your way through the countryside.
This class is the amalgamation of those styles.
Besides, in the beginning, I thought you were going to become a bog-standard stealth archer and that's way too mainstream to entertain me

Selecting the Apex Predator Class unlocks the following skills:
Acid Arrows – Every projectile you shoot from a bow will cause acid damage to the target.

Acid Dhampir Dagger – Gain 10% of inflicted damage with a dagger as HP. Daggers inflict acid damage.

Environmental Hazzard – Killing enemies using the environment awards bonus experience.

Selecting the Apex Predator class will award the following stat points per level:

+7 strength / +5 vitality / +3 perception / +3 agility / +1 intelligence

I still hadn't gotten any bonus experience from the *Environmental Hazard* skill yet, but I was sure that there would be plenty of time.

Bell finished up with the last stump and we rejoined the group at the front of the truck.

"Took you long enough," Panda huffed.

He was sitting on the hood of the truck, apparently trying to use the engine's heat to dry off—though I was pretty sure that'd only work if Sally was plugged into the mana-sucking armband that powered it.

I ignored his comment and looked towards Sally.

"We've cleared a path around the crater, so shall we move on?" I asked hopefully.

"I suppose. It'll get dark in a few hours and we're behind schedule for our first stop so there will be no more fights today," she announced, pushing off the hood with her powerful arms. "Jump in."

I grinned at her and made a beeline for the back of the truck. Jamie was sitting in a meditative pose right at the back, near the cab. He must have been regenerating his mana.

We all piled in and the truck rumbled to life and began trundling around the massive hole in the ground we'd made.

"Oh shit! I didn't loot the boulder." I gasped as we moved away from the clearing. I'd been so busy that I'd forgotten to do any of that adventurer stuff.

"I already did it," Bell said casually, her hair blowing around her as Sally picked up speed.

"Oh, at least someone did," I replied.

I was pretty sure that was my kill by rights, I'd done all the damage. All Bell did was cause a forest fire by trying to burn a big old rock to death. Not that I was bitter or anything.

"Yeah, it only dropped something called an elemental core though. I don't really know what it is," she said, producing the item in her palm.

It was a glowing brown orb. It looked a bit like a shiny marble. I had a much bigger slime core in my own inventory, which I also currently had no use for.

"Cores are used in crafting," Panda said lazily as he rubbed at his head trying to use the wind as a hairdryer. "Hold onto it, if you ever want any custom armour or weapons made they can be pretty handy."

"I thought you weren't talking to Bell," I teased.

"I'm not, I was talking to you."

Bell dived on him and there was a lot of swearing and yelling as he tried his best to get away from her clutches. The girl really had a thing for cute animals, or maybe it was just Panda.

Whilst that happened I opened up my notifications.

Congratulations! You have defeated:
Dhur (lvl 38)
Bonus experience awarded due to level disparity.

I didn't level up from the kill, but that was to be expected. Gaining levels was a lot harder now than it was in the early days. Phase two was a different ball game.

I sat back and stretched my arms out on the uncomfortable side of the truck. I was exhausted, something that rarely happened to me anymore. Working with these people was going to suck.

Who'd have thought that *I'd* have to be the leader? A guy who's only been in this world for a couple of months. How our ragtag little group were going to slay a dragon was beyond me. I could see Bell's use, even if she was a fire hazard, and if Reggie was a healer that'd definitely come in handy.

Jamie though, not so much. So far he seemed like dead weight. I'd have to see what he could do in a solo fight. Then, somehow, we'd need to learn to work as a team. Devising strategies was too much work for my tired mind though, so I figured I'd leave it to the morning.

Luckily, it didn't take us that long to get to the closest village, and what I saw when we arrived woke me right the fuck up.

Chapter 8
Merry Band of Dick Munchers

My heavy eyes were burning with fatigue by the time our mana-powered truck reached the village. It was a small place that reminded me more of an old-western high street than a fantasy village.

With my propensity for getting into duels, I half expected a cowboy to come waltzing through a pair of swing doors to challenge me.

That didn't happen though.

Instead, I was treated to every nerd's dream come true: *elves*.

Long, luscious hair, piercing eyes, and pointy ears. It was safe to say that upon arrival I was fully awake. I focused on the nearest elf, a small girl with mousey brown hair and a bow strapped to her back, and a system notification popped up on my HUD.

You have discovered a new race:
Jungle Elf
Direct descendants from the better-known *Wood Elves*, the *Jungle Elves* tend to prefer the tropics. The story goes that once upon a time a *Wood Elf* lived in the forests of Britania, an island nation sitting just above the central continent.
After years of living a quiet life with his tribe and wife, he looked at the grey, rainy sky and said: "Fuck this I'm out."

After a long sea voyage he eventually came upon a tropical island paradise, promptly got a nasty sunburn, and then the runs from eating an undercooked *Loconut* he'd shaken out of its nest.
And thus the phrase: *barking up the wrong tree* was born.

"Somehow I don't think that's true," I muttered to myself upon reading the notification.

It also told me very little about jungle elves, which was pretty on-brand for the system.

The truck pulled up in a puff of smoke alongside the raised, wooden boardwalk. The village was a single street carved into the jungle and surrounded on either side by large palm trees.

Shops, bars, and trader stalls dominated the right side, the left seemed to be mostly comprised of homes and inns. It was a simple setup.

The elves must have been pretty hygiene-conscious too, considering the raised boardwalks on either side. The road was muddy and torn up by tyre tracks, which we had just added to with our large truck.

Sally popped her head out of the window and yelled: "Everyone out!" and we carefully exited via the rear.

Looking around, I couldn't see too many people. I guessed it was quite late, the sun was already cresting the sky and casting a postcard-worthy orange glow over the little settlement.

The few elves I did see though, were all carrying bows. The short girl with the mousy brown hair approached us as we huddled next to the truck.

"Adventurers?" she asked, coking her head to the side slightly and eyeing each of us up in turn.

"That's right, miss?" Reggie said, stepping towards her and offering out his hand curtly.

"Tilly," she said, ignoring his handshake and moving across each of us in turn.

She approached me and got uncomfortably close. I swear I saw her nostrils twitch as she examined me with her hands held behind her back.

Did she just sniff me? What the actual fuck.

"Use bow?" she asked, grabbing my forearm, and pointing to my bracer.

"It looks like we have that in common," I said, forcing a smile and gesturing to the wooden bow slung on her back.

This is definitely not how I expected elves to act. What happened to the refined elegance I've come to expect from TV? I thought.

She grunted in response and moved past me to Bell who smiled at her happily. The elf's sunburnt skin practically glowed in the orange light of sunset.

I guess the system wasn't making it up after all.

"Hi there," Bell chirped, offering out her hand. "I'm Bell, it's lovely to meet you."

The elf girl simply grunted in response and moved on to Panda, completely ignoring Bell.

"I think she likes me," she chimed in her overly upbeat tone.

The elf girl crouched down and overtly sniffed at Panda's fur. He recoiled slightly, shooting me a pleading look. I had no idea how to help him out, and no desire to, as I stifled a laugh.

"Need bath," she said before standing up and positioning herself in front of the group. Panda looked insulted and opened his mouth to protest but she'd already turned away from him.

Sally walked around the front of the truck and joined us, standing next to the elf girl. Despite talking like a neanderthal, she was actually quite pretty and well-dressed to boot. With the exception of being rather small…and sunburnt, visually she conformed almost perfectly to the elf tropes I was used to.

She had a naturally contoured face; her hair shined vibrantly and she wore a form-fitted leather jerkin and high boots.

Elven shampoo must be great. I thought as I looked her up and down.

"This is Palm Tree Village," Sally announced, gesturing to the settlement around us. "From the looks on your faces, I'm guessing none of you have ever met a jungle elf before.

"They communicate primarily through telepathy, so they don't speak very much. Don't let that fool you into thinking they're dumb. We're only going to be here for one night, so don't go causing any trouble." She glared at me as she said that and I shrugged back at her innocently.

She turned towards the elf and the girl pointed lazily at the small building directly in front of us. Sally walked inside and gestured for us to follow.

The building itself was made of wood. However, the architecture was more like a tree house than the wooden buildings I was used to.

Root-like panels of wood merged and twined together to create living walls that looked like house-shaped trees. The door was a circular knot which swung inwards like a single saloon door.

As I stepped inside I was immediately hit with a cool breeze. The weather outside was stifling, so it was a welcome change to the climate.

The floor was riddled with mismatched rugs and cushions. There were a few tables as well, but they were low down to the floor, explaining the cushions. On the right side was a countertop with an array of twisted glass bottles standing on it.

We stood inside for a moment as Sally leaned on the countertop and the elven girl followed us inside and moved agilely through us, stopping on the other side of the counter.

She held up three fingers and Sally tossed her the corresponding gold coins. The price seemed a little steep to me considering it had only cost me a single gold coin for a weeklong stay at a bed and breakfast in Havar.

Sally didn't seem to care though as she turned back towards us.

"I've rented the entire inn for the night so I can debrief you and not worry about any of you catching a disease." She looked at me again and this time I was actually a little hurt.

"I have a wife you know," I muttered at her. She shot me a fangy grin and continued. "Take a seat."

We all complied and piled around a low-down table in the middle of the room. I sat on a soft green cushion with little beads covering the stitching. It was surprisingly comfortable.

Jamie still looked a little out of it, but his eyes seemed a lot more alert than they had been before so his meditation must have helped him out a bit.

Reggie sat next to him as Bell and Panda flanked me.

Sally came over shortly, bringing six sparkling bottles of glittery...something, and placing them all down on the table.

She gestured to them and we each took one as she plonked herself down at the head of the table, crossed her legs, and leant her head on her fist. Her silver hair flowed over her muscular shoulders.

My bottle had one of those caps on it that were connected to the glass itself by a piece of metal. When I pushed at the bottom of the cap, it flipped open letting a hissing gasp of air leak out.

I took a swig and the carbonation fizzed and popped on my tongue. It was a mild and pleasant feeling that somehow made my mouth warm. I'd describe the flavour but it was so different from anything I'd ever tasted on earth that I honestly don't know how.

The closest thing I could compare it to would probably be cherry aid, mixed with cider and a blue lagoon cocktail. I know that sounds terrible, but trust me, it was great.

"Bell," Sally said suddenly, causing Bell to choke slightly on her beverage. "How do you think your fight with the dhur went?"

"It was a lot of fun," she replied and a glimmer of a sadistic smile tugged on her lips, but just for a moment. "I especially enjoyed being Kaleb's knight in shining armour, the *Mario* to his *Princess Peach,* If you will."

"That is not what happened," I interrupted. "*I* saved *you* and besides, everyone knows *Peach* is fucking *Bowser.* Why would you even want to be *Mario*, the guy's clueless."

"I'll tell you how it went," Sally said loudly, banging her glass on the table and grabbing our attention. "It was an absolute shit show!" She yelled slamming her fist down and earning an annoyed look from Tilly the jungle elf. "You'd probably be dead if Gonads hadn't stepped in. Not to mention that you nearly burned down the entire jungle, putting your team's lives in danger.

"How am I supposed to pass you, when all you gave me was a flaming bag of goblin shit."

Bell shrank back in her cushion; she didn't seem to know what to say but she looked down into her drink shyly.

"Wow, someone finally got her to shut up," Panda commented quietly, glancing sideways at Bell.

"Gonads," Sally began, ignoring Panda. "Rate your own performance."

I straightened up slightly and looked at Sally in her dark blue eyes. She had a fierce look on her face and I gulped before answering.

"It was a solo battle, so I hesitated to act at first," I began. "Once I got into the fight I realised that the dhur had a high defence and my arrows barely seemed to scratch it. I killed it in the end, but it was a more drawn-out battle than I'd have liked."

Booyah! I thought. *Score one for professionalism in the workplace. Not a bad assessment if I do say so myself.*

"Yeah…" she sighed. "You did ok I guess. You did kill it *and* you recognised your teammate's weakness and stepped in to help. Unlike these two idiots who gawked at you both the entire time." She glared at Reggie and Jamie who both shrank down, trying to avoid her heavy gaze.

"That being said," she continued. "You seem to have a habit of draining all of your stamina when you fight. I'd have hoped you'd have figured out how to conserve it better by now.

"You're turning into a one-pump chump and it's going to get you killed. What would you have done if a second monster appeared after you killed the dhur?"

I opened my mouth to reply and she held up her hand to stop me.

"That was a rhetorical question." She sighed again, even deeper this time. "Listen, you merry band of dick munchers have a dragon to kill. You hear me? A real-life, fire-breathing, flying, king of the monsters, dragon. You need to shape up if you want any chance of actually pulling it off.

"Starting tomorrow we'll be walking to the lair. I've obviously been too soft on you by driving you everywhere. You're gonna fight a shit-tonne of monsters, both solo and as a team." She leaned in closer and snarled the last part in a menacingly low tone.

"If I don't see a drastic improvement, I'll send you all home and kill the damn dragon myself."

She slammed the table and the group collectively jumped backwards. Then she stood up lazily, bottle in hand, and walked towards the rooms in the back.

"You'd all better get some sleep. We have an early start tomorrow," she said, leaving us in shocked silence as we nursed our drinks.

Tomorrow. I thought, staring into my drained glass bottle. *That's when this exam will really begin. I need to get stronger.*

Chapter 9
There's Always Some Guy Called Brad

We sat in silence for a while after Sally left, sulkily nursing our drinks. This weird little team of ours desperately needed to improve and we all knew it.

A small part of me swelled with pride as I was the only one who wasn't made out to be completely incompetent. Still, though, I knew my own weaknesses better than anyone and I was determined to beat them.

I needed to get strong enough to protect my wife and kid, strong enough to find a way to bring them to Celestia. That wasn't going to happen any time soon if I didn't get better and increase my level.

Time to channel my inner Goku. I thought, silently wishing that levelling up was as easy as the 80's training montages made it out to be.

After a short while, Reggie stood up and bade us good night. Jamie hurried after him like a lost puppy. I wondered what their relationship was. They obviously knew each other prior to this exam...and that Jake kid. Childhood friends maybe?

It didn't matter. They needed to shape up most of all. Bell had the tactical awareness of an overzealous toddler, but at least she was powerful. The other two were the weakest link.

Starting tomorrow, I'd have to put some work into helping them improve. I'd need backup to fight a real-life dragon. A water mage and healer duo could be pretty useful components in a difficult battle like that.

They just needed to be better.

Panda nudged me from my reverie and nodded towards Bell who was staring absently into her glass. She sloshed the sparkling liquid back and forth and gazed into it like she was in a trance.

I realised what Panda meant.

This was my chance to talk to her in private. She was an outworlder like me, she understood cultural references from Earth, and I needed to know more.

"Bell," I said suddenly and her neck snapped up towards me, startled. "We need to talk."

"Are you breaking up with me?" she replied sarcastically with faux sadness and a trembling lip. "You could have at least taken me to a nicer place to do it. I mean, the drinks here are nice but there's not even a food menu."

"Where are you from?" I asked, ignoring her inability to take anything seriously.

"Oh, you want my supervillain back story," she said, mimicking a tone of realisation. "Well I used to work in *Gotham City* as a psychiatrist until one day I met this guy in clown make up—"

"I'm being serious," I interrupted, raising my voice in irritation. "We're both outworlders, what happened to you, how did you get here?"

What I really wanted to know was if she'd met any other outworlders. I knew it was unlikely, but if there was any chance she'd met Layla…

"Well let's see," she began, holding her forefinger to her chin. "I woke up, ate a banana for breakfast, played *Baldur's Gate 3* for a little bit, then I went for a walk in the jungle, got a surprise tattoo, learnt to cast fireball – the best spell – killed a bunch of monsters, a few other things happened and now I'm here. That's my alibi officer, the whole truth and nothing but the truth."

"Did you meet any other outworlders?" I asked carefully. I didn't want to seem too eager to hear her answer. Bell seemed well-meaning, but she also had an annoying habit of…well, it wasn't a habit as such as her personality. She had an annoying personality.

"Nope, you're my first," she replied chirpily, then she lowered her voice and cupped her hands around her mouth and whispered: "That makes us soul mates."

Damn. I knew it was unlikely, honestly, it was a good thing. The idea of Layla being here was scary. Still, though, a part of me was a little sad that Bell hadn't run into her.

How ridiculous is that? I mean what are the odds anyway? Out of eight billion people on earth, only ten thousand of us came here. Not to mention that they were spread out across the globe.

"How about you?" Bell asked sweetly. "Am I your first too?"

Her phrasing sent an unpleasant shiver down my spine.

"No, there was this guy called Brad," I answered and then trailed off. I wasn't sure if it was a good idea to tell her what happened.

"There's always some guy called Brad," she said, shaking her head slightly. "Let me guess, he said you were the only one for him and then one day you came home to find him shacked up with that bitch Samantha from work."

"No…" I said. "Why, did that happen to you?"

"No, why do you ask?" she replied shifting her tone back to a sweet innocence.

I honestly didn't know how to take this girl. She was so odd. She didn't take anything seriously and it was almost impossible to have a conversation with her.

That being said, she was strong and she was from Earth. She also seemed good-natured and a part of me enjoyed having someone like that around.

"So," she continued. "What happened with *your* Brad?"

I wasn't sure if I should tell her but on a whimsical leap of faith, I decided to do it anyway.

"Not long after I arrived here I was captured by cultists. Brad was in prison with me. I managed to kill a guard by throwing him into a vat of acid but Brad got hit with the splashback and died," I said quickly.

I purposely omitted the part about adsorbing his Celestial Map tattoo. That was dangerous knowledge to share.

"There are so many jokes I could make from how you phrased that," she replied, stifling a laugh. "So I'll just point out the most obvious thing. Throwing someone into a vat of acid is how you turn them into a supervillain. Don't do it again," she said, waggling a finger about like a parent scolding a naughty child. "Also, death by splashback." She giggled.

"She's starting to sound like the system," Panda muttered next to me.

"It doesn't bother you that I killed someone innocent?" I asked, lowering my voice.

"If people actually thought collateral damage was a bad thing *Obama* wouldn't have gotten a second term." She replied. "Sometimes innocents die in the pursuit of justice...or in your case, survival. I can't judge you for fighting for your life. That'd be like judging...well, *Obama* and that guy was great."

I was a little concerned with how easily she condoned drone strikes accidentally killing civilians, but she seemed sincere for once and I was relieved she didn't think I was a bad person.

"Thanks…" I offered, not really knowing how to respond to that.

"No problem," she said. "And thank *you* for putting up with me. I know I'm not always the easiest person to get along with and well…thanks." She looked away and I was so shocked at the lack of weirdness in her statement that I stared dumbfounded at her for longer than was socially acceptable.

"I'm going out for a smoke," Panda said quietly, getting up from the table.

"Since when do *you* go outdoors to smoke?" I asked teasingly.

He pointed at a sign on the wall. I focused on it and the odd language translated into English with help from my language skill: *Speak English Damnit*. It said: *No Smoking*.

Panda left the room and I looked after him. He'd never cared about no smoking signs before. The little guy had literally sat on the reception desk at Adventure Society smoking for an hour whilst I filled in a report.

Something had been off with him since we'd started the exam. My stomach sank as I thought back to our previous quest where I'd ripped an orc's soul out with my mind.

I really hoped he wasn't upset with me about that. He'd seemed ok at the time, but maybe it was bothering him. I swallowed hard and started to get up to go talk to him when Bell spoke again.

"I think teamwork is going to be the key to beating this dragon." She mused. I couldn't tell if she was talking to me or thinking aloud, but I decided to remain seated all the same.

"I agree," I replied and she looked up at me with those big eyes of hers as I continued. "If we can get everyone working together then we might have a chance. The team is pretty well balanced, we just need to learn to work together as a unit."

"Exactly." She smiled. "I wonder if there's an escape room we can book in town, or maybe we could do trust fall exercises?"

Adventure Society was a pretty corporate place, but trust falls and escape rooms weren't really what I had in mind.

"We can work on it tomorrow." I yawned. "For now we should probably get some sleep. Oh, and just so you know, outworlders are pretty much an urban legend in Celestia. Only the more powerful people know that we really exist. So keep it to yourself, it's safer that way."

"Oh, I know," she said casually. "You're the only person who knows I'm an outworlder. I'm real good at secrets." She winked and then stood up, leaving for the rooms in the back.

"How is a blabbermouth like her better at keeping secrets than I am?" I complained quietly to myself.

Both Director Lucas and Sally had discovered my real identity in my first few days of being in Celestia. How had Bell kept it a secret from Lucas?

"Wizard fuckery, it's got to be wizard fuckery," I mumbled.

There was no other explanation. Damn, this world and the system's need to deny me a mana stat. The damned thing probably thought it was funny. I bet it was laughing to itself right now in ones and zeros, or whatever code system's thought in.

Thinking about it, I don't even know what the system is. I thought. *Is it an AI, or a magical entity? Is it even alive? It certainly has a personality but surely it's not just some guy sitting at a magic computer and running the entire world.*

My thoughts spiraled further down that rabbit hole for a little while until Panda roused me by re-entering the inn.

"Oh good, she's gone," he said, pulling up a cushion next to me. "A few sandwiches short of a picnic that one."

I chuckled and turned to him. He seemed a little better, but that annoying inner voice that nags at you to do the right thing kept pressing on my cortex, so I asked him.

"She definitely is." I took a deep breath and swallowed. "Panda, are you alright?"

"Yeah, I'm fine, kid. I mean my fur's a little foisty but I can shower before bed."

"Are you sure? You've been acting a little odd since we started the exam?"

"I said I'm fine," he replied shortly. "Go get some sleep kid, you've got a long day ahead of you."

He got up and headed into the back of the inn and I felt my stomach tumble as I looked after him. He was definitely not alright, but whatever it was, he didn't want to share.

I finished my drink, finally, and went looking for my room. He might have been a bit pissy about it, but Panda was right. I did have a big day tomorrow. I had a team to train, myself to train and probably a whole bunch of monsters to kill.

On Wednesdays, we level up.

Chapter 10
Big, Red, Overgrown Chicken

I awoke the next morning to find Panda conked out at the foot of the bed. He was sprawled out on his back sawing logs in a starfish pose. The vibrations from his snoring shook the bed and resonated around the room, making it even louder.

I was just thankful that he'd actually come to bed. Whatever was bothering him, at least he still felt comfortable enough to sleep around me.

I stretched and yawned, then rubbed my eyes before pulling myself out of the covers, dressing, and leaving the room.

I shut the door quietly, trying not to wake Panda, as I entered the main room. The rest of the examinees were already there, tucking into a breakfast of hard, crusty bread and some kind of soup.

The elf girl was cooking behind the main countertop. Her mousey brown hair was tied in a bun and I was surprised by her adherence to kitchen hygiene protocols.

She grunted at me as I approached and placed a bowl of bright green soup on the counter. Then she threw some bread at me which I deftly caught. I thanked her and joined the others at the low table.

"Morning sleepy head." Bell greeted chirpily.

I nodded to her and began eating my food. The soup tasted delicious, even if it did look like steaming mucus. They say that 90%

of flavour is in appearance, and they're right. Which is why I closed my eyes as I dipped the hard bread into the soup. When I couldn't see it, it tasted great.

Sally joined us around about the time I was finishing my meal. Our group hadn't spoken much, everyone seemed tired as they ate and mentally prepared themselves for the day ahead.

The muscle-bound lycanid curled her lip at the soup and bread and raised a polite but firm hand at Tilly the elf when she offered her some. Sally was practically carnivorous so I wasn't surprised at her reaction.

"I hope you kids are ready," she said menacingly, cracking her knuckles. "The training I'm about to put you through will make you wish that dhur had killed you all yesterday."

"I love a good training montage," I said lazily. "Does anyone have *Eye of the Tiger* on their phone?"

Bell chuckled at my comment and glanced towards me like she wanted to join in but thought better of it.

"What's a phone?" Reggie asked, looking at me with a furrowed brow.

"Don't listen to him," Sally answered. "He's talking nonsense. I'll have to beat that out of him in the training session, won't I Gonads?" She said menacingly, clapping her strong hand on my shoulder and squeezing.

"I think *training session* is code for something not very child-friendly," Bell said to Reggie behind her hand in a loud whisper.

Sally thumped her on the top of her head and she whimpered slightly.

"I think it's time to leave." Sally sighed, letting go of my shoulder and turning towards the counter. "Are you ready Tilly?"

The elf girl nodded, picking up her bow and tipping it towards Sally.

"Good." She continued. "Gonads, go wake up your familiar, you're holding us all up."

"I have a name you know," Panda said sleepily as he entered the main room. His eyes were puffy and he rubbed them gently as he walked towards us.

Sally ignored his comment and left the inn, beckoning for the rest of us to follow with a slight wave over her shoulder.

We did as instructed and as the bright rays of the morning sun hit my eyes, I looked longingly at the truck we were leaving behind. I had a feeling we were all going to miss that thing in a few hours.

We left the muddy little elf village and headed into the trees. It was stiflingly hot inside the jungle. A muggy, oppressive heat seemed to hug the ground in an invisible miasma.

I began sweating almost immediately and regretted wearing all black and long sleeves. The armour I'd chosen wasn't very jungle-friendly – even if it was awesome.

The trek wasn't too bad though, it definitely could have been worse. The palm tree jungle didn't really have any foliage. It was literally just trees and dirt, which made for relatively easy walking.

We trudged along in silence for a long time. I let Panda ride on my back after the first half hour. I felt like *Luke Skywalker* training in the swamps of *Dagoba* as the funny little familiar clung to my back.

Though I'd drop him if he started hitting me with a stick.

Tilly acted as our scout, leading us through the jungle diligently as we followed behind. Our ragtag little group must have been a sight to behold: a forced march of murder hobos and a washed-up female wrestler with a penchant for cosplay.

Tilly held her hand up suddenly in a clenched fist and we all stopped. She must have seen something. My heartbeat quickened as

I anticipated a fight. I hoped for one, anything to quell the boredom of endless walking.

Tilly moved around a tree and I lost sight of her as we waited. She came back a few moments later and spoke to Sally in a hushed whisper which I couldn't make out.

Sally nodded grimly as she spoke, and then turned to us with a fangy smile. She beckoned us closer and we all moved in, creating a semi-circle around her.

"Our guide says there's a pretty tough monster ahead," she said, a fire burning in her battle junky eyes. "It seems like a good chance for me to test your teamwork. I'd advise you not to rush in, at your levels you need to think tactically if you want to win without casualties."

Casualties. I thought solemnly, repeating her words in my head. It was easy to forget that death was a real factor here. It was so easy to see Celestia as a video game, even though it had shown me time and time again that it wasn't.

Sally left us and stood off to the side with Tilly and our semi-circle became a huddle.

"What's the plan guys?" Reggie asked, taking the initiative, and speaking first.

"Before we do anything, I think it might be a good idea to get to understand each other's strength, fighting style and powers," I said and Reggie nodded thoughtfully.

We went around the group and explained everything about ourselves in as much detail as we could. We discussed power sets, fighting styles, special abilities, and experience.

By the end of the conversation, I felt like I understood my team and their uses a lot better. It was a good starting point. Of course, I had kept some of my abilities to myself, I wasn't about to go telling people about my weird soul power after all.

I was sure the others all had their own secrets to keep as well. It didn't matter though; the idea was to understand each other well enough that we could make a plan and use the right people for the right job.

"I'm going to go scout out this monster," I said after we'd finished exposing our skillsets to each other. The group nodded, which I took as them giving me their blessings – not that I needed it.

It made sense for me to be the scout. My armour provided me with a stealth advantage when in shadows and, as long as I had my bow equipped, I could use the *sniper* skill.

Longbow of the Giant Goblin

This bow was carved from the forearm of a unique monster: *Gertrude the Giant Goblin*.
Just as she smashed her old clan into oblivion, you smashed her. You dirty bugger.
I mean, whatever tickles your pickle am I right?
I'm still judging you though.

Longbows can fire accurately over longer distances.
+5% strength
Grants use of the skill: Sniper
Sniper can only be used whilst this item is equipped
Sniper

Not to be confused with sniping, the skill *sniper* allows the user to see further distances. Like a telescope built into your eyes.
Don't go using it to creep on catonids whilst they're changing. I know you're a furry, but at least don't be a creep.

I pulled my hood up, aiding the tropical climate's oppressive heat, and set off in the direction Tilly had gone earlier.

The hood had an enchantment which shielded my aura from people and monsters. I wasn't exactly sure what an aura was, but I had to assume I had one.

As I set out towards our unknown target, I asked the not-so-friendly neighbourhood daemon who was still clinging to my back. He hadn't spoken much since we'd left the elf village, but I wanted his help.

"Panda, do you know what aura is?" I asked in a hushed voice as I crept through the crops of palm trees.

"Of course I do, I'm a sage," he said in a sleepy-sounding voice. "Aura is like a power signature that living things give off. Anyone with mana, which is anyone other than you, has an innate ability to sense a person's aura.

"It basically gives you an idea of how powerful someone is. Some people can hide it and powerful people can learn to hide it, but most wear their aura on their sleeve—so to speak."

I listened to his explanation as I rounded a thick tree trunk, hugging it as closely as I could. There was a lot of shade in the jungle, but I wasn't clear on how much shade constituted a shadow. I needed shadows for my armour to enhance my stealth.

"That makes sense," I replied in a hushed whisper. "Is it possible to sense aura without mana?" I asked, thinking back to recently when I sensed *something* in Sally back at Adventure Society.

"Yeah…" He replied, pausing for a moment as if deciding whether to continue or not. "People with a strong connection to their soul can enhance it and perceive aura through that. Most can't though, even when they break through the level cap and become a jade soul.

"In all honesty though kid, I don't really know much about jade souls or what comes after. It's a closely guarded secret in all the parts of the world I've been to and I've never been summoned by anyone who lived long enough to make it that far."

He finished his sentence with a sad tone and I felt him shiver slightly, but just for a moment. At least he seemed a little less moody. Asking him for information seemed to have cheered him up, even if thinking about his previous summoners was painful.

I didn't know much about his previous life. Taylor had told me that his last summoner was a woman who died about five years ago. I also knew that he'd been in Havar with her around about that time, but that was pretty much it. He'd never really spoken about her himself.

I guessed that for a familiar who was thousands of years old, five years was still a fresh wound. His perception of time was probably quite different to mine.

I rounded another tree, I'd only gone a few hundred meters away from the group, but it had taken longer than usual because I was moving slowly and trying to be all sneaky beaky.

On the other side of the tree I hugged, there was a slight clearing. A little stream of running, crystal water trickled through and next to it I saw our opponent.

A bright red, feathered Tyrannosaurus Rex stood happily wagging its enormous tail as it crunched merrily on a loconut it had bitten out of a tree.

Blood gushed from the carcass in the dinosaur's mouth and dropped in thick globs, staining the ground. I'd heard before that the current theory on Earth was that the T-Rex probably had feathers but seeing it in person was a whole different experience.

Somehow it made the creature even more terrifying. I used the sniper skill to zoom in on the scene, not daring to get any closer without my team.

Its head was so oversized it would have been comical if it wasn't for all the blood and guts. Even more horrifying was that it was actually eating a loconut.

The idea of it made me feel queasy as I thought back to the gut-wrenching smell from the time I had punted one into a tree and its rotten guts had sprayed the floor.

I could barely believe my eyes. I loved *Jurassic Park* as much as the next guy but I never imagined I'd be in a real-life version of it.

If we were going to fight this big, red, overgrown chicken, we'd need a plan.

Chapter 11
The *Weeble Wobble* of Prehistoric Creatures

I zoomed in on the red, feathered dinosaur and a notification activated in my HUD.

> **You have discovered a unique monster:**
> **Tyrannosaurus *Bex***
>
> Part of the T-Rex species, *Bex* was born different from
> the rest. Your average T-Rex has green feathers, but *Bex*
> has red feathers.
> You're probably expecting me to tell a tale of sadness,
> bullying and being an outcast. Well, I'm not. Dinosaurs
> like the colour red, it reminds them of blood, and being
> permanently red means only one thing to them: that
> *Bex* is a strong-ass warrior.
> Many T-Rexs worship her as a god.
> She probably has a complex about that, but regardless,
> she's still a dinosaur, and she will happily munch on
> your corpse.

"What, no jokes or insults?" I asked the sky in a whisper. "You really dropped the ball on this one."

"Is it really a good idea to tease the system?" Panda moaned from my back.

It probably wasn't and honestly, I preferred the notifications being like this. There was actually some information in there instead of bad setups to worse jokes. I still couldn't help but tease the system about it though. It must have struggled to come up with a good dinosaur joke.

I slowly moved away from the tree and headed back to the group to report my findings. They were still huddled around chatting. Sally and Tilly were stood a little way away with folded arms, leaning against a tree. They looked like a right pair.

As I approached the group, Reggie looked up and smiled at me.

"I'm glad you made it back safely." He began as the others turned towards me as well. "We've been talking and we think you should be the group leader."

I stopped mid-step.

Group leader? I've never led anything in my life. I just want to level up, that's all. I thought as the shock of their request bounced around my brain.

"I think he's having a system malfunction," Bell observed. "I had a computer that did that once, damn *internet explorer*, always so slow." She lamented quietly.

I looked up at them and they looked back expectantly.

"Fine." I sighed. I didn't really want the role, but I guessed it was better if I did it than someone else. "Though you might regret your choice when I tell you what we're facing."

"Is it clowns?" Bell asked suddenly. "I hate clowns."

"No, it's a T-Rex," I replied bluntly—to their shock.

Reggie's eyes widened and Jamie literally took a step back. Bell, on the other hand, sighed in relief and muttered something about being glad it wasn't clowns.

We spoke for a short while and hashed out a plan before moving into position. I arrived back at my spying tree and looked out into the clearing. Bex was still there, drinking from the stream as loconut blood leaked from her teeth and contaminated the water.

Kaleb: *Is everyone in position?*
Reggie: *Affirmative.*
Jamie: *Yes.*
Bell: *I'm so in position it'd make the Karma Sutra blush.*

We had all shook hands back in the clearing, adding each other to our contacts. As Sally had shown me before, you can chat with people in your contacts like a text message.

I figured it would be a useful feature for fights where we might not be able to talk freely, or at all. It seemed like a tactically sound choice to me.

I'd left Panda with Sally and Tilly; I didn't want the little guy getting hurt. We had no idea how strong Bex was. Though I was about to find out.

I raised my bow, nocked an arrow, and began charging my Soul Shot power. Usually, I aimed for centre mass, but the dinosaur's head was so large that I just couldn't help myself. If I hit her cranium, I might have been able to end the fight with a single shot.

I fired the arrow with a crack as it shot from the bow like a rocket taking off, blowing me backwards slightly. As I watched, Bex disappeared and the arrow broke through a tree on the other side of the clearing.

Kaleb: *Did anyone see where it went?*
Jamie: *Does it have invisibility?*
Bell: *Maybe it leapt into an alternate dimension, hoping this leap would be the leap home.*
Kaleb: *This is not the time to make old TV references.*
Reggie: *Kaleb look out!*

Trusting Reggie's message, I dived forward and rolled. I'd learnt to do a combat role as a kid, though I never really used it as an adult. It was a skill I was glad I had though as a seismic crash shook the earth at my feet.

I tumbled further than I'd originally intended and ended up near the stream. I turned around, raising my bow with a nocked arrow and was face to face with Bex.

The red-feathered beast had appeared right where I had just been standing, crushing the tree I was hugging. If it wasn't for Jamie, I'd have been dead.

Bex and I locked eyes for a moment and as I opened fire, she charged towards me.

My arrow pierced her chest, but she barely seemed to notice, even as her skin bubbled. She ran towards me, shaking the ground with every step.

I had nowhere to run, she was so much faster than me. I may have had the *Apex Predator* class, but that title truly belonged to her as she pounded towards me.

I had just enough time to fire another shot before she reached me. She screamed as acid bubbles melted the skin around her nose. Her chest had bubbled too, but she didn't seem to care about that.

The nose must have been a weak spot.

"Bad dog," I said as I took a step back and nocked another arrow.

Speaking was a mistake. She stopped thrashing around and glared at me, opening her mouth, and revealing a row of large, isos-celes-shaped teeth. She roared at me so forcefully that my lips parted and my teeth wobbled.

It reminded me of that g-force feeling you get on a fast roller coaster – but without the fun.

"I'm gonna tyrannosaurus wreck this overgrown chicken!" Bell shouted, just as a large, rotating fireball flashed across the mini-clearing and slammed into Bex.

The dinosaur disappeared and all that was left was the smell of ozone and burning feathers. A few of them fluttered around in the air, charred and smouldering.

"Did you get it?" I asked, nocking another arrow, and looking around the clearing suspiciously.

"I don't have a notification, so probably not," Bell shouted back from behind a tree, a tinge of disappointment in her tone.

"It's in the air!" Reggie shouted from his position nearby and I looked up, blinking as I saw her.

Bex seemed to have jumped skyward. Her powerful legs forced her high into the air. I could see the large red blob above us and she was getting bigger by the second.

"Holy shit," I breathed as the dinosaur got even bigger.

"Run you idiot!" Jamie shouted from his position across the stream.

I didn't need telling twice as I sprinted for the treeline. What goes up must come down and that big ass dinosaur was definitely coming down.

CRASH!

I was thrown from my feet as Bex impacted the ground, causing a mini earthquake. She roared again and the trees around us shook.

Kaleb: *Now!*

My head was spinning from the impact of being thrown across the clearing. My HP had dropped slightly as I bashed my head on a thick palm tree.

I had just enough mental faculties to send the message but I also needed to be in the fight myself.

83

I turned around groggily, picking myself up into a sitting position and began channelling a *Soul Shot*. I fired it, taking my stamina down to halfway, it punched straight into the dinosaur's chest.

She howled as a red, gooey hole appeared. Blood spilt out, further contaminating the stream as her flesh and insides burned from the acid. The putrid stench could have given a loconut's innards a run for their money.

Less than a second after my arrow impacted her, a concentrated stream of water sliced into the flesh on Bex's left leg. She hollered and stumbled before regaining her balance, leaning heavily on her undamaged leg.

We'd originally planned for him to take out her legs to stop her from charging at us, but now it served a second purpose. No more jumping...hopefully.

A large fireball exploded on the back of her head and I swear, in my battle haze, I saw yellow cartoon ducks circle her skull.

She still wasn't dead though.

She opened her mouth and looked right at me; the roaring had stopped. In the opening of her mouth, a small, rotating ball of blue energy began to form.

Is she charging up a hyperbeam?

Kaleb: *Keep firing!*

I panicked and added to the chat. Whatever the thing in her mouth was, I didn't want it hitting me. I liked life, I wanted to keep it, and that thing looked dangerous.

I raised my bow and nocked a second arrow as the spinning ball began glowing brighter and bigger. She seemed to be charging it like I did with my *Soul Shot*.

If my skill was anything to go by then this dinosaur hyperbeam thing would spell the end of me. I fired my arrow into the blue ball and it disappeared.

My eyes widened with horror as the meaning of that sank in. This attack had disintegrated my arrow and now it was going to do the same to me.

I thought briefly of my wife Layla and our child who had most definitely been born now, but who I'd never met. I couldn't die here.

Reggie: *Kaleb get out of there!*
Jamie: *I don't think he has enough time.*
Bell: *If you die I'll do weird things to your corpse.*

Well, that's uncalled for. I thought as I looked the rotating blue ball in its metaphorical eye. They say never look a gift horse in the mouth and I was looking an enraged dinosaur in the mouth…and regretting it.

I fired another arrow, this time at the wounded leg. It hit and Bex stumbled but didn't fall. She must have been the *Weeble Wobble* of prehistoric creatures. I mean seriously, that leg had been sliced and shot and she still refused to fall over.

Another fireball bounced off the back of her head at the same time as Jamie used his water powers to slice at her stomach. Blood trickled down her sternum and she was definitely looking the worse for wear. However, it was too late.

I looked towards her predatory eyes in abject horror as she released the blue ball. It was heading right for me, and there was nothing I could do about it.

Chapter 12
Extinction Event

The rotating blue ball of energy was about twice the size of my head when Bex released it from her mouth. It glided through the air towards me and I panicked.

I didn't know what to do, so I did the only thing I could think of. It was more of a reflex action than anything. I fired a barely charged *Soul Shot-infused* arrow at the ball of blue energy.

The arrow impacted and I was blinded by a dazzling, all-encompassing white light. I felt pain in my chest and stomach. It was a cracking and sharp pain like I'd been stabbed.

It was excruciating and likely made worse by my vision being blinded. They say that if you lose one sense the others become more potent, that's why some people use blindfolds in not-so-romantic encounters.

Sadly, it also made everything much more painful.

I screamed out as my insides seemed to be on fire. The pain was intense and not being able to see the damage myself was a huge source of anxiety. How bad was it? Who knew?

I heard Bex roar at a higher pitch than before. She sounded scared and in pain. Had my arrow somehow fought through the disintegrating ball of energy and pierced her face?

I fucking hope so. I thought bitterly as my body convulsed with the pain in my stomach. *I hope my arrow melts the damn lizard chicken.*

"Don't go into the light!" I heard Bell shout somewhere in the distance. Without proper context, I couldn't tell if she was serious or not, but knowing her it was a bad joke.

Her sense of humour was seriously weird.

"Kaleb, stay with me." I heard Reggie's voice and felt cold hands touching my skin. I still couldn't see, but I trusted the healer to do his best for me.

My HP was firmly in the 25% radius, but it wasn't flashing red or anything, so I wasn't too close to death. At least not yet. That was actually a victory for me, assuming we won the fight. I'd ended more than my fair share of monster fights with barely a single HP left. I was improving.

Still though, whatever had happened to me was seriously painful. Why had my arrow made the energy ball explode?

"Did we win?" I mumbled, though my voice seemed slurred as it came out. It barely sounded like me at all.

"Yeah, the dino is dead. I'll fix you up though man, don't worry," Reggie replied, he sounded distracted as he spoke. The sign of a true healer I guess.

Whilst he did his thing I decided to attempt meditation. I did my best to block out the pain and dove into my soul space.

The red rope representing my health was frayed and snapped, almost all of the damage was located in my core. I guess that made sense considering it was where the pain was coming from.

I breathed in and focused on sending energy towards it. The frayed and broken rope began to mend way quicker than normal. I had to assume that was Reggie's helping hand healing me from the outside as I fixed myself from the inside.

I noticed that a thinner, more intricate rope of scarlet was located behind my eyes. I decided to focus more energy there and the red rope began to glow brightly. Then I opened my eyes.

It seemed to have done the trick. The world outside was bright and the light stung as it hit my retina, but I could see.

Reggie was crouched next to me pouring green light into my abdomen. I looked down my chest and saw a gaping wound with large purple bruises on either side stretching up towards my chest.

That explained the snapping pain. My ribs were broken. My chest armour had been all but destroyed, but the self-repair function that all adventurer attire has was already hard at work repairing it.

Strands of black material twined together by themselves and slowly but surely began remaking the armour. Thank God for that, I didn't want to buy another set. This one was expensive enough as it was.

The notification symbol flashed in the corner of my HUD and I decided to open it. It wasn't like I'd be going anywhere until Reggie was done doing his thing anyway. Though I could have healed it myself through meditation, he'd explained previously that his healing power was a lot faster.

You have defeated (Tyrannosaurus Bex) lvl 48.

Bonus experience awarded due to level disparity.

Congratulations! You have advanced to lvl 35

Congratulations! You have advanced to lvl 36

Holy fuck-nuggets. I thought as I saw Bex's level. She was a lot stronger than me and it showed. I was thankful to have had the team's help with her.

She was on the cusp of hitting phase three, whereas I had barely scratched phase two. I got a full two levels from her too which was awesome. It also showed how strong she was, considering how difficult it was to level up in phase two. She was definitely a worthy opponent.

I happily added all ten of my free points into intelligence. The quicker I got that skill up the better considering how it affected my ability to use my new stealth skills.

I had one more notification to open and I braced myself as I realised it was an achievement.

Achievement Unlocked!

Extinction Event
**Why can't a T-Rex clap its hands? *Because it's extinct.*
You murdered a unique dinosaur by shooting a soul-infused arrow into a ball of pure, condensed mana. Poor Bex died in agony, reliving flashbacks to the meteor which destroyed her brethren back on Earth.
Of course, she had never met any dinosaurs from Earth, but you get the picture.
Poor Bex won't be making any more trips to the dino-store, well-fucking-done.
Is that enough bad jokes for you?**

Reward: *Extinction Loot Box*

"I regret teasing you," I said quietly to the sky. "I regret it so damn much."

Though the loot box was pretty cool. I wondered if the system would continue the theme and give me an ancient rarity prize. That would be pretty awesome.

The pain had pretty much subsided by the time I'd worked my way through the notifications and I looked at Reggie who had his tongue stuck out slightly to the side as he worked.

"Am I gonna make it doc?" I said facetiously with mock sincerity.

"Yeah, you'll be just fine." He replied slowly, as he concentrated on the last bit of healing. "Honestly, sleep would have fixed this. It looked painful but you were unlikely to die.

"I don't think any of us wanted to stay the night in this clearing though, so my healing was mostly to save time."

"Jeez, thanks so much," I replied. "Your bedside manner is truly commendable," I mumbled.

Reggie smirked as he finished up the last bit of healing he needed to do and then I sat up. I looked down at my stomach and it looked as good as new, I was even starting to get a faint six-pack.

It turns out that if you wanna get a model-like body, all you have to do is get isekai'd, who knew? The bruising around my chest had gone too and honestly, I felt as good as new.

I sat up and looked towards Bex the dinosaur. Her head had almost disintegrated.

"How did that happen?" I asked, pointing at the corpse.

"When you shot that energy blast with your arrow it blew her face up," Reggie answered. "That's also how your stomach ended up such a mess, but the dino got the worst of it. We left the loot for you since you delivered the finishing blow."

I looked towards his sincere eyes. Reggie seemed like a pretty genuine guy. We might have gotten off to a rocky start with my duel with Jake Milicent, but he was starting to grow on me.

I still didn't think he looked like a healer though. His short and stocky build just didn't seem to mesh in my opinion. I guess it goes to show that you really can't judge a book by its cover.

I jumped up to my feet and approached the sizzling, bubbling dino corpse and the familiar message hovering above it.

Would you like to loot *Tyrannosaurus Bex*?
Y/N

I mentally asserted yes and her body, along with the smell of ozone and burning feathers, burst into confetti. The system didn't seem to be able to make its mind up on what exactly should happen when a monster got looted.

It was different pretty much every time.

You have received a new item:

Scarlet Dino Feathers

Feathers that can be used in crafting.

X1000 gold coins.

"What did you get?" Bell said, appearing from behind me with her hands behind her back and an excited smile on her face.

"I got her feathers, apparently it's a crafting item," I replied nonchalantly.

"That's boring," she whined. "I was hoping you'd get her energy ball power."

"I don't think that's how powers work." I sighed, watching Jamie clamber over the stream to join us.

He crossed very diligently, carefully jumping from rock to rock so he didn't get wet. That probably wasn't a bad idea considering all the blood, gore and crap that had gotten in there, courtesy of Bex.

"I've done a sweep of the surrounding area, there doesn't seem to be any more monsters. We should probably report back now." Jamie said breathlessly.

Apparently crossing a small stream was a bit much for him. The dude obviously needed more cardio in his life.

"No need." Sally's voice boomed across the clearing and we all turned towards her.

Tilly trailed behind her, looking rather uninterested, and Panda was at her side, smoking his bamboo pipe.

"That was a good show, kid," he said, looking at my bare chest and stomach and smirking. "Shame about your armour though."

"It'll grow back," I replied defensively.

"I think it's a good look for you," Bell chimed in sweetly. "Very…progressive."

I shook my head and Sally held up her hand, signalling for us to be quiet.

"That was better than last time," she began sincerely. "Having a leader and a grasp of what each other can do has made a big difference, and that was a tough opponent, so well done."

Jamie and Reggie high-fived and I smiled to myself. It was rare to get praise from Sally and it felt good.

"That being said, you could have done better. It's a few days hike to our objective so you'll keep fighting and training and honing your prowess as we go. Hopefully, you'll be up to the task given to us after that."

Tilly smirked at Sally's words and shook her head lightly. It was obvious that she didn't think much of us. I really wanted to learn some new bow techniques from her. Perhaps, there would be a chance over the next few days, though something in her demeanour made me doubt it.

Sally and Tilly headed out of the clearing and we followed them tiredly. Panda walked beside me silently, something was still wrong with him but he didn't seem willing to tell me what it was.

Sally was a slave driver, but I would be stronger by the end of this quest, of that I had no doubt. Que the training montage.

Chapter 13
Intermission: Isobel Atthill

Isobel was an unassuming girl. A slender build and quiet personality made for a lacklustre impression on others. She'd have been all but invisible to the world if not for her illness, even then, she barely knew anyone outside of the hospital.

The Atthill family was extremely wealthy. The kind of wealth that afforded them the luxury of private doctors, nurses, and their own hospital wing. It was in that hospital wing where Isobel lived her unassuming life.

Her disease was rare. Less than 1% of the entire population of planet Earth had it and because of that, there was no cure. It wasn't that it couldn't be cured, nothing is ever permanent with proper funding, time and the brightest minds working on it, but why would they?

1% of the eight-billion-person population was no small number of people, but next to more common ailments like cancer, why would researchers spend their time researching Isobel's illness?

Medical advancement was a numbers game. There was only a finite amount of time and resources and the general consensus was to work on saving the most people possible from the most common ailments.

Isobel didn't mind though; she'd known she was fated to die young for as long as she could remember and she had accepted it.

It might not have been fair. God knew it was a tragedy for a person to die before reaching adulthood. It is a horrendous misfortune for a parent to outlive their child and naturally her parents fought the uphill battle of saving her life with gusto.

Isobel, however, had already accepted her fate. In a way it was kind of freeing, knowing roughly when you were going to die.

Her fate was no different from anyone else's. Most humans lived their lives expecting to die sometime after seventy. Sure, expecting to die before reaching twenty was a much shorter time frame, but she had never known anything else, so was it really that upsetting?

Death is only sad for those who are left behind.

That was a sentiment that both comforted and distressed her. She didn't want her parents to forget to live their own lives for the sake of trying to extend hers in vain.

Her mother and father were both scientists. They were famous researchers, renowned in their respective fields. Hailing from two powerful families, their arranged union brought another level of prestige and prosperity to the proud Atthill line.

Neither of them cared much for family politics though.

With the exception of playing outside like a normal child, Isobel wanted for nothing. If she desired something and money could buy it, she had it.

Her personal hospital wing was a nerdy hoarder's dream. There were DVDs, manga, books, light novels, and video game boxes stacked to the ceiling in every part of her room.

She had taken to media like a fish to water. It was her window into the outside world, the only way she could experience anything outside of the clinical monotony of hospital life.

It was escapism at its finest.

The thing about being terminally ill is that no one expects any-thing of you. You're a subject of pity, useless to wider society, and that suited Isobel just fine.

Without the burden of schooling, work, social interactions, or physical activity, all of her time was her own. She'd have to be an idiot not to get the most out of it.

So she spent her days playing the latest video games, watching and rewatching movies and reading every book she could find on the internet, ordering physical copies when she could find them.

In the early days when she was growing up, she'd see her parents every day. They'd practically moved into her hospital wing, and when they weren't working they were together as a family.

Her father might not have been able to push her on the swing and her mother couldn't take her swimming, which was her favour-ite hobby, but they were together. A perfect and happy family unit.

Isobel could say with a smile that she had the perfect family life with loving parents who spent time with her. But that didn't last.

By the time of her twelfth birthday, she barely saw her father anymore. He worked constantly. He had dedicated himself to find-ing a cure for his beloved daughter and no matter his wife's concerns of overwork or his daughter's pleas to spend time together, he wouldn't stop.

He was consumed by his desire to save her. That's what Isobel had to believe. She felt awful for him for his endeavour was doomed to fail. She didn't need him to save her, she just needed *him*.

Yet he couldn't see past his single-tracked goal of finding a cure.

Her mother was different. She still worked on a cure, but she balanced her life much better than her husband. She made a point of spending a few hours with her daughter every day.

Though the older she got, the wearier her mother became. Hav-ing a daughter with such a short natural life span must have taken its toll on her emotionally. She wore that agony in the lines on her face, lines that most people didn't get at such a young age.

Her hair had turned grey by the age of 35 and Isobel knew it was because of her.

On her fifteenth birthday, her father had been absent. He was working, as usual. Her mother had spent the day with her however, and they played old video games together, watched *The Princess Bride*, their favourite movie, and even played some old board games that Isobel's mother had bought her as a surprise.

It was truly a great birthday, but Isobel was much more perceptive to the feelings of others than she let on. So she noticed the tiredness behind her mother's eyes. She saw the smiles that didn't quite reach them. She heard the tinge of sadness behind her every word.

It was heartbreaking. To cause so much pain to those around you by simply existing was a fate she wouldn't wish on anyone.

As Isobel moved into her later teens she would not get to experience the usual coming-of-age celebrations that most adults the world over enjoy. She would not share her first alcoholic beverage with her parents because her condition wouldn't allow for it.

She would not meet someone, fall in harmless teenage lust, call it love and then cry when her partner inevitably moved across the country to attend a different college to her.

Nor would she take a gap year and go backpacking around Europe or South Asia, meeting new people, experiencing new cultures, and *finding* herself.

All of these things that movies had trained her to expect, would never come to be. Her life was not finally beginning as the Hollywood tropes so often suggested, it was ending.

At the age of eighteen, she entered her twilight years. Her condition worsened and even engaging with the media she so loved was a challenge.

Her body began shutting down. She lacked energy. The end was closing in, and yet she was at peace with it. It would be easy to curse her short life. To look at the world around her and feel bitterness.

There were so many experiences that others took for granted. A first kiss, playing football in the street with your friends, going to parties, being able to walk unassisted.

Yes, it would be easy to be overcome by jealousy. To look to the sky and curse God for abandoning her. But what use was there in that?

There was no happiness to be found in comparing her life to the lives of others. Despite what people like to tell themselves, equality is, and will always be a lie.

People are not born equal and they never have been. So comparing oneself to others is a fool's errand.

Isobel genuinely believed that, and as she made peace with her death, hospital machines beeping angrily around her as worried doctors and nurses burst into her room and began trying to save her, she had only one regret.

She wished she'd have been able to spend more time with her father.

The panicked voices of the hospital staff began to fade as her vision turned to black. She'd soon be at peace, having lived a life of escapism and multi-media indulgence. She was sure that to many it sounded like paradise.

Then she woke up.

She found herself in a jungle, surrounded by...palm trees.

Isobel had never been in a jungle before, she'd never even been outside. How had she gotten here, and where the hell was here anyway?

She pushed herself off the ground and moved towards the nearest tree, stroking it with her palm. It felt firm yet smooth with small, evenly placed ridges running the length of the thin trunk.

Amazing, who would have thought that this was what palm trees felt like? She thought to herself, marvelling at the simple pleasure of nature. A pleasure she had never known, until now.

"Wait, am I walking?!" she exclaimed, looking down at her legs with wide, excited eyes.

She tried jumping and it…worked. Her legs worked, without any assistance or anything. There was no pain, no exhaustion, just…movement.

So this is what jumping feels like. I've really been missing out.

She hopped around the little clearing where she had woken up, giggling to herself like a maniac as her hospital clothes flapped merrily up and down.

If anyone had been watching her they'd have thought she was an escaped mental patient, but she didn't care.

Then time stopped. Like, literally stopped. Isobel was floating in mid-air, frozen. A phenomenon that defied all scientific logic as she knew it.

An overly happy voice filled her ears and words appeared in her vision, like a notification from a video game:

Welcome players, to Celestia!
You are the newest residents of this little slice of
heaven, lucky you.

This is a world filled with peoples of all races, monsters,
magic and even the odd dragon or two.
How great does that sound? It's literally every nerd's
dream come true right?
So, what's the catch?
You're being hunted!

That's right folks, all 10,000 of you have been gifted a
brand-new tattoo, completely free of charge. Each tattoo
is a wholly unique and different part of a map. The
Celestial Map to be precise, not that I expect you to
know what that means.

Our prestigious hunters are oh so very eager to put that
map back together again, piece by agonising piece.

They see you when you're sleeping. They know when
you're awake. They want to skin you all alive so run or
you'll get flayed!

The map is on your skin and starting now, the hunt is
on.

Good look out there, players. We hope you enjoy your
stay in the idyllic and welcoming world of Celestia.

"Well, that settles it then," she said to herself as time resumed
and she dropped to the floor. "I've been isekai'd…awesome!"

Isobel was aware that talking to one's self aloud would have been
considered a little unhinged back home, but if there was no one
around to hear her did it really make a difference if she spoke to
herself or not?

She ran around in a circle some more, enjoying the freedom of
movement which she had never before experienced.

Once she ran out of breath and had to take a moment to calm
down, she smiled.

"This is my second life." She grinned up at the clear blue sky.
"I'm going to live without fear and I'm going to try and make some
real-life, honest-to-goodness friends, and I'm going to do all the
things I never could back on Earth."

She grinned from ear to ear as she looked around the palm tree jungle. This was her chance to experience something new. Who needs escapism when you can live it? Fantasy was her favourite genre. Maybe there would be a wise old wizard with a pointy hat and white hair to guide her.

Maybe *she* could be a wizard and learn spells and shit.

Who knew?

"I'm gonna need a new name if I'm going to start a new life." She mused to herself. Her mother had always called her Izzy for short. She'd liked it well enough, but she didn't feel much like an Izzy anymore.

Izzy was her hospital name and she wasn't sick now.

"I guess I could just shorten my name the other way?" She said with a shrug. "Yeah, that works. In this world, I'll be known as Bell, and I'm going to be a mother fucking wizard! I wonder if they have the fireball spell in Celestia. That spell was always super OP in games."

Chapter 14
Spider Bukkake

I dived to the side, narrowly avoiding a swipe from the huge spider's hairy leg, slashing out with my daggers as I went.

The overgrown arachnid howled with pain as my dagger tore into it and the skin around the leg started to bubble violently.

I saw my reflection in its eight, crimson eyes as it glared at me. I'd say it was shooting venom with that glare, but why use a metaphor when it literally shot venom from its hairy, horror movie mouth.

The purple liquid fired from its fangs in little spit balls of death as I narrowly avoided them with a matrix-style dodge. Sadly, I was no Keanu Reves and as I leaned backwards to avoid the venomous glob, I fell on my ass and had to roll to the side as the spider tried to impale me with its front leg.

I slashed at that leg too, but the arachnid was too quick and all I managed to do was slice through some of its thick hairs.

"That was a close shave!" Bell quipped from the sidelines as she and the rest of the team watched my struggle.

I was battling solo at Sally's request. She wanted to see us all in action against various types of monsters. We'd been at it all day and I was the last one to perform.

"I've been in hairier situations," I shouted back as I threw myself to my feet and pressed my attack.

Sally had forbidden me from starting the fight with a *Soul Shot*. She'd said I was becoming too predictable and she wanted to see how I fought when I couldn't use a sneaky power attack.

Naturally, I instead produced both of my daggers and ran at the overgrown spider like a madman. I wasn't the best melee fighter, the bow was definitely my speciality, but that didn't mean I couldn't fight without it – or at least, that's what I'd hoped to prove to her.

I ducked under the spider's carapace and slammed both of my daggers into the underside of its body as I ran between its legs. A shower of bloody, purple gore gushed from its belly behind me, giving me all the more reason to keep going.

There were no showers in the palm tree jungle and I did not want to be known as the guy who smelled like spider guts and put everyone off their dinner.

The arachnid screamed in a distorted, high-pitched, monster voice as I opened its stomach. Its blood mixed with venom and burned at the grass below it. The hissing sound and burning smell were terrifying, but as long as I didn't get any of it on me, I should have been ok.

I reached the other side of the carapace and combat rolled the last few meters, turning around swiftly and raising my blades across my face to block an incoming kick.

However, spiders don't kick, they web.

And as I raised my blades to protect myself from an incoming attack, I realised I had made a big mistake. I was on the wrong side of the spider, with the wrong weapon to help me.

A thick, gloopy web fired from its backside and hit me straight in the face. My daggers did very little to prevent the spider bukkake that covered me from head to toe.

So much for staying clean. I sighed internally.

The underside of the spider burned as the acid made short work of the arachnid's guts and innards. It stank like rotting flesh and burnt arm hair. Hopefully, it would be dead soon, reduced to a steaming pile of venomous goop. I'd barely taken any damage either. However, I was still going to be known as the guy who took fresh webbing to the face.

"Hey, Kaleb!" Bell shouted, cupping her hands around her mouth as she struggled to contain her laughter. "Do you spit, or swallow?"

Yup, I'm never going to live this one down.

"Ask your mum Bell," I yelled back. I didn't have time to waste thinking up a better comeback, and mum jokes were classics.

I heard Panda chuckle at my retort as I dove back in and slashed at the arachnid's spinnerets. I didn't need to continue attacking. The spider was as good as dead, but I had frustrations that could only be taken out on eight-legged creatures, and frankly, I needed the violent therapy.

The spider dropped to the ground with more of a whimper than a scream and the familiar notification filled my HUD.

You have defeated *Giant Spider* (lvl 39)
Bonus experience awarded due to level disparity.

The giant spider was three levels above me, yet I defeated it with relative ease and without using my bow. I'd take that as a win, even as I pulled chunks of thick, sticky web off my face.

You know that feeling you get when you think about spiders, or maybe you see some web as you're walking through a wooded area, and suddenly it feels like you have web on you.

I bet you're doing it right now, aren't you? Maybe a loose strand of hair has brushed your forehead and for some reason, it feels like a spider web, so you brush it away and then the same feeling happens again except on the back of your neck.

I felt like that. Except it wasn't a phantom web, it was a real, tangible web from a giant motherfucking arachnid who had webbed all over me, and now I was never going to be free of that feeling again.

Oh god, how I hate spiders. I shivered as I moved in to loot it.

Do you want to loot *Giant Spider*?
Y/N

You have received a new item:
Spider Silk
Venomous Sack
X1000 gold coins

The silk and sack were both crafting items, according to the system. I was getting more and more crafting items recently and I made a mental note of hiring someone to make something for me with all of my new materials when I got back to Havar.

I was sure Panda knew a guy. Probably a small shop on that same street where all the other shops were. The scope of his Havarian contacts was pretty limited now that I thought about it.

My theory about coins also seemed to be proving correct. As with the last monster I looted, I received 1000 gold coins, instead of the usual 10 which I had become accustomed to.

The only thing that those two monsters had in common was that they were both phase two. As was the slime queen I'd killed ages ago, which also gave me 1000 gold coins.

I think it was safe to say that the amount I looted correlated to the phase the kill was in. Phase one's netted 10 gold per kill. Phase two's netted 1000. If I could get to a point where I was regularly killing phase four's I'd be super fucking rich in no time.

Maybe I'd be able to hire someone to isekai my family to me with that kind of money. I could buy my own skull-shaped island and sit on a swivel chair with Panda in my lap. As my arch nemesis entered my lair, I could turn around menacingly and tell them I'd been expecting them.

Pulling myself from my *Bond* villain fantasy, I opened my penultimate notification.

Achievement Unlocked!
Arachnophobia

So you've taken web to the face? Now you know what all those poor girls on *Porn Hub* feel like. You're a dirty little slut, aren't you?
Seriously though, spiders are gross and you need to kill more of them. If I could shiver, I would, but I'm the system and I don't have normal bodily functions.
Anyway:
Did you hear about the spider who ate a fly? He was a real buzz kill.
Reward: *Bukkake Loot Box*

"Oh come on!" I shouted up at the sky to the backdrop of Panda's howling laughter as he saw my reward through his ability to see my HUD as my familiar.

I shook my head and pulled up my final notification.

Dagger has advanced to lvl 11.

Well, at least that was good. I needed to improve my dagger as much as possible if I wanted the skill to evolve as the *bow* skill had done.

Theoretically, if I got the *dagger* skill to level 25, it would evolve into a better skill. At least, that was what had happened with my *bow* skill.

"The system called you a whore didn't it?" Bell smirked as she and the rest of the group strolled towards me.

"Something like that," I grumbled, picking web off my face and out of my stubbly hair.

"See, this is why I always thought *Spider-man* was a creepy dude." Bell mused. "Shooting web at people, it's just a bit of a gross metaphor."

"You leave *Spider-man* out of this!" I gasped, pointing at her face. "He is a national treasure. There's a reason his franchise has been rebooted so many times in such a short period of time."

"…Because the writers lack creativity and the shareholders love a good cash grab?" Bell replied innocently.

"Well yeah, probably," I sighed, scratching the top of my head where loose bits of web were still clinging to me. "But they do it with Spiderman because he's such a great character."

"*Wolverine* is better," she said folding her arms and giving me a deadpan look. "He's not tied down by annoying morality. He smokes, drinks *and* is an all-round badass and they got *Hugh Jackman* to play him, which means he has the voice of an angel…and the claws, can't forget about those."

"In the most recent *Spider-man*, they got all three of the actors who played him together and recreated the meme," I replied arrogantly. "Did *Wolverine* do his meme in his movies? No, he didn't. He just used crappy CGI and butchered *Deadpool's* character so badly that *Ryan Reynolds* had to reprise the character in his own movies to try and salvage the hatchet job that was done to him."

"Shut up!" Sally yelled, thumping us both on the tops of our heads. "Quit talking nonsense and let's move on."

My brain literally rattled around in my skull as I looked up and saw multiple Sally's pointing and shouting at me. Damn, that steroid kitty could hit.

"Honestly, it feels like you two talk in code sometimes," she sighed, rubbing her palm on her face. "Your performance was pretty good Kaleb," she said with a fangy grin. "Next time though, try not to get bukkaked. You're an adventurer, not a porn star."

She walked away as Reggie and Jamie doubled over with laughter, clutching their stomachs. Tilly and Panda followed her and he also giggled, but less enthusiastically.

Something was still wrong with him and I knew I needed to find out what it was. He was acting so strange, normally he'd have been the first to tease me. The little guy loved banter. Yet he barely ribbed me at all during, or after that fight.

"Come on," Sally yelled as she left the battle site. "There's a small village at the foot of the mountain. We'll rest up there for the night."

We had been travelling through the palm tree jungle for about a week. After our fight with the dinosaur, we had plenty of chances to fight as a team.

Slowly, we'd honed our teamwork and our solo ability with instruction from Sally. I'd hoped to learn a thing or two about bowmanship from Tilly the elf, but she'd refused to take me along on her hunts.

I didn't know how she did it, but every night she left for an hour or two and came back with a bountiful collection of meats whilst we set up the camp.

The woman was a genius at living off the land. Maybe she'd give me some tips before we fought the dragon, though considering its lair was at the top of the mountain, I doubted we'd have time.

I trudged after the rest of the group as they followed Sally out of the clearing, wondering if we had what it took to defeat something as legendary as a dragon.

One sleep, and then we'd fight it. It was like counting down the days until Christmas.

Chapter 15
Never Trust A Man Who Tries To Sell You A Caravan

We only had a short walk until we reached the village at the foot of the mountain. We hadn't slept since we'd left the elven inn a week ago.

We meditated in shifts when we needed to recover stamina or health, usually after a few battles, but that was the only rest we got. At my level, I could put off sleeping for a long time as long as I meditated enough.

I was getting quite good at it too. I could recharge my HP and stamina in half the time it took everyone else to. Bell was still in the early stages of her meditation technique.

She didn't really seem to understand how it worked fully. Reggie had spent a lot of time talking her through it, sometimes for hours, as she struggled to navigate her soul.

I had taken to it right away back when Sally and Panda first talked me through it. However, according to the others, I was a bit of a special case. Meditation and tapping into the soul were apparently techniques that most people struggled to get to grips with.

I guess my natural talent for it kind of made up for my lack of mana...actually, on second thought, it definitely didn't. Magic was way cooler than meditation.

Thanks again System, you ass.

We walked for about an hour after I finished off the giant spider. Reggie had dropped back to chat with me for a bit, he voiced some concerns he had about the make-up of the team.

According to him, a well-balanced adventuring team should have at least one dedicated melee specialist, and we didn't have one. He raised a good point. Apart from myself, everyone was a mage. So we were three long-range attackers and a healer.

Not very balanced at all.

After some pleading from Reggie, I promised to mention it to Sally later. I didn't really want to have that conversation with her, but who knew, maybe it'd get me some bonus points on the exam for thinking critically about tactics.

We pushed through the final layer of palm trees and found ourselves facing a sheer cliff face. The mountain reached past the clouds and was made of a dark grey rock. It looked pretty foreboding and I hoped it wasn't a sign of things to come.

At the foot of the rocky mountain stood a small mining village which could easily have been mistaken for a full-blown town. There were rows and rows of medieval-style stone houses with thatch roofs.

They reminded me of the little cottages I'd drive past in the English countryside in my old job as a truck driver. It was a quaint little village, but lively, much more so than the elven village we'd stayed in along the way.

As we walked through the main square, a small, bearded fellow came over to greet us. He had black soot on his face and carried a pickaxe which looked way too big for him.

His legs were short but his shoulders and arms were huge! Seriously, he could have given Sally a run for her money and if they arm wrestled, I wasn't sure who I'd bet on.

I focused on him and a notification popped up on my HUD, confirming my suspicions.

You have discovered a new race:
Dwarf

From *Tolkien* to *Sapkowski*, every fantasy author on Earth has written about dwarves at some point. You know what they are, so you don't need a notification to tell you about them.
Seriously, do some of your own research for once.
Interestingly though, *dwarves* are a part of Norse Mythology back in your world and were adopted into fantasy stories most famously by *Tolkien*, and then everyone else started doing it too.
Did you know that in his famous series, he decided that the plural for *dwarf* would be *dwarves*? At the time, the accepted plural was spelled *dwarfs* but the man refused to change it when challenged by his editor. I guess when you're the father of fantasy you can get away with that stuff. Though I heard his editor got a little *short* with him about the whole ordeal.
Get it?

"Well lookie here!" The dwarf exclaimed as he strutted towards us, swinging his pickaxe. "It seems we've got us some adventurers, boys." He called over his shoulder and a few others looked our way, a few of them heading towards us.

"We're from the Adventure Society, yes." Sally began tentatively. "We heard you've got a dragon problem?"

"You heard right missy." The lead dwarf replied. "That scaley fuck has been terrorising the village he has. Keeps stealing our livestock whilst we're working the mines. Mighty rude of him if you ask me."

Bell covered her mouth, her eyes betraying a stifled laugh. It was probably his west country accent; it was pretty comical.

"But where are my manners." He continued, placing his dirty hand over his heart. "My name is Ale, the mayor and chief miner in these parts, and these two idiots are Whiskey and Vodka." He added, almost as an afterthought, gesturing to the two gawping dwarves watching us from a few feet away.

At the mention of their names, Whiskey and Vodka trotted sheepishly towards us.

"Those are some…interesting names," Reggie said sceptically, taking Ale's hand in Sally's place as she backed up hesitantly. Apparently, the overgrown kitten wasn't overly fond of non-violent physical contact.

"Aye," the dwarf mayor replied. "It's customary in our village for kids to be named after what their da was drinking when they were conceived. Been doing it for generations, we have."

"You must run out of names pretty quickly," I said, walking towards the dwarf, who stretched out his hand as I approached.

I took it and he squeezed as we shook. It was a proper dad handshake. I couldn't help it, I'd never met a dwarf before, much less one with a west country accent—I'd always expected them to be Scottish.

I knew I'd regret it for the rest of my life if I didn't speak to him, it was just too good of an opportunity to pass up.

"I'm Kaleb by the way," I said as we shook.

"Nice to meet you. But, Nah, we've got a naming system in place." Ale replied, gesticulating wildly as he spoke. From the smell of him, he was probably a little drunk. "Take Vodka over there. He just got his lass Brandy up the duff whilst off his tits on whiskey. So naturally the bairn will be called Whiskey-Two since we've already got a Whiskey." He gestured loosely towards the shy-looking dwarf standing a few meters back. He waved awkwardly as I looked at him.

"What does Whiskey-One think about that?" I replied, keeping up easily with the west country drawl.

"Oh he's over the moon he is," Ale replied. "Vodka and Whiskey have been best mates for ages now, he was the best man at his wedding you know? He's actually going to be Whiskey-Two's godfather, how cute is that?"

"I'm getting a migraine," Reggie complained, rubbing the front of his head.

"Kaleb!" Sally shouted and I jumped, snapping my head in the direction of her drill sergeant voice. "Stop talking nonsense with the dwarf and ask him to set us up with some rooms for the night."

"He *has* a name," I replied, raising my eyebrows at her.

"I'm sure he does, but I can't understand much of what he's saying so I'm promoting you to my dwarven liaison officer whilst we're here," she retorted, crossing her arms, and sounding rather proud of herself.

The *promotion* sounded more like being shafted to me, but I didn't mind too much. I was growing pretty fond of Ale; he reminded me of home—even though I'd never been to Somerset before.

"Sorry about her," I apologised to the dwarven mayor. "Do you guys have an inn we can stay at for the night?"

"Nay worries mate, catonids and dwarfs aren't known to be chummy." He placed his hand to the side of his mouth before continuing with a whisper and eyeing Sally. "If you ask me, it's because they can't handle their drink. Word to the wise young Kaleb, never trust a man who can't handle his booze.

"Oh…and never trust a man who tries to sell you a caravan either. One minute you're looking around the place and the next he's nicked off with your shoelaces."

"I'll take that under consideration, Ale," I laughed, "so, about those rooms?"

"Oh aye, we've got plenty of rooms we do," he replied with a friendly smile, "inn's over there. If you get some time before you slay our dragon, come find me and I'll treat you to my namesake."

"I might just take you up on that," I said, shaking the mayor's dirty hand again before leading the group towards the inn he'd pointed out.

"We're going to have to call you the dwarf whisperer from now on," Bell mused happily.

"They do say everyone's a genius at something," Panda added. "Shame your talent is talking to little alcoholics."

"That's why me and you are such good friends," I replied, earning a chuckle from some of the group.

The inn we'd been directed to looked like a typical fantasy anime inn. It was a Tudor-looking building with whitewash walls held together by wooden beams, and it had a little sign hanging above the door that said: *Drink Inn*.

I smiled at the name; it definitely suited the residents of the village. I pushed open the wooden door with Sally hot on my heels.

It was surprisingly busy inside, wooden tables and booths were filled with rowdy dwarven customers clanking tankards, talking, and just generally having a good time.

Sally nudged me towards the bar which was manned by a fancy-looking dwarf in a checkered, tweed suit. He had one of those moustaches that was twirled at the ends and he wore a bowler hat.

"Ask for six rooms, ideally in the quietest section of the inn," Sally asked, pushing me towards the bar with a forceful hand. She

115

seemed pretty uncomfortable around the dwarves. It was odd, I figured that straight-talking, hard-working drinkers like them would be exactly the kind of people she'd like.

"Hi, can I get—" I began.

"Six rooms, as quiet as you like?" The dapper-looking bartender cut in. "I heard her, and yes you can. They'll all be on the top floor and it'll be three gold please."

I turned back to Sally to translate but she seemed to get the picture. The dwarf held out his hand with a big smile plastered on his face but Sally ignored it and placed the money on the countertop.

"Thanks," I said sheepishly as Sally pushed away from the bar and headed straight for the stairs. I followed behind her, struggling to keep up as she took them three or four steps at a time.

Her tail was tucked between her massive thighs as she bounded away from the bar.

I finally caught up to her on the top floor, panting after basically sprinting up twelve flights of stairs.

"What the hell is wrong with you?" I yelled, hands on my knees and panting.

"Nothing!" She replied defensively, throwing open the nearest door and checking the room. She looked like she was in a spy movie as she picked up lamps and squatted down to look underneath the bed.

"I doubt it's been bugged," I said, following her inside as the rest of our group began to catch up.

"An adventurer can never be too cautious."

"Cut the crap kitty cat," I interrupted. "Don't try and pass this off as a lesson. What's your problem with dwarves? They all seem super friendly to me," I asked, placing my hands on my hips.

"They *are* super friendly. That's the problem," she replied, squirming slightly as she spoke. "It's creepy."

116

"Like clowns," Bell added from behind me, folding her arms and nodding her head knowingly. The rest of the group had caught up too and seemed to be enjoying the spectacle.

"Wait…are you scared of dwarves?" I asked incredulously, struggling to hide my snickering.

"Of course not!" She replied adamantly. "I would just rather not be around them…especially in enclosed spaces."

"You were just checking for dwarves under the bed weren't you?" I continued, the laughter becoming much harder to hold back.

Sally didn't reply. She stared at me with hard, dark blue eyes. I stared back for a long moment, trying to hold back the giggles.

Then she slammed the door and I couldn't hold it in anymore.

Chapter 16
...And You Can Take That Straight To The Bank

I bent over with my hands on my knees as I laughed. I couldn't help myself. The idea of the big, strong catonid silver ranker being terrified of a few little dwarves was just too amusing.

"I think you hurt her feelings," Reggie said from behind me, sounding genuinely concerned for Sally's emotional welfare.

He was such a nice guy. Too good for the likes of us. It didn't prevent me from laughing even harder at his serious tone though.

Bell giggled beside me, though she didn't seem to be quite as amused as I was.

"Reggie," I began, struggling to speak through the giggling fit I'd succumbed to. "I think she might be scared of you too."

I turned and looked him up and down. He was barely taller than a dwarf himself and his stocky shoulders didn't exactly help his case. Jamie smirked at this and Reggie's cheeks turned a deep shade of crimson.

"Fuck you, Kaleb," Reggie replied indignantly before turning on his heels and marching back down the stairs. "I'm getting a drink."

"Yup, he's definitely one of them," I called after him, practically howling at my own terrible joke.

Jamie flashed me a grin before hurrying after him. Even the moody Panda seemed to be enjoying the scene. Nothing put him in a good mood like verbally ripping into someone.

After a few moments of agonising laughter, I finally managed to regain control of myself. I turned to Bell and Panda; the latter was purposely facing away from the former as he looked up at me with cute, plushie-like eyes.

"In all seriousness, I actually do need to talk to Sally," I said, gesturing towards her room door. "I'll meet you downstairs."

Bell nodded and skipped away from us like a school kid playing hopscotch. Panda glanced towards her and shook his head.

"Good luck in there, kid." He snickered, before heading back to the bar as well.

With a sigh, I turned back to the door and knocked loudly. After a moment it was wrenched open and the towering catonid leaned over me, her scowling expression was the stuff of nightmares.

"What?" She huffed in a hostile tone.

"I need to talk to you about the make-up of the team," I replied earnestly. "Reggie and I spoke about it earlier and as team leader, it fell to me to speak with you."

She looked me up and down with her dark blue eyes as if deciding whether or not to entertain me. Then she quickly glanced up both sides of the hall as her silver hair swished from side to side, before stepping back and gesturing for me to come inside.

I entered her room and moved towards the window as she closed the door, applying a security chain which reminded me somewhat of a feature you'd expect to see in a shady motel.

The window was small, with no way to open it. It overlooked the village square where we'd met Ale. The sun was starting to drop below the peak of the mountain casting an idyllic orange glow over the quaint little mining town.

It reminded me of a typical postcard photo as I smiled to myself, basking in the natural beauty of it all. Directly opposite the inn was an entrance which seemed to lead underground.

It looked like a mine shaft. A thick, wooden frame crested the outside of a large tunnel that led into the mountain.

I wonder if the dwarves sing Hi-Ho as they walk single file down the shaft on their way to work. Now that would be a sight to see.

"Alright Gonads, what's your issue with the team," Sally said, half sighing as she plonked down onto the bed. It creaked with her weight and she crossed her legs and pulled out a thick cigar.

"Well," I began nervously, turning to face her and leaning back against the window ledge. "Reggie and I got to talking and we realised that the make-up of the team seems a little skewed.

"We have a healer, two casters and an archer, but no melee specialist. It just seems like a bit of a design flaw to me. Three long-ranged attackers and their healer don't exactly make for the most balanced adventuring team. Especially when our target is a dragon."

She looked at me, letting out a puff of thick, black smoke which spiralled soothingly into the air. The smell was all-encompassing and I just knew it was going to stick to my armour. I'd spent enough of my life smelling like a chain smoker, I wasn't keen on the idea of reliving that once I left the room.

I guess it can't be helped, I sighed internally.

"Yeah, you're not wrong," she said thoughtfully. "A standard team of four should have a melee fighter, a healer, a mage, and some kind of specialist to fill the final spot.

"The thing is Gonads; you *had* a melee fighter in your team. But, in your infinite wisdom, you decided to shoot his fucking hand off and send him to the healers."

Jake fucking Milicent. I thought, remembering the stuck-up noble brat who had challenged me to a duel at the first examinee meeting.

"Oh," I managed to say, struggling to find the words.

"Oh indeed," Sally smirked, flashing me a momentary fangy grin. "I wouldn't worry about it too much though. If that idiot noble challenged you to a duel the first time you met, then I doubt he'd have been a good team member for you anyway.

"Besides, you have those daggers of yours. There's a reason I forbade you from using your bow in your last solo fight." She smiled wickedly at me, taking in another drag from her cigar and pausing as her words sank in. "*You* are the team's melee specialist now."

Well, shit.

She'd really planned it all out, hadn't she? I was alright with my daggers, but the bow was where my powers and class skills really shone.

"...And you can take that straight to the bank." She smirked, rising from the bed, and opening her door slightly. "Now get out Gonads, I need my beauty sleep."

"More like a cat nap," I muttered as I marched past her with my shoulders slumped and my head hung low.

"What was that?" She growled and I disappeared down the stairs without answering.

As I re-entered the bar, I noticed that the rowdy dwarves were even more numerous. Most of them were dirty from the mine's soot, but they didn't seem to care.

They were simply drinking their fill and having a good time. It was admirable in a way, to see hard-working folk having a good time. The simple life was a far cry from my own these days.

"Kaleb, over here!" Bell shouted chirpily, waving to me from a small booth in the far corner. Panda and the rest of the team were with her.

He sat on the edge of the booth with his arms folded and a scowl etched onto his face. I waved back, asked the moustached bartender to send a round of drinks to the table, and joined them.

The booth they'd found was a little cramped, I guess it was dwarf-sized, but we all managed to cram in somehow.

"Well?" Reggie said after a few moments of silence.

"She said that it was my fault we didn't have a melee specialist because I kinda…shot his hand off," I replied, rubbing the back of my stubbled head awkwardly.

"Jake can be a real ass," Jamie muttered, shaking his head, and placing a cold hand on my shoulder.

I looked towards him. His eyes had large black rings underneath them and he looked pale. Perhaps other adventurers had a harder time going without sleep than I did.

"I guess we'll just have to make do," Reggie sighed and began loudly slurping ale from a wooden tankard.

I felt bad. It was technically my fault that we'd have to face the dragon with a sub-optimal team, but jeez, that Milicent guy was an asshole and he deserved to have it handed to him.

"Don't worry guys," Bell said sweetly. "I'll just use my fireball and nuke the lizard."

"Yeah…thanks," I replied, taking a swig of my own drink as the bartender placed the round I'd purchased on the table.

It was a thick, amber liquid with white froth on the top. It looked and smelled just like a beer back home…but it definitely wasn't.

It tasted like lukewarm motor oil and as the fizzy bubbles popped in my mouth, an overwhelming barley flavour lit up my taste buds.

It was awful. Definitely a far cry from the ale we had back home. I stuck out my tongue with disdain and placed the tankard back on the wet table half-heartedly.

"Not much of a drinker?" The bartender asked slyly as he watched me. "You know what they say: never trust a man who can't handle his booze." He winked at me and then walked away shaking his head and muttering something about sketchy sober humans.

"I think he likes you," Bell snickered. "Just like how my fuzzy little buddy over here likes me!" She reached across the table to scratch Panda behind the ears and he batted her hand away irritably.

"What's gotten into you lately?" I asked him as he glared at the sad-looking fireball mage.

"Nothing." He replied in a gruff tone, facing away from the group with folded arms.

"It's obviously not nothing," I replied.

I didn't want to push him if he didn't want to talk about it, but this was getting ridiculous. If he didn't like Bell that was fine, but he didn't need to be so moody to the rest of us, especially me. We were supposed to be friends.

He growled and hopped down from the booth bench, trotting through the crowd with clenched paws.

"Maybe you should talk to him in private?" Reggie suggested, offering me a shrug as he closed his thin lips together and widened his eyes.

He was probably right, so with a heavy sigh, I stood up and left the group just in time to catch my familiar heading up the stairs.

I squeezed through the growing crowd of drunken dwarfs to follow him. I took the steps two at a time in a concerted effort to catch up and as I rounded the corner of the last flight I heard a door click shut.

I opened it and realised it led out onto a flat, wooden roof. It was pretty barren but offered a nice view of the town.

Panda sat on the edge of the room, slumped over slightly, and lighting his bamboo pipe. If he knew I'd followed him, he didn't show it.

I moved next to him and plonked myself down on the edge, letting my legs dangle off the side. The breeze was quite nice and I looked over the top of the dwarven settlement as small, bumbling figures, staggered around on the streets below.

"You know," I began hesitantly. "If there's something bothering you, you can talk to me."

"It's stupid." He muttered, refusing to meet my eyes as I looked towards him.

"If it's bothering you then it's not stupid to me," I replied, choosing my words carefully. "We're partners in all this."

"Yeah but…for how long?" he said, looking at his lit pipe, but not smoking it.

"What do you mean?"

"Listen, kid." He sighed deeply. "I wasn't born yesterday, I'm a goddamn sage, and I can see that I've outgrown my use to you. Hell, I'm already being replaced."

I looked at him in silence. I wasn't sure what he meant but at least he was finally opening up to me.

"I'm a daemon." He continued slowly. "Yeah, I can be a useful guide in the beginning, but the more you level up and learn about this world, the less you need me.

"And now…" He sniffed slightly and took a breath. "…And now, you've got other people who can help you better than I can. I mean for fuck's sake; I can't even fill the role of comic relief anymore with that stupid fireball fuck around. I'm completely useless to you, and honestly, I'm just waiting for you to realise it and get rid of me."

I looked at him as he looked away, still refusing to meet my gaze. He took a long drag of his bamboo pipe and blew the smoke out into the pleasant night breeze.

"Yeah…" I began in a whimsical tone. "I guess you are pretty useless." His shoulders dropped and he finally turned to face me, I don't think he expected me to be so blunt about it. His big eyes looked up at me, shimmering, even in the dark.

"…But only a sociopath chooses his friends based on how useful they are to him. You're not just a tool to be used up and thrown away Panda, you're my friend…and honestly, I'm not the brightest bulb in the lamp, I could use some sagely advice from time to time."

I smiled warmly at him and placed my hand on his soft shoulder. He shook his head slightly and let out a slight chuckle.

"You're a real asshole, kid, you know that?" he said, taking another drag and blowing the smoke in my direction.

"I never claimed to be anything else mate."

Chapter 17
Molotov Cockatiel

We sat in comfortable silence for a while after our heart-to-heart. It was one of the most peaceful moments I'd had since arriving in Celestia, as we watched the sunset together.

Panda smoked his pipe and the intangible tension that had been growing between us finally dissipated. I was happy to understand him better, I guessed that even millennia-spanning daemon sages had insecurities.

That was an oddly comforting thought. No matter how old they get, people still suffer from bouts of self-doubt every once in a while.

As we stared out at the beautiful orange glow cresting the mountain peak, a strange bird flew over the horizon. It looked like a living flame as its orange and red ombre-patterned wings flapped leisurely.

I tried to focus on it, but it was too far away to elicit a system notification.

"Do you know what kind of bird that is?" I asked Panda quietly. "It's mesmerising."

Panda looked up from his freshly lit bamboo pipe which he had been refilling and gasped as his eyes locked onto the mysterious creature.

"If I'm not mistaken, that's a Molotov Cockatiel." He replied in hushed, awed tones. "They're really rare."

"*Molotov Cockatiel?*" I replied incredulously. "There's no way that's what they're called. You've got to be yanking my chain."

"No kid, that's their species name." He replied earnestly. "The system names things, not me. If that name sounds funny to you then blame the system."

Now *it makes sense. That damned system would do anything for a cheap laugh.*

"Hundreds of years ago the continental humans hunted the cockatiels to near extinction. Their feathers are super valuable." Panda explained as we watched the magnificent bird crest the sunset sky. "They're endangered now…their feathers were used to enhance weapons and they were supposedly quite powerful. Though hurting them has been outlawed for a long time now.

"Multiple governing bodies and societies got together to make it official. Don't mistake that as an act of kindness though. Those guys are ruthless, they're just waiting for the birds to repopulate so they can hunt them again for more feathers."

I grunted and shook my head. It sounded just like how things worked back on Earth. I guessed that no matter where you go there will always be rich assholes trying to expand their empires on the suffering of others.

"See," I said lightly. "Your sagely wisdom will always be useful…even if it's just for bird spotting." I chuckled and he shook his head, but I could see the faint flicker of a smile forming on his lips.

We sat for a while longer before retiring to our shared room. I had some business to attend to once I was finally in the comfort of a safe room.

You have entered a safe zone; would you like to open all loot boxes?
Y/N

Naturally I mentally asserted yes. I had two boxes to open and this was the first safe zone I'd entered in weeks. I wondered what would be inside them.

Extinction Loot Box

The small, golden sphere, which most definitely was not a box, descended from the wooden roof. It hit the floor, cracking a few floorboards and exploded into tiny ribbons of scarlet confetti as a scroll was left in its place.

Unlike with previous loot boxes, this the scroll didn't immediately disappear into my inventory. Instead it hovered in front of my face, giving me a choice.

Choose one:
X1 Cursed Mystery Seed
X1 Blessed Mystery Seed

That was it.

There was no description, no terrible jokes, no…nothing. I wasn't sure which I should choose at first, until I remembered that this was a world filled with obnoxious and annoying gods like Chrysus.

With that in mind, it made sense that the blessed seed would have something to do with one of them…maybe.

Either way, it wasn't worth the risk of having to indulge any of them with my time, so I chose the cursed seed and a description popped up in my HUD before it disappeared.

Cursed Mystery Seed:
This seed is a consumable item with a one-time use. You probably shouldn't use it unless you're in dire straits. It *might* save your life, but there *will* be a cost.

Well, that's not ominous, I thought to myself with a sigh just as the second box began to descend from above.

Bukkake Loot Box:
Given to those who like to be surrounded by the enemy, and who go out with a bang.

A white, rectangular box hovered above me. It glowed brightly, the hue intensifying as it shook. A small clasp was located on the front of the box and it seemed to be trying to break free but couldn't undo itself.

Against my better judgement, I reached out and undid the clasp. "UWU!"

The sound of an anime girl moaning filled the room like an unsolicited video opened in the middle of an important meeting to the embarrassment of the unsuspecting recipient.

As the lid blasted away from the top of the box, thick, white liquid shot out from within, covering me from head to toe.

You have received a new item:
Wet Wipes

"I hate this place," I said, reluctantly retrieving my *gift* from my inventory and using it to clean myself up before bed.

The next morning we woke early to the sound of Sally's fist beating on our door. I definitely didn't get enough sleep, but luckily I barely needed it these days.

Panda and I hurried downstairs as he protested the early awakening. The bar was deserted when we arrived, with the exception of the moustached bartender who sported black rings under his eyes. The dapper dwarf must not have gone to bed yet.

"Where is everyone?" I asked through a yawn as I entered the bar area.

"Work." He muttered in a groggy tone. "Boss wants to see you."

He lifted his head in a backwards nod towards the door and I left the inn.

The morning sun had risen and the light was blinding as the heat haze sent shimmering air cascading off the roadside. The palm tree jungle was stifling during the early hours, but it got much worse at midday.

Sally stood awkwardly at the back of the group with Tilly looking nervously around the town square. My team were chatting happily amongst themselves, though Jamie still looked exhausted.

He'd regained some colour from the previous night, but his eyes were terribly bloodshot. I wondered if he was struggling to sleep, or maybe it was simply the lack of sleep from trapsing through the jungle the past few days on meditation alone.

I'd heard once that a person can be sleep-deprived but never in a sleep surplus. So, after a week of being constantly awake, the poor mage probably needed a lot more shut-eye than Sally had allowed him.

It was just part and parcel of the adventuring lifestyle though. Thankfully, it didn't really bother me. I'd trained for sleep deprivation for most of my adult life after all. Working sixty hours a week as a truck driver was no joke, so this was actually a nice break considering my level and meditation slowed down natural fatigue.

"Gonads!" Sally shouted harshly as she spotted me exiting the *Drink Inn*. "Do your job and liaise with the dwarf."

"He *has* a name you know?" I said as I marched past her towards Ale.

He was stood talking to my team, his bushy beard swaying as he laughed animatedly.

"Morning Ale," I said, approaching the mayor and extending my hand for him to shake.

He took it and performed his dad squeeze once again before gesturing for me to follow him. I looked back at my team and gave them a look telling them to wait.

"So, today's the big day eh?" He said as we strolled towards the mine entrance.

"It seems like it," I replied. "What can you tell me about our dragon?"

"Aye, I thought you might ask." He smiled knowingly as we stopped in front of the mine and he leaned against the wooden frame at the entrance, folding his arms. "Yer dragon is a big bastard he is.

"He's a red'un and his lair is at the top of the mountain. There are two ways to get there you see? Climb up from the outside, or…since I've taken a liking to ya, you can use our mine tunnels."

"Are the mine tunnels faster?" I asked eagerly, brushing the remnants of sleep from my eyes.

"Oh aye. We have a tunnel leading straight to his lair we do. How do you think we found him? Digging away as we do, one day we came out in this large cavern right near the top of the mountain.

"It was filled with shining, shimmering gold. Enough to turn this village into a resort. We'd all be rich, never have to work the mine another day we wouldn't.

"But, alas, the big red fuck breathed some fire at us and we ran away. Damn near singed my beard off he did. Naturally, we posted the quest the very next day."

I nodded appreciatively and thanked the dwarven mayor before returning to the group who eagerly crowded around me.

"Well?" Sally asked agitatedly as she glanced around the square with her huge arms folded.

"He says we can use the mine shaft to reach the dragon's lair," I answered, looking around the group as I delivered the message.

"Apparently the dragon is big and red and breathes fire. There's also supposedly a large pile of gold up there that the dwarves want."

"Fuck what dwarves want!" Tilly exclaimed, gesticulating to the surrounding area with a frown. "We kill dragon. We take spoils. Way of world."

It was the most she'd spoken since the day we'd met her. I guess money really does talk.

Sally put a calming, oversized hand on the elf girl and nodded to her.

"Don't worry, any spoils are ours to claim. The quest doesn't say anything about handing the gold over to anyone," she said in a low voice. "That being said, this is an adventurer exam and how you handle this battle is more important than any potential spoils…if you want to go full-time with the society that is." She added, looking over each of us in turn.

I wouldn't say no to a dragon's horde of gold, but we had to actually kill the thing first. No use getting ahead of ourselves.

"If this thing breathes fire, then Bell's attacks might not do much," Reggie said thoughtfully, crossing his arms with his hand lightly rubbing his chin.

"I told you before," Bell said chirpily. "It's called fighting fire with fire for a reason. My flames are stronger, so I'll win." She flexed a bicep and her arm barely looked tense at all, but I got the picture. Her eyes were lit with passionate flames – a battle junkie through and through.

"We can talk tactics as we walk," Panda said from my side, his moody demeanour had pretty much disappeared after our conversation the previous night.

He looked towards Sally who widened her eyes at his sudden proactivity and then nodded.

"The furball is right." She announced, pushing through the group. "Let's go."

We followed behind as she led us into the mines. She glanced warily at Ale as she walked past him and I thanked him and bade him goodbye. He wished me good luck in return.

It was cramped inside the mine. I guess that made sense for a dwarven work crew. Sally had the worst of it, being a goliath of a catonid and all.

It didn't take long for us to reach a fork in the road, one led down towards the sounds of voices and pickaxes hitting rock, the other led up.

We took the obvious choice.

The path was steep and the further we walked the less wooden bracing was there to prop up the cave walls. It looked like the shaft had been made in a bit of a hurry.

We strategized as we navigated the cramped, awkward shaft. It was sweaty and dirty in the mine shaft and it didn't take long for our clothes, faces and hair to become thick with soot.

Shame I had to use up all those wet wipes, I thought bitterly, *they'd have come in handy right about now.*

My sweat acted like glue to the black powder that clung to my skin like a caked-on foundation. It wasn't very pleasant and I soon found myself longing for a shower.

It was stifling in the mine and it only got hotter the higher we climbed. Perhaps that was a sign that we were closing in on the dragon's lair.

"Dragons," I said wistfully, lost in my own thoughts. "I still can't believe they exist."

"I always thought they might." Bell said, looking back at me with dirty, sooty streaks across her teal hair and cheeks. "I mean, there are stories of dragons in every culture imaginable on Earth right? So those legends must have come from somewhere."

"I guess," I replied. "You can also apply that argument to most major religions though. A lot of them have similar creation mythos with a prophet and a singular god and stuff. I still don't believe in it though."

"I preferred the mythological religions myself," Bell said as we continued our trek. "Loki is great, imagine, a god of mischief who can transform into pretty much anything and lives to fuck up everyone else's day. Sounds way more human to me than a big man in the sky no one has ever seen."

"What are you two going on about?" Reggie interrupted irritably from further ahead. "How can you even begin to debate the validity of the divine? Athena is real and powerful."

"We weren't talking about *your* gods," I replied. "We know they're real…though I'm still not sure they're actually gods per say," I mumbled the last part as we wandered into a widened section of the tunnel.

"He worships Athena," Jamie said, dropping back to talk quietly with me. "He gets a little sore when people talk about theology so flippantly."

I was about to reply when I noticed a light at the end of the tunnel. The sides of the shaft were blackened with much thicker soot than before, like the entrance had been scorched with flames.

Sally crouched down and held up her hand in a fist. Wordlessly we did the same and stuck close to her as she crept forwards.

I crouched at her shoulder as we crested the edge of the tunnel and looked out into the dragon's lair. Piles of glimmering gold decorated the place and sitting peacefully atop them, was the dragon.

A red scaled beast, roughly the size of a house, and we had to fight it.

Chapter 18
Gold Eyes Red Dragon

I felt my mouth gape open as I peered into the lair from over Sally's shoulder. The room was filled with gold, so much that even a share of it would likely make us the richest people on the island.

However, my gaze was drawn more firmly to the gold's owner: a large, red dragon the size of a house. It sat atop the gold pile, eyes closed and snoring.

Its fearsome snores caused the entire room to vibrate with a deep, bassy hum. Its scales hung regally around its body, but most shockingly of all, it seemed to be a hybrid of both western and eastern mythology.

The dragon had the fat body of a western beast, but the head and arms of the eastern dragons of legend. Its slender face looked out of place atop such a large frame, and the thin white moustache fluttering with the breath of every snore was…a little strange.

Sally: *A sleeping dragon should make for easy prey.*
You've lucked out.
Kaleb: We'll see.

Sally wisely spoke to me through the group chat. Keeping the volume as low as possible was a sound strategy.

I wasn't so certain the battle would be as simple as a sleepy assassination, but it should definitely give us an advantage.

I opened up my own chat with the team and we carefully planned our opening move. It was quite simple really. The three attackers among us would all charge our most potent attacks and release them at exactly the same time.

Theoretically, that should make for an extreme amount of opening damage to sway the battle in our favour. Our healer, Reggie, would hang back in a support role and provide assistance where necessary.

Before we moved into position, I focused on the dragon activating the pop-up notification on my HUD.

You have discovered a mythical monster:
Gold Eyes Red Dragon

This flame throwing beauty is everything a *Charizard* aspires to be. Elegant, tough, powerful and...greedy. The *Gold Eyes Red Dragon* is a fearsome hoarder of wealth, like a better-looking *Jeff Bezos*. Dragons are solitary creatures by nature and rarely take kindly to intruders visiting their home unannounced. Like a Floridian with a shotgun, they will happily take out home invaders with self-assured, extreme prejudice. I don't want this notification to *drag-on* so I'll end it here. Good look player, you'll need it.

I didn't have the time to spare admonishing the system for its terrible jokes and Earthen cultural references, instead focusing on the tidbit of information that was actually useful.

Dragons being solitary creatures was good to know. Hopefully it would mean that this fight wouldn't have any unexpected visitors crashing the party.

I took a deep breath and activated the stealth mechanic provided by my armour. I had very little time before it would run out, but with the extra ten free points pushing my intelligence stat up, I was sure it would be enough to reach my position.

I would be stationed across the room, drawing the most attention after the initial attack, and helping our group to hit the beast from all sides.

My heart fluttered as I quickly crept past the mountains of gold. I had to tread a careful path as not to accidentally cause the clanking of metal coins which would no doubt wake the dragon up.

Luckily though, the room was quite small so I didn't have far to go. Once I reached my position on the far side, I drew my bow. My stealth skill had run out halfway across the room, but luckily it didn't seem to matter.

It was more of a precautionary activation anyway, just in case my steps caused the sleeping dragon to rear its head.

I aimed my bow, nocking an arrow and drawing the string. I activated my *Soul Shot* skill and began channelling energy into the arrow.

At the same time, Bell's hands began glowing crimson as she held them out before her, forming a pushing stance with her wrists touching and her bottom hand inverted. It reminded me of a *Goku* move as fire started to circle and grow between her palms.

Jamie had the least amount of movement to make, stopping near the entrance with Reggie right behind him.

Sally, Tilly, and Panda watched with bated breath from the dwarven mine shaft as he dropped into a half-squat stance. He held a single arm, pointed out towards the dragon in a fist, using his spare hand to steady it by gripping his forearm tightly.

I'd only seen him do this once before; in his solo battle. Apparently it was quite draining for him, but as a team we decided that water attacks were likely going to give us an advantage against a fire breathing dragon, so it made sense to have him use his most powerful skill from the off.

Reggie: *Are you all ready?*

He was in charge of timing the simultaneous attacks since he was the only one of us that was free to use his full mental faculties to assess the situation objectively.

None of us replied to his message, but he took our silence as a yes as he issued the command.

Reggie: *Now!*

I released my arrow which soared so fast my eyes couldn't keep up with it as it sank into the dragon's face. Its scales bubbled and hissed as acid melted through the skin.

At the same time Bell's spinning fireball launched through the air, colliding with the opposite side of the dragon's face. It probably wasn't very effective, but I could feel the heat from all the way on the other side of the room. It seemed to simply bounce off the dragon's flame-retardant scales, but it did so in a brilliant show of force and flame.

From the front, Jamie opened his hand and a powerful, firehose-like stream of water erupted from his palm. It struck the dragon directly on the nose, simultaneously putting out Bell's fire and causing a cloud of sizzling steam to fill the room, obscuring our vision.

"Burn motherfucker, burn motherfucker burn!" Bell half yelled; half sang as the steam caused a moist film to cover my skin.

"Are you singing *Five Finger Death Punch*?" I asked incredulously from across the room.

"Hell yeah!" She cheered.

"I always figured you'd be more of a *Taylor Swift* fan."

"Don't be sexist Kaleb, it's not a good look on you." She chided and though I couldn't see her through the steamy haze, I imagined an admonishing look on her anime-like face.

"Just because I'm a white girl doesn't automatically mean I like *Taylor Swift*." She continued, blasting another fireball in the direction of the dragon.

"…I mean, statistically it's pretty likely…" I muttered, as I fired a few arrows into the steam.

Our little chat didn't last long.

A large gust of wind pummelled me and I went flying into a large stack of gold to my rear. The mist began to dissipate and the unharmed dragon stood proudly atop his mountain of treasure, wings spread wide and moustache twitching.

"How dare you!" It bellowed in a deep, commanding tone. The voice bounced around the cave, almost deafening me. "Only cowards attack when their foe is a'slumber."

Jesus who is this guy? He sounds like an Arthurian knight.

I scrambled to my feet and raised my bow once more, nocking an arrow.

"Sit down you insolent cur!" The dragon shouted, its gold eyes flashing dangerously as it swept its wing towards me like a backhand.

I fell back into the gold with a clinking crash, staring up at its face. Merely moments ago it was bubbling, skin melting where my arrow had hit. Yet now it looked fully healed, barely a scratch on it.

What the hell was up with this thing?

I heard a scream and looked to my side as Jamie launched a second water attack. He looked ill, the fatigue finally getting to him.

"Die you big fucking lizard!" He yelled as a torrent of water shot from his palm, hitting the dragon in its open mouth.

I was pretty sure that was the first time I'd heard him swear. It was definitely the first time he'd sounded anything more than meek or humble, though his quipping definitely needed work.

"Impromptu waterboarding?" Bell asked, a little too casually for mid battle. "The C.I.A would be proud."

The dragon spat out the water but didn't look overly perturbed by the attack. I had a sinking feeling, deep in my gut, that this dragon was way more powerful than we had been led to believe.

"Well I never." It began, its voice rising in volume as its anger raged. "The rudeness of the youth today. Fucking humans!"

It looked at Jamie with fiery eyes and snorted in his direction. Two small fireballs hurtled from its nose towards the water mage.

"Jamie!" Reggie shouted, pushing him aside from behind and taking both hits directly in the chest. His body roared into flames as he screamed.

It was painful to watch.

Jamie looked up from the floor and held his hands out like he did with his water spells but nothing happened. Reggie writhed in agony as his hair burnt off and his skin began melting.

The smell of burning skin and viscera filled the lair and I had to cup my hand over my mouth to hold the vomit back. It was revolting.

I rushed towards him, looking through my inventory to find anything that might help. If only I hadn't used all the slime condensate on the forest fire.

The dragon batted its wing at the space between me and our healer, blasting me backwards to the floor once again. My health had taken a surprising battering from the wind attack which barely seemed more than offhand gestures from our opponent.

I was sitting at less than half of my maximum HP as the dragon loomed above me, a shadow casting a menacing glare from the beast's narrowed golden eyes.

Reggie's fire was put out by the wind and he struggled to his knees, looking lost and confused.. His skin looked like ash and his lips had peeled back to reveal his bleeding gums and teeth. One of his eyes had popped in the intense heat and bloody gore leaked from the eye socket.

"Reggie!" Jamie screamed as he scrabbled towards his friend, catching him just as he couldn't kneel anymore.

Tears crested the water mage's face as he looked down in horror at his charred friend.

Reggie wasn't dead just yet though and I pulled a healing potion out of my inventory and threw it towards them from my prone position.

Jamie noticed and scrambled to catch the potentially lifesaving liquid, fumbling, but managing to pull the potion into his chest.

The dragon sneered, snorting steam and took a step towards us. The lair shook as gold piles started falling, like a landslide, but of coins. It didn't seem like our foe was going to give us any time to take a breather.

I looked up and nocked another arrow, still prone and covered in gold. The dragon glanced towards me out of the corner of its eye.

I fired my arrow.

Chapter 19
Not Bad For A House Cat

My arrow soared through the air towards the malevolent dragon, but he was too fast for me. He lifted his clawed hand and batted it away, like swatting a fly, before turning his full attention to me.

I was laid prone, half covered by a stack of coins which had buried me during the landslide. They were heavy and I struggled to move under the weight of the dragon's financial might.

I'd heard the saying *money is power* before, but this wasn't exactly what I'd had in mind.

The dragon took a thundering step towards me, shaking the ground and causing more of the gold to slide down the money mountain.

I lifted my bow and nocked another arrow, my stamina running dangerously low. The dragon sneered, curling its lip beneath the odd white moustache which hung off the edge of its muzzle.

Its glaring, golden eyes peered dangerously at me, daring me to try it. I could tell that if I loosed my arrow it would be the last thing I ever did.

I thought of my wife Layla and our child who I had never met. They had given me strength before, literally in one particular case, and they gave me strength now.

My wife wasn't the most caring women, but she was a straight-shooting pragmatist who had always cared deeply for her loved ones. If she was here, she'd have told me to cut my losses and run. Of course, if she was in my position, that would be the last thing *she'd* do. She'd fight to the end, and that was exactly what I planned to do.

I didn't want to die. I wanted to protect them, to bring them here so we could be a family again. That being said, nobody would be able to say that Kaleb Akabane died a whimpering coward.

If I was going to die, I would die fighting.

I gritted my teeth, narrowed my eyes, and fired my shot.

The dragon sighed like a disappointed father scolding an unruly child for the umpteenth time as it snorted a tiny fireball which collided with the arrow, burning it to a crisp in mid-air.

"Why are all you humans so stupid?" The dragon asked as it shook its head and looked down on me. "It's like you only have two brain cells and they're so preoccupied in fighting each other over third place, that even they are useless to you."

It sounded fed up, not at all what I expected as it lifted its three-clawed foot above my head. There it was, I was about to be made into pate.

I fucking hated pate.

"Not on my watch you overgrown garden skink!" Sally yelled and the dragon turned away from me just as her oversized, black blade slammed into the top of its skull.

It stagged backwards dazedly, its huge foot landing mere inches from my face. I gasped, looking wide eyed between Sally and the dragon, and blinking slowly.

That was way too close.

"Get out of the way Gonads," Sally scolded me. "The pros are here now."

She offered me her hand and I grasped it firmly as she pulled me out of the coins so hard I felt my shoulder creak as my arm nearly came out of its socket.

I staggered towards her and she let go of my hand, side stepping me deftly as I stumbled behind her. Tilly scowled at me as she walked past, her hips swaying with practiced swagger.

The dragon looked at them with disgust, like a man who had taken a bite of a juicy beef burger only to find out it was actually some vegan replacement shit. Its eyes burned with a contempt-fuelled hatred and Sally sneered back, baring her fangs.

"Phase four are you?" It growled, barely opening its mouth as it spoke. "Not bad for a house cat." It spat as fire exploded from its mouth in little, simmering globs of spittle. "It's a shame I don't keep pets."

It dived towards them in a flurry of wings and claws as Sally lifted her sword to block and was flung across the room into a pile of gold near Bell and the rest of the team.

I looked at her open mouthed and then back towards the dragon but in that split second, Tilly had made her move. The elf girl fired a myriad of arrows, her hand nocking, drawing, and releasing the string faster than my eyes could comprehend.

The dragon's claws moved just as fast and when she finally let up, it held an entire quiver's worth of arrows between his claws. The dragon sneered and pulled its red, scaled arm back for the haymaker.

I knew I had to do something, even if it wasn't much, so I slammed down on the stamina potion icon in my inventory and poured almost all of my remaining stamina into the *Perception Of The Apex Predator* skill.

Perception of the Apex Predator (rare)

Slow down time for a period determined by the amount of stamina you use on the skill. Cooldown determined by the amount of stamina used on the skill.

It was a skill I hadn't used too often as it seemed to be geared towards people with much higher stamina than myself, but I was at a loss and this was all I could think of.

Time stopped and I dived towards Tilly, knocking her out of the way with my shoulder and falling to the floor. Then I rolled away from her as fast as I could. It wasn't much, but perhaps it would save her life.

Time resumed after barely a second and the dragon altered his aim slightly, scowling as he flung the arrows across the room. They hit Tilly before she even had time to gasp. I looked towards her still standing body, acupuncture hadn't terrified me this much since I'd watched *Final Destination 5* as a kid.

"When I asked Santa for a good dicking this Christmas, this is not what I had in mind!" Bell yelled from across the room.

I barely heard her as I stared up at the deathly beast, ready to face my end. We were well and truly fucked, up shit's creek without a paddle didn't even begin to describe our situation.

Just call me Nagasaki cause I'm about to get wrecked by a fat man, I thought dourly, looking up at the belly of the beast above me.

I tried to find words, or the strength to keep fighting but my body wouldn't move and my mouth wouldn't mouth.

"Dirty, venerable lesser races!" The dragon bellowed as I stared up at it from the floor, unable to speak, unsure what to do. "It doesn't matter where I go, this always happens.

"Why won't you odious cretins leave me be? All I wanted was a peaceful life. I should have listened to my mother when she told me that it simply wasn't in the cards for a dragon.

"What did I ever do to you?" It screamed, but I thought it might be a rhetorical question so I didn't even try to reply. I was right. "I just wanted to live out my days, hoarding my wealth and eating the occasional dwarf or two. Is that too much to ask?"

I looked up at it in disbelief, my fear quickly turning to shock. Was this thing really throwing a temper tantrum? It seemed so regal before, now it reminded me of a toddler in a fancy restaurant, or a toddler on a plane, or a toddler being denied access to a toy store.

Ok, I think I might have had a bit of a hang up about screaming kids in public places, but this was a god forsaken dragon for crying out loud! What in the ever-loving fuck was happening?

"That's it." It continued, its voice suddenly cold and menacing. "I tried to live the peaceful, solitary life, but you lesser life forms couldn't leave me be. There's only one solution now.

"I'll have to rid this island of your filth all together." Its eyes glinted as it looked slightly above me, like it had a sudden lightbulb moment and had completely forgotten we existed. "I'll just have to eradicate you all, then I can finally get some peace and quiet."

Its voice sounded distant, psychotic even, as it grinned like a madman and flapped its powerful wings.

It hovered above us for a moment and the entire team stared at it, unsure what to do or say. Then it opened its mouth and spewed a firestorm of a cyclone at the side of the lair, blasting a hole through the side of the mountain.

It flew through the new exit it had created, seemingly forgetting we were even there. It had obviously gotten pretty caught up in its *Bond* villain monologue.

The room was silent.

I stared at the hole in the wall in disbelief. Had that really just happened? How was I still alive? We needed to warn someone, anyone, *everyone*. The gold eyes red dragon was pissed and every person on the island was about to be its punching bag.

Shit!

I stumbled to my feet and turned towards Tilly the elf. Her body laid next to me; more arrow than elf at this point as dark, pooling blood spilled out around her.

The only part of her body which didn't have holes in it was her face. She was beautiful, serene in death as her gleaming eyes stared into the void which I was sure was staring back at her just as passionately.

"Reggie, stay with me!" Jamie's trembling voice pierced through my melancholic ponderings of elven death, bringing me back into the room.

I turned on my heels and rushed towards him, sliding on my knees, and arriving next to Reggie. He looked like *Anakin Skywalker* at the end of *Revenge of the Sith* and for a split second I was surprised that Bell wasn't standing on top of the gold pile shouting: "You were my brother!"

It certainly seemed like something she would do, but instead she simply stared blankly at the scene before her. It seemed that even she wasn't callous enough to crack a joke as our friend struggled to cling on to life.

Reggie's head turned towards me slightly, it was hard to make out his facial features through the charred flesh but I swear he smiled at me. It was only a flicker of his lips through ragged, slow breathing. Yet as I looked at our dying healer, I took it as him telling me to keep the rest of them safe.

We hadn't been together long, but still, watching the light as it left his eyes and his body turn to ash was heart wrenching. I'd gotten used to killing, but seeing a friend die before my eyes…I wasn't sure I'd ever get used to that.

The floor rumbled and I lost my balance slightly as the entire room shook. It was like an earthquake had started out of nowhere.

The sound of clattering, clinking coins filled the room as the mountains of gold began sliding over each other.

"We need to get out of here!" Panda shouted, poking his fluffy, black and white head through the mineshaft hole.

I looked at him for a moment before fully comprehending the situation. He was right. We needed to skedaddle right the fuck now. I stood up, grabbing Jamie's shoulder and yanking him with me.

He looked at me with hollow, teary eyes.

"I can't leave him." He muttered, clearly in severe shock. He pulled against me but it was a weak effort.

I tugged his arm more firmly, ushering him towards the tunnel. He wouldn't budge. He just kept repeating the words: "I can't leave him," over and again every time I tried to get him to move.

We didn't have time for this. I felt bad for him, hell I was upset and I'd not even known the guy all that long, still, the living had to come first.

I slapped Jamie hard across the face, snapping his head to the side as his faraway eyes snapped back into focus.

"He'd want you to live!" I yelled, trying desperately to be heard over the rumbling of the collapsing cave as I grabbed his shoulders.

He stared back at me, barely comprehending and I tossed him towards the hole. There was no time to be nice about it and he wasn't the only one who needed my help.

"Strike!" Bell yelled as she jogged towards me.

I didn't have time to admonish her for the poorly timed bowling joke as I shook my head and rushed towards the closest gold pile.

She bent down and touched Reggie before heading to the escape hole herself.

Mere seconds after she moved away from our former healer's ashes, rocks rained down and a boulder crashed into his corpse, scattering him around the lair.

I reached the gold pile and could just about make out a single, muscular arm trapped beneath the mountain of coins. I grabbed it and began pulling when a notification popped up on my HUD and I'd never been so happy to be living in a world with a looting system.

Do you want to loot *gold coins*?
Y/N

Chapter 20
Yerma

I immediately mentally asserted yes on my HUD and the mountain of gold in front of me disappeared. A new notification popped up and even though we were seconds away from a cave in, I couldn't help but look at it.

Loot successful! 1,250,000 gold has been added to your inventory.

"Holy shit," I breathed, glaring dazedly at the notification. I was a millionaire. I was rich. I was filthy, stinking, tory scum, duck island, trump tower building rich.

A loud groan interrupted my train of thought. I looked down to see Sally siting on the floor, rubbing the back of her head.

Oh yeah, that was why I looted the gold in the first place. I remembered.

Sally had been flung into the gold pile by the dragon and I'd rushed over to pull her out of it before the cave collapsed.

"The cave!" I shouted, startling myself as I remembered the dire predicament we were in. Being rich as fuck was good and all but I couldn't spend my copious amounts of looted dragon gold if I was crushed to death in a cave in.

I looked down at Sally and offered out my hand. She looked back at me with a puzzled expression but took it anyway. I hoisted her from the ground, and by that I mean she stood up entirely unassisted whilst I held her hand and made a show of helping.

She nodded at me and opened her mouth but the imploding cave was too loud to hear anything. I took it to be a thankyou though and I nodded back with a smile before gesturing towards the dwarven mineshaft.

We turned and began running towards it as ceiling rocks and wall debris crashed all around us.

I dived into the tunnel after Sally just as the final Jenga piece toppled the tower. The dragon's lair caved in with a mighty crash sending dust and debris flying into the tunnel.

It was like my own personal action movie moment.

I picked myself up off the ground and checked on my team. They were dirty, scared, battered, and bruised, but they still lived, and so did I…somehow.

"Where's Reggie and the elf?" Sally asked innocently, looking around the dark mineshaft as if they might be hiding in the shadows ready to pull a prank on her.

"They…" I began, struggling to meet her inquisitive, deep blue eyes. "…They didn't make it."

She looked at me for a moment and I looked away. She opened her mouth to speak, perhaps to comfort me, or maybe to admonish me for not doing better, but we were interrupted.

"Listen, I called dibs!" Bell shouted, raising her hands up and backing away from Jamie.

He was stalking towards her with his fists raised and his teeth gritted. Whatever was going on, he was furious at her.

"It's fucking disrespectful!" He shouted, spittle flying from his mouth. "He was our friend you loopy, psycho-bitch!"

"Well yeah," Bell replied, as if she couldn't quite comprehend what the water mage's problem was. "He'd have *wanted* us to loot him, and *I* called dibs."

I stared on, not quite sure what to say.

"He was my best friend! You can't just take his stuff like that. He fought for us, died for us and before his body is even cold you decide to loot him? It's fucking...it's just...heartless." Jamie's rage began to cool into frustrated despair as he lowered his hands and sobbed whilst staring at the fire mage in disbelief.

She didn't reply, choosing instead to look at me and shrug nonchalantly before walking back down the mineshaft slope towards the dwarven town.

I felt hair tickle my neck, accompanied by the smell of lavender. I turned towards it to see Sally leaning uncomfortably close to me.

"I'll make sure he's alright, go check on her," she whispered.

I nodded and trotted after Bell, Panda hot on my heels.

"What should I say?" I asked him quietly before I caught up with her.

"Honestly." Panda began, looking a little awkward as he spoke. "I know it's not very nice to say, but I don't think the girl did anything wrong. She looted that Reggie kid's corpse on the way out of the lair right?

"I actually think it was pretty quick thinking. Healer boy probably had loads of useful things on him and the cave was collapsing. Taking it was better than leaving it if you ask me."

I wasn't so sure myself, but I nodded my thanks at him as I caught up to the fireball mage.

"Hey, wait up!" I called as I jogged the last few steps towards her. She turned to me, slowing her pace slightly and smiling in her usual cheery fashion.

"Oh, hi Kaleb." She greeted me. "That was one hell of a shit show back there huh? Who would have thought that dragon would be so strong?"

"Uh...yeah," I replied, brushing off the small talk. "Listen, I just wanted to check on you, to see if you were alright?"

"Why wouldn't I be?" She replied, a puzzled look in her eyes. "Wanton death and destruction is my middle name." She winked casually.

I was at a bit of a loss for words. Was she truly not bothered by the deaths of people we'd travelled with for over a week? Maybe this was just her way of coping. I couldn't tell.

Before I had a chance to continue my conversation with Bell, a new notification appeared frantically on my HUD and the entire group came to a halt.

A group system notification?

Emergency Quest!
The Sacking of Havar

A dragon is coming! A dragon is coming!
Thanks to the misguided deeds of *certain* members of
the Adventure Society, a large, red dragon is currently
on his way to the city of Havar.
This dragon is pretty upset and intends to genocide the
fuck out of all sapient life forms on the island.

Objectives:
Prevent Havar from being destroyed 0/1
Kill the dragon 0/1
*Protect the citizens 0/1 (Remaining Population
1,732,192/1,732,192)*

This is a group quest given to all inhabitants of the area surrounding Havar

"An emergency quest? Well, shit," I said aloud as I read through the notification.

Bell turned to look at me, she looked worried, concerned even, as her big eyes shimmered oddly in the low light of the mineshaft.

"Kaleb," she said, her voice cracking slightly in a small, frightened whisper. "There's no reward listed."

I stared back at her, dumbfounded.

"I'm sure there will be one," Panda said, approaching us cautiously. He gave me a meaningful look which I didn't quite understand.

"Keep moving!" Sally shouted from behind us. "This new quest is now part of your exam. We need to get the fuck out of this dwarven cesspit and back to Havar."

I looked back at her to see a piercing, battle-junkie gaze staring back at me, a fangy, exhilarated smile sat underneath. She marched towards us, and the exit, practically dragging Jamie behind her like a lazy dog that was refusing to walk.

I nodded and turned back to the exit, before breaking out into a little jog. She was right, there would be time for grieving later, right now we needed to save Havar.

"Come on," I said to Panda and Bell as I left for the exit, they followed, but with less enthusiasm than I'd hoped.

As I saw the light at the end of the tunnel, I heard a few screams and groans from outside.

I picked up my pace, rushing towards the sounds of anguish and exited the mine tunnels into the blinding, midday sun.

It was carnage.

The bustling dwarven village we'd spent the night in was a sea of flames and blood. The aggressor was nowhere to be seen, but the devastation left in its wake was evident.

The town square was littered with tiny, charred corpses. Children cried over their fallen parents, dwarves huddled around their dead friends and the mayor, Ale, stood in the middle of it all, unharmed and sporting a thousand-yard stare.

I rushed towards him, grabbing the dwarf by the shoulders,

"What happened?" I asked, shaking him. "It was the dragon wasn't it?"

"Aye." He replied, his voice as distant as his stare. "He burst from the mountain like a god of death, he did. That big…fucking…lizard.

"He…he breathed fire all across our village. Our homes, our people…gone. Then, then he just fucking left! No words, no…nothing."

I let go of the dwarf, he was clearly in shock and there wasn't anything I could do for him. The scene around us was horrible, the smell of burning flesh would surely haunt me later down the line, but right now, I didn't have time to think about it.

All I could think about was getting back to Havar before this happened there too, on a much larger scale.

The others caught up to me and I looked around the village square. I needed a dwarf who wasn't in shock and as my eyes settled on a familiar face, I found one. Vodka stood off to the side, holding his wife. She was alive and it seemed that the entire family was unharmed.

"Vodka!" I shouted and he looked towards me with alert, but sad, eyes. "I need a fast way back to Havar, does anyone here have a car I can use?"

"Aye." He replied. "I got the quest too. You can take Yerma, she's parked over yonder." The sullen dwarf gestured towards a building which seemed to have been spared from a fiery death.

It was an unassuming, wooden, barn which sat just far enough from the rest of the town to not quite be a part of it.

"Yerma?" I asked, before leaving.

"Aye," he replied, still obviously a little dazed and speaking stoically, his voice completely monotonous. "She's the town's only car, we use her for supply runs and the like. Naturally, everyone's ridden her at least once…just like Yer Ma."

I shook my head, unable to suppress the tug of a grin on my lips. I uttered a few words of thanks before turning back to my team and gesturing for them to follow me.

Without words, they did and I sprinted towards the barn on the edge of the small mining town. It looked pretty Amish to me, a typical, red, wooden barn with white structural beams on the outside and presumably, copious amounts of space on the inside.

I began sliding one of the doors open whilst Sally grabbed the other. As the midday sunlight streamed through the open doors, I caught a glimpse of our commandeered transport.

It looked like an old jeep. It was black with a roll cage and just about enough room for the five of us to squish inside.

"This will do." Sally said, a smile curling on her lips. "This will do nicely."

Chapter 21
Humans Know Nothing Of Polite Society

Director Lucas sat back in his hand-made, leather office chair that was imported from the mainland. He breathed out leisurely and took a sip of his favourite amber drink.

Life was good.

It had been over a week since the last time Diako, his god, had invaded his mind and demanded something from him and he was glad for the reprieve.

The only critical voice he wanted in his head was his own. He wondered absently how the examinee team was getting on with their quest. In all honesty, he hoped it would take them a little while longer to complete it.

He wasn't mean spirited by nature and he didn't hold anything against any of them, but his life was just a lot more…simple, without Kaleb Akabane in town.

It wasn't the outworlder's fault of course, and he'd never hold it against him, but Diako mostly left the director alone when Kaleb was away and he liked the peace that came with that.

Of course, peace never lasted.

He sat bolt upright, woken from his lackadaisical serenity by a disturbing quest notification: *The Sacking Of Havar.*

"What the hell has that outworlder done now?" Lucas said aloud after reading the quest, rushing towards a shelf at the side of his office.

It was obvious that the reference to *certain* Adventure Society members meant Kaleb and the examinees.

That boy is addicted to causing trouble, he thought exasperatedly.

The office was pretty bare, he liked the minimalist approach to decoration. The shelf, however, had a purpose.

He was a practical man after all, and as he placed his favourite glass, half-full of his favourite alcoholic beverage onto an intrenched coaster on the shelf, he realised that practicality was best served with a dash of flourish.

The shelf dipped lightly as the wall slid smoothly to one side, revealing a hidden room. Lucas stepped inside; he loved this part.

No matter how many times shit hit the fan, the act of opening a secret door and walking out as a superhero, never got old.

That is exactly what he did. Inside the room was a walk-in wardrobe where he kept his most treasured and expensive adventuring gear.

Of course, he didn't need a wardrobe. No one did. Celestia was a system planet and everyone had access to an internal storage space, but what's the point of being rich and powerful if you don't get to indulge yourself every once in a while?

Nothing made Lucas feel like more of a badass, than walking into his secret room to put on his expensive gear and then walking back out looking like a completely different person.

He stepped back into the office and he was no longer Director Lucas. He was The Hero of Havar. Dressed in golden armour like Athena herself, with a white cloak draped down his back and a matching masquerade mask covering his eyes, he felt awesome.

Ah, I see you're already dressed. Diako said, entering Lucas' mind and completely ruining the good mood he had cultivated for himself.

"I am." He replied. "How long do we have?"

Not long. You can travel the entire island by car in less than a day, flying is faster. I would estimate a few hours at the most.

Lucas looked out of his penthouse window and sighed. It was hard to stay pumped up when he'd have to wait for his fight.

Oh well, I guess it can't be helped, he thought, pouring himself another drink and sinking into his chair to watch the skies. When the beast arrived, he would be ready.

***

Yerma roared through the jungle as we skidded along the dirt roads. Sally poured so much power into the vehicle that it felt more like a supercar than a jeep.

"Are you sure this is a good idea?" Panda asked her sceptically. "You're the strongest one here and you're draining your mana to make this rust bucket go faster than it has any right to. What happens when we get there and you're too exhausted to fight, or worse, when Yerma falls apart on us and we get stranded in the jungle?"

"Shut it, furball," Sally yelled. "If we don't get there on time then none of this will matter anyway."

I rolled my eyes at them and folded my arms. If we were chasing down the dragon I'd need to be as fresh as possible.

The rickety jeep wasn't the best environment to meditate in, but I had to try. My stamina was practically non-existent after the last bout.

With a bit of concentration, and a lot of pretending I was the only one in the vehicle, I managed to dive into my soul view.

I quickly fixed my stamina coil. Doing so was second nature now. However, my attention was more firmly drawn to the little blue and green ball circling in the depths of my core.

It felt more tangible than last time, almost as if I could touch it, manipulate it, if I really wanted to. I reached out with my mind towards it, it was so close now. I almost had it when a shout woke me up.

"Gonads!" Sally shouted.

I opened my eyes with a start and saw Panda's face mere inches from my own. I gasped and pushed him away as Sally's voice cut through my surprise.

"Get rid of that fucking thing before it destroys our car!"

I looked around and, to my surprise, a huge spider was chasing us through the jungle. It was twice the size of the jeep and its mouth frothed white, bubbly foam as it sprinted after us.

I immediately conjured my bow and started charging my *Soul Shot* ability.

"Why can't Bell take care of it?" I asked incredulously as my shot charged.

"Because she's a fire hazard and we don't have time to prevent the inevitable forest fire she'd start." Panda said, sighing and shaking his head. "And before you ask, Jamie's recharging for our fight with the dragon and he doesn't meditate as well as you do."

He wasn't as openly hostile towards the fireball mage anymore which was an improvement on his part. I still wasn't sure if he actually liked her though. Hell, I wasn't sure if I did either. She was nice most of the time and I enjoyed having someone to talk Earthen pop culture with, but she was also completely fucking nuts.

As we spoke, she pouted on the back seat. Her arms were folded and her chin was tucked into her chest as she stuck her bottom lip out and narrowed her eyes, it would have been kinda cute, if she wasn't an adult.

I sighed as my *Soul Shot* infused arrow charged up with about half of my stamina. Then I took aim at the spider's face and fired.

The green-tinged arrow flew through the air and sliced through the spider's multi-eyed face, practically cutting it in two.

I guess that's what happens when a speeding arrow collides with a charging spider. Force multiplication makes the impact that much more deadly.

The spider crashed to the ground and a few moments later it disappeared from sight as Sally continued to drive the jeep like a formula one car.

The notification announcing its death came but I didn't level up. It was much harder to do that these days, gone were the days of gaining multiple levels from every single fight.

I kind of missed them, but at the same time, it was much easier to track my progression now each fight wasn't a near death experience. Looking back, I really got through some of those early fights by the skin of my teeth.

Now though, I was beginning to feel like I kinda knew what I was doing. I felt strong…for my level at least.

"We'll be arriving soon." Sally announced.

I nodded and immediately dived back into mediation. I'd wasted too much stamina on that damned spider.

***

It's here. Diako sang into Lucas' mind. He didn't need the warning; he'd sensed the dragon's extreme mana signature from a few miles out.

He stood up and opened his penthouse floor window, flying out to meet the creature. The dragon was massive and as it approached the city of Havar it let out an ear-splitting roar and fire shot from its mouth coating the nearest bridge and gate in sticky, purple flames.

"I don't think so." Lucas said, flying towards the dragon at a ferocious speed and pulling back his arm for the haymaker.

He threw the punch, just as his speed hit maximum velocity, and socked the big red bastard right in the jaw.

The dragon flew backwards slightly, recoiling from the impact, and looked at Lucas inquisitively, rubbing its chin with a clawed hand…paw? It didn't matter.

"Are you this settlement's defender?" The dragon asked in a deep, intelligent growl.

"Nah…" Lucas mused, stroking his chin as if he was searching for the right words. "Your face just got in the way of my regularly scheduled flight training."

The dragon chuckled. It was a deep, throaty sound that re-minded Lucas of the sound a dog makes right before it throws up on your mum's new carpet.

Poor Mimsy. He thought, remembering a time when that exact scenario had happened. *May you rest in peace.*

"What is your name human?" The dragon asked as the two hov-ered above the city.

Lucas wasn't one for mid battle small talk, but this fight was go-ing to be very destructive and if a little distraction would allow more civilians to get to safety then he'd happily take one for the team.

"In polite society, the person asking gives their name first." He replied to the dragon.

"Humans know nothing of polite society." The dragon chuckled amusedly. "But I'll play along. My name is a Soromir."

"Lucas." The director replied, struggling not to laugh at the dragon's ridiculous name. He may as well have said Frank or Dave. Why did a dragon have a human-like name?

It made no sense.

"It is nice to meet you Human Lucas," Soromir began, looking below himself as people the size of ants scurried through the streets, desperately fleeing from him. "And it will be a pleasure to kill you."

"It's just Lucas." The director replied cooly. "Human Lucas is my father's name."

Then he placed his hands together in front of him, like an artsy cameraman lining up the perfect shot, and fired.

A beam of pure, tangible, white light shot from the space between his hands like a hyper beam. It crashed into the dragon's chest who was forced backwards with a yelp. Lucas had caught him off guard.

"This is why I fucking hate humans!" Soromir screamed as he caught himself in midair. "You always fight so dirty. Have you not heard of honour?"

"Honour doesn't win battles, power does," Lucas replied as he lined up another shot.

Soromir was faster. He snorted at the director and two fast fireballs shot towards him. Lucas quickly disabled his flight skill, dropping a few feet, before reengaging it again.

Dodging in midair was never easy, but he had good control over his abilities. He sneered as he went back to lining up his next shot, but something impacted the top of his head and he went flying towards the ground.

The fireballs were chasers, designed to follow their target. Lucas hadn't accounted for that as he smashed through the walls of a lycanid couple's home.

You're losing your edge, Diako sneered in his mind, *actually, I think you might have put on some weight as well. That armour seems a little tight around the mid-section.* Lucas ignored him.

He shook his head and checked his HP. It had dropped but it wasn't too low just yet.

"Sorry about that," he muttered before flying back towards the fight, leaving the bewildered couple to stare after his golden visage.

His light powers were ill suited to fight a fire dragon, but he was the only person for miles who had a gold rank adventurer card, the highest rank attained in Havar. If he couldn't kill this thing then no one in the city stood a chance.

He poured all of his mana into a single shot. His first hit had barely tickled the dragon. Soromir was too powerful it seemed. Lucas had more than one trick up his sleeve though.

He held his hands out in front of himself and channelled all of his stamina into the shot. Soromir sensed his attack and turned towards him, a smile forming on his scaled lips. His moustache twitching in the breeze.

At the same time, the two unleashed their attacks.

Lucas' beam of pure light energy poured from his chest. It was amplified by the position of his outstretched hands and focused into a condensed laser beam of pure light energy.

Soromir roared and a condensed stream of black, all-consuming fire, shot from his open mouth to meet his foe.

The two attacks met in the middle, pushing against each other as their owners struggled to push their power further and further towards the other.

It was too much though, and as the black energy fought with the light, a huge ball of mixed mana erupted from the centre engulfing everything in sight.

Chapter 22
Dragonborn

Sally drove Yerma hard down the main road towards Havar. The city was in sight and the bridge was engulfed in purple flames.

I couldn't see the lycanid guard who was usually posted there, hopefully he'd gotten to safety. The main road was deserted and I tried to prepare for the worst as I steeled myself for as many awful possibilities as I could.

High above Havar the gold eyes red dragon idly flapped its wings as it faced off against a small figure in golden armour that reflected the sun's rays in a gleaming star of light. I recognised the look; it was the same attire Lucas had worn when he'd come to my rescue on the cliff entrance to the Goblin King Ballroom.

The two stared at each other for a moment and then, without warning, they both fired off powerful, tangible attacks.

A solid white beam of light exploded from Lucas' chest. At the same time the dragon breathed pure, black fire from its mouth.

The two forces met in the middle and the build-up of power began to grow outwards in a ball until it blocked out even the shining sun above them. The attacks moulded and pulsed against each other forming a sphere that reminded me of a Ying and Yang symbol.

Then it was silent.

I felt wind rush past me from behind as if all the air in the vicinity was being pulled into the epicentre of the mass of pure power that formed above the Adventure Society skyscraper.

I couldn't hear anything at all. Sound seemed to have vanished from the land. There was no road noise from Yerma, no wind sounds…not even the chirping of birds or my beating heart created noise.

It was as if the ball of melding power was a blackhole, an abyss, consuming everything around it.

Then the noise came back.

It exploded all at once with a powerful crack, followed immediately by a thundering boom which shook the road as small chasms began to form all along the surface.

Sally struggled with the wheel as I was jerked against the jeep's roll bars and we were in very real danger of being thrown off the road as the earth beneath us split into multiple fissures of cracked stone.

Despite all of that, my gaze was locked firmly on the battle above the city. The sphere of energy exploded outwards in a flash a bright light and simultaneous darkness.

I couldn't see anything for a few seconds. Then the scene returned, though it had changed drastically.

The skyscraper had been sliced in half and fell, almost in slow motion, towards the centre of the city. Glass shattered and sprinkled down like snow threatening to slice up anyone unfortunate enough to be in the immediate vicinity.

From that height, I wasn't even sure that the civilian's wooden homes and stores would save them and I was certain that many lives had been lost in an instant.

The black energy from the dragon's fire catapulted all around the city and large flames erupted all over the capital. It was as if hell had come up to meet the earth and I could only imagine the carnage and terror the citizens were feeling.

Lucas and the dragon still flew high above Havar facing each other. They stared at each other for a long, silent moment, then a victor was declared as Lucas fell from the sky, crashing into the ground like a meteor.

At that moment, Sally slammed down hard on the brakes and I was nearly thrown from the jeep as we skidded to a halt in front of the burning bridge. We'd made it, but not fast enough.

The catonid warrior vaulted from the vehicle, ripping her armband off.

"Hurry!" she yelled before sprinting over the bridge and into the fray.

I didn't need telling twice. I jumped out of Yerma and was hot on Sally's heels as I dodged the sticky, purple flames which spread along the wooden bridge. It was getting pretty rickety and I half expected the planks below my feet to disintegrate at any minute.

Thankfully they held though, as I made it across the bridge and through the entrance archway. I looked around at the sheer devastation. Taylor's Tailor was demolished, the remnants of her sign fuelling a jet-black flame.

The store itself may as well have never been there. It had all but vanished as the mana-fuelled flames jumped from building to building like a swarm of angry, hot locusts destroying everything in their path.

I felt a twinge in my chest and hoped that the plucky, young catonid had made it out in time. I'd only met her once, but she was kind to me and no one deserved the kind of death that the black fire promised.

"Watch out!" Bell screamed as I was knocked flying to the side.

I turned back to see what was going on just as the red dragon crashed into the ground, right where I'd been standing a moment earlier.

She'd saved my life. I kind of felt bad for not being sure if I actually liked her or not earlier, but now was not the time for feelings. It was the time for actions.

I jumped to my feet, equipping my bow, and taking aim at the dragon. It looked worse for wear; Lucas had done a number on the flying lizard fuck.

Good job golden boy. I though as I stared up at the haggard beast.

Its scales hung limply on its chest like broken, cracked armour. One of its eyes was missing and the other looked dazed and unfocused. The right wing had a myriad of holes through it and viscera and blood leaked from the broken skin, leaving trails of black gore in its wake.

Surely, weakened this much, even I could finish it.

I didn't have time to shoot my shot though as Sally flew towards it with a speed that my eyes could scarcely keep up with.

"That's my sister's store you bastard!" She howled as her brilliant black sword cleaved into the back of the dragon's neck.

Her sister? I thought. *Wait, does she mean Taylor?*

The dragon howled either in pain or rage, I couldn't quite tell which, as it lifted a claw and batted Sally away.

She flew through the air, disappearing into the smoke. Her sword did not go with her, it was still sticking out of the back of the dragon's neck.

He didn't seem too happy about it either as he tried in vain to remove it with his tiny arms. It reminded me of the T-Rex from *Meet The Robinsons*, but unfortunately, the humour of that was lost on me as I channelled all of my stamina into a single *Soul Shot*.

Surely, a full powered blast aimed at the weakened chest would do the trick. It couldn't have had much HP left could it?

There was only one way to find out. I released the bowstring and my arrow soared through the air leaving a strong trace of green energy in its wake as dirt flew from the ground as it passed by.

It collided with the dragon's exposed chest and sank in, but only to the tip. How powerful was its skin? The exposed chest skin bubbled and the dragon grunted in dismay as it turned its hateful, single eye towards me.

"You again?" he growled in a choking sound, breathing in rasps.

It lifted its claws above me and I dismissed my bow, summoning my daggers and raising them above my head. It was all I had time to do. The only form of defence I could think of in the split second before the dragon ripped me in two.

"Hey ugly!" Jamie shouted from the side, launching a fierce water cannon at the outstretched claw.

The dragon halted, turning its gaze towards the water mage before idly swatting him away like a fly. Jamie flew into the archway which hung over the bridge with a sickening crunch. A smear of blood was left in his wake as his limp body slid down the stone like a slug and dropped limply to the ground.

"Jamie!" I cried involuntarily and the dragon turned back to me.

I saw roaring flames erupt from its back as Bell screamed and fired shot after shot. The dragon ignored them like a man ignores a single bug as he walks down the road.

It grinned maliciously as it took a slow step towards me. I slashed out at it with my daggers but I could barely raise my arms. I'd put all of my stamina into that single shot and my daggers didn't even scratch the beast with the paltry power I had left.

Lowering its huge head towards me, it opened its mouth revealing rows of sharp, serrated teeth. It was terrifying.

I stood stock still, a deer in the headlights of a semi-truck. I couldn't move my body at all as its hot, putrid breath stung my face and snapped shut.

I closed my eyes.

Nobody would be able to say Kaleb Akabane died a coward. Though that was a small solace in the face of an unfulfilled life. I'd never get to meet my child. I'd never hold my wife again.

I felt something soft slam into me and my eyes snapped open as I staggered to the side waking from my dying thoughts and turning back to see a scene unfold in slow motion.

It was Panda. He had shoulder barged me out of the dragon's reach. He looked towards me with a grin as the dragon's teeth snapped closed on his neck.

His body evaporated into silver light and he was no more. However, the image of his smiling face as he'd saved my life was burned into my retina.

He was gone.

My friend...The closest thing to family I had in this godforsaken place.

Gone.

My stomach churned and my vision turned red. I recognised the feeling instantly and I leaned into it.

I had promised Panda that I wouldn't use this power again. It was dangerous, it could kill me.

I didn't care.

I felt powerful energy welling up inside of me. My body became a nuclear weapon, armed and ready to devastate everything around me.

I reached out towards the beast who looked stunned as its one remaining eye widened in shock and horror at the puny human with the soul power.

"How?" It asked, stunned. "You're only a human...not...not even close to the level cap."

"I am going to destroy you," I said, interrupting it in a calm and cold voice that I barely recognised as my own. "When I'm done no one will remember you even existed. I will erase you from history, even your own mother won't remember having such a pathetic, disappointment as a son."

As I rambled, the dragon's expression changed. It looked... scared.

Good.

I reached inside of it, seeing a black outline of the beast that had killed my closest friend, and I crushed it with an ethereal hand of inner power.

The hand was a swath of circling green and blue energy and it closed around the startled dragon like it was a mere insect. I felt its soul crunch like bone in my metaphysical hand.

The dragon yelped like a wounded puppy as I squeezed it with all of my might. Somewhere outside of the soul realm I felt my teeth crack as I clenched them, my hands broke and my legs snapped at the femurs.

My entire body was so tense that it couldn't support the weight of the strain I was putting on it, but though I was aware of it, I felt no pain.

The ball of energy inside my stomach that I'd tried so hard to touch whilst mediating earlier leaked out and snaked along my bones, overtaking my ligaments and threading lines of power into my muscles.

I felt nothing but a primal rage as I squeezed the very life essence out of the terrified dragon.

It screamed a final, piercing death cry as I opened my eyes and saw its scales evaporate into the air. Its white skeleton was all that remained as a veiled blood red essence poured out of the beast and into me.

It must have looked like I'd sucked its soul out of its body like some kind of energy vampire. I felt the power course through me as I stole the last of its life essence which settled neatly into the ball at my core, tinging the blue and green circulating power with a touch of crimson.

"D-dragonborn." Bell stuttered quietly from somewhere beside me as the world faded to black.

Chapter 23
The Desert Samurai: Taking Out the Trash

The Samurai and Pocco, her wolf familiar, spent some time meditating in Chrysus' temple after her fated meeting with the god.

He had left her with basic instructions on how to do so and she'd spent days on end in a Buddhist pose trying to decipher the inner workings of her soul.

She had eventually worked out how to replenish her HP by breathing in natural energy from the air around her and manipulating the way it interacted with her inner circulatory system.

Once she had cracked that nut, the rest was easy, though it still took some time to fill her bars. Concentrating her willpower for such a long time on such a menial task drained her mental faculties quickly and she had to take breaks regularly.

It wasn't wasted time though as she practiced with her newly fixed and upgraded katana. She smiled fondly at the weapon with its gleaming black blade and fancy crimson wrap.

It looked truly demonic, which sat perfectly in line with the persona she wanted to portray to the world. She chose a skill which allowed her to summon an Oni mask, after all.

She fondly opened her system interface and read lovingly through the katana's upgrade notification for the umpteenth time that day.

Katana of Unyielding Prosperity
Upon taking up the mantel of retainer for Chrysus, God of Wealth, he rewarded you with a weapon upgrade token.
The *Katana of Unyielding Prosperity* is the personification of Chrysus' violent will. Perhaps you will think on his teachings as you slay your enemies.

Loot gold from enemies killed by this weapon.
Mana cost for sword-based skills is halved.
+20% mana whilst wielding this weapon.
+10% stamina whilst wielding this weapon.

Her new god had given her a serious boon to her offensive strength with the gift of the upgrade token. Not only would being his retainer grant her wealth, but also some serious power.

With the halved mana cost to her sword-based skills alone, she would become an unstoppable force in the midst of battle.

Previously, she had used her active skills sparingly as they had a particularly high mana cost. That would change though, with her new weapon.

She practiced with the sword and meditated for a few more days as Pocco merrily hunted around the oasis. Their little spot in the desert attracted all kinds of wildlife which the wolf familiar would happily chase, kill, and eat. Sometimes he even brought The Samurai entire birds as presents and he always wagged his tail proudly as she praised him for his accomplishments.

Eventually though, she did leave the temple.

Chrysus had given her a new mission and she intended to enact his will fervently as she made her way to the Western Continent to take part in his High Priest Tournament.

What those in Celestia referred to as the Western Continent, she knew as the USA, Mexico, and Canada. Of course, those countries didn't exist in this world but the map was comparatively the same as Earth's was.

It struck her as odd that the land masses in Celestia mimicked the ones on Earth, but it wasn't her place to question things that she couldn't control. Maybe one day when she became a god herself she'd get an answer as to why they bore such striking similarities to one another, but that was a task for another day.

As The Samurai travelled across the desert, heading to the western coast with her faithful wolf companion, she thought on her newest quest.

The Celestial Map.

Her new god had given it to her immediately and his snake-like eyes glinted with hunger as he spoke about this task. It was quite a simple one, though it would possibly take her a lifetime to complete.

She was to hunt down and eliminate all 10,000 of her Earthen compatriots who had been isekai'd into the world with her. Supposedly, once she'd killed them, she could adsorb their map pieces, eventually piecing together the entire thing on her own body.

She wasn't overly keen on the idea of marring her flesh with 10,000 tattoos, she was a samurai, not a yakuza. However, if her god willed it then it would be done. That was their deal and so far he had more than kept up with his side of the bargain.

Besides, amongst that vast number of humans, there was sure to be a few worthy opponents…and their experience points would certainly help her in her personal quest for power.

175

She was no assassin though, so she planned to challenge these people to honourable duels like the great warriors of old.

One such duel happened faster than she had anticipated.

After a few weeks of traversing the desert, levelling up and killing monsters, she arrived at the unimpressive port town of Arkesh.

It was a simple place of clay huts and wooden, ancient Egyptian watercrafts. Colourful cloths adorned the streets, keeping the beating sun away from the precious skin of the dark locals.

It was quite refreshing, she had to admit, even if it was a little tacky.

It was whilst perusing the markets, in search of a trustworthy vessel to traverse the sea with, that she found her first prey.

He was a tall man with a beer belly and a fez hat perched atop his blading head. He didn't look like much of a fighter, but the men he commanded certainly did.

She had stumbled upon him accidentally after fighting off some thugs on the outskirts of town. Nobody had deigned to tell her that the outskirts were bandit territory.

After despatching them easily, she asked the last one where the rest of his scummy band of merry men were hiding and the injured, terrified man had pointed to a compound of unassuming clay huts.

Naturally, upon seeing the plethora of guards in their murder hobo attire, she waltzed straight through the front door.

Samurai's do not sneak...at least not when their foes are weak.

After kicking down the door to the biggest hut in the cesspit of a bandit hideout, she stood face to face with the fat old man.

"A samurai?" He said questioningly. "So...they have those here too?" He pondered, stroking his invisible beard with his stubby little pig fingers.

It was at that moment that she knew she had found her first target. Chrysus would be pleased.

"Outworlder!" She declared boldly, pointing her sword towards the man. "I challenge you to a duel."

He looked up at her, pointed at himself with a single raised eyebrow. "Me?" He scoffed incredulously. "What do you think I have all these minions – I mean guards around for. Get rid of her." He gestured lackadaisically to his goon squad. "If you manage to take her alive then you're free to *play* with her as a reward."

The man's black eyes glinted as his pink cheeks flushed red at whatever nefarious thoughts he was having.

Disgusting. The Samurai thought to herself.

If all the humans that had been isekai'd were like this one then she'd be doing the world a service by murdering them.

She drew her sword as the lecherous goons charged, an evil grin hidden by her Oni mask. Pocco stood in the door, guarding her flank. He was a good boy.

The Samurai would dispatch these cretins in an instant.

Midnight Slash (common)
Unsheathe your blade in an instant 10-foot leap to slash through foes. This skill imbues the wielder's blade with dark mana.
Activating this skill has a medium mana cost.

Her *Midnight Slash* ability took hold and she leapt through the air in a millisecond, leaving severed torsos, shocked expressions, and a swimming pool of blood in her wake.

The pig's cronies never stood a chance.

"Pathetic." She spat as she stood face to face with the outworlder. "The idea of adsorbing the tattoo of such an immoral, and frankly disgusting, cur such as yourself makes my very soul shudder." She announced in a regal, old fashioned nature. She had seen enough samurai dramas back home to know that she was nailing the dialect.

Before the man could protest she swiped her blade across his neckline, severing his head from its body. As the head fell to the floor she kicked it into the wall where it crunched and splattered gross old man juice in a stain that reminded her of psychiatry test cards.

A notification popped up asking if she wanted to adsorb the man's map piece and she begrudgingly mentally asserted yes.

Thank you! Chrysus said into her mind, his snake-like hiss a warming presence on her raging internal discord. *I knew you wouldn't disappoint me Yuki. I am quite literally sitting on the edge of my seat in anticipation of where your journey will lead you next.*

She wasn't keen on people using her real name. Her moniker: The Samurai, was a promise she had made to herself, the person she wished to be in this world. Yuki was her dead name, as far as she was concerned.

However, she gave the god a free pass owing to the respect and reverence she gave him as the most powerful being she had ever met.

Yuki bowed at the waist after sheathing her sword and she knew that the god had seen her acknowledgement of his praise.

Later that evening she purchased lodgings for Pocco and herself in a small, unassuming inn near the port. Upon entering her room she received an unexpected notification.

Would you like to open loot boxes?
Y/N

She hadn't even realised that she had loot boxes to open, but she quickly mentally asserted yes all the same as she sat down on the dirty bedsheets.

PKing Loot Box
Only the best murder's get rewarded. Consider yourself initiated.

Reward: *Entry to the Morning Star Hotel and Spa.*

A bright, crimson light appeared in front of her as a small, oriental, black box floated down from the ceiling, landing in her lap.

She looked at it, cocking her head to the side, and as she reached out to open it, the lid evaporated and a mild, burning pain lit up the back of her hand.

She unsummoned her armoured glove and saw a black pentagram lined across her hand.

Oh great anther tattoo. Just what I wanted. She sighed and went to bed, not even waiting for the loot box to burst into golden flames before disappearing.

Chapter 24
Scales Of The Apex Predator

I awoke in an unfamiliar place, my head pounded and my entire body was on fire. Not literally, that would have been worrying, but figuratively.

My muscles burned, they felt deflated and there was a heavy weight pressing into my chest. When I opened my eyes, the world seemed eerily bright. Like there was a new depth to every colour, every shadow...everything.

I was in a small room with bare panelled wooden walls. There was only one other bed in the room with me and its occupant looked to be in a bad way. I could hear laboured breathing from the figure who was wrapped so tightly in fresh, white bandages that you'd be forgiven for thinking they were an Egyptian mummy.

By contrast, my bandages weren't as all-encompassing. They were mostly centred around my limbs and hands. Though from the look of my HP, any injuries I'd sustained in the battle with the dragon should have been long gone.

"Well look who's finally awake." A cheerful voice rang out from beside me. I turned towards them and gasped as a sharp pain exploded from my neck.

Bell lounged on a chair next to my bed with one leg dangling over the arm. She looked as comfortable as ever, though I was surprised to see her.

"Where am I?" I croaked through a cracked and irritated throat. My voice sounded awful, like I'd chain smoked for the last fifty years. That would be quite the achievement, considering I was only 28 years old.

"You're in the afterlife. Our evil overlord Lucifer is kinda into extreme bondage, but he always gives out cookies afterwards so it's not all bad," she said with a practiced straight face. "If I were you, I'd just lay back and think of England. That's where you're from right, with an accent like that?"

"It is," I croaked back slowly. "But seriously. Where the hell are we?"

"A makeshift hospital," she replied, grinning at my seriousness. "Well...technically we're in a big inn near the palace, the part of town near the Adventure Society was completely demolished so we all got relocated after..."

She trailed off and in my mind's eye I saw the black flames tearing through the stores I'd visited. I saw the Adventure Society tower fall, glass shards plummeting to the ground.

I saw Panda.

That stupid hero's grin on his face as his head was bitten off.

Bell must have seen the look on my face because her reassuring, playful smile turned into a grimace.

"I don't know what you did to that dragon," she said, leaning in and whispering. "But I'd keep it to yourself when people come asking, and they *will* come. Sally has kept them at bay for the time being, but until Director Lucas recovers, they'll be hounding you any chance they get.

"Me and Sally are the only ones that saw...*that*...but no one believes our little tale about how Lucas killed it so bad it took a few minutes before it knew it was dead."

I took a moment to digest the information. Sally and Bell knew about my weird-ass soul power. That was unfortunate, however they seemed to be going out of their way to help me keep it under wraps,

I already knew the adventurer district had been decimated, I'd watched it happen. Though if we'd been moved into the heart of Havar then that would mean we were in the noble district. I'd have to be careful.

"Sorry," I began sheepishly. "I...I should have kept myself under control. It's just Panda...Panda was the closest thing I had to family in this damned place." The floodgate opened and as I began to apologise, it all came out.

"My wife was pregnant before I was isekai'd, our kid has probably already been born. The first time I used...*that*..." I said, mimicking her not-so-sly way of referencing my soul power. "It was after I saw this kid's mother get killed in front of her. I saw it like she was my own child and it was my wife on the floor in place of her mother...and I just got so angry.

"Everything I've done since arriving here was to protect them, to bring them here and reunite with them. Panda had been the only one helping me with that. He was my closest friend...he was family."

I looked up at her with bleary eyes, my throat was throbbing from overuse in my weakened state. Surprisingly she listened to the whole thing without interrupting. Then she opened her damned mouth.

"Yeah alright, calm down *Dom Toretto*." She began with a smirk. "He's your familiar not *tu familia* just summon him back. Also, there's no judgment here for your little psychotic break, things like

182

that keep people interesting." She winked as I stared back at her with what must have been a pretty pitiful gaze.

I blinked the wetness out of my eyes as my brain kicked into overdrive. How stupid could I be? She was right of course. He was a familiar, he wasn't dead, he was just sent back to his waiting room, sage school place until I summoned him again.

He'd literally told me that the first time I'd met him. If I could move my arms I'd have face palmed right then and there.

With that sudden and obvious realisation dawning on me, I felt a huge weight lift off my chest. I'd have never expected Bell to be the one to provide *me* with sound advice, but I guess everyone has their moment.

"Thanks," I replied, my mind churning with possibilities. I needed to find someone in the know to perform the summon for me. I bet it'd be expensive as shit but with the money I'd gotten from the dragon's lair it shouldn't be a problem.

I could bring him back!

I *would* bring him back.

"Glad to be of service," she replied, grinning at me. "Oh, by the way. Sally said to tell you to check your stats when you woke up. Apparently you're not very good at reflecting after a big battle."

"I'll have you know I'm the best at reflecting after battles," I croaked back, trying to add an edge of playfulness to my *Fallout* ghoul-sounding voice. "I'm also the best at being humble."

She gave me a pointed look and I dived into my HUD. There was a fair few notifications waiting for me.

You have defeated *Gold Eyes Red Dragon* (lvl 100+)

Bonus experience has been rewarded due to level disparity.

Bonus experience has been negated due to low damage caused by player.
Once again you stole the final hit. I can't give out the same achievement twice, you know? Stop trying to game the system for loot boxes!
Congratulations! You have reached lvl 37

Congratulations! You have reached lvl 38

...

Congratulations! You have reached lvl 42

"Holy shit!" I gasped. "That dragon passed the level cap."

Even with the bonus experience negated, I still rose six whole levels from that single kill. I didn't even know that was possible in phase two. I'd been grinding away for ages trying to level up and it turned out that all I needed to do was beat a city destroying flying beast with almost all of its health depleted. I couldn't believe I hadn't thought of that sooner.

"Yeah I know." Bell replied cheerfully. I looked at her with a blank expression and she continued. "It'd have to be at least past the level cap to shrug off my fireballs like that...and Sally might have mentioned something." She professed confidently, folding her arms, and muttering that last part.

I ignored her and dove back into my notifications.

Congratulations on reaching level 40 player!
You have a new active skill to choose.

You may pick one of the following skills:

Limit Break (uncommon)
Are you tired of those pesky stamina and mana costs stopping you from unleashing your most powerful

attacks? Well fear no more! With *Limit Break*, once per day, you can push past your limits and *Captain Yami* the fuck out of any opponent.

Using Limit Break can and will induce the following symptoms: nausea, vomiting, fatigue, drowsiness, headaches, migraines, loss of hair, skin irritation and general irritability. Please consult your physician before using Limit Break.

I had only one thought upon reading that skill: *why did it sound like a pharmaceutical advert?* I immediately noped the fuck out of it and moved onto the next one.

Arrow Volley (common)

Like the archers of old, unleash a one-man volley of arrows onto your enemies. This comes with a high stamina cost but can also take out multiple foes at once. *This skill can combine with Soul Shot at later levels. The amount of arrows created is determined by amount of stamina used.*

Now that was more like it! I needed an area of effect attack and one that could one day combine with Soul Shot would be a brilliant investment in my skill list.

I was a little perturbed by the common rarity, but I had been pretty lucky with my skills so far. It made sense that I wouldn't be unlocking unique and ancient skills every time I levelled up.

...Right?

Scales of the Apex Predator (Ancient)
Having defeated a dragon more than double your own level, your soul has learned some of their kind's tricks. Namely, the ability to use scales as armour.

Summon dragon scales once per day and coat your skin in the red, semi-impervious scales of the *Gold Eyes Red Dragon*.
Quit *dragon* your feet and choose this skill already God damn it!

The system didn't need to tell me twice. I immediately asserted yes on the HUD and accepted the skill. *Arrow Volley* would have to wait until next time.

I guess I really do get offered ancient skills every time. I thought, smiling widely. *I wonder if it's like this for everyone.*

"You just got a super rare new skill didn't you?" Bell asked, folding her arms.

I nodded like an idiot, grinning from ear to ear. I was so pleased with my new upgrade that the pain of moving my neck didn't even bother me.

Speaking of pain, I still had a few notifications left to look into. I opened them up, hoping for an explanation.

WARNING
You have unlocked the ability to weaponize the soul before your level is high enough to protect you from it.
You are suffering adverse effects from the strain your soul has put on your body.
If you keep doing this before reaching the level cap. You will die.

Well shit.

I guessed that was what Panda meant when he warned me against using my soul attacks. I'd really have to reign it in if I wanted to live long enough to make it a proper trump card.

Hopefully I wouldn't have to face any super powered enemies any time soon. Of course, there was always the option of learning to reign in my emotions, but who wants to spend time working on themselves when there are monsters to fight?

Emergency Quest Complete!

The Sacking of Havar

A dragon is coming! A dragon is coming!
Thanks to the misguided deeds of *certain* members of the Adventure Society, a large, red dragon is currently on his way to the city of Havar.
This dragon is pretty upset and intends to genocide the fuck out of all sapient life forms on the island.

Objectives:
Prevent Havar from being destroyed 1/1
Kill the dragon 1/1
Protect the citizens 1/1 (Remaining Population 1,473,005/1,732,192)

This is a group quest given to all inhabitants of the area surrounding Havar

I felt a little numb as I read the completed emergency quest. Over 250,000 people had died in the attack. I knew that overall, it had been a miracle to save as many as we did, but still.

I didn't want to think about that, nor why my original quest to slay the dragon hadn't completed yet. So I continued onto my next notification.

You have gained a new title:
Dragonslayer

You have slayed a dragon that was infinitely more powerful than you. That's no easy feat, even if someone else *did* do most of the heavy lifting.

You have gained some of its power by adsorbing its soul.

Dragons are more likely to talk to you and less likely to annihilate you the moment they see you, like they do with most humanoids.

Gain the skill: Eye of the Dragon

New Skill:
Eye of the Dragon (rare)

You have been gifted with a single golden eye from a gold eyes red dragon. This will allow you to see mana in the world around you, like literally everyone else on Celestia.
Well done, you finally hit puberty you late bloomer you.

Increase intimidation effect by 50%

I gained another new title and a fancy new eye to boot. Wait…did that mean I had one golden dragon eye in my eye socket? What the hell happened to my other eye. I looked up at Bell questioningly and went to open my mouth before being interrupted by her giggles.

"I take it you got to the eye notification?" She said, fighting through a giggle fit as she looked at me.

"How did you know?" I asked.

"Because you've got a golden eye now. It's been staring at me lecherously this entire time. Seriously dude, it looks like half of your face wants to devour me…though you could at least take me to dinner first." She winked, still struggling to control the laughter.

"You could have told me!" I shouted, or at least attempted to shout, my throat was still sore and wasn't exactly playing ball.

"What would be the fun in that?"

Chapter 25
Magic Feds

Before I'd finished admonishing the giggling fireball mage, Sally burst through the door, slamming it shut behind her.

She looked as perky as ever, that cat really knew how to bounce back from being batted across the city like a homerun ball. Her silver hair bounced on her shoulders as she looked around with shifty blue eyes and then focused on me.

"Good, you're awake," she said, summoning a bottle from her inventory into her hand and thrusting it at me. "Drink this."

I began to focus on it but she cut me off rudely.

"You don't have time to worry about notifications, just drink the damned thing!" She grabbed the bottle, ripping the cork out with her teeth and practically force feeding it to me like I was a newborn, or a CIA hostage.

I gasped in surprise and coughed half of the shimmering blue liquid back up, but Sally persisted and I gave in, swallowing the rest like a good little captive.

"Good. That'll heal your soul," she said, slumping onto the end of my bed. "The royal inquisitors are on their way and if we want to keep up the charade that Lucas killed that dragon, we need you to be as unassuming as possible."

I opened my mouth, so very full of questions, but Sally continued before I could say anything.

"They're going to examine you and question you about the attack. Tell them that you fought with me and the rest of your team but do not mention that freaky soul ripping crap you pulled. Hopefully this potion will fix you up enough to hide that gaping wound in your mana flow before they get here."

She finally stopped, taking a deep breath, and leaning back on the bed. I had so many questions, but I asked the first thing that popped into my head.

"What's mana flow?"

"It's the aura people give off. Those of us with mana can see it in untrained whelps like yourself." She turned to look at me, seeming slightly calmer now. "After you decimated that dragon your flow looked fucking huge, like, untethered Lucas huge. I think it's because your soul got damaged…that was a soul attack right? I've only seen them used a few times."

I nodded.

If the potion she force-fed me could really fix me up then there was no reason not to take it. Though I wondered if I would also be able to see mana flow now with my new shiny dragon eye.

"What's a royal inquisitor?" I asked next, trying to remember the many questions I wanted to ask. This time Bell answered.

"They're like the king's detectives. Fucking feds." She groaned. "Just remember not to speak to them without a lawyer."

I nodded slightly at that, but despite Bell's *unique* way of speaking, I got the general gist.

"Ok cool, thanks for covering this up for me," I said a little sheepishly as the two women stared at me with wildly differing expressions that both somehow still seemed incredulous.

"Don't be stupid Gonads it's not a good colour on you." Sally said, rolling her eyes. "Besides, I owed you a life debt...consider it repaid."

She was, of course, referring to the time I saved her from a huge goblin motherfucker during our first quest together. I'd literally dragged her unconscious body away from a goblin horde and then held them off until help arrived.

"You never owed me anything. Friends don't count stuff like that," I replied with a smirk.

She looked at me for a moment and then her cheeks turned a faint shade of pink. It was an odd look for a woman of her...physique.

"Friend's huh?" she asked slowly. "Thanks."

There was a moment of awkward silence between us until Bell saved the day with her inability to read a room.

"Oh, by the way Kaleb. We *may* have stolen all of your dragon loot." My head snapped towards her and my neck crinkled slightly. It was, however, noticeably less painful than it had been an hour ago, so perhaps that potion Sally gave me had begun to work.

"There were billions of gold coins!" She continued oblivious to my frown. "But Sally made me give them away."

"You're damn right I did!" Sally roared. "That amount of money singly handedly paid for the reconstruction of the part of town destroyed by that monster."

"Yeah..." Bell replied. "But it also could have bought me my own personal dragon to ride on, or a big boat, or even a palace made of the bones of my enemies. Just think of the amazing, wealthy future you just robbed me of."

"You mean the wealth *you* robbed from *me?*" I asked, shooting her a deadpan look which finally got her to shut up.

We sat in silence for a little while after that and I spent some more time in my HUD figuring out how to spend my free points.

In the end I put 10 points into intelligence and 20 points into strength. I still wanted to increase my intelligence as it directly affected my stealth abilities which I'd gained from my armour.

However, strength gave me more stamina which I desperately needed. I still hadn't even scratched the surface of my *Perception of the Apex Predator* skill yet and that would surely be OP as fuck once I had the stamina to make it work properly.

The ability to stop time was a life saver. It had already saved me back at the dragon's lair and I'd barely gotten to use it for a single second then. The possibilities were simply staggering…as was the amount of stamina needed to fully utilise it.

Once I was done, I took a look at my stat sheet and smiled at the progress I'd made.

Status Sheet:

Name: Kaleb Akabane
Race: Outworlder
Class: Apex Predator (unique)
Adventurer Rank: Temp
Level: 42
Map Pieces 2/10,000
HP: 434/376 (434)
Stamina: 449/409 (449)

Strength: 365 (382)
Agility: 148 (169)
Perception: 144
Vitality: 296 (354)
Intelligence: 68

Personal Skills: *Speak English Damnit!, Eat Anything, Minor Poison Resistance, Usurper (unique), Health Sense (common), Eye of the Dragon (rare)*
Class Skills (Passive): *Newly Qualified Bowman (59.1%), Dagger (lvl 11), Novice Apex Skirmisher, Acid Dhampir Dagger, Acid Arrows, Environmental Hazzard*
Active Skills: *Perception of the Apex Predator (rare), Soul Shot (ancient), Scales of the Apex Predator (Ancient)*

Blessing: *Blessing of Wealth*
Familiars: *Panda (Daemon)*
Titles: *Audacious Soul Expander, Dragonslayer*
Admission: *Pentagram [Right hand (Morningstar Hotel and Spa)]*

All in all I was pretty chuffed with my upgraded stats. The sheet was starting to get pretty long now. I smiled at my *Newly Qualified Bowman* skill which had finally passed the halfway point on its percentage.

I did feel like I'd improved with the weapon with all the grinding and practice I'd been doing. I wondered what it would evolve into at 100%.

Oddly though, my adventurer rank still said *temp* even though I'd passed the quest. I *had* passed the quest right? I looked towards Sally.

"Hey Sally," I said and she looked up at me. "Did I pass the exam? Because it's not updated on my stat sheet yet."

"You did." She blinked a few times, seeming to be slightly caught off guard. "It hasn't updated because you haven't handed the quest in yet, and you need to do the induction seminar first anyway."

"Induction seminar?" Bell and I both asked in complaining and groaning voices.

From my previous experiences with the Adventure Society I could only guess at what kind of torturous corporate bullshit we would be subjected to this time.

"Yes." She replied. "Though that'll have to wait for now. The tower hasn't been rebuilt yet and we have an audience with the king tomorrow."

I looked at her, blinking slowly.

An audience with the king? I thought. *Am I about to be knighted?* Sir Kaleb did have a nice ring to it, but somehow I doubted that was what was going to happen.

Sally must have read my look because she continued un-prompted by either myself or Bell.

"He wants to reward us for our part in slaying the dragon." She explained. "Lucas will get most of the prestige of course, but I'm sure you'll get a nice little trinket or something." She paused, taking a deep breath. "Reggie will receive his recognition posthumously."

I opened my mouth to speak but the words wouldn't come. We'd been forced to leave his ashes inside the dragon's lair which had caved in.

I hoped his family wouldn't be there. It sounded self-centred but I just didn't know if I could face them. I knew I made the right choice in prioritising the living, but still, how do you tell a parent that *you* made the decision to leave their son's ashes somewhere that they can't be recovered from?

"What about Jamie?" I asked solemnly, the image of his limp body slapping into the wooden arch, blood leaking down, burning the backs of my eyelids.

"He's alive for now." Sally said hopefully.

"Where is he?" I asked suddenly, siting up slightly. I barely knew the guy but if he was still breathing I wanted to see him, to thank him. If he hadn't attacked the dragon when he did I'd have been squished.

Sally lifted a muscled arm and pointed to the bed next to me. I turned towards it with my mouth hanging open. I'd noticed the patient when I'd first woken up, wearing full-body bandages like a mummy cosplayer.

"He's in a coma." Bell said quietly. "Honestly, it's a miracle he's not dead after what happened to him."

I looked at him gravely. Even if he did wake up he'd likely never be the same. As far as I knew, physical disabilities didn't exist in this world. Magic healing kinda did away with all that stuff.

The mental strain though? I don't think even mana or HP recovery can cure that. Nobody would be able to go through the trauma he did and come out the same way. Hell, I'd noticed myself change bit by bit since this all started and I hadn't even been made into a human pancake.

As the three of us looked sadly towards our comrade there was a sudden knock at the door which jolted me awake from my depressing thoughts.

It opened, and two men walked in wearing black, embroidered suits and sunglasses. One of them flipped a badge open at me.

"Inquisitor Miles, I'm here to speak with a Mr Akabane."

Holy shit. They really are magic feds. I thought, struggling to stop my mouth from lolling open at the strange intrusion.

Chapter 26
Bell of the Ball

Inquisitor Miles and his silent and larger partner entered the room standing at the edge of my bed. Sally moved out of the way for them without saying a word, which told me everything I needed to know.

These guys were dangerous.

"Mr Akabane, I'm glad to see you're recovering well." The sunglasses wearing man said in an official *I don't really give a shit* tone.

He really did look like a magic FBI agent in his black suit. It was embroidered with black stitching which swirled down his arms. It was the kind of suit I'd imagine *Dumbledor* might have worn if he was trying to be a little less conspicuous.

"I'm certainly getting there," I said, playing up the croak in my throat. The pain had mostly subsided now, likely due to Sally's potion, but the more pathetic I seemed the less they'd harass me...hopefully.

"You sound awful," Miles replied casually, cupping his hands in front of him. "However, we do need to ask you a few quick questions if that's ok?"

I nodded, eyeing up his partner as slyly as I could. The man was as tall as he was broad. Definitely the type to give Sally a run for her money. The steroid abuse must have been rampant in Havar.

He hung back near the door. Mimicking Miles' stance and staring directly ahead, looking over the top of the rest of us. He looked more like a shady nightclub bouncer than a fed. I wondered if he was the bad cop when informants refused to play ball.

"Can you tell me, in your own words, what happened when you fought the dragon please Mr Akabane?" Miles asked, shooting a warning glance at Sally.

"Which time?" I croaked.

"When you killed it."

"I didn't kill it, I'm pretty sure that honour belongs to Director Lucas," I replied smartly.

No son-bitch is gonna catch me out with leading questions like that.

"Is that why you're the one sporting the dragon's eye then?" he asked coyly, gesturing to my newest title reward.

I feigned a look of shock, looking around the room at the others. Bell struggled to keep a straight face.

"What dragon's eye?" I practically shouted. "I've only just woken up! Someone get me a mirror."

The inquisitor sighed, rubbing a slow palm across his face.

That's right buddy, you wipe the stress headache away. Where I'm from we call those the Kaleb special.

"Mr Akabane, please can you take this seriously. I understand that this isn't the best time but I'm just trying to do my job." Miles said exasperatedly, peering at me through pleading eyes.

Before I could answer, the indomitable fed by the door glanced my way and, in a deep voice, said:

"We can always do this the hard way." There was a menacing undertone to his rumbling voice.

Sally tensed up and I could see she was ready for a fight. I felt the same way, mentally hovering over my daggers in my HUD. Bell, however, had a different plan.

"We have ways of making you talk." She repeated in a bad German accent. "Jesus, I didn't know we were dealing with the gestapo. I heard this place was socialist but I didn't realise that meant national socialism."

I chuckled as the tense air in the room abated slightly. The tall man looked confused but before he could retort Miles held up a silencing hand.

"It's alright." He let the words hang for a moment, shooting his colleague a look before continuing. "My friend here has a poor sense of comedic timing, please accept my apologies." He took a breath before continuing.

"So, am I right to say that you *didn't* kill the dragon Mr Akabane?"

"Nope," I lied. "I'm only a temp adventurer, in fact we were out on our exam when this happened. I could barely scratch the thing. The Director was the only one powerful enough to stop it.

"Between me, Sally and the rest of the team, we must have used up all of our collective stamina and mana and we barely left a scratch on it."

I put on the most earnest voice I could muster. After all the effort Sally had put in to helping to hide my soul attack power it would be disrespectful of me to fuck it up now.

Inquisitor Miles looked at me with appraising eyes. They flashed a blue colour for a moment and somehow I instinctively knew that he was using a skill.

It must have been the effect of my dragon's eye. It didn't tell me what that skill was, but I guessed that it was some kind of appraisal skill. It was likely that he was examining my stats or something – though I doubted he could do that in anything other than a limited capacity.

"Are you a communist sympathiser, Mt Akabane?" he asked, narrowing his eyes.

"I am not," I replied evenly.

"Alright then," he said, once again leaving his words to hang in the thick silence that followed. "Thank you for your time Mr Akabane. I've also being instructed to give you this letter." He passed me an envelope with a wax seal on it and then left.

We waited a few moments before speaking. I eventually broke the silence myself.

"Do you think he bought it?"

"Hopefully." Sally replied, perching back on the edge of my bed, and slumping her shoulders slightly. "At the very least, I don't think he has a way to prove otherwise and in Havar, that's good enough."

"So they weren't really nazi's then?" Bell asked innocently.

"I don't know what that means." Sally sighed. "I need to make a call." She stepped out of the room, closing the door quietly behind her.

Whilst she was absent, I took a better look at my letter. It had a sparkling, purple wax seal of an orca on it which I greedily tore into. The tri-folded, thick parchment dropped open.

**Dear
MR AKABANE,
KALEB**

His Majesty the King cordially invites you to attend a banquet tomorrow evening at the royal palace as a reward for your part in the defence of the city of Havar. You will be granted an audience with our illustrious ruler as well as a reward befitting of your heroism. Please dress accordingly.

Yours Faithfully,

Herbert Codswallop,
Secretary to the King and first minister of the
independent nation of Havar.

"Dress accordingly?" I asked the room quietly.

"Oh, you got your king letter?" Bell chimed sweetly. "From the guy with the funny name?"

I nodded, passing her the letter which she scanned briefly and passed back to me.

"I wonder what our rewards will be?" I asked her, already having an idea of what I would like to ask for.

Hopefully this king would be amenable to my request. I doubted it would be difficult or costly for a ruler of a nation, still, I had no idea who this guy was. I'd only recently discovered that Havar *had* a king and I'd been here for months.

"I think I'll ask for a yacht." Bell said thoughtfully. "I mean they've got enough of them in the harbour right?"

Before I could answer, the door opened and Sally walked in. Behind her was a familiar face I hadn't seen in ages.

Talyor of *Taylor's Tailor* followed behind the huge catonid, looking as vibrant as ever. She wore a fitted suit, that kind of reminded me of a zebra, with the sleeves rolled up and a catonid friendly skirt which allowed her fluffy ginger tail the freedom to sway slightly as she walked.

"Well, if it isn't the town hero," she said merrily, perching on the end of my bed where Sally had previously sat. "Sis here told me you need something fancy for your audience with the king?"

"Yeah…" I began hesitantly. "But before we get into that, how in the ever-living fuck are you two sisters?"

Sally growled as Taylor held a delicate hand to her lips to stifle her laughter.

I just couldn't wrap my head around it. For one, Sally had silver hair and tanned skin, yet Taylor had ginger hair and pale, freckled skin.

And of course, there was the obvious elephant in the room...

"So..." Bell began. "You got all the personality and Sally got the compensatory steroids?" She asked the duo innocently.

Sally growled even deeper this time and I was surprised she didn't hit the fireball mage. She wasn't exactly known for her *lack* of violent tendencies after all.

"Something like that." Taylor replied earning her own growl from her sibling. "Yes, we are sisters. Twins actually."

I just gawped. I knew that not all twins had to be identical but this was just ludicrous.

"I thought cats gave birth to a full litter?" Bell said, placing her index finger on her chin and tapping lightly. I couldn't tell if she was thinking really hard, or if she was constipated.

"We're not cats." Sally growled, her voice deep with anger.

"What Sal is trying to say." Taylor interrupted much more patiently. "Is that catonids aren't the same as cats. We give birth like humans do, usually just one at a time.

"But anyway, that's not what I came here for. Kaleb, I hear I have you to thank for revenging my store?"

I looked to Sally and she nodded. She must have filled Taylor in on what had happened. I wasn't sure I was overly pleased having more people knowing about my little secret, but Panda liked her and I trusted Sally so hopefully her sister could keep a lid on it.

"Yeah, something like that," I replied cagily, scratching at the back of my head in discomfort.

"Well, if it *was* you, then thank you," she said earnestly. "That thing nearly killed me when the shop caught fire. Honestly, I was lucky to make it out alive. I was still fleeing from the adventurer district when you guys got here. If it wasn't for you…then I probably wouldn't be sitting here right now."

I looked at her silently as she gripped my hand in both of hers. They were warm and soft and she smiled genuinely at me as her yellow eyes looked deeply into mine.

Unsure what to say, I stayed silent, holding her gaze as best as I could. I wasn't overly comfortable with professions of thanks like this, especially when she was so…alluring.

I had no intention of breaking my wedding vows of course, but I was still a man…and a bit of a nerd at that. Who wouldn't be at least a little stunned sitting so close to a beautiful cat woman?

If Panda was here he'd be calling me a furry. I admonished myself as I felt a slight heat rise to the surface of my cheeks.

"Well," she began, letting go of my hand softly and flashing me a fangy smile. "I've come to pay my debts and I promise you won't be disappointed. You're going to be the bell of the ball by the time I'm done with you!"

"Won't I be the Bell of the ball?" The fireball mage asked, raising her hand like a schoolgirl.

Taylor ignored her interruption and continued. "I know you like black, so I'll keep the colour scheme dark. I have a nice enchantment to use as well, which I expect will come in handy for a gentleman such as yourself."

That's the first time anyone has called me a gentleman. I'm common as muck. I thought, taken aback. That was probably the strangest thing to happen to me since arriving in Celestia.

"I'll just need to take your measurements again." The ginger catonid continued. "It looks like you've filled out a bit since last time. I take it you've been putting your free points into the strength stat?"

I looked down at my chest and then across at my shoulders and arms. Now that she mentioned it, I had developed some muscles. I looked more like an athlete than a bodybuilder, but still, that was a far cry from the beanpole I had been.

Wait did she say measurements? I groaned internally. *Not again!*

Chapter 27
Shit-Eating Nobles

The rest of the day passed in a relative haze as my measurements were taken and I further rested to aid my recovery.

I decided to try meditating, but I couldn't keep it going for long as diving into my soul view was excruciatingly painful. I guess that's the price one pays for batting above their average, so to speak.

In the few agonising moments that I managed to meditate; I saw something strange. My HP rope looked like electrified wire. Cracking green stalks buzzed around it, like they were eroding my heath in a constant and terrifying stream.

My rope would fray and then fix itself only to be struck by the green lightning once again as the process repeated.

I was thrown out of my soul view pretty quickly due to the pain. Left with a migraine, I decided to try and sleep it off. Sally's potion had already made me feel much better, but it seemed that only time would fully heal this wound.

The odd sight made me uncomfortable. I sincerely hoped that I hadn't caused permanent damage to myself by using a soul attack on the dragon.

Though I knew that even if that was the case, there was nothing I could do about it from a hospital bed. Eventually my tired mind succumbed to the sweet release of the dark abyss we call sleep and I was at peace for a fleeting moment of serenity.

I didn't dream of anything in particular, an affliction I'd suffered for most of my life. I very rarely seemed to have dreams, which is why it was so concerning for me when on the rare occasions that I actually did. The last one I remembered was traumatic as fuck and a part of me still wondered if it was caused by an outsider.

I could recall that dream as vividly as if it had really happened. The sight of my pregnant wife laying in her own blood, a cultist standing above her.

The sound of a familiar voice in the back of my mind urging me to get stronger.

After I woke up I finally left the makeshift hospital to see that it was getting quite late in the day. I must have slept for much longer than usual, I felt pretty normal again though. My limbs didn't ache, and though meditation still hurt, the green sparks seemed to be more sporadic, which could only be a good thing.

As arranged the previous day, I met up with Sally, Bell, and Director Lucas at a small bar on the outskirts of the palace district. They were all dressed for the occasion, as was I with my new suit, courtesy of Taylor.

My suit was pretty understated compared to Lucas'. It was black with some light embroidery and I wore a forest green shirt with the collar undone slightly. I'd never liked ties.

More importantly though, was the enchantment Taylor had sewn into the hem. The suit would increase my recovery rate tenfold. That wasn't even close to the buffs my armour gave me, but as a recovering patient, it was better than nothing.

"Ah, there you are Gonads," Sally purred. "I was starting to think I was going to have to come drag you from your hospital bed myself."

She was wearing a turquoise pant suit with the sleeves rolled up in an oddly 80's style. Except those weren't shoulder pads making her torso look so broad, they were just her roided-to-fuck shoulders.

By contrast, Bell was dressed in a red and black ball gown. It was a stark difference to her usual white robes and something about it made her look almost regal, like she was used to the wealthy life. Perhaps it was the long black gloves that reached up past her elbows.

"Ah, perfect, we're all here." Lucas said in his soothing baritone voice. "Shall we?" He asked, gesturing away from the small bar they'd stood in front of.

He was wearing a golden, sparkling suit like a noughties host in a fancy Japanese club. More noticeably though were the scars over his left eye and the bruises on his face.

Looking like a failed boxer, he waltzed purposely in the direction of the palace and we followed after him.

We rounded a corner in tense silence. Even Bell hadn't so much as made a peep since we'd met up. I wondered if she felt as nervous as I did. I'd never met a king before, and though I wasn't the biggest fan of a monarchy-based system, there was still something to be said for the grandeur it inspired.

One such example, being the palace itself.

We strolled casually up to the regal building, its visage a square towered complex with a sparkling dome in the centre, like a jewel of the sea from some *Disney*-esq movie.

The entrance was well guarded by humans dressed in the same garments as agent Miles and his dumb lacky. It struck me as odd that they were all humans considering that Havar was most densely populated with lycanids and catonids.

However, that thought quickly left my mind as we walked to-wards the entrance: a large archway set with glittering gems of emerald, ruby and sapphire. The arch itself was probably worth more on its own than the cost to rebuild the entire adventurer district.

So much for socialism. I sighed internally as we approached the sparkling entrance.

Lucas approached one of the guards and handed him our letters. The bald man nodded, keeping a neutral expression, as he waved to his colleagues to let us through.

I felt a twirling storm in the pit of my stomach, as if we were entering a lion's den. Bell walked close to me and I could feel the tension oozing from her aura. She was obviously as uncomfortable as I was.

On the other side of the archway was a sprawling garden with tables, wait staff and a luxurious circular bar in the centre. On top of the bar were multi-coloured spotlights. It was about as tacky a spectacle as I could imagine, yet it was also incredible to experience firsthand.

"Our audience won't be for a little while yet." Lucas said, stopping in the first spot he could find that wasn't filled with people in expensive-looking attire. "You two should go get a drink or something, you look like deer in headlights." He chuckled, shaking his head slightly.

I nodded and Sally flashed me a fangy smile. She looked nervous too, but her discomfort made her look all the more aggressive. I guessed that wasn't a bad thing, what better way to keep people away from you than projecting an aura that spelled violence?

"The bar then?" Bell asked me, glancing towards the crowded circular eyesore.

"Why not," I replied and together we moved towards it, pushing and delicately manoeuvring our way through the bustling crowd.

I had to assume that most, if not all, of the guests in attendance were nobles. I had no idea that Havar had so many rich assholes living in its humble city.

Once again, they were mostly humans. Though there was the occasional lycanid. One such man caught my attention. He must have been at least seven feet tall and wide enough to level a house. His fangs were as long as my daggers and he dressed in a red and gold military-style jacket with odd ribbons decorating his chest.

"Well, look who it is." I turned towards the sound of a sneering, self-assured voice to see an unfortunately familiar face. "What, did they hire you on as a waiter? You're not doing a very good job of it; I ordered a drink at least ten minutes ago now."

"I'm sorry, who are you?" I asked, looking at the pest through my brow as I stared down at him.

"Wha—" he began, sputtering slightly, a response that gave me no end of pleasure. "I am Jake Millicent. Surely you remember me?"

"Jake…Millicent?" I replied nonchalantly. "Nope, sorry, never heard of you. Though I'm pretty sure that's a girl's name."

Bell snickered at the boy's flustered face. His cheeks flared an unflattering scarlet colour which clashed awfully with his closely cropped brunet hair.

"We duelled only a few weeks ago!" He replied in an exasperated voice.

"Oh," I replied, feigning remembrance. "I'm sorry Millie, I didn't recognise you with both of your hands. Small world isn't it? Who'd have thought we'd meet again in a place like this eh?"

Jake's cheeks burned even brighter as he gritted his teeth and set his jaw. Before he could say anything though, Bell joined in.

"We're getting awards from the king tonight Millie," she said in her usual, innocent, and cheery tones. "Did he invite *you* here to be *our* personal waiter? Because I'd love a tequila sunrise."

"You slight me for the last time peasant!" He squeezed out through his unfounded rage. Honestly, the boy had even less emotional control than I did. "I challenge you to a-"

"No, you really don't Millie," I said cutting him off and adding an icy tone to my voice as I moved towards him and put my lips close to his ear. "I was merciful last time, but if you challenge me again I'll kill you. First I'll shoot off your legs, then your arms and finally I'll take your head. And I'll do it in front of all of these people, and not a single one of them will care, do you know why?"

He opened his mouth to answer me but I pressed on, the guy obviously didn't understand the concept of a rhetorical question. "Because personal power is the *only* thing these people care about. They don't care about your money or your family name. They only care about your ability to fight. So whilst I dismember you in front of all of these people, the only thing they will think is 'wow that Kaleb guy sure is strong'. So take my advice and get the hell out of here."

I backed up a step and flashed him a smile which I didn't allow to reach my eyes. He stared at me for a moment, the red flush rushing from his cheeks, chased away by a ghostly white.

Then, he did something I honestly never expected: he left. Without a word or any kind of pompous retort, he simply turned on his heels and walked away.

"I guess you don't need that *Batman* rip-off armour to be an edge lord after all." Bell smirked, watching after the embarrassed noble.

"I guess not," I replied, feeling a lot less anxious all of a sudden. "Was that too much?" I asked her as we continued towards the bar.

"Just a little bit." She giggled. "It was pretty fun to watch though and I can't say he didn't have it coming. He was mean to Panda when we first met, I'd have killed him if it was me."

"Yeah…sure." I winked as we joined the queue for a drink.

It took us way longer than we'd anticipated to get a beverage and we drank them much too quickly for the time spent to be worth it.

By the time we made our way back to Lucas and Sally, the real party was beginning in earnest. I barely had time to sit down at the table they'd precured before the palace doors swung open in a flourish of flashing golden light. A voice boomed through the courtyard, seemingly from thin air, and suddenly the garden was deathly silent.

"Welcome to his majesty's humble abode." It said, echoing across the palace grounds. "We would like to invite you all to begin making your way inside, our opening ceremony is about to begin."

The gathered crowed began moving towards the doors like sheep as I turned towards Lucas.

"Opening ceremony? That better not be about us." I frowned, a new pit of anxiety bubbling in my stomach.

"Who else would it be about?" The dark-skinned man beamed. "We're the heroes of Havar my boy. This entire night is about us. It wouldn't be an audience with the king if every shit-eating noble in town wasn't there to stare at us with jealous eyes now would it?"

Well shit. I thought, sighing outwardly as we stood and joined the queue. This was not what I'd signed up for.

Chapter 28
Royal Seal of Havar

As we approached the grand palace doors a large lycanid man stopped our little procession. I recognised him instantly; it was the same man who had caught my eye earlier.

He was huge. Dressed in a red and gold military coat with odd ribbons and medals dangling from his chest, he held out a sturdy arm to halt us.

"Come with me, your party is to enter through a different door." He growled in a low and menacing tone.

I knew already that lycanids had vocal cords that made them sound threatening, but despite being aware of that, I still thought the military garbed man's entire visage oozed danger.

I swallowed hard as I strained my neck to look up at him, his shaggy main billowing in the breeze around us.

"Of course." Lucas said, squeezing between myself and the lycanid and offering out his hand. "It's been quite some time Raphiel.

"Indeed." He growled, taking Lucas by the arm, and shaking it once with a powerful stroke. "I am to escort you to the side door where you'll enter, bow and kneel before his majesty."

"Lead on then, my good fellow." Lucas said, smiling as he gestured away with his palm. If it wasn't for the scratches and bruises all over his face you'd never have known he'd just gone toe to toe in single combat with a dragon.

"I know he looks like a big bad wolf." Bell said, whispering in my ear. "But he's really more like a puppy once you get to know him."

I turned to her raising an eyebrow. Did she know this guy?

She didn't offer me an answer, simply trotting after Lucas and Raphiel as he led us around the side of the palace.

"That guy is massive," I said in low voice as Sally moved to walk beside me.

"He's the head of the royal guard." She grumbled. "We used to work together, a long time ago. Don't let his appearance fool you, he's only the third strongest in this little group of ours."

I thought for a moment as we walked in silence. I had to assume that she meant both herself and Lucas were stronger. That was all well and good but it was me and Bell who were most likely to piss him off.

We marched along the outer path for a short while before stopping before another, much smaller door. I could hear chatter and horns playing inside the palace itself. The opening ceremony must have already started.

I felt my stomach do another summersault as I mentally prepared for an audience with the king. I needed to ask him for a favour and I honestly had no idea how that would go down.

If he refused then I wasn't sure what I'd do. There would surely be another way but finding it might take time. I took in a deep breath as the cool night air filled my lungs.

"It's time." Raphiel said, opening the side door and gesturing for us to go through.

Lucas went first, followed by Bell, Sally, and me. Raphiel brought up the rear, closing the door behind him.

We walked through an understated corridor before rounding a corner which opened up into the palace hall. The nobles flooded the place in neat rows, leaving a gap in the middle to walk through. It reminded me of a wedding ceremony.

They stood at attention, beady eyes following us as we marched ceremoniously along the isle. The hall itself was gigantic and sparse. The ceilings were high and decorated with chandeliers and paintings of ships and the sea.

At the end of the hall was an oversized, golden throne with red cushioning on it. Behind that was a pair of expensive looking stained-glass windows depicting a man being crowned and city next to the ocean with light beaming down on it from the heavens.

I get the feeling I'm not going to like this guy. I thought as I took in the grandeur of the falsely proclaimed socialist palace.

The king sat formally on his oversized throne. He had golden hair which was braided and tied in a fancy bun at the top of his head. He wore no crown, but from the scarlet and golden robes covering his shoulders, he was obviously a monarch.

He had a beard which was perfectly trimmed into a thin line which cut along his jawline ending at his chin which had a thin, single braid.

We walked towards the throne and Lucas stopped us. He bowed deeply before moving to the side and kneeling. Bell then copied him with a curtsey, Sally bowed and then it was my turn.

Now, I've heard the saying when in Rome before and I knew I needed to ask for a favour. However, I simply wasn't raised to bow to others. There was something in me that simply wouldn't allow it.

So when I reached the line of my kneeling friends, I nodded politely at the king before taking a knee next to them.

I was respectful, but I also wouldn't bow to anyone. It just wasn't in my nature. Maybe I had a chip on my shoulder from growing up poor, or maybe my *Usurper* skill compelled me to defiance. Either way though, I was sure it wouldn't be that big of a deal.

But, of course it was.

The entire room erupted into a pompous cacophony of gasps and mutters, Nobles turned to each other with shocked expressions, looking at me with disgust. It was, quite frankly, hilariously over the top.

"My word, I can't believe *him*."

"I heard he's a communist."

"Why of course he is, look at that disgusting face of his. Everyone knows communists have awful faces."

"The king should execute him for his impertinence."

"He's a communist spy."

"I bet he barely even helped with the dragon problem."

"What a horrible young man he is."

The king didn't allow their chatter to go on for long however and he raised his palm shutting them all up as they returned to their places in silence.

Why do they keep mentioning communism? I wondered, before remembering my *Torch of Eternal Communist Supremacy*. That damned system had made me a social pariah.

"Young adventurer." He began in a loud and commanding voice. "Perhaps you are unaware, but in our culture it is respectful to bow before a monarch."

As he spoke I felt something niggling at the back of my mind. It compelled me to bow, to be compliant and docile. I waved it away with barely a thought.

"I meant no offence, but where I am from we don't bow," I said, putting on my poshest voice and hoping to sound respectful.

"Expecting a bow because of one's station is subservience, not respect. At least that's how it is thought of modernly in my country."

The king looked at me and furrowed his brow. Perhaps I had gone too far, bowing would have been the easier solution, but as I mentioned before, something inside of me just wouldn't allow me to. The entire act of bowing to someone means you place them as higher than you and no matter who this guy was, no one was higher than anyone else in my opinion.

At least I hoped it was my opinion. For all I knew it could have been a side effect of my *Usurper* skill. Could skills alter a person's personality?

A man has to live by a code. It doesn't have to be the same as the law, it doesn't even have to make sense. But everyone should have things that they believe in and will fight for no matter the consequence. Without that, we're nothing more than robots or animals.

The king's eyes squinted slightly as he looked at me, they seemed to pierce right through me and I felt the niggling feeling in the back of my mind once more. Once again, I brushed it away.

He leaned forwards slightly, a twitch on his lips revealing some kind of emotional reaction. Meanwhile, the nobles watched us in stunned silence.

Then he chuckled.

It was a light, Santa-like laugh and a few beats later the entire hall erupted into forced, awkward laughter until the king held his hand up again.

"Very well," he said loudly. "As you have done Havar such a great service I will permit your humorous impudence as a difference in culture."

I let out a sigh of relief and nodded courteously to the man before glancing to my side. Bell had her head bowed but I could tell she was doing all that she could to hide her giggles.

"These brave adventures knelt here before you." The king began, standing from his throne and looking out over his many nobles. "Have been summoned here today to receive my favour and thanks. Were it not for these brave souls our fair nation would be in tatters at the hand of an evil, benign dragon.

"This kingdom owes these honoured warriors a debt of gratitude and I would not be worthy of ruling such a fine nation as this if I did not reward our most prestigious allies and protectors.

"Please arise adventures and look upon my face as equals."

Some of the audience members gasped at this as my party and I rose from the floor as one. The king stepped forward, standing barely an arm's length from us, then he continued.

"Lucas Regina." He began, moving towards the Director with his hands clasped behind his back. "As recognition for your achievements in slaying the dragon which pillaged our lands, I award you the title of Baron.

"You will be gifted the land around the mountain lair and a suitable staff to run it for you whilst you continue your duties as Director of Adventure Society. Do you accept?"

"Yes, your majesty." Lucas said with a wide grin. "Thank you."

The king nodded and moved down the line to stand in front of Sally.

"Silver Ranked Adventurer Sally, for your bravery in leading a team of adventurers against such a vicious and overwhelmingly powerful monster, I award you 1,000,000 gold pieces and reinstate your seal of royal favour. Do you accept?" He said, offering out a small silver token.

"I do." She replied, taking the token, and placing it in her inventory. "It is good to be back in your good graces."

The king nodded cordially.

217

I wonder what all that is about? I thought inquisitively as the king moved down the line to stand in front of me.

"Adventurer Kaleb Akabane." He began, looking me dead in the eyes. "For your bravery in fighting the dragon, a foe which vastly outstripped you in power, I award you a seal of royal favour. Do you accept."

"Yes, thank you," I said, awkwardly taking the small silver token.

The king leaned in close and whispered to me.

"After this is done you should join me for a drink. I'd quite like to chat with you."

I gulped as he moved on to Bell.

I glanced down at the silver token; it was round and looked like a coin. Of course, the only currency in Havar was gold, so I knew it wasn't one.

I focused on it and a notification popped up in my HUD.

You have received a royal seal:

Royal Seal of Havar

This is a seal awarded to those who have gained favour with the royal house that rules *Havar*. It doesn't actually do anything, but it can open a lot of doors.

Holding the Royal Seal of Havar will negate the negative effects of The Eternal Torch of Communist Supremacy whilst interacting with Havarian officials

You are now considered friendly with the socialist states in Havar.

That was interesting. I'd almost forgotten about the torch and its weird effects which supposedly made me an enemy of any non-communist faction in Celestia.

The explanation seemed kind of cryptic but I figured that if it was important it would become clear eventually. I put the seal into my inventory and zoned back into the room as the king stood in front of Bell.

"Adventurer Bell of no last name," he began. "For your bravery in fighting the dragon in the defence of Havar I award you a seal of royal favour. Do you accept?"

"Yup, thank you, your kingliness," she said, smiling sweetly and curtseying.

The king rolled his eyes, seemingly ignoring her reply, and handed her the seal. Much to the horror of every noble in the room.

Chapter 29
No System Is Perfect

With red and gold robes billowing behind him, the king returned to his throne as we watched. The hall was completely silent.

"We have two more decorations to hand out," he said solemnly, "sadly, not all of our heroes are able to be with us this evening. One young man is in hospital and another sacrificed his life for the good of this nation. I am awarding them both a seal of Havar for their dedication to protecting us all, and I would like to direct you all in a moment of silence to remember the sacrifice made by young Reginald, a true hero of this fine nation of ours."

The room went silent and many of the nobles placed their hands over their hearts, Lucas did the same and I mimicked his body language, bowing my head.

After a moment, the king raised his eyes and continued with his speech.

"As further thanks for your dedication in the protection of Havar," he said, opening his arms widely towards the crowd of gathered nobles. "Please enjoy these humble celebrations."

The doors creaked open and wait staff flooded the room carrying tables and chairs and drinks galore. The nobles began to filter away from their formal standing positions, many moving back outside.

To the side of the hall a small stage was uncovered and a band set up and began playing fast jazz that reminded me of the roaring 20's I'd heard so much about. Their instruments were strange to me, but the sounds they made were familiar enough as not to be jarring.

The king sat back in his chair as a group of FBI-like mages began using some kind of skill to lift the platform the throne was on. It rose into the air and moved across the room until it was in the middle of the hall.

A spiral staircase of floating wooden steps appeared and a large table and a few chairs floated to the top of the platform. Simultaneously a semi-transparent bubble of blue swirls encased the king and his private platform.

"His majesty wishes for you to join him." Raphael growled, gesturing towards the staircase.

I nodded to him and headed towards it; Bell tried to follow but was stopped by the large lycanid who took up a bouncer-like position at the bottom of the spiral staircase.

I guess I'm the only VIP at this party. I chuckled to myself as I began climbing the floating, wooden steps. My stomach churned slightly as I climbed, not from the vertigo, but because I had a lot riding on this conversation.

At the top of the stairs, the king's platform had become a private booth straight out of a gang-flick night club.

Leather benches with high backs surrounded a low square table with the oversized throne at the head.

The mages, who doubled as security, stood guard, facing away from the king and his booth. He looked up at me, leaning back in a relaxed manner, and gestured for me to join him with a tilt of his head.

One of the mages, who dressed in a magic fed uniform, moved to the side allowing me entry and I took a seat near the king on the soft, leather bench.

"Thank you for joining me Mr Akabane, there's so much I wish to speak with you about." The king said in a much more relaxed tone than his earlier address. "But first, let us have a drink."

He snapped his fingers and one of the mages turned and lifted his arms. A cooler with a large, golden bottle floated up from the hall floor and landed softly in the middle of the table. Two sparkling glasses accompanied it.

The mage flicked his wrist again and a fizzing, amber liquid was poured from the bottle into the two glasses, which floated through the air towards both me and the king.

I took my glass and raised it slightly in his direction before taking a sip. It tasted like champagne. In fact, the taste was so similar that it was almost indistinguishable from the real thing...at least to my uncultured tastebuds.

WARNING

You have ingested a neurotoxin which will make you more perceptible to the effects of monarch-based soul manipulation skills.

This effect has been negated by your Usurper skill.

That crafty bastard, I thought smugly as the notification flashed up on my HUD. *I can use this to my advantage.*

"What do you think?" the king asked jovially.

"It reminds me of a drink from my homeland," I replied, downing the entire glass in one go and smiling at him. "I like it."

"Good I'm glad," the king continued, leaning forward. "That's actually part of the reason why I called you up here. It's not every day one such as I gets to have a cultural exchange with an out-worlder."

I stared blankly at him, at a slight loss for words.

For fuck's sake! Is there anyone in this place who doesn't know? I thought scathingly.

"An outworlder?" I replied, trying to keep an even tone to my voice. "I'm nothing so outlandish. I'm simply a foreigner visiting new and strange lands, nothing more."

"That tattoo on your back begs to differ." He replied coyly before taking an arrogant sip of his drink. I felt the familiar tingling at the back of my mind and I knew he was trying to use his manipulation skills again. "You have a tendency to get beaten up during your fights Mr Akabane. Clothing and armour so often…rip."

Well, shit. I thought. *I guess there's no weaselling my way out of this one. Maybe I should play along for a bit, make him think he's got me hooked.*

"You need not worry." He continued, a pleased look in his eyes as he took in my obvious discomfort. "I serve Athena and she has no interest in claiming the Celestial map. You have nothing to fear from me."

"Athena," I began tentatively. "I've heard that name a lot. There's an Athena where I'm from as well, or at least there was a long time ago."

"How intriguing," the king said, leaning back in his throne once more and crossing one leg over the other. "Please, do tell me about *your* Athena."

"Well I don't know much," I began, trying not to meet his eyes. I still needed something from him and if he wasn't trying to skin me then maybe it didn't matter that he knew what I was. Though it was obvious that he wanted something from me as well. I just needed to figure out what it was. "But she was a Greek goddess in the ancient times. The goddess of war, knowledge, and beauty I think."

"It sounds like your goddess may have much in common with my own." The king said thoughtfully as he rubbed his thumb and forefinger down his braided chin beard. "However, I have not asked you here to talk about gods. Their understanding is not for mere mortals like us, even kings, to ponder." He chuckled and I gazed at him expectantly.

"No..." He continued contemplatively. "I want to know how you killed that dragon. I know it wasn't Lucas. He may be stronger than most on this island but even he couldn't destroy that thing."

And there it is, I thought smugly, *he wants me to confess to killing the dragon. I can use this to my advantage if I can make him believe that I'm under the influence of his skill and this wine.*

"It wasn't me," I protested but the king cut me off with a raised hand.

"Don't misunderstand dear boy. This is a transactional conversation. You want something from me don't you? I can give you it, all I ask in return is the answers I seek."

I leant back in my comfortable seat and took a long sip of the bubbling champagne, feeling the niggling of his skill trying to worm its way into my head, and pushing it off with ease.

I did need something from him, but I'd been warned by almost everyone close to me not to disclose my soul attack power. This was a dangerous game I was playing and my stomach dropped and lurched as I tried to think of a way to win.

"My familiar was killed during the attack," I said slowly. "I can resummon him, but I have no mana of my own. I was hoping you might have a mage who could help."

"No mana at all?" the king asked, leaning forward again. "Why, that's unheard of! Very well. What you ask for won't come cheap.

Summoning one's own familiar is an easy feat, but summoning one on behalf of another requires a very skilled and high levelled mage indeed.

"I will allow you access to my court mage, though you will have to pay for the materials needed out of your own pocket. The nation is in disrepair at the moment and we don't have the money to spare."

"Obviously," I said dryly, gesturing at the grand party below us.

"In return though, you must tell me how you defeated the dragon." The king said, ignoring my sarcasm and staring at me with glinting, predatorial eyes.

Despite his obvious propensity for charisma, there was something lurking in those eyes that I hated. He wanted more from me than he was saying and I knew I would be falling right into his trap.

I was a fly caught in his spider's web with no choice but to submit. I could have walked away, but then how would I have gotten Panda back? That being said, I didn't have to tell him *everything*, just enough to make him think I had.

"Ok," I began tentatively. "I don't know exactly how I did it, but right before I passed out I charged my arrow up with stamina…more stamina than I had left. I didn't see the death, but when I woke up I had a notification saying I'd killed it, though it also said that it took most its damage before I finished it off, likely from the Director."

It was the best lie I could think of. There was no way I was going to tell this obviously dubious monarch about my soul power. I wasn't always the brightest bulb, but I did trust my friends and they'd all told me to keep it secret.

The king sat back once again considering my answer. He stroked his thin, braided beard thoughtfully as he stared at nothing in particular.

"Hysterical mana," he breathed. "I've heard of it before, but to meet someone who has experienced it firsthand. Remarkable."

I took another drink, consciously stopping myself from sighing in relief. He seemed to have bought into my lie. Either that or he was shrewder than he let on.

"Answer me one more question," he said suddenly. "Why hide this from my inquisitors?"

"I'm an outworlder," I replied, barely having to fake it at all. "I don't know what is considered abnormal in this world. Everything here is an unknown to me. The last thing I want is to stand out and have the cults and gods home in on me for using some weird hysterical power."

He considered this for a moment and then smiled widely.

"That was wise. You can trust me with this, I won't share your secret."

He gestured towards one of his mages and whispered into his ear. The man nodded and disappeared.

"I have sent for my court mage. He will begin setting up in the summoning room. I'll have you escorted there once it is prepared." The king said, throwing a leg across the arm of his throne and leaning back in an extremely relaxed manner. "In the meantime, would you indulge me in some more casual conversation?"

"Why not?" I shrugged, holding out my glass. "Assuming there's more drinks to be had?"

The king laughed and clicked his fingers and a mage refilled our glasses with his magic telekinesis skill.

Kaleb one, king zero.

"So Mr Akabane," the king said.

"Call me Kaleb."

"Very well, Kaleb, what do you think of our little nation so far?"

"Honestly I quite like it here," I replied earnestly. "It's got its problems, but it's an interesting place. I've met a lot of great people, been on a few adventures, you know, the usual."

"What are those problems as you see it?" he asked, raising a single eyebrow.

"Well, your people seem to call this place a socialist state, "I began. "I see the comparison. Basic goods like food and shelter are dirt cheap and that's certainly a good thing. However, you are a king living in a grand palace and throwing expensive balls whilst your people are still reeling from a dragon attack. Where I'm from, socialists believe that the government should be owned by the people, a monarchy like you have here stands in complete contrast to that..

"You don't seem to have any non-humans on your staff either which seems a little odd considering most of the citizens are nonhuman. Also, you have a noble faction who, from the limited interactions I've had with them, seem to be quite entitled. The whole notion of greatness by blood seems to go against the foundational ideology of a world that says it values personal power above all else."

The king considered my words for a moment and I gulped. Perhaps I'd gone a little too far. His nation seemed to be doing better than many back on Earth, even with its flaws, maybe it wasn't my place to criticise.

"No system is perfect Kaleb." The king said carefully. "I can see how, to an outsider, our country may have...*problems*. However, how do you think we fund basic amenities?

"Have you, for example, paid tax since arriving here? We sell basic necessities so cheaply that we make a loss with every sale. We do that to allow the people to live without worry of starvation or homelessness. It is, however, at great cost to the nation itself.

"As the king, I tax the nobles a lot of gold so that I might make life easier for the peasant classes. In return, I allow them to feel special, to fit in at the top of our class-based system and have their entitlement. Without that...with a classless society, prices would surely go up.

"What is the sense in being equal if that equality is in name alone? Would you prefer that my people die in the streets from hunger simply so that they could sit at the same table as me, figuratively speaking?"

I looked at the king, unable to form words. He made sense, but I still wasn't convinced.

"I understand your meaning, but I'm not sure I agree. Moreover, I wouldn't call that socialism at all," I said after a long moment.

"That's mere semantics my dear adventurer, the name doesn't matter, it's the ideology that does," he replied, leaning forward conspiratorially.

I was about to continue when a mage leaned over and spoke into the king's ear. He nodded and then sat back up, looking me dead in the eyes with a piercing gaze.

"I have thoroughly enjoyed our conversation, but alas, my court mage is ready for you." He sighed, seeming genuinely sad at the prospect of our parting. "Perhaps you'll indulge me again some time?"

"It'd be my pleasure," I said, standing and offering him my hand.

The king took it and shook once with a firm grip and I was led back down the floating spiral staircase. It was time to resummon Panda.

Chapter 30
Vietnam All Over Again

At the bottom of the floating spiral staircase I was greeted once again by Raphael, the huge lycanid royal guardsman. He looked me up and down, his ferocious eyes drinking me in as his muzzle salivated slightly.

I felt like Red Riding Hood's grandma.

"I am to escort you to the summoning chamber." He growled, his warm, wet breath tickling my nostrils.

He turned and began marching across the hall and I followed. His golden and scarlet military jacket billowed as he marched. He wore it slung across his shoulders, presumably so he could throw it away in a dramatic anime-like show of strength during battle.

We crossed the dancefloor, the party now in full swing, and exited through a small, unassuming, wooden door in the far corner of the room.

Through the door, we walked down some dungeon-like brick stairs which led out into a subterranean ceremonial room. It looked sketchy as hell.

Water dripped ominously from the roof, a metal pentagram was built into the floor and there were shelves covering the walls with all kinds of magical herbs, bottled body parts and general magical confectionery.

Hunched over a workbench in the corner was a small, wrinkled man with wispy, greying hair and bushy eyebrows that looked like long, dark caterpillars.

"I leave now." Raphael said and I heard his heavy footsteps crack against the brick as he headed back upstairs.

"Shall I take it that you're the court mage?" I asked tentatively, moving towards the hunched man.

"I am." He replied in a voice that sounded much too young to belong to a man of his obviously old age. "Cicero is my name, and you are Kaleb Akabane. My king seems to have taken an interest in you."

He turned towards me and I saw that one of his eyes was missing. He made no attempt to hide his gross eye socket, which was sealed over with scarred, grotesque skin.

"Yeah," I replied, taking an involuntary step back. "He seems to have taken a shine to me."

"Indeed," the mage said, walking towards me with a creepy grin on his face. "We are to re-summon your familiar no?"

I nodded, consciously deciding to stand my ground. I didn't want to show weakness in front of this man, after all, I *was* his king's guest. What was there to be afraid of?

"Good," he continued in a slow and slivering voice that reminded me of a snake's hiss. "How would you like him?"

"What do you mean how?"

"You are a phase two are you not?" Cicero replied, furrowing his brow. "You would surely want to summon the familiar at a phase two rank no?"

Summon him at a phase two rank? I thought confusedly. Did this mean that I could re-summon Panda every time I hit a new phase and increase his phase alongside my own?

"Yes," I replied. "I would like to summon him to the highest rank available."

"Phase two is the highest rank you are capable of summoning him to." Cicero hissed. "It will be expensive though; the material cost is great."

"How much?"

"800,000 gold pieces should do it." The side of his thin lips curled upwards slightly. I couldn't tell if he was fleecing me or not, but something about that look told me he was.

"Is the price negotiable?" I asked more confidently, stepping towards the man, and forcing myself to meet his eye.

"No," he said succinctly, moving back towards his bench and fingering an abacus. "800,000 for phase two, 300,000 for phase one. Make your choice."

"Phase two it is then." I sighed. "Though, I still need to set up my transfer account with Adventure Society, so I'd have to pay you physically."

The mage turned towards me with a deep smile on his face. He croaked a few times and I think it was his attempt at laughter, it sounded jarring.

"The payment is not for me Mr Akabane. It is for the gods," he said, gesturing to the pentagram on the floor. "Place the coins there, you'll see."

Silently I did what he asked, mentally ejecting all 800,000 coins from my inventory. I expected that much money to flood the entire room but instead something weird happened.

As the coins left my inventory they melted into pure, liquid gold which ran into the etchings of the pentagram itself. The symbol sucked them up like a vacuum, the etchings getting brighter and brighter as the gold vanished into the pentagram.

The mage pottered around the shelves, bundling oddities into his arms. He moved carefully around the pentagram, scattering the items around it in an oddly calculative fashion.

"Stand in the centre and do not move." He ordered and I obeyed, watching the weird ritual take place.

It was nothing like the first time I'd summoned him. Had something similar to this taken place prior to my wandering into the cultist library? Had I stolen someone else's summoning ritual?

Fuck them. They were cultists. I hope I did steal all their resources. I thought defiantly.

"Are you ready?" Cicero asked and I nodded once. Doing my best to stay as still as possible.

Suddenly there was a flash of light and I was enveloped in swirling colours all around me. This was closer to what had happened the first time I'd summoned the daemon.

Almost as suddenly as it started, the ritual ended and the oddities the mage had placed around the pentagram disappeared, melting into the floor and giving off a stench of burning.

"Yeah that's right." A familiar voice said. "I'm a bonafide war hero toots and I need all the help recovering I can…Kaleb?"

Panda stood before me at the edge of the pentagram wearing a white cast on his arm and a crutch under his armpit. His bamboo pipe hung limply from his mouth and he looked shocked to see me.

"Good to see you buddy," I said, looking down at the furry little bastard with affection.

Whilst I'd been laid up in hospital, lying and dodging kings and their subordinates to get him back, he seemed to be chasing women in his waiting room world.

I didn't really mind, but I was definitely going to give him some shit for it.

"Well this is awkward; I was just in the middle of-"

"Lying to women to get them to sleep with you?" I interrupted, finishing his sentence for him.

"I don't lie, kid; I saved your life remember?" he said, ripping off his cast and dropping his crutch to the floor. "It's good to be back."

"It's good to have you back," I replied. "Feel different at all?"

"No...wait!" He gasped. "I'm at phase two! Kid this is great. They struck me down and now I'm more powerful than they could possibly imagine!"

"Don't get too excited mate." I laughed. "You're only phase two, it's not like you're at the level cap or anything."

"Don't take this away from me, kid! I haven't been this strong in years." He protested, throwing an air punch, and twiddling his bamboo pipe between his fingers. "You could have chosen a nicer place for my welcome home party though. This dungeon stinks of old people."

I looked awkwardly at Cicero who seemed to have returned to his workbench and was completely ignoring us. It was probably for the best.

"Actually, this is just the summoning room." I grinned. "The real party is upstairs?"

"Well then what are we waiting for?" he replied gleefully, hopping up the brick stairs before I had a chance to speak to him further.

I muttered my thanks to Cicero who completely ignored me, then followed Panda up the brick stairs and back into the palace hall.

The party was getting loud. Drinks were spilled, people laughed, danced, and talked in quiet circles in the corners. I spotted Sally and Lucas at a small table on the outer edge of the room, Bell didn't seem to be with them though.

It seemed Panda spotted them as well and made a beeline for them, stomping right through the centre of the dancefloor. I guessed his insecurities had vanished after his heroic sacrifice to save my life from the dragon.

I followed after him, content to enjoy the evening and get back to work in the morning. What that would actually mean in the wake of such destruction, I didn't know.

"Sally!" Panda shouted as he shuffled along the floor towards her.

She turned to him with a dower expression on her face and a drink her hand. Her 80's style suit jacket with the rolled-up sleeves flaunted her thick, vascular forearms.

"Oh you're back, are you?" She asked dryly. "Sorry furball but there are no pets allowed in the palace."

"I'll have you know that I fought and died for this country!" He said with faux outrage. "Honestly, it's like Vietnam all over again."

"How do you know about that?" I asked him, raising an eyebrow.

"I'm a sage, I did some studying whilst I was away. Figured it would be good to know more about your culture." He replied with a shrug.

"You just didn't want to be left out of the banter I have with Bell."

"That harpy has nothing to do with my endless thirst and pursuit of knowledge, kid."

"Speaking of Bell." Lucas interrupted. "Do you know where she is? I haven't seen her since the award ceremony."

I shook my head. The last I'd seen of her was just before I was summoned by the king. She tried to climb the stairs with me but Raphael wouldn't allow it.

Knowing her she was probably off galivanting in the garden and chatting shit to some poor, clueless noble.

That was when I heard a scream.

It was the shrill kind of scream you'd associate with a posh, sheltered woman and, naturally, the four of us rushed in the direction it was coming from without hesitation.

I didn't know when I became the kind of guy who ran towards danger, but apparently I had changed, because I didn't even think about it, I just ran.

We raced into the garden just in time to see a fireball light up the circular bar. It exploded in a searing blaze of flames, blasting everything away from it.

Nobles flew through the air, one man rolled desperately on the floor trying to put out the fire that had erupted on his suit jacket.

I barely took any of that in however, my eyes were focused squarely on something else.

Just behind the inferno that raged around the bar was a hooded figure with silver eyes. Draped over his shoulder was a young girl with teal hair and black, elbow length gloves. She was unconscious.

"Bell!" I shouted, sprinting towards them.

Chapter 31
That's A Lot Of Bravado For A Mere Phase Two

I raced passed the fleeing, screaming crowd of nobles in my pursuit of Bell and her kidnapper.

So much for personal power. I thought scathingly as the cowardly societal elites ran, screamed, and generally caused carnage in their desperate attempt to reach safety.

The hooded figure walked casually away from the sea of flames which erupted from the top of the circular bar. They looked back at me with menacing, silver eyes hidden behind a mask.

Something about the way they held themself seemed oddly familiar to me, but I didn't have time to think about that.

Pulling my bow from my inventory and nocking an arrow, I fired a warning shot to the side of the figure who stopped dead in their tracks.

"Stop, or the next one won't miss," I said cooly, channelling my inner action hero.

"How scary," the figure replied in a deadpan, unimpressed voice. "That's a lot of bravado for a mere phase two."

They then turned and began walking away once more, completely ignoring, and underestimating me. Bell's limp body lolled on the figure's shoulder and they carried her like she was made of paper.

I fired another shot, this time aiming directly for the back of the kidnapper's head. They moved ever so slightly to the left and my arrow sailed past them. I fired another and another after that, all of them easily dodged.

I felt my blood begin to boil over with rage at the ease with which this kidnapper dismissed me, and I began charging a *Soul Shot*.

Let's see you dodge this you arrogant fuck. I thought, gritting my teeth as I felt the soul energy flow through me, lighting up my arrow in a sickly green glow.

It was painful, which would have been odd if not for my recent trouble accessing my soul view. Still, the pain only served to add to my rage as I pushed through the physical torment and continued charging my attack.

"Stop!" Panda shouted, finally catching up to me. "If you hit them with that it'll hurt Bell."

I knew he was right, but I wanted so badly to hurt this bastard. I looked down at my familiar and saw his large, rounded eyes. They looked concerned. Though whether that concern was for me or Bell I couldn't tell.

I breathed out slowly and lowered my bow, glaring at the back of the kidnapper.

"Good choice." They said, before vaulting the twenty-foot palace wall like it was nothing and disappearing into the night.

"Damn it!" I yelled, kicking the ground in my frustration.

"It might not seem like it, but you made the right call there, kid." Panda said, resting a comforting paw on my leg.

"Where the hell is Lucas?" I asked the familiar. "He could have stopped this."

Panda shook his head and glanced behind me, I turned, following his eyeline. A few feet away, Lucas stood, carrying a limp body, and looking up at me.

I walked towards him; fists clenched. He looked distraught, his face was scrunched up and there was something in his eyes...fear maybe?

As I approached I gasped as I realised who it was cradled in his arms.

The king's body hung limp and lifeless in Lucas' arms. Raphael followed a few meters behind; he had one less arm than the last time I'd seen him and from the wounds covering his chest and neck I was surprised he could stand at all.

"What...how?" I asked, stunned as I looked upon the pale face of Havar's monarch.

I hadn't known the man long, or even liked him all that much. Still, it was shocking to bear witness to such an important and likely pivotal assassination.

"The assassin chose the perfect time to strike." Lucas said, his words hanging hollow in the thick air between us. "Havar in ruins, the palace understaffed, a ball to honour us warriors. They knew exactly when and how to pull this off."

We were interrupted by the heavy patters of Sally's footsteps as she caught up to us.

"I lost him," she said, looking at the ground and clenching her fists.

"Don't blame yourself," Lucas said in a measured tone. "Someone with the skills and planning to pull this off was never going to be easy to catch."

"Wait, I'm confused here," I said, putting myself between the two of them. "I understand assassinating a king, he's an important political figure and I'm sure he had enemies, but why kidnap Bell?"

Sally and Lucas shared a look before she placed an arm over my shoulder and led me away from the others.

"We don't know for sure if her kidnapping and the assassination was related, but if it was, then only one faction fits the bill." Her voice was hushed and she spoke softly, stopping occasionally to check that no one was listening.

"Who?" I replied, barely allowing a breath to escape my lungs.

"Have you heard of The Morningstar Collective?" she whispered.

I nodded slowly.

I had received a quest to check out a place called The Morningstar Hotel and Spa and back when I'd purchased my armour one of their criminal lackies had come by to shake down the shopkeeper for protection money or something like that.

I lifted my hand and showed Sally the pentagram tattoo etched onto the back of it. I had received it in a loot box shortly after I'd accidentally killed another outworlder. Supposedly, it would allow me entry to the hotel.

"I thought I recognised that symbol the first time I met you," she said thoughtfully, grasping my hand and pulling it closer to take a better look at the marking.

"Where is it?" I asked slowly, staring into space in the direction of the wall where the masked kidnapper had left with Bell.

"It's everywhere," she replied. "The Morningstar Hotel and Spa is a pocket dimension. It exists everywhere and can be accessed by going through a number of portals scattered around the planet. There's one in every major city, or so the rumours state."

"So where is the Havar portal."

"I don't know for sure, but I've heard that it can be accessed in the red-light district. I'd start there." She tapped me on the shoulder and stood up straight, brushing her flowing silver hair from my shoulder.

"You're not coming with me?" I asked, looking up at her perfectly sculpted and muscular jaw.

"I can't," she said sombrely. "You can only get in if you've been marked. If you do manage to find it though, see if you can find out who orchestrated all this. I know saving Bell is the top priority, but anything that can shed some light on the king's murder will yield a good reward."

She patted me on the shoulder and returned to Lucas and the others. I stayed put, staring up at the large wall. My head was swimming. I guess I was going to have to tackle that quest earlier than expected.

***

Diako sat alone in his throne room. It was a dank, dark place filled with shadows and deep black columns which guided a wide path to the entrance doorway.

From his seat of power he kept tabs on all of his retainers and members of The Organisation, *His* Organisation.

He was in the business of assassination, theft and controlling the goings on of the mortal world through shadow puppetry and manipulation. Prior to godhood, Diako was a skirmisher type fighter, he was shunned by the Adventure Society for his *callous* methods.

Diako cared only for getting the job the done. The end result was all that mattered in the end. The Adventure Society, however, cared very much for the means by which such ends were achieved.

What he considered to be collateral damage, they often called murder. Something he believed to be very short sighted. He was a diamond class adventurer when they exiled him.

However, the joke was on them, considering he now held influence over many of the mortals who oversaw the Adventure Society. He was now a god, and their petty organisation, his pawns.

One of which, he was watching very closely from his dark throne.

He saw as Lucas Regina carried the limp body of Havar's ruler into the courtyard. The man was a mess, covered in scars and bruises from his pathetic battle with the dragon.

"Lucas." Diako said, speaking directly into the director's mind. "I have a new mission for you."

My Lord, now is not the time. He protested, stopping, and staring blankly as he held the king, surrounded by his guardsmen. *The king has been assassinated and I—*

"I am aware of your petty mortal politics and recent events." The god interrupted. "My needs outweigh those of you and your king, or are you forgetting our agreement?"

No, My Lord, of course not, Lucas relented, sighing internally.

Lucas was unaware of this, but when Diako was connected to his mind, he could sense the feelings the man was emitting. Most often he sensed loathing for the god, but also fear and a resigned feeling of duty.

It was one of the things Diako liked about the man. He lacked ambition, but he was content in being a salve to that which he called fate.

Of course, there is no fate but that which you make. Diako knew this for a fact. However, if Lucas was too blind to realise that, then he would serve the god all the better.

"The outworlder is about to traverse dangerous waters." Diako continued. "I will watch over him, however, when he returns I want you to send him on a new quest."

If that's all My Lord, couldn't it wait until later? Lucas asked and Diako could sense that the man was preoccupied with the events surrounding him in the mortal plane.

"No." The god replied, making no effort to keep the venom from his lips. "You will leave the body with its guards and begin making preparations at once. He is to leave as soon as he is able."

Lucas sighed and Diako watched as he made excuses and handed the body to a lycanid guard with one arm missing.

The beast was strong enough to take the cadaver in his single, muscled arm and he nodded to the director before leaving.

Diako leaned back in his throne. All was going according to plan.

Chapter 32
Jazz Is For Losers

Not long after my talk with Sally I slipped away from the palace. The guards had kept it locked down for a short while but at Lucas' insistence they eventually began allowing people to leave.

He had argued that since they'd all seen the killer flee, there was little to be gained by holding the party guests against their will.

No one was under suspicion, after all. The unknown quantity was the killer themselves. Lucas and Sally had seen them running from the scene wearing a full-face mask and hood.

None of it made sense to me. Why assassinate the king now? I didn't understand Havar's internal politics well enough to fully grasp the situation, but it just didn't add up. How was Bell involved and why did they take her.

The natural conclusion was that she was taken because she was an outworlder, but she'd seemed to have kept that secret to herself much better than I had, yet I hadn't been a target.

I needed to know more and I wanted to get her back. So, after leaving the palace, I headed towards the red-light district, guided by Panda.

It was dark out as we passed through the deserted streets of the noble district. It felt almost like an entirely different world from the adventurer district I was used to.

We rounded a corner and that world changed once again.

Bright neon lights lit the walkways, mansions and stately homes turned to dive bars and window-shop brothels like the ones in Amsterdam. It was quite the culture shock to say the least.

"I think when they built this place they took the term *red-light* district a bit too literally," I said to Panda as we stood at the brightly lit entrance.

Streetlights glowed red casting the pavement in a scarlet glow as purple and green neon signs added to the cyberpunk-fantasy hybrid atmosphere in the district.

"Yeah," Panda replied slowly. "It's a bit of a step away from the fantasy setting you were expecting huh?"

I gave him a curious glance which he answered with a simple: "I spent some time reading up on your culture whilst I was in the waiting room."

"So you did more than just chat up the nurses then?" I replied with a smile.

He nodded and we walked down the bustling hub of sexual depravity and debauchery. We passed by large glass windows, each with their own occupant.

In one, a slender catonid pranced around on all fours wearing a spiked collar and not much else. In the window next to her, a male lycanid stood in a *Superman* pose wearing nothing but a golden G-string.

Unsurprisingly, most of the clientele roaming the streets were humans in expensive clothing with flashy jewellery adorning their necks, wrists, and fingers.

"I told you all humans are furries." Panda sniggered as a timid looking man approached the catonid's window and began swiping his finger in the air, likely conducting a system bank transfer.

"Any idea where we should start looking?" I asked.

"Oh honey," a seductive female voice chimed from the side of me. "You can start by looking right here."

I turned to my right and saw a latex clad lycanid woman leaning against a dark, wooden wall. She had lipstick on her muzzle and enough eyeliner to make you think she was cosplaying Panda.

My eyes went wide as she stepped towards me and began lightly stroking my arm with her clawed fingers.

"No thank-" I began but was immediately cut off.

"What a cute little familiar you have there. I know a nice little bar just down the ways. We could drop him off there with a few bottles whilst we...get to know each other." She leant up and whispered the last line in my ear and I shivered, not in a good way.

Panda was in full blown hysterics at this point, clutching his stomach and wiping tears from his eyes as he laughed. I turned towards him, hoping to convey my need for urgent assistance through my gaze.

He shook his head slightly and approached the lycanid woman, patting her lightly on the leg. She looked down at him, raising an eyebrow.

"Thank you for your interest in this Kaleb." He began. "However, we are going to go in another direction. We thank you for your application and wish you all the best going forward."

What the actual fuck.

She looked down at him and then slowly removed her hand from my shoulder. Looking back at me, she shrugged and moved back towards her spot against the wooden wall muttering: "your loss, hun."

I turned sharply and began walking away before she changed her mind and Panda had to shuffle-run to catch up.

"I am so confused," I complained when he finally caught up.

245

"What's so hard to understand?" He laughed, "this is a business for them, it's really not that difficult."

I didn't reply as we walked a little further into the district, passing all kinds of weird and wonderful things. It was not my idea of a good time. I felt awkward just being in the vicinity of so many brothels, let alone actively looking for the proverbial needle in a haystack within them.

I pulled up the quest in my HUD to see that it had been updated.

A Good Time, Not A Long Time

You've been marked as a guest of *The Morningstar Hotel and Spa*. I wonder what mayhem and fun awaits behind its doors.

Updates:
You have discovered that *The Morningstar Collective* are a syndicate who run a racketeering operation in Havar.

You suspect that *The Morningstar Collective* have kidnapped another adventurer and are holding her at The Morningstar Hotel and Spa

It is possible that *The Morningstar Collective* are involved with the regicide of the local king.

Objectives:
Enter The Morningstar Hotel and Spa 0/1
Uncover the secrets of The Morningstar Hotel and Spa 0/1
Rescue the kidnapped adventurer 0/1

Find out if The Morningstar Collective are connected to
the regicide 0/1

Reward:
X1 Skill Upgrade Potion
X1 Weapon Upgrade Potion

It had updated significantly since the last time I'd checked it. It now included finding Bell and investigating the king's murder.

I guessed the reward was pretty good. It made sense this quest wouldn't be quite as straight forward as it originally seemed to be. Still, it begged the question, how was I going to find this damned hotel?

"How are we going to find this place?" I eventually asked my daemon familiar.

The red-light district was pretty big and I had no desire to walk into every building in the immediate area.

"Why could try asking around?" He offered with a shrug. "There's a bar I know a street over, it's a venerable mecca of gossip. If anyone around here knows how to find this place, you can bet your ass they'll be in that bar."

I shrugged and followed Panda around another corner to the front of an unassuming crimson door in between two high profile brothels. He knocked on the door with his paw and took a step back.

A slit slid across the door with a clank and two beady eyes peered out at us.

"Password."

"Jazz is for losers," Panda offered the voice.

The slit closed and I heard multiple locks click out of place before the door swung open. A dwarf in a spiked leather jacket stood in the opening, politely holding the door for us.

We stepped inside and he immediately locked it up again. We stood at the top of a sticky staircase the led down into the ground.

"Jazz is for losers?" I asked Panda incredulously.

"You'll see," he teased as I followed him down the stairs.

Upon reaching the bottom, I did see.

The underground bar thumped loud with the raucous tones of medieval metal music – at least that was the best description I could give it. It sounded like *Amon Amarth* mixed with *Dandelion* the bard from *The Witcher 3*. It was actually pretty good.

"Is that an electric lute?" I asked, looking at the slender Svartalf on the stage. He had long purple hair and a bushy black beard with a plethora of earrings in each ear and a studded bracelet on his right wrist.

"It sure is," Panda smirked, hopping onto a barstool as a svartalf bartender approached him wearing a leather vest with various runic patches on it.

The musician on the stage launched into a speedy lute solo as the small crowd gathered in front of him screamed and someone threw their underwear at him. He caught it deftly with the headstock of his lute and twirled it as he continued playing, garnering even more vigour from the excited crowd as distorted notes rang out.

"What is this place?" I asked, a smile tugging at my lips as I sat next to Panda.

"It's a speakeasy," he replied nonchalantly. "You will never find a more wretched hive of scum and villainy."

"Don't quote *Star Wars* at me," I chided, "besides, the *Cantina Band* played jazz."

"Jazz is for all those pretentious noble pricks in their palaces," the bartender said, butting in on our conversation. "Down here we play real music. Our tunes are by the people, for the people."

"I thought that was more of a punk thing?" I asked jokingly.

It seemed to go over the svartalf's head as he shrugged and grabbed two glasses from the bar.

"Drinking?" He asked.

"Sure, what do you have?"

"Oil."

I shot him a poignant look and he sighed in an overly dramatic way.

"It's dark ale. The most metal drink around, it's our own brew and it's the only brew we sell," he explained in an exasperated and practiced tone.

"Ok sure, we'll take two of those then please," I said, dropping a few gold coins onto the bar. I deftly sprinkled a few more on top of the pile and pushed them towards him. "We're also looking for some information. Do you know how to get to the Morningstar Hotel & Spa?"

The entire bar went silent. Even the lute playing rocker on stage stopped mid song as everyone turned to look at us.

"This isn't a detective movie kid," Panda said. "That is not how you ask for delicate information in this part of town." He rubbed his temples as if trying to dispel a sudden headache, and I gulped.

I turned back to see the bartender pointing a loaded crossbow at my face. He didn't look pleased.

Chapter 33
I Get Cranky When I Don't Get My Nap

"Woah," I said, raising my hands in a submissive way. "It was just a question, there's no need for the hostility."

The bartender glared at me through the sights of his raised crossbow. The bolt was practically touching my face, there was no chance he'd miss from such a close distance.

The rest of the bar felt tense as a deadly silence washed over the interior. From the corner of my eyes I could see multiple patrons moving their hands to their blades and cudgels.

"A newcomer in a noble's suit walks into our bar and starts asking about *The Morningstar Collective*'s famed headquarters. That's pretty damn suspicious to me," the bartender growled. "You'd better start talking *Outsider*."

His last word sounded as if it left a bad taste on his tongue as he spat it out. I took a deep breath, I needed to calm down.

"Would you prefer it if I wore my adventuring gear?" I asked politely as I quickly dove into my HUD and changed back into my armour. Being able to equip clothes with a mental click sure could be useful.

I felt better as soon as I felt the cushioned leather against my skin. If it came to it, I might be able to slow time for long enough to dodge his initial shot. It would be risky though, but at least with my armour back on I was ready for a fight.

"Stop playing games Outsider." The bartender hissed, tightening his grip on the trigger of his crossbow. "Who are you and why do you want to know about *The Morningstar Collective*."

"They kidnapped a friend of mine and I'm looking to get her back," I said, keeping my eyes locked on his. "Also, they might have just assassinated the king."

He took half a step back, confusion lighting up his dark eyes as quiet murmurs broke out behind me.

"The king is dead?" he asked slowly, suddenly seeming much less sure of his actions.

"Yes," I replied. "Now, from the looks of this place I'm sure none of you will shed a tear for your ruler, but if this was *The Morningstar Collective* then you can bet your ass that they'll be making a power play. From what little I know of them, that wouldn't be very good for anyone here."

I was lying through my teeth at this point. I had no idea if the illusive underworld mobsters were involved in the assassination, or if they had any interest in running the government.

Still, I got a vibe that a revelation like that would shock these wannabe anarchists and I hoped that would ease the tensions a little bit.

The bartender looked uncertain as he loosened his grip on the crossbow. He looked around at the people behind me and the muttering stopped.

"How do I know I can trust you?" He asked, a bead of sweat trickling down his brow. "You could be one of *them*."

"Why would I ask how to find them if I worked for them?" I replied, frustration beginning to show in my tone.

"Not *The Morningstar*, the royal inquisitors!" He shouted, gritting his teeth afterwards. "They've been trying to pin us for treason for years. How do we know that this isn't just their latest ploy. Send in someone new, get him to tell us the king is dead to gauge our reactions and then use that as evidence against us. What assurances do we have?"

Oh great conspiracy theorists, I thought, sighing internally.

Kaleb: What now?
Panda: Beats me, the guy's clearly off his meds. The royal inquisition doesn't use underhanded tactics like that, they just kill and interrogate people they don't like. They don't need to lie about it.

The HUD's messaging system was useful, especially since it allowed you to transfer thoughts into a text-based system without having to type it out.

"The royal inquisition doesn't need to trick people," I began slowly, trying to figure out what I was going to say as I said it. "They just kill and interrogate whoever they want to and they do it with impunity. Everyone knows that. Besides, if you don't believe me just wait until morning when they announce the king's death."

It was a bluff, but I trusted my familiar's knowledge of the local systems and I was willing to try just about anything to avoid getting a new hole in the head.

On that note, I also hovered tentatively over my daggers in my inventory. I wanted immediate access if it turned out that I couldn't talk my way out of this one.

Panda: Hey that was my line.
Kaleb: Thanks buddy, hopefully it'll save our asses.

"I guess…" The svartalf replied slowly, easing his trigger finger slightly. "Still, how do we know for sure? I have a family, we all do. If I let you go, I need assurance that I won't die."

"Who said anything about letting me go?" I replied cooly. "I just want to know how to get into the Morningstar Hotel and Spa. Show me to it, let me go inside and then I'm no longer your problem to deal with. If I was an inquisitor I'd be killed by them right? So it's a win-win."

He lowered his crossbow and stared at me for a few moments. Then he chuckled. It was awkward at first as I stared at him, but soon the entire bar burst into raucous laughter.

"Yeah you're definitely not with the inquisition, Outsider," he laughed. "Everyone knows they're in deep with the syndicates. Not even they would try to deny that so openly in a bar full of our kind."

He grabbed a glass with one hand whilst he wiped away a tear with the other and began pouring a dark, viscous liquid into it.

"Here," he said, sliding the glass towards me. "I'm gonna need to introduce you to the owner before I can let you leave, but you should drink first."

I nodded, still unsure of exactly what was going on, but I was happy that the intensity was dropping all the same. I raised the glass to my lips and took a deep gulp of the oil. I immediately regretted it.

"I guess they call it oil for a reason," I spluttered as the foul tasting, thick liquid made its way down my gullet, burning my throat as it went.

I slid the glass towards Panda who finished it off, licking his lips. That bear would drink anything. His stomach must have been made of cast iron.

After a few short moments the bartender returned, picking up his crossbow once more but in a much less threatening way.

"Come on then, the boss is in the back." He gestured to a door next to the bar with the tip of the crossbow and I stood, walking through it with Panda at my heel.

The bartender followed me, closing the door behind him and directing me through the kitchen towards a small office at the back.

It was dark and the walls were covered in satanically stylised posters of local metal bands with their electric lutes and studded leather. It was actually kind of cool.

Sat behind a shabby looking desk was a beautiful female svartalf with midnight purple skin and black eyes with red pupils.

"Ah Kaleb, good to see you again. Though I have to say I didn't expect to find you crawling around this part of town," she said, looking up from a weapons manual.

"Wendy?" I asked. "What are you doing here?"

Wendy was the owner of *Wendy's Wonderful Weapons* in the adventurer district. I had met her a little while ago when I needed my bow fixing and some new daggers, which she'd absolutely fleeced me for.

I didn't know much about her, but what I did know hadn't left the best impression. She was a shrewd and calculating business owner and she hated Panda because he had found out that she was cheating on his previous summoner and, being a dutiful familiar, he had ratted her out.

"I own this bar," she said dourly. "The real question is what are *you* doing here and why are my employees so up in arms about it?" She looked at me over the top of her manual, raising a single eyebrow and scowling at Panda. "Also leave your pet outside please Kaleb, we've been over this."

"Not this time Wendy," I said sternly. "I'm only here for one thing. I need to know how to get into The Morningstar Hotel and

Spa. If you know where the Havar entrance is then kindly tell me and I'll be on my way."

She leaned back in her chair and placed the weapons manual down on her desk. Smiling slightly, she looked me up and down and rolled her eyes exaggeratedly.

"Well, well. Look who finally grew some balls?" She purred, holding onto every word as if she was dropping them off for their first day at nursery. "Alright Kaleb, I'll play ball. Say I do know how to get in, what's it worth to you."

I sighed, shaking my head, and rubbing my eyes with my thumb and forefinger.

"Listen Wendy, I don't have time to play these games today. Give me a price, or say I owe you a favour or…whatever. Just don't waste any more of my god damned time."

"Wow, someone's not had his baby formula this morning," she chuckled, "ok, sure I can tell you where it is, but it's going to cost you a lot. One million gold to be precise."

"I don't have that much," I said bluntly.

"Then come back when you do," she said with a dismissive wave of her arm.

"No," I said, feeling my frustration rising. "I don't have time to play a game of 'whose dick is bigger' with you Wendy. Tell me what I need to know or I'll tell the royal inquisitors that you're all anarchists. I'm sure that a random tip off from a renowned adventurer would be enough to make sure they'd give you guys a pretty hard time, wouldn't it?"

"Shame you're not a renowned adventurer then isn't it?" She replied calmly.

I felt the bartender tense up suddenly and begin to raise his crossbow at me. Perhaps unwisely I used *Perception of the Apex Predator* for less than a second and snatched the weapon away from him. When time resumed I was pointing it squarely at Wendy's face.

"Haven't you heard?" I asked cooly. "I'm the hero of Havar."

I fired the bolt. Wendy sat stock still, staring at me with her cold, calculative eyes as it sailed past her head and stuck into the wall, leaving a shallow cut on her cheek.

Shit, that woman is infallible.

The bartender glanced from her to me and back again. He looked so confused, the poor guy. He probably had no idea that I'd never sell them out to the royal inquisition, I didn't like them either.

My threat had definitely fooled him, but I wasn't sure if it had worked on Wendy. The svartalf seemed a little too clever and cunning for her own good.

We stared at each other for a tense moment until she eventually broke the stalemate with a heavy sigh.

"Fine, fine, I'll tell you where the entrance is," she said, leaning forward on the desk, pushing her palms into her eyes. "Jeez kid, I don't know what the hell happened to you since the last time we met but you're almost someone worthy of respect now...*almost.*"

I tossed the crossbow back to the surprised bartender who fumbled with it in the corner.

"It's been a long week and I get cranky when I don't get my nap," I replied with a half-smile.

Chapter 34
El 'Dorado

"If you want to find the entrance to The Morningstar Hotel and Spa you'll need to get inside El 'Dorado." Wendy said, sitting back in her chair as if my previous outburst and the blood trickling down her cheek weren't bothersome in the slightest.

I raised my palm, gesturing for her to go on.

"El 'Dorado," she continued, "is an elite entertainment establishment here in the red-light district. It's renowned for only serving a *high standard* of clientele."

"So, in other words, it's pay to play?" I asked, crossing my arms, and sighing openly. Why was nothing ever simple?

"Not quite," Wendy replied with a half smirk on her purple face. "The buy in is expensive, but anyone can raise some gold. No…El 'Dorado refuses to serve anyone who isn't a noble, even if they do have money."

I sighed again, rubbing my forehead as a deep, throbbing pain began to ruminate inside my skull. I dove back into my HUD and re-selected my party suit.

"So, if I dress like this it'll help?" I asked.

"Maybe, though if you were friends with a noble who could vouch for you it'd be easier," she replied. "At least you have the mark though, that saves me some explaining."

Wendy gestured to the pentagram tattoo on the back of my hand and leant in closer to inspect it.

"How did you get that?" She asked, reaching out to grab my hand which I snatched away quickly.

"It's a long story."

"Well, regardless. You won't get anywhere near the entrance if you can't get into El 'Dorado." The svartalf smirked and leant back in her chair, crossing her arms, and eyeing me up.

"I suppose you know an easier way inside?" I asked, my headache worsening as I guessed where this conversation was going.

"How perceptive of you," she chuckled, "it just so happens that I do. I know a guy who works there and for a price, maybe I'll vouch for you and see if he can add your name to the list of nobles they give to the bouncers."

"Well, I saw that coming a mile away," Panda groaned, pulling out his bamboo pipe and lighting it to Wendy's displeasure. "Once a snake, always a snake. Ain't that right kid?"

"How much?" I asked through clenched teeth.

This whole charade was getting ridiculous. I was wasting so much time by having to jump through all of these hoops. Time that Bell might not have.

"100,000 gold," she replied cooly without hesitation.

She'd been leading the conversation towards this from the start. If there was one thing I knew about Wendy for certain, it was that the only thing she ever seemed to care about was cold hard cash.

I mean honestly, a weapon's merchant moonlighting as a sketchy bar owner. Who does that?

"Deal," I said, delving into my inventory and depositing the gold directly onto her desk.

100,000 gold coins began to spill from my palm. The desk cracked under the weight and gold coins spilled out, filling the room. The svartalf jumped back, nearly falling off her chair as the unstoppable tide of gold ruined her office.

"Oh, sorry about that," I said with a grin as I jumped back to avoid my mess. "I haven't had a chance to set up my system banking with Adventure Society yet."

Wendy wasted no time in sucking the gold into her own inventory and within moments the coins were gone. Her desk, however, was completely destroyed, even the floor had cracked slightly under the weight.

"I'm glad I didn't raise the price," she muttered, quickly composing herself and standing in front of her broken chair. "My contact's name is Gav, I'll let him know you're coming. Once you get in, meet him by the bar on the second floor and he'll show you to your hidden syndicate entrance."

"Nice doing business with you," I replied, moving towards the exit whilst the bartender watched, aghast at the exchange. "I'm sure it doesn't need saying, but if you're fucking with me I *will* be back here, and my next visit might not be so amicable."

I left the office before she had a chance to reply, grinning smugly to myself.

"*My next visit might not be so amicable?*" Panda repeated slowly as we moved back through the crowded bar and left the establishment. "Who are you?"

"That's the kind of thing people say in shady back-office dealings," I replied nonchalantly. "Why, what kind of threat would you have made?"

"I'm a sage, we don't need to make threats," he replied.

"More like you can't back them up," I chuckled as we reached the top of the stairs and returned to the pleasant night's breeze.

The red-light district was still bustling with prostitutes, creepy nobles, and commoners window shopping for the pleasures of the flesh.

"I take it you know where this place is?" I asked Panda as he began walking in the opposite direction to me.

"Yup, it's pretty hard to miss, kid," he replied, "you'll see."

We strolled in silence up the busy street trying to avoid any unwanted social interactions with the locals. The entire area made me feel uncomfortable. It was just so out in the open.

Where I was from, solicitation and prostitution were illegal so those who partook tended to keep it on the down low. I'd heard that it was quite different in other places, namely Amsterdam, but I'd never actually been there myself.

The glowing neon signs that lit the cramped streets were a far cry from the medieval fantasy theme I'd gotten used to in the other districts.

There were *some* neon signs and of course the Adventure Society building was a glass skyscraper, but this place felt...different.

We rounded a corner and suddenly I understood what Panda meant when he'd said that El 'Dorado was pretty hard to miss.

Standing tall at the heart of the red-light district was a multi-tiered, golden building that looked more like a Japanese temple than a high-end brothel.

In place of neon, it had a large sign written in fancy, curly, calligraphy that said El 'Dorado in bright, silver letters. Large stone steps surrounded the building on all sides and there was an ornate stone fountain directly in front of it.

"Well this place certainly...stands out," I muttered to Panda as we approached.

"I told you so," he replied, "now let's just hope that dirty, conniving, cheating, svartalf held up her end of the bargain."

260

I nodded and we approached the front entrance. There was a long queue stretching back halfway down the street filled with chattering people in normal clothing.

It was obvious that none of them belonged to noble families. I was no expert on nobility, but I knew enough to know that no self-respecting rich bitch would be caught dead in *peasant's clothing*.

"I thought this place was nobles only?" I said quietly as we strolled casually to the front of the line.

"It is, but that doesn't stop people from trying their luck anyway," Panda replied, offering a casual wave of his paw.

As we walked past the queuing people, I began to notice some of them gawking at us whilst others gave us dirty looks. I could hardly blame them, I'd be pretty pissed off myself if someone cut the queue in front of me, but needs must and all that.

I forced my way through a small gathering of young human men and found myself standing in front of a large lycanid bouncer. He looked me up and down with bored, appraising eyes as his muzzle twitched ever so slightly.

"Name?" He asked cordially.

"Kaleb Akabane," I replied. I could feel my palms beginning to sweat, this contact of Wendy's had better have pulled through.

The lycanid spent a moment scanning a list on a long scroll in his hands. It seemed oddly medieval considering the neon signs that littered the district. I'd have expected him to have used some kind of magic iPad or something.

"You're on the list," he muttered in a low, yet somehow polite, growl. "Go on in and have a nice evening sir."

I nodded to him and accepted his offer, walking hurriedly through the open, sliding paper doors.

"I guess Wendy's guy was real after all," I whispered to Panda.

He huffed back at me as we stepped into the entrance of El 'Dorado, it was like a whole other world. Inside the odd, golden oriental temple was a refined and lavishly decorated establishment.

There were private booths filled with suit wearing nobles, each with a skimpily dressed girl on their arm. Well dressed, beautiful waitresses roamed around with golden bottles of bubbling liquid cradled in their arms.

There was a small bar in the corner, dancers on small platforms dotted about and three of the four walls were covered with sliding, paper doors which I could only assume led to private rooms.

It certainly wasn't what I'd expected. With the exception of the private rooms and the dancers, it reminded me of a cabaret club – not that I'd ever actually been to one of those, but I'd seen them in manga.

"Good evening gentlemen," a charming and overtly feminine voice said as we took a step inside. "Welcome to El 'Dorado, where your wildest dreams come true. How may we serve you this evening?"

I looked to my left-hand side and saw a white furred catonid in a yukata staring up at me. She had her hands cupped delicately in front of her and she wore a light contouring makeup on her face which gave it the impression of being longer and more angular.

"We're not quite sure just yet," Panda said, thankfully taking over for me, "but we were thinking we might start with a drink, perhaps somewhere on the second floor? I've heard it's nice up there."

It was in times like these that I was thankful for my familiar's oddly high charisma ability. I would have definitely stumbled on my words and sounded like a virgin if I'd have answered.

"Oh, you're looking for one of *those* kinds of evenings?" The catonid replied coyly, looking me up and down and fluttering her long eyelashes. "That shouldn't be a problem. Though you might be a tad overdressed for the second-floor sir. Perhaps you'd allow me to help you change into something more…fitting?"

I looked at her, at a complete loss for words as I felt my heart jump into my throat.

"That sounds great," Panda said in my stead, "please lead on."

The woman smiled and grabbed my arm delicately, hooking her own around it and pushing herself into me.

I hope Layla never finds out about this; she'd kill me.

Chapter 35
Never Trust A Leprechaun

The voluptuous catonid escort led Panda and me into a private room in the back. My heart pounded in my chest as she opened the sliding paper door to reveal...a shower room.

"Please take a moment to wash yourselves and then change into our complimentary bathrobes," she said courteously, "I'll be back in a few minutes to escort you to the second floor."

I nodded my thanks as she left the room and Panda started giggling.

"Once a furry, always a furry," he said through the laughter.

"You knew this was all she wanted from us didn't you?" I asked, turning towards him with a frown etched deeply into my face.

"Yup," he chuckled, "but it was worth keeping it to myself to see you get all flustered like that. This is a fancy place Kaleb. The sex workers here expect to be wined and dined first, not to mention that they demand proper hygiene. People don't come to a place like this for a quickie, they want the full *El 'Dorado experience.*"

"Well you could have given me a heads up at least," I sighed before delving into my HUD to unequip my clothing. I stepped into the shower, relishing the luxury of warm water drenching my hair and body.

Afterwards I slipped into the provided robe. It was black and seemed to be made of a silk-like material that hung lose and comfortably.

Once the escort returned we followed her to the second floor which was laid out in a much more personal setting. Pillows and low tables littered the floor with bamboo shielding surrounding each area for some privacy.

The men all wore the same robes as I was, but the women were dressed in a plethora of varying garments from refined kimonos to sequined bikinis. There was a look for every mood it seemed.

"I will leave you gentlemen in the capable hands of the second-floor servers," our escort began, "thank you for your patronage and please enjoy your evening."

She bowed before leaving. The entire set-up seemed oddly oriental to me, even the way the girls spoke and acted was all very eastern. Despite the name, El 'Dorado was a facsimile of what I imagined a Shogun's personal brothel to be like.

After the catonid had left, I took the opportunity to try and meet Gav. He was supposed to be our second-floor contact and was the man who had gotten our names on the list outside.

I approached the bar casually and leaned over the countertop, pretending to peruse the selection of beverages, but really trying to decide how to ask the bartender for our contact's location.

"What can I get for you sir?" A well-dressed human bartender asked.

She was dressed in tight pants and a white shirt with a waistcoat, unbuttoned just enough to remind us that we were indeed in a brothel.

"What do you suggest?" I replied.

"Our specialty this evening is called a Mandrake's Petal. It's a lovely blend of dark liquor, blue fizz, and purple draconic juice served with a mandrake's petal on the top to add some fiery zest," she replied in a practiced voice.

"That sounds delightful," Panda said, climbing up onto a barstool beside me. "We'll take two please."

As the bartender nodded and began mixing our drinks I slid a little closer to the bar and popped the question.

"Is Gav working tonight?" I asked as nonchalantly as I could.

"He…is," she replied slowly. "Are you well acquainted with our manager?"

"I am, he's an old friend. I haven't seen him in a while but I'd heard he was working here now," I replied, hoping I wasn't digging myself a hole with such a detailed reply.

"I can let him know you're here if you like?" The bartender asked, sliding the first drink across the bar towards me.

"That would be great," I said, "tell him Kaleb is back in town."

She nodded and left after sliding a drink to Panda who nearly allowed it to slide off the end of the bar as his undexterous paws fumbled with the bulbous glass.

I smiled over at him and then took a sip from my taller glass of swirling blue and purple liquid. It tasted sweet with a fiery kick at the end that was just enough to warm the tongue.

The bartender returned a few moments later with a short, well-dressed man in tow.

"Kaleb!" He exclaimed, opening his arms, and walking towards me like an old friend. "You didn't tell me you were in town." He pulled me into a hug and urgently whispered in my ear, "play along, we can talk properly in private."

"Gav, I haven't seen you in ages," I said in an obviously fake voice. Acting wasn't really my strong suit but I spied the bartender minding her own business as she moved back behind the bar so hopefully it worked well enough.

"Come, come," Gav said, gesturing towards his office in the back, "I've got a lovely Athenile 1500 sitting on the shelf in my office and I can't think of a better reason to crack it open than reuniting with an old friend after such a long time."

As he turned away I focused on his small frame and a notification popped up in my HUD.

You have discovered a new race:
Leprechaun

**The Leprechaun are a humble race famous for their pranks and mischievous personalities. Often said to be found hunting for multicoloured cereal at the end of rainbows, the *Leprechaun* are a rare people who usually show up at the worst possible time and disappear as soon as you realise you've been bamboozled.
Do not attempt to steal their *lucky charms*.**

Ignoring the system's comments about well known cereal adverts, I followed the man with the slight Irish accent into a back room. It looked just like any other office room with the exception of the sliding paper doors.

He sat behind a large desk and gestured for us to join him.

"Wendy says you're after infiltrating The Morningstar Hotel and Spa," he began, immediately changing his tone to a less forced one. "Nasty business that, but who am I to judge eh?"

"That's right," I replied, "we were told that the entrance is inside the El 'Dorado and that you can show us the way."

"Indeed I can," he said coyly, "considering it's right here in my office."

He turned to the side and pulled a book halfway out of a bookcase to his right. The case slid to the side revealing a door which was blacker than the abyss.

There was a grinning gargoyle head jutting out of the door with an open mouth.

"Stick your hand in there and if you have the mark it'll open," Gav explained, "if not, then there's nothing more I can do for you."

I stood up and glanced at Panda out of the corner of my eyes. I delved into the chat function in my HUD.

Kaleb: *Something doesn't feel right about this.*
Panda: *Yup, you can't trust a leprechaun.*
Kaleb: *Not that! I mean that the door is in his office. He must have ties to the Morningstar Collective. This could be a trap.*
Panda: *Oh yeah, that too.*

I walked towards the door, trying to mask the irritation on my face. Something was definitely off, but I didn't have much of a choice now.

I placed my hand into the gargoyle's mouth and felt a slight burning over the place where my pentagram mark was. I removed my hand quickly as the pain made me jump and the door swung inwards revealing a swirling green portal.

"Well, would you look at that," Gav crooned, "a marked man are you? Off you go then and pleasure doing business with you."

"Before we go," I asked, turning towards the man, and quickly changing back into my armour with the instant effect of my HUD's equip function. "What kind of trap are we walking into?"

Gav jumped back in his chair at my sudden outfit change and gasped in an overly dramatic way.

"Trap?" He said, sounding offended. "There're no traps in there from me, I can assure you. I might work with the Morningstar Collective but believe you me, there's no love between us. I collect my pay and let their customers through the door and that's that."

"Ok," I said calmly, "but if I find out you're lying to me…I'll be back." I gazed at him hard for a few moments as his bemused smile turned into a slight frown.

"You're really playing into that whole edge lord look today aren't you kid?" Panda said as he stepped up to the portal and peered at it sceptically.

Without replying I stepped through the portal, leaving just enough time to glare back at Gav a second time.

I felt my stomach do a somersault as I whirred through the green abyss, but thankfully it was over quickly as I was thrown out on the other side. I felt queasy, like I might vomit at any second but I managed to hold it down.

Panda stepped out next to me.

"It can be rough the first time," he said, patting my leg sympathetically. "Not the first time I've had to say that."

The portal had dumped us in a small and empty foyer with red walls and a marble flooring. There was a large concierge desk right in front of us with a bored-looking man sat at it reading a book.

"Welcome to The Morningstar Hotel and Spa, is this your first time visiting us?" He asked without taking his eyes off the crinkled pages.

"It is," I replied, approaching the desk.

"Oh, really?" He asked, looking up at us and folding the edge of his page over before shutting the book and placing it under the desk. "It's been a while since we've had any new patrons."

At that moment my HUD flashed and I opened the notification.

Achievement Unlocked:
666

So you've finally bitten the bullet and said goodbye to those pesky morals that have been bothering you your whole life.
You've entered *The Morningstar Hotel and Spa* **a place for player killers, bandits, outlaws, ne'er-do-wells, and other scum. You'll fit in just perfectly.**
Please check your tommy gun and fedora at the door and collect your cigar from the front desk.

Reward: *ne'er-do-well loot box*

"...And in the back you'll find the casino which also has a bar and that's about it, any questions?" The receptionist asked and I realised he'd been explaining the layout to me whilst I'd been busy reading my notification.

Most notifications stopped time, or at least slowed it down. However, for some reason, achievements didn't work that way. I guessed it must have been because they weren't urgent or something.

"No, that's fine thank you," I replied and walked past him towards the double doors at the back. "Oh, actually, just one thing," I said, stopping short of the door and turning back, "do I come back here when I'm ready to leave?"

"Yes sir," the man said, "just come back here and I'll open a portal back to where you came from."

"Can I go through a portal to somewhere else?" I asked, an idea brimming in the back of my mind.

"No sir, only platinum members can use that service I'm afraid," he replied.

I looked at him for a long moment waiting for him to continue but he didn't.

"How do I become a platinum member?" I asked poignantly.

"You don't," he said in a deadpan tone, "that privilege is reserved for the capos and above and you're not even in the syndicate."

Well, that's helpful, I thought with an internal sigh.

I thanked the man and opened the large double doors. It was time to find Bell and then get the hell out of this place before someone killed me and stole my skin.

Chapter 36
Jack The Reaper: Don't Fuck It Up

Having finished up his most recent mission on the northern continent, Jack headed quickly towards the local church of Diako.

He had been instructed to meet his handler there and he didn't want to cause any delays. Jack had spent the last week mostly assassinating famous merchants across the continent and he'd jumped a serious number of levels because of it.

He'd also assassinated a king on some small island nation who was a level 56 which netted Jack a cool amount of experience, now he was well on his way to hitting phase three.

That had been quite a job. Luckily for Jack some local syndicate guys had been running their own operation to kidnap some outworlder who was attending the party there. That provided Jack with the perfect distraction so he could take out the big man.

It had been a bit of a rushed job; the place had just suffered a dragon attack and was in shambles. The idiotic king had chosen then of all times to throw a lavish party.

What a prick, Jack had thought. He had absolutely no remorse for killing a ruler like that. *I mean seriously, who throws a party when his people are reeling from half the town being destroyed?*

The assassin didn't really understand the need to take out merchants, the king he understood, politics and all that, but the merchants didn't make much sense to him. However, his was not to reason why so he did as he was instructed and headed home.

Home, that had a weird ring to it. He couldn't remember the last time he'd had a place that he genuinely considered his home. It was an alien feeling and not one he welcomed.

The Reaper had grown up in an orphanage where he'd learned to fight to survive. Food was scarce, love and attention were non-existent, and his only education was from the school of hard knocks.

Naturally, he'd joined the military as soon as he was old enough and the rest was history. He couldn't exactly say that he'd had a good life, or even been a good person, but he had survived...somehow, and that was enough.

Meeting the god Diako had changed all of that though. He was still killing people for a living sure, but now he felt like he had a purpose, like he was serving a true higher power and not just doing the dirty work of rich bureaucrats.

Having spent much of his life fighting wars against religious fanatics, he never expected to become one himself. Well, fanatic was a strong word, it's not like he'd throw on a suicide vest and run into a school just because Diako asked him to. In fact, if his new god did ask him to do that then he'd likely leave The Organisation behind.

Still, he felt like he had a purpose again and he was happy to make himself useful to such a powerful being. Not to mention the personal power boosts he'd received by working for him, that certainly sweetened the deal.

As Jack entered the church he was met with the familiar cool feeling that washed over all who entered. From what he had gathered, Diako was a god who wasn't well known in most places, but in the city of Diopolis his flock were everywhere.

Diopolis was a safe haven for members of The Organisation and that was partly due to the heavily fortified walls which surrounded the city.

"Boss wants to see you," Bert grunted as Jack walked into the main church hall.

"Why?" The Reaper replied.

"Hell if I know," Bert shrugged, "he's in the back talking to our Lord."

With a nod, Jack marched past the brutish man and entered the back office. Clint, his newest handler, sat with his feet up on a desk and a bottle in his hand. His eyes were closed, but they were moving behind his eyelids which Jack had come to learn, meant that he was talking with Diako.

The god was able to talk to his vassals telepathically, which was something Jack still wasn't completely comfortable with, despite how useful it could be.

Take a seat Jack, Diako whispered into the assassin's mind.

It was a strange feeling to commune with a god like this. It felt invasive and unnatural yet somehow comforting. Jack wasn't sure how he felt about the odd way of communicating just yet but he hoped one day he'd get used to it. The feeling of shivers going down his spine every damned time was not one he enjoyed.

Dutifully he took a seat opposite Clint and waited.

A few moments passed and then Clint opened his eyes and took a long swig from his bottle. His sighed satisfactorily and then cast his gaze on Jack.

"You have new orders Rook," he said, "come with me."

The broad man removed his feet from the table and stood up, leaving the room with Jack dutifully in tow. He wasn't overly keen on Clint, he seemed too unprofessional, but for the time being he was in charge so Jack did as he was asked.

One day, I'll be at the top, he thought greedily as he followed Clint downstairs into the basement.

Tied up inside the small, dingy basement was a man who had been stripped down to his underwear. He was fat and hairy and he looked terrified.

"Kill him," Clint said, stepping to the side.

Without hesitation, Jack summoned the sniper rifle he had made back in Britania and, drawing on his mana reserves, fired a clean hole through the man's skull.

He didn't even give the prisoner time to plead for his life.

Achievement Unlocked:
Killing In The Name Of

You have taken the life of another player, you rascal. If Diako asked you to bend over and *take one for the team* I bet you'd do that too.

Reward: *PKing loot box*

Jack had gotten used to the systems strange way of communicating. At first he got annoyed at its constant attempts to berate him. Now though, he mostly just ignored it.

Loot box rewards could be quite useful and he'd happily take a bit of slander if it meant he could get more useful items.

"Good, now loot the body," Clint instructed.

Jack moved closer to the corpse of the man he'd murdered and looted him. He didn't get anything special and began to wonder what this was all about.

"What now?" he asked.

"You didn't get the absorption notification?" Clint asked, a thin bead of sweat cresting the top of his forehead.

Jack shook his head.

His brain felt like it was on fire all of a sudden as he felt the sheer force of Diako's anger. He had no idea what he'd done to upset the god so much but he dropped to the floor clutching his skull as waves of agony rushed through him.

Then, as suddenly as it had started, the pain went away.

We're going to have to skin him, he heard in his head. It was Diako's voice but it sounded more like a raspy, angry hiss than his usual baritone.

Clint must have heard it too because with a shaky sigh, he hoisted the corpse over his shoulder and left the room, beckoning Jack to follow.

Without a word, Clint laid out the dead man on a large X which seemed to be made of two wooden beams which crossed at the centre. There was a vat of bubbling acid in front of the X.

"We're going to have to do this quickly, he should be alive for this part," Clint said in a worried voice as he tied the man to the X. "Acid is the only way to remove the tattoo from the soul as you cut…the cutting is your job."

He handed Jack a small knife which glinted in the eerie green glow that emanated from the acid pot.

Clint began pouring acid all over the body, well, everywhere apart from the odd tattoo which looked like some kind of unreadable code.

As Jack began to cut, all he could think was how lucky it was that the man was dead. If this procedure was supposed to be performed on the living…*well, let's just say it wouldn't be very pleasant.*

***

New Quest: *The Celestial Map*

Collect all the pieces of *The Celestial Map*. Upon completion of this quest you will unlock another quest.

Objectives:
Map pieces collected 2/10,000

Reward: *Vast Cosmic Power*

Vast Cosmic Power? Jack thought as he reread the last line of the quest. He had no idea what that meant but 10,000 kills, which he'd presumably have to hunt down individually and skin, sounded like a lot of work for such a vague reward.

He wondered what all that talk of absorption was about. Was he supposed to be able to do that as an outworlder? Would Diako order him to be skinned once he outlived his usefulness? That wasn't worth thinking about right now, so he pushed it from his mind.

Assuming some outworlders had this strange absorption power it was possible that someone already had half the map completed – unlikely, but possible. It was also possible that Diako would use that person to take Jack's tattoo. Did he need to be dead for that to work? He'd give it up willingly if asked, but he wouldn't allow himself to be killed in the process.

"I'm glad that's over with," Clint said, wiping his hands and carefully placing the collected skin into a sealed box. "The big man says to go to your bunk and open that box. Supposedly it'll let you into some club run by the syndicate and he wants you to get in there. Your orders are to infiltrate and then hold for further instruction. Our Lord Diako will be running this op personally so don't fuck it up."

"Understood," Jack replied and turned to leave the basement. The less time he had to spend in Clint's presence the better.

He retired early and opened his loot box. It floated down from the ceiling in an eery red glow and then popped open with a squelch as red confetti shot out everywhere.

Great, something else for me to clean up, Jack sighed internally.

PKing Loot Box

Player killing, what a despicable pastime you have. Do you know what player killers and Rishi Sunak have in common? No one likes them.
Welcome to the party pal.

Reward: Entrance to The Morningstar Hotel and Spa.

The Reaper smirked at the comment, he wasn't too fond of the UK prime minister either. Then again, he wasn't fond of anyone who grew up with a silver spoon in their mouth, especially one who had it out for dogs. Animals were one of the few things on his old planet that Jack actually liked.

He had adopted an XL Bully a few years back. It was a dopey-ass motherfucker and it went ballistic whenever he'd get back from operation. Having that kind of greeting for your homecoming was a nice, albeit rare, feeling.

He missed that dog dearly.

I wonder if he's still running the country, Jack thought absently. They weren't too far away from the next election when he'd been teleported to Celestia. Hell, maybe the country had finally risen up in revolt and removed him themselves? ...*Nah, stiff upper lip culture doesn't promote revolution.* He thought with a fond smile, that way of thinking had kept him sane all these years. He couldn't exactly admonish it now.

The red light emanating from the box grew stronger, breaking jack out of his reverie and practically blinding him, then he felt his hand begin to burn.

When the box had finally disappeared and his vision returned, Jack looked at the painful area to see that a pentagram tattoo had appeared on the back of his hand.

He focused on the red lines marring his skin and a notification appeared on his interface.

The Morningstar Hotel and Spa

Hello player! Do you like murder, debauchery, and depravity of a sexual nature? Why of course you do! Just like a mid-noughties tween teabagging a fresh kill on Call of Duty, you've become a player killer! Yippee, those are the best kind! What's the only thing better than a player killer, I hear you ask? A serial player killer! So come on down to The Morning Star Hotel and Spa and try out our...facilities...completely free of charge!

He read over the words a few times before dismissing the notification.

The Morningstar Hotel and Spa, he thought, *so that's where I'm going for my next assignment. Sounds sketchy.*

Jack had no idea how to get into the hotel, but he trusted that full details would be provided in the morning. For now it was time to get some rest. He had no doubt that this next assignment, like the many before it, would be a long one.

Chapter 37
That Last Part Certainly Sounds Ominous

I opened the double doors which led from the foyer into The Morningstar Hotel and Spa and was immediately bombarded with flashing lights and loud, thumping music.

The main room seemed to be a club and it was full to the brim with shifty looking patrons dancing, drinking and, in the case of the weird slime guy off to the left, blobbing.

I considered focusing on him to see what he was but decided against it. I'd already wasted enough time trying to get here so finding Bell had to be my only priority for the immediate future. I didn't have time for distractions.

There was a bar in the corner so I headed in that direction. Bartenders always had the scoop on local goings on.

As Panda and I squeezed our way across the crowded dancefloor I noticed a person in strange samurai armour talking to a group of men in a booth. They had a wolf with them, which was odd. I hadn't met anyone else with a familiar so far. Unless it was a wild wolf they'd somehow trained? That would be cool as shit.

Why would there be samurai armour in Celestia? I wondered, *the similarities between this world and mine are so weird.*

Sitting to the far side of the bar was a shady-looking man in a trench coat. He seemed to be watching me out of the corner of his eye. Naturally I avoided him and made a beeline for the bartender instead.

"What can I get for you?" The bartender asked, placing both hands on the countertop and leaning in.

"Some information would be nice," I began, "if I was looking to hire someone to say…precure a certain *biological* item for me, could that be arranged?"

Panda: *Biological item?*
Kaleb: *I'm trying to be cagey, that's how criminals talk*
isn't it?
Panda: *Maybe if they were buying chemical weapons…*

The bartender scowled at me for a moment before sighing and shaking his head, mostly to himself.

"Look pal," he began, "I don't know what you've heard about procurement of Celestial Map pieces but I'm telling you, it's not true and The Morningstar Collective don't have anything to do with it. So kindly buy a drink or fuck off." He turned away from me muttering and walked to the other side of the bar, literally as far from me as he could without leaving his post.

"Well that was rude," I mumbled to Panda.

"Sounded to me like you hit a nerve," he replied, "there's definitely something going on here."

"Perhaps I can help?" The trench coat wearing man asked in a hushed tone. He had moved closer to us and I hadn't even noticed. We were practically touching when he spoke and I had to use all of my willpower to prevent myself from jumping back or punching him in the face in shock.

"Who are you?" I asked tentatively, looking up at his squared, action hero jaw.

"Most people call me The Reaper, but my friends call me Jack," he replied casually.

"*The Reaper?*" Panda snorted, "what kind of moniker is that? Do you live in a retirement home praying on old folks or something?"

"...Or something," Jack replied casually, a slight smirk twitching on his thin lips.

He was a well-built man. Not quite bodybuilder level like Sally, but muscle still showed through his trench coat and it looked like the kind of muscle that one attained through practical use rather than through lifting weights – like a soldier.

How do I know that? Is this the work of my perception stat going up? I wondered.

"Why would you help us?" I asked, keeping my eyes trained on him, he was obviously dubious.

"The why doesn't matter," he began, "what does matter is that I know where they're keeping your friend and how you can get to her."

"Where is she?" Panda and I yelled almost in unison.

A few members of the crowd glanced our way at the sudden outburst, including the odd samurai person in the corner. After a few seconds everyone went back to minding their own business though and I tempered my emotions, keeping my voice low.

"Where is she?" I asked again in a hushed and measured tone.

"This place is a lot bigger than most people realise," Jack replied, "it has a subterranean level where the most...nefarious activities take place. Your friend is being held down there."

"How do we get in?" I asked, growing more and more impatient by the minute.

"The subterranean area is only open to platinum members," he replied.

I'd already spoken to the receptionist earlier about becoming a platinum member and he'd said that it was only available to capos or above within the syndicate itself.

"I can give you the membership," Jack continued, "my employer is…affiliated with the syndicates and has higher level access than most. However, I will need something in return."

Here we go, this is what he's been leading up to, I thought.

"What do you want?" I asked, trying to keep the annoyance out of my voice.

"I can't tell you right now," he said, "let's just call it a favour. I need your word that you'll help me when the time comes."

I looked towards Panda who shrugged. A favour could mean anything from spotting him a few gold pieces to helping him destabilise the local government, and from the look of this shady-ass dude it was more likely to be the latter.

Still, I didn't really have much of a choice if I wanted to help Bell did I?

"Fine," I replied, crossing my arms, "but if you ask me to murder children or do something that will hurt my friends then I'm out."

"What kind of guy do you take me for?" Jack replied lightly, opening his arms in mock offence. "Take this, if you keep it in your inventory it will allow you access to pretty much anywhere in the hotel. That's all I can do for you, good luck."

Jack passed me a small business card which looked like it was made of paper but felt as hard as metal.

You have received a new item:
Platinum Membership Card

This card allows platinum level access to all amenities at *The Morningstar Hotel and Spa*. We hope you enjoy your debauchery; you now have access to the following:

- *Penthouse suit*
- *Teleportation to other entrances (please see the receptionist)*
- *Basement level access*
- *Discount on syndicate hiring services*

"That last part certainly sounds ominous," I said as I finished reading the notification. "Let's go find this basement level."

***

Jack retreated back into the crowd after giving Kaleb the card. He kept the two in his sight line but used his abilities to blend into the crowd enough that the outworlder and his pet would think Jack had disappeared.

Well done, Jack, the familiar and unsettling presence of Diako said, entering his mind. *My plan is set in motion.*

"What exactly do you want with that guy?" Jack asked quietly, moving to an empty booth so that people wouldn't notice him talking to himself. He hadn't mastered the art of telepathic communications yet. One might think that it would be as simple as thinking a response but it wasn't, so Jack still had to speak aloud.

Let's just say I need him for a future plan, Diako replied, *for now Jack, watch him closely and keep him alive.*

"Are you demoting me?" Jack asked, feeling the frustration rising within him. "Last week I was an international assassin and now I'm what? A babysitter?"

I've assigned you this role because your work has pleased me and you are well suited to the task, Diako replied, an air of annoyance seeping into Jack's mind as he spoke. *Complete this task for me, stay close to the boy, and I will give you further instructions when the time comes. Try to get into his good graces, perhaps you can engineer a situation where you save his life. I will leave the details up to you.*

With that, Diako left Jack's mind and he shuddered, flopping back unceremoniously in his booth chair, and sinking down.

After a long moment Jack sat back up straight again and began examining the crowd.

Where has he gone? Jack wondered as he scanned the area. Only moments ago his target was heading away from the bar but now he had completely disappeared.

Surely he hadn't ventured down to the lower levels already? Even a complete amateur wouldn't waltz into the lion's den without completing any preparations.

Jack knew that he himself was a professional and was under no illusions that his work was far superior to that of mere adventurers but still…the idea of a single man and his Panda strolling right into the heart of The Morningstar Collective without any information was ludicrous.

What was he planning to do, stroll up to the first guard and ask about their newest outworlder prisoner?

On second thought, that's exactly what a guy like that would do, Jack thought to himself with a gulp. *After all, isn't that the exact thing he just tried with that bartender.*

Jack jumped up from his seat and pushed his way across the dance floor as he hurriedly made his way towards the lower levels. If he wasn't careful his new assignment would be over before it even began.

If the panda guy wanted to get himself killed then that was no skin off Jack's back, but he would not fail his mission because of the incompetence of others.

Chapter 38
Did He Just Say Butchery

Finding the entrance to the basement level was surprisingly easy. There wasn't a blinking neon sign with an arrow on it which said, "nefarious activities this way," or anything like that, but there was a magic elevator.

I stepped inside it and the elevator must have registered the platinum card in my inventory because when I had Panda use his mana to activate the control panel, it worked immediately.

Lacking any mana of my own, I considered myself lucky to have my magical daemon familiar along for the ride as we descended into the bowels of the hotel.

The doors opened with that familiar department store *ping* and I stepped out into a small room with two guards.

"Let me guess," I said, strolling towards them in my nobleman's party suit, "one of you always lies and the other always tells the truth?"

"I don't recognise you," the large one grunted.

He was a dark-skinned human dressed in an embroidered black suit and sunglasses. Considering we were indoors I had to assume that the sunglasses were part of the uniform...at least I hoped that was why he was wearing them.

His attire reminded me of the magic feds who had interrogated me before.

Maybe there just aren't that many fashion trends in Havar, I thought to myself as the man looked at me and scowled.

I turned away from him and spoke to his friend instead.

"I'm looking for a girl," I began, gesticulating like I was some confident nobleman who frequented sketchy underworld hotels. "Teal hair, round face, likes fireballs, goes by the name of Bell…" The guard stared at me blankly, "I take it that's not ringing any then?"

"Who are you?" The large man said whilst his companion simply stared at me like a gormless cretin.

"A platinum member," I replied, channelling my inner spoilt rich kid – or at least what I imagined one to be. "And a well-respected member of a great noble house. I need you to tell me where the girl is…I have business with her captor."

I really hope this works, I thought. I was starting to get tired of all the red tape. I could feel the pressure rising in my chest. If I didn't get to Bell soon I was going to have to start using violence: a plan that was more likely to get me killed than get her out of chains.

"Which noble house?" The large man asked slowly.

"Millicent," I replied confidently. They were the first noble house that popped into my head. Jake Millicent was the only noble I actually knew by name, which was kinda funny considering the circumstances in which we met.

"You're not permitted into the butchery…*Mr Millicent,* that area is for syndicate personnel only," he replied through a smug expression.

Shit, did he just say butchery? I thought, an air of panic twinging inside my head.

"Kid," Panda said, tugging on the sleeve of my suit jacket, "he just said she's in the butchery, these guys must be cannibals, we need to get her out of there!"

I didn't think that was what the term implied considering that Bell was an outworlder and it was much more likely that they were after her map piece, but he was still right. No more playing around, it was time to take this rescue operation to the next level.

I took a step forward and the large man moved in front of me, folding his arms and blocking my way through. His slender, silent friend moved to my side and placed a firm hand on my shoulder.

"Take another step and we'll have to eject you forcefully," the large man said with a cruel grin as he cracked his knuckles.

I summoned my daggers into my hands and slashed the throat of the slender guard at my side. It was a quick, fluid motion as I calmly lifted my hand, stuck the blade into his gullet and flicked the edge through the sinew and skin.

Blood sprayed from the wound like a faucet, covering my nice new suit and the side of my face as the surprised guard gargled.

"Amateur," the unphased large man sneered, "he's a phase three, a severed windpipe won't kill him. It'll be healed in a second."

"I didn't realise acid was so easily healed," I replied cooly, noticing the bubbling, pulsating skin flapping where the man's gullet should have been.

His desperate eyes glanced between the large guard and me as he clawed at his gushing neck.

I grinned and dashed towards the large guard. I was upon him in a second. My enhanced strength had allowed my legs to push off from the floor at an inhuman speed.

The large man lifted his arms to block me, but it was too late. I hammered my first dagger through his eyeball and he threw his hands over it, clawing at my fist and the dagger clutched tightly in it.

At the same time he opened his mouth to scream but before any sound could leave it, I thrust my second dagger through his throat. His screaming died in a pathetic fit of gurgling and flailing.

The large man died quickly. Horribly, but quickly.

By the time my acid had finished doing its work his face was barely recognisable as something even remotely human.

There was a time not so long ago where I would have recoiled at the actions I'd just taken, but this was a world that relished violence and personal power and I had a friend to save.

The slender guard died shortly afterwards and I received two no-tifications in quick succession.

You have defeated *Morningstar Collective Guard* (lvl 49)

Bonus experience awarded due to level disparity.

You have defeated *Morningstar Collective Guard* (lvl 53)

Bonus experience awarded due to level disparity.

I found it mildly amusing that the larger, more intimidating guard was the weaker of the two. I guess his bark really was worse than his bite.

Both of them were higher levels than I was, yet they went down with relative ease. Perhaps it was because I was an adventurer? Kill-ing monsters was a lot harder than killing humans if these two clowns were anything to go off.

Considering how easy the fight was, I was pleasantly surprised when the level notifications came.

Congratulations! You have advanced to lvl 43

Congratulations! You have advanced to lvl 44

Congratulations! Skill: *Dagger* has advanced to lvl 12

...

Congratulations! Skill: *Dagger* has advanced to lvl 16

I couldn't believe my luck, not only had I gained two whole levels, but my *dagger* skill had increased by quite a lot as well. It was still trailing behind my *Newly Qualified Bowman* skill, but at this rate it would evolve sooner than I'd planned.

Whilst we'd travelled towards the dragon's lair for the exam I had tried to use my daggers more often, but in a team environment my bow was better suited.

I couldn't wait to see what my *dagger* skill would be like after it evolved though.

Quickly, I assigned my ten free points from levelling up to the intelligence stat. I was beginning to consider min-maxing my strength stat and just pushing that as far as it would go since the added power was obviously useful.

However, intelligence directly affected the amount of time I could leverage my full set armour bonus to stay invisible for and that too, would be extremely useful in a fight.

I quickly looted the two guards and gained some gold, a soiled suit, and a pair of tacky sunglasses. It was a disappointing haul, but I'd prefer to level up anyway.

"Jeez kid," Panda said as he tiptoed over the blood-soaked floor, "that was ruthless."

"Sorry buddy," I replied quietly, "but I'm done wasting time. We've been wading through bullshit since she was taken and now...we're just so close..."

I trailed off, unable to say what was on my mind, and stepped into the corridor the guards had tried to prevent us from entering.

The carpet below my feet was sticky as I entered my HUD and changed into my armour. Considering the nefarious locale, that was pretty suspicious.

We passed by a few locked doors, one of which had a window. I peered through to see a freezer of some sorts with strange meat stacked in neat rows. Maybe these guys really were cannibals, wouldn't that be something?

The corridor itself was actually quite short with a door at the very end. It was placed in such an obvious position that I almost didn't believe that we'd finally made it.

I tried the handle and it opened easily.

Who leaves a prison door unlocked? I thought, but when I walked inside that thought drifted away.

Held on a huge X made of wood was a naked, bleeding, Bell. I quickly checked my surroundings just in case her kidnapper was still there, but the room was empty.

Everything about the room reminded me of the time I was kidnapped by cultists...the time I'd killed Brad. The X was the same, there was even a vat of acid close by. It was as if the various groups attempting to flay the outworlders all shopped at the same freaky version of *Bed, Bath and Beyond.*

Without a word I began using my daggers to cut the bindings which were holding Bell's arms and legs. It was a thick, tight rope which must have been painful in and of itself.

As I began trying to free one of her legs I noticed that Bell's map piece was on her stomach rather than her back. I had assumed that everyone's tattoos were in the same place as mine but it seemed that wasn't the case.

It was my first time properly looking at one since I couldn't see my own. It was made of thick black lining and looked more like some sort of runic writing than an actual map. The skin around the map piece was red and cracked as if the torturer had focused on doing something specifically to that area…preparations for extraction maybe?

As I moved onto her final arm, Bell began to stir.

"Kaleb?" She asked in a feeble and uncharacteristic voice. It set my heart on fire to hear her sound like that when she was usually so full of life.

"Yup it's me," I replied with forced cheer, "here to save your useless ass."

I finished cutting through the final restraint and her body flopped forwards, she didn't seem to have the strength to stop herself.

Deftly, I caught her and pulled my bloodied suit from my inventory. It wasn't perfect, but it was something. I wrapped the jacket around her and scooped her up into a princess carry.

My eyes burned, but this time it wasn't with the threat of tears, it was with a furious hatred. It was time to end this Morningstar Collective for good.

"B…" Bell began feebly, I looked down at her swollen eyes with concern, "being tortured is not as kinky as anime had led me to believe."

I chuckled and smiled to myself as we prepared to leave the room. Inside though, I was a furnace.

Chapter 39
A Beautiful Femur

I carried Bell back down the corridor and towards the secret elevator, being careful not to trip on the two corpses I'd slaughtered on my way downstairs.

Just as we were about to reach the subterranean foyer a blaring alarm rang out around the room deafening me. It filled the room with an air raid-style siren that rose and fell in a way that made it impossible to tune out.

Shit, I must have triggered the alarm! I thought, picking up the pace as I headed purposely towards the elevator.

I felt a hard prod to my cheek and looked down with a furrowed brow. Bell gazed up at me and opened her mouth but I couldn't hear anything over the blaring siren.

She looked frustrated and then her eyes brightened and a chat notification popped up on my HUD.

Bell: *Go down the corridor to the left.*
Kaleb: *Why? The exit is this way.*
Bell: *They have a vault down there, it's where they keep the skins.*

I thought for a moment, suppressing the urge to shudder, and then nodded. If I could reach that vault I could adsorb whatever

293

map pieces the Morningstar Collective had acquired and that would piss them off royally.

Also, it would help me in my never-ending quest to complete The Celestial Map, which I had no interest in ever pursuing because, despite a certain system achievement I once got, I was not a genocidal maniac.

The system had given me the quest after I'd accidentally killed an adventurer named Brad and adsorbed his map piece. It sounds worse than it was ok?

Bell smiled feebly back at me and we headed down the corridor she had indicated, a confused-looking Panda trailing behind us. I rounded a corner and pushed through some swing doors to find an absolute blood bath.

The corridor was littered with the sliced and diced corpses of guards and casino staff alike. Blood and viscera splattered the walls and the floor was slippery and scarlet. It was hard to tell where one body ended and another began as limbs and torsos were mixed and matched in the carnage.

It was like a horror movie and the stench was inescapable.

Carefully, I picked my way through the mess and headed towards the open vault door at the end of the corridor. It was a typical metal vault door that loosely resembled a gear and was way too thick to blow open with dynamite or a skill.

Yet, the door hung loosely off its hinges as if someone had done exactly that. Stepping inside I saw rows of empty shelves. Whoever had done this had stolen the skins.

I was beginning to think that someone else had set off the alarm that rang all around us.

***

Approximately 30 minutes earlier...

"Where is she?" The short haired man and his panda exclaimed simultaneously attracting the attention of the bustling crowd in the main club room.

The Samurai also couldn't help but stare in their direction as they spoke a little too loudly with the man in the trench coat.

From the expression on his face, he wasn't used to working with such amateurs. He seemed to be a man to which subterfuge was second only to breathing. The batman wannabe, on the other hand, was loud and obvious—a man after her own heart.

The Samurai valued forwardness, it either showed a distinct confidence in oneself and a willingness to tackle things head on, or idiocy. She had yet to see which one of these applied to the armoured man.

It's almost time, Chrysus spoke into her mind.

He had been with her since she had entered this god-awful hive of scumbags.

The boy with the panda will lead you to the vault, just don't let him see you, her God continued.

She didn't reply. Chrysus was a god, he was inside her head, he didn't need her to speak to be able to understand her intentions.

The feeling of his mind touching hers was strangely intimate and took some getting used to. However, it was also comforting to carry a divine being of such great power inside of her. She accepted him fully and when he was with her it was almost as if their souls merged. They were one.

He was also a constant reminder of her goal. She would become a god – the strongest being in this world capable of challenging anyone, even Chrysus.

"...But yeah little lady, that armour of yours would look great on my bedroom floor, what do you say?" A small, broad, and rich noble asshole said from the opposite side of the booth she was oc-cupying.

He and his friend had joined the Samurai a short while ago and though she had no intention of engaging in such frivolous conver-sation, he did make good cover to help her blend in better.

"Your insides would look great on my bedroom floor," she re-plied calmly, "what do you say?"

The nobleman's eyes widened as he realised he'd been hitting on the wrong type of person and began to shrink down in his seat.

The Samurai smirked and made to leave, signalling her wolf fa-miliar with her hand. The man with the panda had left and she in-tended to follow him. He was her ticket into the subterranean facil-ity.

Dancers, servers, and patrons alike, moved willingly to the side as the Samurai walked across the club. Noticing the man and his panda summon a discreet elevator in the corner, she decided to keep her distance lest they spot her.

Once they entered the elevator, she made her move.

Midnight Slash (common)

Unsheathe your blade in an instant 10-foot leap to slash through foes. This skill imbues the wielder's blade with dark mana.
Activating this skill has a medium mana cost.

Activating her *Midnight Slash* skill, the Samurai leaped forwards, slicing through the doors like butter and landing with light finesse on top of the elevator.

She winced as Pocco jumped through the opening and she caught him. Had she missed, her familiar would have hit the roof loudly, alerting the man and his panda to their presence.

Secrecy was less important now that she had a way into the basement, but Chrysus had insisted that she stay as far away, and as unobtrusive to the man and his activities, as possible.

Once the elevator reached its destination she waited for a moment, peering through the small gap between the edge of the roof and the open, elevator door.

She watched as the man gesticulated in his exchange with the two guards before mercilessly slaughtering them with…was that poison?

The men he had killed all had bubbling lesions on their skin. She felt herself grin as she looked over the bodies from above. He was dangerous. She liked that.

Then, after he left, she pulled herself from her hiding place, dropping through the elevator roof hatch.

Good work my vassal, Chrysus said. His presence had never left her mind and she knew that he had been watching her every move. *What we're looking for should be down the corridor to the right. No need for secrecy now. Eradicate anyone that stands in your way, get what we came for and leave.*

She nodded, her grin widening as she brazenly pushed open the door that had been indicated to her. Stood before her was a group of twelve guards who all turned towards her with wide eyes.

Catching them off guard certainly took the sport out of the slaughter, not that she enjoyed it any less. The Samurai drew her blade menacingly as the guards fumbled with their own.

"Sic 'em Pocco," she said and the wolf darted forward, latching onto the leg of the closest guard who screamed like a little girl.

"Shit! Get her!" Another guard yelled and the rest charged towards her.

She ducked underneath a slash from the first guard, then had to roll out of the way of a second, slashing at the ankles of her attacker as she rolled.

He screamed and dropped to the ground like a sack of bricks startling his comrades. Before they had time to gasp, the Samurai was back on her feet and she let out a myriad of two-handed slashes which she controlled perfectly.

Blood splashed and drained from wounds, severed limbs and a single decapitation. Guards screamed and she laughed maniacally as her red armour glistened with the crimson blood of her foes.

She parried an attack, kicking out at a guard who stumbled back into the waiting jaws of Pocco the wolf. Then, a different guard locked blades with her. He was stronger, but she had more skill. As the blades were held in a stalemate, she moved one of her hands to the back of her katana's tip and leaned in with all of her bodyweight.

As she leaned, she felt contact with the neck and shoulder of her opponent and she dropped down, pulling away in a devastating slashing movement. The man dropped to the ground, bleeding out from a deep cut that split him open shoulder to chest.

The fight lasted moments and she didn't even need to call upon her active skills. It was a little disappointing.

However, she was there for a specific purpose and fighting was secondary to that. At the end of the blood-soaked corridor was a large, metal vault door.

Use your new skill, Chrysus said.

She nodded and drew her blade, holding it firmly above her head before activating the skill.

Heavenly Slash (Rare)
Channel mana into you blade to unleash a devastating single strike. The more mana you add, the more effective the attack.

This skill has a high mana cost.
This skill has a high stamina cost.

Imbuing as much mana as she could into the strike, she slashed down with devastating destructive force, forcing the vault door from its hinges. With a smirk, she sheathed her katana and pulled the broken door open.

Inside the vault was shelves upon shelves of skins, just as her master had said there would be. It was gross, but useful.

Perfect, he said inside her head, *as I thought, the Morningstar Collective has been busy. If anyone was going to have the resources to begin collection in earnest it would be them. After all, they do have portals to every major city. Adsorb them all and return to me.*

"Yes master," she said, replying for the first time since she entered The Morningstar Hotel and Spa.

A notification popped up in her interface almost immediately and she accepted it.

Do you want to adsorb 4,837 map pieces?
Y/N

The sheer amount of death that went into collecting this many wasn't lost on her. That was almost half the pieces needed to complete the map in a single raid.

I bet that idiot Yaldabaoth never expected someone as skilled as you to come to loot his hoard, Chrysus chuckled in her mind. *The fool probably didn't even know the value of what he'd been collecting.*

"This puts us one step closer to achieving your goal," The Samurai replied.

Indeed it does, Chrysus said proudly, *if everything goes to plan we'll be ready by the end of the year. The next phase relies on my high priest tournament going to plan. I'll need you at the top of your game my…disciple.*

"I thought I was a vassal?" The Samurai replied, her voice was reserved but her mind was racing.

You have too much potential to waste on a mere vassal, he replied and then exited her mind.

The feeling of the god leaving her was a dizzying experience. She felt an odd sense of loss, but at the same time was ecstatic at the new promotion. With Chrysus' help, she would ascend to godhood and rule this world.

He would regret helping her when she cleaved his head from his neck one day. However, until that day came she would serve and revere him to the best of her abilities. That was her duty as a Samurai.

As she exited the vault Pocco came trotting up to her wagging his tail which sprayed blood with every swish. The wolf brought the Samurai a beautiful femur and it was very proud of it too.

She bent down to pat the wolf. It was so cute. Then headed back to the elevator. An alarm blared out mere moments after it began ascending back to the main floor. She hoped she would get to fight her way out.

Chapter 40
Yaldabaoth

We'd barely been inside the vault for more than a minute when the alarm finally shut down.

"I'm glad that's over," I muttered as I carried Bell back down the corridor.

"Does anyone else still hear ringing?" Panda asked as he trailed clumsily behind me, "I think I've caught tinnitus."

"I don't think you *can* catch tinnitus, buddy," I replied. "It's not a disease."

"Well I *have* caught it, kid," he complained as he tiptoed through the viscera filled corridor. "The ringing won't stop. It's like no matter what I do it follows me…like a lost puppy but without the cuteness."

"I know what that's like," I muttered in response as we re-entered the room with the elevator.

I got Panda to channel his mana into the panel on the wall, calling the elevator down to our level, then we entered it and my pass must have registered once more as we were heading back upstairs within moments.

"Someone must have used this whilst we were away," Panda said, scratching his chin.

"It was probably whoever killed all those guards," I replied seriously. "Stay alert, we don't know what we'll be walking into up there."

I had planned to cause some mayhem of my own in the hotel after seeing what the Morningstar Collective had done to my friend. I needed to ger Bell to safety first though, she was in no condition to fight.

Even as I mentally prepared myself for whatever was to come when we reached the main floor, my mind was racing. Where was the silver eyed man who had kidnapped Bell and why weren't there more guards? To my understanding the hotel and spa was accessible from every major city in Celestia. Surely it shouldn't have been this easy to break in and free Bell. Something wasn't right.

The elevator doors opened with a ding and we stepped back out into the club area. It was deserted. Whereas previously it had been filled with people dancing, drinking and debaucher-*ing*, when we exited the elevator there wasn't a soul in sight.

I took a step forward and nearly tripped on something soft and squishy. Looking down I saw that the floor was littered with blood and human body parts. There must have been at least twenty corpses spread across the room, or at least, there were enough pieces to make twenty corpses.

"I don't know who robbed that vault," Panda began, "but if we ever meet them you should buy them a drink, kid. Looks like they've just saved you from an impossible fight."

"Why me?" I replied absently as I looked sceptically around the room. It seemed a little too easy and my Kaleb-senses were tingling, who was the thief and how were they *this* powerful?

My eyes darted towards the bar as I saw something move out of the corner of my eye.

"Well aren't you a perceptive one?" A familiar voice said from behind me, "most people don't notice my presence at all."

"How about instead of playing games with us," I replied irritably, "you fill us in on what happened whilst we were gone, Jack?"

The trench coat wearing man smiled as he fell into step with me. I didn't exactly like him tagging along, but I wasn't in the best position to protect Bell on my own. I couldn't exactly carry her *and* fire a bow.

"Oh it was quite the spectacle," Jack said in his crooning tones that could melt butter. "That walking suit of armour and their wolf wreaked havoc. They came back up just before you did. The hotel was mid evacuation due to the alarm and the armour didn't hesitate for a second.

"It ran straight towards the reception, slaughtering guards as it went. It was really something, it's been a while since I've seen someone do that kind of damage."

As he spoke I began to notice even more bodies. They were less obvious than ones I'd tripped over, but tucked between a booth and strewn in front of the bar there were bloodied corpses, these ones were more intact that the others.

One of them looked like it had been mauled by a feral beast, guts were strewn across the floor and a look of sheer terror was etched permanently into the man's face.

"Well, as long as the armour has taken care of them, at least I won't have to fight my way out of here," I replied, picking up the pace slightly.

"How very pragmatic of you," Jack said with a smile, "now let's get this young lady home shall we?"

"Are you coming with us *L.A Noir*?" Bell asked quietly from her place cradled in my arms.

I sniggered at the nickname.

"I certainly am," Jack replied, ignoring the joke, "your boyfriend owes me a favour and I need to collect."

"I'm married," I replied with a sigh.

"Sorry, your *husband* owes me a favour," he said, rolling his eyes.

"Not to her," I began, but thought better than to offer any further explanation. It really wasn't the time or the place.

We reached the double doors leading to the reception a moment later and I shouldered my way through them.

The reception was piled high with bodies strewn across the foyer floor. It was a scene straight from a horror movie.

Whoever this armoured person that Jack had mentioned was, they were brutal.

"Fuck!" a large man yelled from close by.

His body was grotesque and covered with scars and abrasions. The man was clearly no stranger to a fight but from the look of his many healed injuries he wasn't very good at them.

Sporting a green mohawk, the angry man wore a suit with the sleeves cut off. Yup, you heard that right. What a weirdo.

He was flanked by two lycanids with large swords and he held a strange spear which glowed an eerie purple colour.

He faced a portal which snapped shut a few seconds after we entered the room, then he turned towards me.

"Who the fuck are you?" He demanded, thrusting his spear in my direction.

"Who me?" I replied, "I'm just a boy standing in front of a fashion disaster and asking him to stop needlessly removing the sleeves from clothes."

Bell chuckled, but it quickly devolved into a cough reminding me of her dire need for medical treatment. I poured a health potion down her throat quickly and that seemed to help a bit. In all honesty, I wanted to slap myself for not thinking of that earlier.

"You look more like a thief to me," he said menacingly. "Do you know who it is you mock boy?"

"No and I don't really care, I just want to get the hell out of here," I replied with a shrug, though internally I was scouting the room for a spot to place Bell down. It was obvious that I was going to have to fight my way out.

"You stand in front of Yaldabaoth!" One of the lycanids growled, "a capo in The Morningstar Collective and the overseer of our affairs in Havar."

"Does that make him like a mini boss or something?" I asked as I edged towards a bench off to the side, "because from what I hear, Havar isn't exactly a powerful place."

"Kaleb," Jack said from my side, "as amusing as this back and forth is, you should be careful. He may be a low rung on the Collective's ladder, but he's still a higher level than you."

"Did you just assume my level?" I asked him in mock offence.

"Enough!" Yaldabaoth yelled, veins popping on his scarred face. "I will not suffer these ridiculous insults anymore. The boss is going to have my head for this disaster, but if I take yours first maybe he'll be forgiving. Kill them!"

He gestured towards us and his lycanid guards raised their oversized swords and began advancing.

"Hey Bell, do you have any mana left?" I asked as I retreated towards the bench I'd spied.

"A little," she croaked.

"In that case," I began, "Bell, use fireball!"

She smiled slightly and raised a shaky arm towards the lycanid guard on the left. A medium sized ball of spinning, sparking flame fired from her hand and shot into the lycanid's face.

305

His fur set alight and he dropped his sword, throwing his hands to his face and batting at it whilst he screamed in agony. The smell of burning hair and flesh filled the room, stinging my nostrils.

"It was super effective," I muttered as I placed Bell down on the bench and drew my bow.

I turned back to fire on the second attacker but Jack had already beaten me to the punch. He had, what looked like, a magic sniper rifle in his hands. Pulling the stock firmly into his shoulder, he calmly looked down the sights and squeezed the trigger.

A beam of red light erupted from the gun like some kind of energy beam and the second lycanid's chest exploded. Goop, gore, blood, and guts blasted out in all directions.

"That was badass!" Panda exclaimed as he shuffled towards me and Bell. "I'll stay with her; you go back up *John Wick* over there."

I nodded and jogged towards our new, shady ally.

As I stepped up next to the trench coat clad man, we both aimed our respective weapons at the scarred capo.

"Who are you really?" I asked him as his eyes widened and he raised his hands.

"I am Yaldabaoth, how did you kill my men so easily?" He asked, a shocked tone in his voice.

"I don't think you are," I continued, "I heard that Yaldabaoth was the chairman of the entire organisation not just some two-bit capo asshole."

Jack snorted laugher and I glanced at him, being careful not to take my eyes off the scarred man in my sights.

"Yaldabaoth, the chairman?" Jack howled; it was the most emotion I'd seen from him since we'd met. "The chairman calls himself Nyx and I'm pretty sure he's a god, though a pretty minor one. This asshole is just a wannabe gangster on his pay role. His real name is Jimmy. Yaldabaoth is an alias he uses."

"You watch your mouth!" Jimmy exclaimed, pointing his spear at us. "Don't you dare say his name!"

"Oh great," I sighed, "so he's a zealot and an idiot."

"Aren't they all?" Jack replied.

In that moment and without warning, Yaldabaoth – or Jimmy…whatever his name was – charged towards us with his spear levelled at my chest.

I fired off an arrow which he deflected with the tip of his spear. Jack shot a magic bullet at him but at the same time, Jimmy threw a dagger at him.

Jack blocked it with his rifle and then tried to fire off another round but nothing happened.

With an almighty scream, Jimmy rammed his spear through my side, impaling me. I dismissed my bow and summoned my daggers, gritting my teeth as the ripping pain in my skin burned through me.

I had let my guard down and now this asshole had gotten the better of me.

Not for long, I thought angrily.

Slashing at his face with my left dagger, I brought the right one down hard on the shaft of the spear that was sticking out of my side.

It snapped in two and I was free from Yaldabaoth's grip. Down a weapon, the deranged gangster pulled a glittering yellow potion from his inventory and tipped it into his mouth.

His face was bubbling in a half-Chelsea grin where my slash had connected with the edge of his lips. He grimaced as he downed the liquid and I took that moment to yank the severed haft of the spear out my body.

I yelled out as I pulled and it came free with a splattering of blood and what looked like a piece of kidney.

Great, my alcohol tolerance will never be the same, I thought grimly as I clicked on a healing potion in my inventory.

The broken skin began to heal, pulling itself back together and I once again focused on Yaldabaoth.

Having consumed the yellow potion his, already sizable, arms doubled in size giving him the appearance of a hulking, disproportionate monster.

I dashed forwards and slashed at his neck, but he was faster. Despite his abnormal size, his speed was something to be reckoned with and he blocked my slash with his oversized forearm.

The daggers barely penetrated his hardened flesh, hitting the forearm felt like trying to cut steel and my wrists jarred with the unexpected impact. His skin bubbled slightly but it didn't seem to bother him.

I dropped to the floor and attempted to sever his Achilles tendon but he predicted my actions and kicked out with devastating power, launching me across the room and into the far wall.

The world went black for a moment as I gasped for breath. A second later I watched as Jack, his weapon now fixed, fired a volley of magic glowing bullets into the juggernaut.

Raising his scarred arms, Yaldabaoth blocked most of the bullets. One, however, got past his defence and imbedded itself into his eye with a loud pop.

Body moving on automation, he threw his hands to his face, clutching at the eye socket and howling as blood and eye fluid dripped through his oversized fingers.

Whilst he was distracted, I took my chance.

I summoned my bow from my inventory once more and channelled my stamina into a *Soul Shot*. The arrow rocketed from my bowstring and cut a hole straight through Jimmy's chest.

Grunting, he moved one of his arms to the hole as if trying to prevent the blood and viscera from leaking out.

"I won't die like this!" He growled in an unnaturally deep and distorted voice.

"You bloody well will," Jack replied from behind as he fired off another few rounds.

They ripped through Yaldabaoth's body and he grunted with each impact. Falling to his knees he looked up at me with a fierce hatred in his eyes. I dismissed my bow and summoned my daggers once more.

"Nyx will avenge me, then you'll be sorry," he spat in my general direction, laboured breath sounding more like wheezing.

"I doubt that," I replied coldly, "I doubt he even knows your name."

I strode up to the dying, ugly monstrosity and gripped the back of his head. Pressing my lips close to his ear I said: "this is for Bell," and plunged my dagger into his throat.

His lips pursed and he gasped and gurgled as he choked on his own blood. In the end, his wide eyes pleaded for help that he was never going to get.

Chapter 41
Tell Him How Rare Ancient Skills Are!

You have defeated *Yaldabaoth* (lvl 60)

"Wow, that guy was no slouch," I said aloud as the notification flashed up on my screen.

At level 50 you hit phase three, so Yaldabaoth was well on his way to becoming a phase four. Sally was past level 90 the last time I'd spoken to her about it and I still had a long way to go before catching up to her.

Congratulations! You have advanced to lvl 45

Bonus experience gained due to level disparity.

Previously I had been dumping all of my free points into intelligence to try and boost the time I could spend invisible: a skill I'd gained from a full set armour bonus.

In the last battle though, I realised something. Ignoring my other stats wasn't the best idea. They got raised significantly with every level, which was why I was putting my points into intelligence.

It was my lowest stat and the stat which progressed the least with each level up. My class *Apex Predator* gave a mere plus one to intelligence per level, whereas it gave a generous plus seven to strength, plus five to vitality and plus three to both agility and perception.

With that in mind, this time I split my free points a little differently, adding two to intelligence, two to perception and one to agility.

It would take longer to raise a single stat this way, but after facing Yaldabaoth I spotted a critical weakness in my skill distribution.

How had I let him get so close to me? The beast had stabbed me before I'd had the chance to dodge. If I had higher perception and agility stats then maybe I would have noticed sooner and had the skill to dodge out of the way of that attack.

If he had been a stronger opponent then there was a good chance I would have died, and I wasn't about to let that happen.

After quickly assigning my new free points my HUD flashed once more with a notification that left me grinning.

Quest Complete!

A Good Time, Not A Long Time

You've been marked as a guest of *The Morningstar Hotel and Spa*. I wonder what mayhem and fun awaits behind its doors.

Updates:
You have discovered that *The Morningstar Collective* are a syndicate who run a racketeering operation in Havar.

You suspect that *The Morningstar Collective* have kidnapped another adventurer and are holding her at *The Morningstar Hotel and Spa*

It is possible that *The Morningstar Collective* are involved with the regicide of the local king.

You have discovered that the entrance to *The Morningstar Hotel and Spa* is located inside *El 'Dorado*.

You have gained a platinum pass to access the lower floors where you suspect the prisoner is being held.

You have discovered that *The Morningstar Collective* are secretly kidnapping outworlders and collecting their skin.

Objectives:
Enter The Morningstar Hotel and Spa 1/1
Uncover the secrets of The Morningstar Hotel and Spa 1/1
Rescue the kidnapped adventurer 1/1
Secret Objective: Kill Yaldabaoth, the capo responsible for Morningstar interests in Havar 1/1
Find out if The Morningstar Collective are connected to the regicide 0/1 (objective failed)

Reward:
X1 Skill Upgrade Potion
X1 Weapon Upgrade Potion

Secret Reward...negated as not all objectives were completed.

There was a lot to unpack in there and I didn't have much time to dwell on it. Most of the notification was a running quest log of the things I'd done and discovered.

I wasn't surprised to see that defeating Yaldabaoth was a secret objective and that was kind of cool. I was, however, pretty disappointed that I failed to shed some light on *The Collective's* involvement with the regicide.

My secret reward was taken from me and that was a bitter pill to swallow, still I gained a skill upgrade and a weapon upgrade potion and I knew exactly how I wanted to use them.

"It'll take me a few minutes to work out how to get their portal system open," Jack said from behind the reception desk. The receptionist was nothing but a pile of bloody goop after the armoured assailant had torn through the room.

"No problem, I have some quest rewards to apply anyway," I replied half-heartedly as I continued moving through my HUD.

First up was the weapon upgrade potion, not that I knew how to use it. Did I drink it or did I pour it over the weapon I wanted to upgrade? I looked towards Panda who shook his head at my confusion.

"Isn't it obvious?" He asked behind a cocky smirk. "If it's a skill potion you drink it because the skills are inside you, if it's a weapons potion you pour it on the weapon you want to upgrade. That is, unless the weapon is your fist, in which case you'd drink it...probably."

Taking his advice, I summoned my bow from my inventory and applied the potion. My HUD lit up immediately.

Longbow of the Giant Goblin (common)

Longbow of the Giant Goblin (uncommon)

This bow was carved from the forearm of a unique monster: *Gertrude the Giant Goblin.*
Just as she smashed her old clan into oblivion, you smashed her. You dirty bugger.
I mean, whatever tickles your pickle am I right?
I'm still judging you though.

Longbows can fire accurately over longer distances.
+10% strength
Grants use of the skill: Sniper
Sniper can only be used whilst this item is equipped

I furrowed my brow as I tried to work out what had changed besides the rarity. It took a moment, but I realised that the strength increase had gone from 5% to 10%.

It wasn't much, but the higher my percentage bonuses got the more bang for my buck I would get at each new level and that would definitely be useful going forward. As far as quest rewards went I couldn't really complain.

Next came the big one. I had an upgrade potion for skills and I knew exactly which one I wanted to use it on. This skill had been the backbone of my fighting style for a while now and improving it even further was the obvious choice.

I drank the potion and a new window popped up on my HUD asking me which skill I wanted to apply the potion to. Naturally, I chose Soul Shot.

ERROR
Soul Shot is already an *ancient* rated skill. It cannot be upgraded to unique artificially.

"What!" I shouted, turning the heads of Jack, Bell, and Panda at the same time.

"You tried to upgrade Soul Shot didn't you?" Panda sighed as the other two watched in bewilderment. "You can't use an upgrade potion to push a skill past ancient rarity, kid...sorry."

"You have an ancient skill?" Bell blurted out and then coughed a few times. Her frailty seemed to be subsiding with time but she was far from her usual self.

"Yeah, don't you?" I asked with a shrug.

"No!" She shouted, forcing herself into a seated position and looking at me like I was an idiot. "*L.A. Noir*, tell him how rare ancient skills are!" She demanded and Jack looked between the two of us with widened eyes.

"Kaleb," he said diplomatically, "as the lady says, ancient skills are exceedingly rare so people like you and I who are fortunate enough to have them shouldn't go around bragging about it."

"You have one too!" She screamed, practically falling off the bench I'd laid her on. "Well this is just great."

With a slight smirk, I delved back into my HUD to choose a different skill to upgrade. I didn't have the heart to tell her that I had two ancient skills and a unique skill.

Do you want to upgrade the skill: *Acid Dhampir Dagger*?
Y/N

Acid Dhampir Dagger is able to merge with the class skill *Acid Arrow*, would you like to merge these skills?
Y/N

I mentally asserted yes for both questions.

Acid Dhampir Dagger has merged with *Acid Arrow*
You have unlocked the skill:

Acidic Dhampir Weapons (uncommon)

Acidic Dhampir Weapons (rare)

A Dhampir is the offspring of a human and a vampire.
They can't turn into bats or anything but in some

earthen mythos they drink blood to gain power, or
because they think they're edgy or whatever.
Anyway, the point is that the *Dhampir Weapons* will
steal HP with every hit you make. That's right, attack
them and heal yourself in the process!

Gain 10% of damage inflicted by weapons as HP.
Due to the nature of your class, Dhampir Weapons
refers to skirmisher class weapons only.
All Dhampir Weapons inflict acid damage.

The upgraded skill added an interesting development. It seemed that the upgrade specifically merged the two skills, applying the *Dhampir* effect to my bow.

Gaining back health with every shot was a good bonus. It was useful on the daggers but I barely used them. If I'd have had this skill during The Goblin King Coronation quest then I wouldn't have needed Lucas to save me when I was neck deep in goblins.

With the bow being my primary weapon it made sense to upgrade it, and the skills surrounding it, as much as possible. Still, I had no idea that upgrading a skill could cause it to merge with another skill.

"Almost...done," Jack grunted from beneath the reception desk when a blue portal suddenly sprang to life. It looked a sickly, pale color. A far cry from the vibrant portal we'd entered to get here.

I scooped up Bell who was still sulking and headed across the room towards the portal and our way back to Havar.

"Thanks for that Jack," I said, stopping next to the reception desk, "you've been a big help. I really appreciate it."

"Appreciation is nice and all, but don't forget our deal," he replied smugly.

I looked at him sceptically and then sighed. He had earned my favour, as shady as he might have been. Without his help I wouldn't have been able to save Bell, and he helped me take down Yaldabaoth.

"I won't," I replied earnestly, "whenever you need me, I'll be there."

"Good," he replied, offering his hand out to shake and then thinking better of it when he realised my hands were full from carrying Bell. "I think we'll meet again sooner than you might think."

I nodded at him in lieu of a handshake and entered the portal.

"I wonder what happened to that silver eyed guy who kidnapped Bell in the first place," Panda said with a shrug, "we never found him."

***

Jack leant back on the blood slick desk and sighed deeply, rubbing his temples with his palms. "You can come out now," he said into the shadows.

On cue, a hooded figure with a pair of piercing silver eyes emerged from the nearby darkness, his body shimmered as he exited the shadows themselves using a power that was unfamiliar to Jack.

"Our deal is complete Reaper," he said mechanically, striding towards Jack with a swagger that portrayed his arrogance.

"It is," Jack replied, "your service to The Organisation won't be forgotten, thank you for sealing the portals. If the higher ups of The Morningstar Collective had been able to get here the kid would never have survived."

The silver eyed man nodded, perching himself next to Jack against the receptionist's desk.

"Your god has convoluted plans," he murmured more to himself than to the assassin, "kidnapping a girl so that you can pretend to help some guy save her to trick him into believing he owes you a favour. What a roundabout way to get things done."

"I don't pretend to fully understand Diako's vision," Jack said wistfully, folding his arms, "but the boy had to be willing to do almost anything for me. We needed him in my debt, it is part of the grand design. And...if we happened to take out Chrysus' vassal in the process then all the better."

"Yaldabaoth was a good capo," the man growled, "Nyx won't be pleased with this."

"Nyx is a minor god," Jack replied coldly, "he has not the will or the power to defy *my* lord. Watch your mouth."

The silver eyed man snorted derisively and shook his head. "I guess your work here is done then?" He asked suggestively, "I have a lot of work to do if I'm to take over the Havarian branch."

The Reaper nodded and the man gave him a meaningful look before leaving the room and heading towards the bar area. Jack smiled when he thought of the arduous task of cleaning that was ahead of the arrogant prick.

Good work Jack, Diako said entering his mind as the man left. *I'll open a portal for you now, it's going to take you to the continent. I have a new mission for you.*

"No rest for the wicked then boss?" He said aloud with a smile.

Diako had opened the portal to Havar for Kaleb using Jack as a vessel to channel his mana through. Jack was clever and good at using mana, but he wasn't a genius, nor was he a high enough level to strong arm his way through a complex portal system.

You can rest when my goal is met, that was our deal. The god's presence made Jack shiver; it was becoming a nervous tick of sorts. He hated not being let in on the full design of Diako's plans. Though he talked a big game to the arrogant man, he himself knew very little of the plans of gods.

It was a new feeling for the old solider. He'd spent his entire life following orders without question, so it irked him how much he was annoyed by not knowing more of his god's plans.

A bright scarlet portal sprang to life, much more potent than the one Diako had opened for Kaleb, and Jack stepped through it.

The continent awaits, my vassal.

Chapter 42
Results May Vary

When I arrived back through the portal to the *El 'Dorado* office, our little leprechaun friend almost fainted. He was shocked that I'd survived, and even more so to hear of the decimation of *The Morningstar Collective*...or at least the Havarian branch of it.

I didn't stick around for long though.

Hurrying through the city streets to the orange glow of dawn, I made a beeline for the building that Adventure Society had been using as a makeshift hospital in the wake of the dragon attack.

There, I finally managed to offload Bell. She was ordered to take a week of bedrest to fully recover from the trauma of being tortured. On Earth, trauma wasn't so quickly healed, but the Society healers assured me that with some good meditation and bedrest, her emotional scars would heal almost as well as her physical ones.

I wasn't so sure it worked that way. Meditation was useful, but the kind of suffering she'd endured...that stuff leaves lasting damage.

I slept like a baby that night in the room adjoining hers. I checked on her periodically over the next couple of days but she spent most of her time meditating and I didn't want to disturb her rest.

Supposedly the hospital didn't count as a safe room so the next day I made a point of visiting *The Winking Giant* inn. Fortunately, it hadn't taken too much damage in the attack and, as usual, the lycanid landlady flashed me a shiver inducing smile as I made my way to my room to open the loot box I'd received from entering *The Morningstar Hotel and Spa*.

Would you like to open all loot boxes?

Y/N

Yes, I mentally asserted.

As usual, a crack of bright light bounced around the room and this time a disco ball appeared on the ceiling. Funky, 70's style music rang out as the ball descended and then the bottom fell off and a small parcel descended heavenly into my outstretched hands.

Ne'er-Do-Well's Loot Box
Loot awarded only to the most despicable of people. The system knows what goes on in that hotel. The system sees all. The system wishes it could gouge out its eyes, but alas, the system does not have eyes...because it is a system.

"Well that was an unexpected notification," I mused aloud, "since when do you refer to yourself in third person?" I asked the ceiling.

"Kaleb!" Panda snapped, "stop talking to the system, it's weird."

I shot him a dirty look as the descending parcel warped away into my inventory. I dived into my HUD half-heartedly expecting a joke item like hemorrhoid cream or something. However, what I got was even more unexpected.

You have received a new item:

Chaos Seed

Summon a chaos demon for 60 seconds.
Results may vary.

That was all it said.

No jokes, no weirdly elaborate backstory, no farcical whimsy of any kind, and that was a little bit...worrisome. Still, at least it wasn't hemorrhoid cream.

I kept the seed in my inventory and left the inn.

It was nice to finally have some downtime and Panda and I used it to explore the city some more, stocking up on potions, books, and rations for future quests.

I stopped by the Adventure Society the day after returning and informed Director Lucas and Sally of what I'd found inside *The Morningstar Hotel and Spa*. Lucas ordered a cleanup crew to search the premises but by the time they got there the place had been cleared out. Apparently there was no subterranean level to speak of and they couldn't find any connection to the regicide.

The government of Havar was in shambles after the untimely death of the king. The infighting and power grabs that began in the wake of the incident was threatening to destabilise the city, but that was nothing a soon-to-be iron rank adventurer should be worrying about so I tried to keep the local politics out of my mind.

The Adventure Society building was well on its way to being completed and, though I finally managed to set up my system banking, I still couldn't hand in my quest for slaying the dragon.

Lucy, the catonid receptionist, promised me that they would be ready to give out rewards in a few days and at that time I would be officially recognised as an iron rank adventurer...even though I was close to becoming a phase three and qualifying for bronze rank.

Not one to sit still, I took a mediocre quest in the nearby palm tree jungle and fought some mid-level monsters. The quest was nothing to write home about, but it kept me busy. Disappointingly though, I didn't gain another level from the copious amounts of monsters I'd hunted.

After Bell's week of rest was finally up, we both returned to Adventure Society to officially hand in our completed quests and become fully fledged adventurers.

"It feels like forever ago since we piled into Sally's truck to go slay a dragon," Bell mused as we entered the building.

"It's hard to believe that was only a few weeks ago," I replied, "ready to become an iron ranker?"

"Oh, you know it!" She said with a grin.

"I'm glad to hear it," Lucy commented as we approached her desk.

We were finally able to claim the rewards for the dragon quest and it was oh, so satisfying.

Quest Complete!

How To Slay Your Dragon

There have been reports of a dragon nesting at the top of the big mountain in the middle of the island. The Havarian local government have tasked the Adventure Society to handle the issue.

Remember when you first got here? I told you there would be dragons.

Objectives:
Find the dragon's lair 1/1
Kill the dragon 1/1

Reward: *X1 item upgrade token, adventurer rank-up*

****Speak to the Adventure Society to claim your reward.
Reward payable upon the successful completion of the
above objectives****

Lucy handed me an item upgrade token and explained that to apply it I needed to enter my inventory tab and mentally assert which item I wanted to add it to.

I asked what the difference between upgrade potions and upgrade tokens was. Apparently the potion variant was awarded directly by the system and its origins were unknown, whereas the tokens were man made.

Supposedly the effect was the same though.

Since it was an item token I couldn't apply it to my armour or weapons, which sucked. However, I did have one idea of how to use it. Delving into my inventory I took the first piece of adventurer gear I'd ever bought and upgraded it.

Item Upgraded!

Quiver of The Infinite (uncommon)
**This quiver contains an infinite number of iron arrows
and you can withdraw its contents directly from your
inventory. This means you can shoot arrows almost as
quickly as you shoot...well, you get the idea.**

It was a minor upgrade, but one that I was pretty satisfied with. Arrows formed the backbone of my attack power, so even a minor upgrade in arrow quality would boost my damage output.

Though not explicitly stated, iron arrows were sturdier than I was used to and I expected they could hold more *Soul Shot* power than the previous ones. I'd have to test that out when I got a moment. Previously the arrows had been described as *inferior* and their brittle tips hadn't been great. Hopefully the upgraded iron variant would do more damage.

As I pondered my upgrade, a shining light glimmered in my peripheral vision and I turned around just in time to see Bell's robes transform.

Before my eyes, her white robes were dyed a cascading scarlet, black trimming outlined the edges and a hood sprouted onto the back.

"I thought item tokens didn't work on armour?" I asked as the glow began to fade.

"I got an armour upgrade token," she replied with a cocky smile, "I negotiated my reward before taking the quest."

"What!?" I practically yelled, looking between the self-satisfied fireball mage and the sheepish catonid.

Panda giggled mid drag and began choking on the smoke from his bamboo pipe. Shaking my head, I turned back to the receptionist.

"So, are we officially iron rank now?" I asked, trying to keep my dissatisfaction out of my voice.

"Not quite Mr Akabane," she replied curtly, "you both need to be officially onboarded first. You can use the room where you chose your class if you like? It's free now and by the time you're done I'll have gotten your paperwork in order."

Bell and I sighed almost simultaneously.

"Hell is a corporate seminar," I muttered.

"This feels more like a punishment than a reward," Bell added, "I just got out of the hospital, why would you do this to me now?"

Lucy offered a sympathetic look before disappearing into the back office, turning to call us just before she left, she said, "oh, the Director wishes to see you once you've finished the seminar."

"I guess we're doing this then…again," I moaned, turning with slumped shoulders towards the stairwell.

"This is why it took so long to be able to hand in the quest after the dragon attack," Bell said as realisation dawned on her, "they needed to fix the corporate stuff didn't they? I thought it was weird that they couldn't just give us our tokens and change our ranks immediately."

"It was all leading to this," I replied, lowering my head.

"Will you two quit your whining," Panda said as we began ascending the stairs. "It's just a video, it'll only take an hour and then you can start taking all these cool quests." He pointed towards the iron rank board as we passed the second floor.

The quest room was a bustling hive of activity, starkly different to the relatively desolate newbie board downstairs.

The board was practically overflowing with requests too. These were the quests that would help me to break through to phase three. I had to admit, even amidst the bureaucratic drudgery, I was excited.

Holding myself a little bit higher, we climbed past the other floors and exited into the office floor. It still surprised me just how closely the bureaucracy of Havar mimicked Earth.

Office cubicles, tired workers with forced smiles, a soul sucking atmosphere. It was everything I hated about the modern world and seeing it in my new fantasyland was a little frustrating.

Still, I'd rather it was them than me.

The surly receptionist grunted at us and nodded towards the same room I'd used to choose my class. That seemed like so long ago and I almost looked fondly upon her attitude for the memories it conjured.

With a polite nod, I led Bell and Panda towards the room and opened the door. Our seminar was about to begin.

Chapter 43
Hell Is A Corporate Seminar

Are you ready to take the next step in your career with Adventure Society?

Damned right you are!

With Adventure Society your medical bills will be subsidised, your taxes will be paid and, in the likely event of your untimely death, we'll endeavour to return your corpse (or whatever is left of it) to your next of kin.

"What, no death in service payout?" I muttered, hand resting on my cheek as we sat in the room watching the crackling screen before us.

The entire seminar was set to the backdrop of an odd, poorly drawn cartoon. The cheery voice of the narrator did nothing to help quell my boredom as each passing minute felt like an eternity.

The first video seemed more like a sales pitch, but the second was a straight up pharmaceutical-style warning. The only thing it was missing was the mandatory "please consult with the surgeon general before taking this" that I'd seen in oversees adverts.

Congratulations on passing the iron rank examination. As promised, your contract is now eligible to advance from temporary to permanent (terms and conditions do apply and you will be accepted on a probationary period of six months starting from the day you sign your paperwork. You will not be entitled to holiday pay, pension, or tax exemption by signing the Adventure Society contract. Adventure Society is in no way liable for loss of limbs, loss of life, mana-based sickness, mental health issues, rehabilitation, trauma counselling, sudden blindness, spontaneous combustion brought on by looking into the eyes of an eldritch horror, or any other ailments that may befall you in the enactment of your duties. Adventure Society also maintains the right to terminate this contract at any time, without notice).

"I'm beginning to think that this isn't actually a very good deal," Bell said, shifting restlessly in her seat.

"I'm inclined to agree," I replied, "though it does make me kind of nostalgic for home in a weird way."

"Will you two be quiet!" Panda said, turning around in his seat and shooting us a dirty look, "I'm trying to watch this."

"Why would *anyone* want to watch *this*?" I asked him incredulously.

"I'm a sage, I love new knowledge," he shot back, "besides, *someone* needs to understand the rules so you idiots don't accidentally get yourselves kicked out." He turned his head back to the seminar video with a greedy look in his eye.

Bell and I shared a look.

As you embark on your journey up the ranks in our illustrious, globe spanning organisation you can expect to take on some challenging quests. In this video we'll cover the basic policies of the Adventure Society, including: what to do when facing a vicious pack of man eating Harpies, how to talk to quest givers, and most importantly, the correct procedure for filing paperwork at your local branch office.

The third collection of videos were mostly bureaucratic rubbish and I began rubber necking about halfway through. By the time I woke up we'd moved onto the final video.

Now that you've completed this introductory seminar, we can explain the rank structure which helps keep our company running smoothly.

The rank system:

Initial guild ranks coincide with the basic phases. At phase one (levels 1-29) you will only be eligible to enlist as a temporary adventurer. As a temporary adventurer you will only be eligible for the most basic types of quests.
At phase two (levels 30-49) you will become an iron ranker, as you all well know by now! Iron rankers make up the bulk of our worldwide operations and are given access to more challenging quests. At this level you will also be able to take quests above your current rank as long as you are in a party with at least one member of the correct rank for the quest you intend to take.
Phase three (levels 50-89) will see you promoted to bronze rank. At this stage you will be given access to quests of a multifaceted nature. This includes politically sensitive and long-term quests.
At phase four (levels 90-99) you will rank up to silver and be among our most elite members. You will be expected to tackle some of the hardest work we have available as well as mentoring rookies and running exams.
Phase five (100+) will see you promoted to gold rank. Though common on the continent, in Havar, the director is the only person of this rank.

There are also diamond, platinum and mithril ranks
which can be reached after achieving the level cap, but
we'll cover those another day.

For now, get out there, new iron ranker, and keep our
city-state safe!

Adventure Society: killing the monsters under your bed.

With that, the farce was finally over. Despite sleeping through most of it, I felt physically and mentally drained. Corporate life definitely was not for me.

In front of me, Panda stretched out his arms and made a satisfied groan as he hopped from his seat.

"Wasn't that invigorating?" He asked, lighting up his pipe which he had refrained from using during the seminar.

"No," Bell and I both replied as we vacated our seats groggily.

"Hold on a moment," Director Lucas said, entering the room with a swish of his cloak. "Before you leave, I need to update your cards."

I'd almost forgotten I had a card. It was supposed to serve as my identification if I visited other branches but since I still hadn't left Havar, I'd never actually used it.

I pulled it from my inventory and passed it to Lucas.

"My, my, it still says level nine on your card Kaleb," Lucas said. "We really need to get something in place to allow you to update these more frequently. On the continent they have card readers at reception, maybe we should trial that here as well."

He seemed to be speaking more to himself than to me, but his musings reminded me of the cards I had used as a wagon driver in my previous life. I had a digi-card which recorded my hours and needed to be docked periodically.

Of course a place that runs mandatory seminars would want to implement something like that, I thought, then again, it would make it easier for me to take better quests.

Director Lucas slotted my card into the funny machine on the wall which spat it back out at him. The card had changed colour to…was that iron?

Even I have to admit that's a nice touch.

"Level 45?" Lucas asked, raising an eyebrow as he returned my ID to me. "You'll be bronze rank soon; you've almost completely skipped iron rank."

He seemed pleased, though I thought he'd be more surprised.

I quickly checked my updated card before returning it to my inventory.

Adventure Society ID:

Kaleb Akabane
Level: 45
Rank: Iron
Class: Archer / Light Skirmisher

I was pretty satisfied with the upgrade. It was nice to see all my hard work in one place…well, two places since my stats screen showed it in much greater and more satisfying detail.

"Bell, you have progressed marvellously as well," Lucas said with a smile, "hitting level 42 is no small feat. You and Kaleb are going to be some of our top adventurers before you know it."

"You know it!" She replied with a chirpy smile, "in fact, I think we should go out to celebrate right now."

"Actually, I know a place we could go for food if you want to?" I replied.

"I'm afraid I'm much too busy organising everything in the aftermath of the dragon attack," Lucas said, his face sporting a few wrinkles around his bloodshot eyes. "Please come and visit me later though, I have something important to discuss with you, but that can wait. The two of you deserve to take some time to rest after everything you've done for this city."

Bell was eager to feast and I was in a pretty good mood myself, so despite wondering what it was Lucas wanted to discuss with us, we left the society and headed to the street where *The Wandering Giant Inn* – and pretty much everything else – was located.

Not so long ago I was attacked by an agent of Chrysus down a back alley not far from the inn. I'd fired off a *Soul Shot* and destroyed a local restaurant. That agent had gone on to invite me to take part in something called a *high priest tournament*, which I had no intention of going to.

As we walked down the busy street I saw a myriad of different construction crews working on damaged buildings and filling in cracked street paving. Despite that, many stores were still intact and commerce was flowing. After a short walk we came across a store with a little sign hanging above it: "*Renegade Restaurant, Bar & Grill*". I thought I'd only given him enough to fix the door I broke, but the entire shop front was new.

"He certainly put that money to good use," Panda mused as I approached the entrance.

"Good afternoon and welcome to…" a burly lycanid greeted us, before stopping in his tracks, "It's you! You're the stranger who paid to repair my restaurant. Please, come in and be seated, let me treat you and your friends to a meal, it's the least I can do."

The man flashed us a fangy smile as he gestured inwards. He was a flashy looking lycanid in a waistcoat and shirt. He certainly looked the part.

Inside nearly all the tables were filled with customers, happily chatting away as they ate their meals. In one corner though, the atmosphere was quite different.

"Hi, Sally!" Panda yelled, waving a stumpy paw at the muscle-bound silver ranker, "mind if we sit with you."

Looking up from a stack of paperwork, her expression lightened a little as she waved us over.

"What are you three doing here?" She asked as we slid into the booth with her. We all had to cram into one side because the mountain of paperwork she was working on took up so much space.

"We're celebrating finally reaching iron rank," Bell explained, "no more fetch quests for me."

"*I* never really did any fetch quests," I mused, thinking back on the three mandatory quests I'd undertaken.

"You were basically already doing iron rank quests as a temp, Gonads," Sally said in between scribbling on paper, "you can thank me later for that."

"I can thank you now," I replied cockily, "the owner has fully comped our meals for today, so, since we're sat with you, your food is on me."

"Wait…" Bell began, glaring at me through her large, anime-style eyes, "you *never* had to do fetch quests?"

"Not really, no," I replied.

"I hate you," she whispered ominously, "do you have any idea how annoying it is being asked to go halfway across the island to pick berries? There's no fast travel in this world Kaleb, it takes days sometimes."

Ignoring her outrage, I flagged a waiter down and we ordered some food. They returned quickly and a huge piece of meat with a white bone sticking through it was placed in front of each of us. It smelled divine and looked even better.

"Oh my god," Bell breathed, "it's the manga meat on a bone that every human dreams of! I've always wanted to try this."

The browned, succulent meat practically melted off the bone and was every bit as satisfying as it looked in anime and manga. Bell was right, I too had wanted to try it since the first time I'd watched *One Piece* as a kid.

After we finished our food, we stayed a little while for some free drinks. The ale in Havar was divine, at least it was a damn sight better than the motor oil the dwarves served, and I had no reason to dread having a hangover the next day.

"So, what kind of quest are we doing next?" Bell asked as we supped our second round.

"What do you mean *we*?" I asked.

"Well, we're basically a party now aren't we?" She replied, her cheeks turning a light reddish colour, "I just figured we'd continue working together after everything we've been through."

The thought hadn't really crossed my mind, I'd never considered us as a party, hell, I didn't even know how to set one up.

Then again, Bell was pretty strong and she did make for good company. Moreover, I'd feel pretty bad leaving her on her own after everything we'd been through together. She had a knack of getting into trouble and I didn't want her death on my conscious.

"Well I guess it's ok," I replied, looking over to Panda who nodded back at me. "So, Panda, how do you even start a party?"

"Usually," he replied, rubbing his chin with his paw thoughtfully, "you'd invite some friends over, maybe buy some chips and dips, put on some music and get some kegs…"

"You know that's not what I meant," I replied monotonously, narrowing my eyes at his amused expression.

"It's pretty straight forward," Sally interjected, "you can create a party in the chat function of your HUD. It'll open a party chat which you then have to name. To make it official, you'll need to register that name with the guild."

Following her instructions I dived into my HUD and invited Bell to a party chat. The only sticking point was the name.

"How about, *Bell's Banditos?*" The fireball mage offered.

"That's stupid, we're not even bandits," Panda said, "it should be *The Travelling Sage and his Lacklustre Companions.*"

"That's not a name, it's a sentence," Sally muttered across the table from us. "You should call yourselves, *Wild Cards*, because you all have such different abilities."

"This isn't a deck builder, or an 80's teen superhero show," I replied with a shake of my head. "How about *Dissident Flame?*"

The others took a moment to consider my idea, which I took to be a good sign. Panda nodded slowly as he thought it over and Bell looked a little confused. In the end, it was Sally that spoke first.

"I like it, it sounds very official," she said, "just don't go getting full of yourselves just because you have a team now."

After a little more back and forth which was mostly Bell putting forth names like: *The B Team, B-Men* and *Bell's Company*, we eventually settled on *Dissident Flame* as our team's name.

"Great, I'll get it filed with Lucy tomorrow," I said, after finishing my fourth ale. It had taken us a while to agree on a name and we'd gone through our fair share of freebies.

Chances were that Bell was going to be the more memorable of the three of us anyway, and I was happy to lead from the shadows and let her take the spotlight. I just wanted to level up and get more powerful and I didn't need to paint a target on my back for rival teams and cultists.

"So, back to my original question," Bell began, "what kind of quest are we going to do next."

"Actually," I began tentatively, "I was thinking about going to the continent."

Chapter 44
A Friend In Need...

"You want to go to the continent?" Panda gasped, spluttering his ale all over the table, "you know I've only been there once right? My sagely knowledge won't be much help to you over there."

"Yes," I replied, cupping my hands in front of my chin. "My goal is to get stronger and I think it's time to leave Havar behind and go travelling. There's an entire world out there after all."

Bell's eyes lit up as she listened to me, then she lifted her wooden tankard in my direction and said: "let's do it!"

With a smile, I hit her tankard with my own and we both turned to stare at Panda who looked more uncertain than I'd ever seen him.

"Just think of all the new knowledge you'll be able to pilfer," I said slowly, like I was enticing a dog to come to me.

Panda stared back at me through the lids of his large eyes. He held up his tankard tentatively as if cogs were turning in his brain.

"I do like the sound of that," he began, "but the continent is dangerous and...ah, why not." He shook his head lightly as he hit his tankard into ours.

"That settles it then!" I announced gleefully, "tomorrow morning I'll register our party with the guild and then team *Dissident Flame* will set out for new horizons."

"Cheers!" We all shouted as we hit out tankards together once more and downed our drinks.

"There's just one problem," Panda said, "how are we going to get there?"

I lowered my tankard slowly as realisation struck. I hadn't actually thought about that part. Perhaps we could hire a yacht? I had plenty of gold, though I didn't know what the going rate for yacht hire was...

"You're in luck," Sally said quietly from behind her mountainous stack of papers. "It just so happens that I have some business on the continent myself. I'll let you hitch a ride if you help me out with a little *errand* I have to take care of along the way."

"That sounds great!" Bell chimed happily.

"It does...that's not like you," I said slowly, "what kind of *errand* is this exactly?"

Sally looked up at me, her dark blue eyes flashing dangerously as her fangs crested her lips in a familiar way.

"Oh nothing much..." she began, "just a little monster extermination quest."

***

I awoke the next morning with a hangover to end all hangovers. How was it that in a world brimming with magic and potions that could literally heal you from the brink of death, there was no hangover cure.

It seemed like a bit of a lapse in judgement to me. Surely an alchemist somewhere must have discovered the cure.

As I placed a warm palm against my throbbing temple, I vowed to track down that alchemist and covet the cure for myself. It could quite possibly be the single most valuable treasure in this world...

After downing a few tankards of water, courtesy of my lecherous, lycanid landlady, I set off to the guild and registered our party. Team *Dissident Flame* was officially recognised as a guild sanctioned party and was added to my adventurer card.

Kaleb Akabane
Level: 45
Rank: Iron
Class: Archer / Light Skirmisher
Party: Dissident Flame

It felt kind of nice to be part of an official team. Sure, there were only three of us and Panda was *my* familiar, but there was something comforting about someone to back me up.

Turning to leave the society behind and set off on our voyage, I heard a shrill shout from Lucy the receptionist.

"Wait!"

I looked behind me, raising an amused eyebrow at her and she smiled at me. "The director needs to see you," she said warmly, "assuming the hero of Havar has the time to spend with us lowly mortals."

Oh yeah, I thought groggily, *Lucas did say he needed a word.*

"I'll always have time for you Lucy," I said, blushing slightly as she smiled at me once again.

Maybe I am a furry...

Lucas' office was as drab as ever when I arrived in the lift, courtesy of Lucy's mana activating it for me. He sat formally behind his desk, his face told the story of his fight with the dragon, though those bruises were gradually fading.

It reminded me just how powerful the beast was, to not only be able to best Lucas, but to leave marks that he couldn't heal instantly. I shuddered at the thought of how disastrously *my* fight with the thing could have turned out.

"Kaleb," he said warmly, indicating the seat opposite him, "thank you for coming. I hear you're to head out for the continent today?"

"Yup," I said, struggling to hide the excitement in my voice, "new horizons and all that."

"Indeed, well in that case I won't take up much of your time," he said, offering me a glass of his favourite amber alcohol which I swiftly declined, the mere smell churning my stomach after the previous night. "To speak plainly, I have a quest I would like you and your team to take for me. It's on the continent so it shouldn't be out of your way."

"I don't see why not," I said with a shrug, "as long as the society is offering a good reward."

"Actually, this quest is a more personal one," he replied, looking down at his drink, "off the books strictly speaking."

Growing more intrigued by the minute I raised my eyebrows at him, indicating for him to continue.

"Do you remember when we spoke about my father?"

"You mean the super powerful bloke who shunned you and banished you to Havar?" I replied, "sounded like a bit of a prick if I recall."

"That's the one," he smiled sadly, "I recently learned of a plot to assassinate him. I believe the hitman in question is the same person who killed our king. The thing is, I'm not on the best of terms with my father as you well know. So I was hoping you could look into the matter for me.

"He lives in Castalor and I'm quite friendly with the director there. If you agree to this, all I'd ask is that you go to the city, keep your ear to the ground and touch base with the director there."

"Of course I'll help you," I said, looking him in the eyes, "you've helped me out plenty, I'd be happy to return the favour."

He nodded solemnly and though his mouth was smiling, his eyes harboured a deep sadness. There was something he wasn't telling me and the hairs on the back of my neck stood up as if warning me to probe deeper.

Before I could, the quest notification popped up on my HUD and I read it.

New Quest:
Lucas, I Am Your Father

Lucas Regina has asked you to travel to the city of Castalor in order to root out an assassin who he believes is going to kill his father.

Objectives:
Go to Castalor: 0/1
Prevent the assassination: 0/1
Speak to the local Adventure Society Director
(optional): 0/1

"There's something you're not telling me isn't there?" I asked, dismissing my HUD.

"As astute as ever," Lucas sighed, "yes there is. This quest will be putting you and your team, congratulations on that by the way, in great danger. Not only is Castalor home to some very high levelled individuals, I have reason to believe that the cult has its hand in this whole affair."

"So you're asking me, a newly minted iron ranker, to take on high level cultists who want to skin me alive, in a dangerous city. All to protect a father who was a dick to you and who is infinitely more powerful than anyone I've ever met?"

"Yes," he said, looking into his glass once more. "I understand if you don't want to do it. It's a rather unreasonable request when pu-
"

"We'll take it!" I said, banging my fist on the table and standing up.

"You will?" He began, his voice cracking slightly as he began to raise his head. "But why?"

"A friend in need is a friend indeed," I replied as I began to leave his office. "When a friend needs help you don't ask questions and you don't turn them down. You just do it."

***

I left Adventure Society feeling pretty positive about the future for the first time in a while. That warm feeling disappeared as soon as I boarded Sally's flying ship.

"How fast can this thing go?" Bell asked as Sally finished the preparations for take-off.

"Fast enough," she responded, "this is one of the only flying vessels in the Havarian port you know."

"I bet I can make it faster," the fireball mage grinned as she held both of her hands out over the rear of the ship.

Sally flashed her a fangy smile and as we took to the skies, Bell fired endless streams of fireballs behind us.

I had to hold onto the mast for dear life as the two adrenaline junkies doubled over with laughter at my precarious predicament. They laughed even harder once we reached cloud level and poor Panda spent a solid hour with his head over the side railing, polluting the waters below.

Yup, having a team definitely wasn't all it was cracked up to be.

I spent the next week training with Sally. The demonic cat woman had me running around the ship until I felt seasick. We trained in melee combat, we worked on stretching the capacity of my *Soul Shot* ability, and we worked on my quick fire and accuracy.

By the end of it, almost all of Sally's dinner plates had been destroyed and my *Newly Qualified Bowman* skill reached the 70% mark. I wondered what it would evolve into, just as I was also contemplating how my *dagger* skill would improve once it reached the percentage evolution stage.

I was nearing that milestone as the days passed and almost two weeks into our voyage, I got what I was after.

It seemed that specialised and well-thought-out melee training did wonders for my *dagger* skill. It gained a level at least once a day, though it was hard fought for. I puked, ran out of stamina constantly, and felt like every muscle fibre in my body was set alight.

However, with blood, sweat and tears, after the second week I finally hit the goal I was after.

Dagger has reached lvl 25

Would you like to evolve Dagger? Dagger will merge with Novice Apex Skirmisher in order to evolve.

Y/N

I'd been waiting for this for so long. I'd spent ages training specifically with my daggers in the jungle, I'd used them to kill plenty of monsters and people alike, but it was the specialised training with Sally that finally pushed it over the edge.

Without hesitation, I mentally asserted yes.

Newly Qualified Apex Skirmisher (Dual Wield) (0%)

The Newly Qualified Apex Skirmisher has started on his path to truly mastering small blades. What it lacks in reach, it makes up for in speed – a description that would also accurately describe your love life.

The *Newly Qualified Apex Skirmisher* will have to complete greater feats in order to evolve this skill. Upon reaching 100% proficiency, the skill will evolve.

Damage proficiency improved.
Dual wielding proficiency improved.
A minor bonus to the effect of agility will be added when a small blade is equipped.

I grinned the entire time I was reading the upgrade, even the system's attempt to shame my manhood was like water off a duck's back to me. It seemed that as I progressed, my skills began to merge together to create a more tailored skillset.

That certainly made it easier to navigate my stats sheet.

It made sense that my agility would increase marginally when I was using my daggers and that was a useful boon in melee combat.

Mostly though, I simply felt that my overall knowledge and ability with the daggers was solidified.

I wondered if any of my other skills would eventually turn into percentage-based levelling? So far it seemed that it mainly effected my passive fighting skills as my active skills all came with specific grades such as uncommon or rare.

I'd probably need to get my hands on more upgrade tokens or potions to further advance those skills, though I was feeling pretty good about my overall progress so far anyway.

As the second week of our voyage whittled away and I continued my training, I checked my map to see a little coloured line cutting through the shadowed sections.

My map acted much like the kind you would get in a game. It showed the places I'd visited in colour, whilst everywhere else was shadowed and dark.

I could see the outlines of the various continents, but nothing more than that. A small line of colour now showed, cutting through the shadows from Havar in the direction of the continent.

The map itself was a facsimile of Earth, so, with my mediocre geography skills, I knew that we were approaching the area where the Florida Keys were back in my world.

Previously our days had been extremely regimented: wake up, eat, train, eat, train, eat, drink, sleep, repeat.

It wasn't the most exciting of journeys but it certainly helped me to progress. Bell was doing well too; she was training to failure every single day with her fireball magic.

She'd spend most of the day channelling as much mana as she could into a single blast which she'd fire from the rear of the ship.

The sudden jolts of random speed made my training harder, but I gradually became surer footed from it. She was trying to increase the potency of her spells. She'd gotten the idea from my *Soul Shot* and in lieu of having a specific skill herself, she decided to train her resilience to be able to pump more mana into each shot in the hopes of being able to create her own high-powered attack.

If she managed to pull it off she'd be a force to be reckoned with considering her fireballs were area of effect attacks. Between the two of us we'd be nearly unstoppable on quests. Theoretically, Bell could take out the small fries in a single move, leaving me to deal with the more potent enemies using my more specialised attacks.

Of course, we were quite a way off from realising that goal.

As our journey took us closer towards the Florida Keys facsimile on the map, Sally began acting strangely.

She had shortened our training sessions and began spending more and more time on the bow of the ship, staring off into the distance as if she was looking for something.

After a day of this I decided to approach her and ask about it.

"What are you doing?" I asked harmlessly as I leant over the side, trying to match her eyeline.

"Scouting," she replied.

"Scouting for what?" I probed.

"Our target."

Target? I thought.

She had mentioned that she needed our help with something and that it was a monster extermination quest, but what kind of monster would we be exterminating up in the sky above a vast ocean?

"If we're about to get into a scrap, the least you could do is share the details," I huffed, still struggling to see anything through the cloud canopy that obscured the ship in all directions.

With a flick of her wrist and a sigh, a notification popped up on my HUD.

**Adventurer *Sally* would like to share a quest with you.
Do you accept?**

Y/N

Nervously I mentally asserted yes.

**New Quest:
*Kraken Skulls and Taking Names***

**The Adventure Society in Havar has received an urgent
request from a smaller branch located in Asquith Town.
The local fishermen have been unable to ply their trade
for weeks due to an unknown threat in the nearby
waters. They've requested aid to deal with this.
Society intelligence suggests that the monster in
question is both large and at least as powerful as a high-
level silver ranked guild member.**

Objectives:

Investigate the waters near Asquith Town 0/1
Kill the monster 0/1

Rewards: Adventurer Sally has set the terms of this quest as [subcontracted]. As such your reward will be the terms agreed upon by your party [Dissident Flame] and Adventurer Sally.

"I didn't know you could subcontract quests?" I murmured as I read through the notification.

"Yup, and we already agreed that you'd help me with this in return for travel to the continent," she replied, flashing a fangy smile my way.

I had the distinct feeling that we'd been played.

"What's going on kid?" Panda asked in a huff as he waddled up the stairs behind me. "I just saw the quest notification, did something happen?"

"I got one too!" Bell shouted from halfway across the vessel as she too made her way towards us.

"Oh, something happened alright!" I exclaimed, "this damn cat played us like a fiddle!"

However, my last few words were drowned out by the sound of a crashing wave as water crested the side of our ship, soaking me thoroughly.

What the hell? We're flying, how could a wave have reached us all the way up here?

That was when a slimy, black tentacle slapped onto the deck of the ship, cracking the wood with a terrifying creaking sound.

Chapter 45
Not The Time To Be *Kraken* Jokes

A slimy, black tentacle slammed onto the deck of the ship just as I was brushing my short hair out of my eyes from the salt water that lashed my skin.

CREAK.

The ship jolted and dropped down in the sky before regaining its composure and halting our untimely descent. The wooden slats on the ship's deck cracked under the pressure of the tentacle and before I had chance to summon my bow, Bell was raising her arms.

"No!" I shouted, diving from my position atop the stairs and slamming her to the ground, "if you fire that here you'll set the damned ship on fire you idiot."

She looked up at me with glistening eyes before cancelling her spell. Looking sheepish, she muttered an apology and we untangled ourselves from one another.

My head snapped in the direction of a second crack as another tentacle slapped onto the ship, wrapping around the bow where I was stood only moments ago.

For a second I was worried for Sally, who was also up there, but the silver ranker had wasted no time gawking at the slimy append-ages that assaulted our vessel.

She had leaped into the air, drawing her oversized sword from her back, and crashing down onto the first tentacle. She cleaved it in half as inky blood sprayed across the deck, creating a slip hazard worthy of a "slippery when wet" sign.

Where's Bon Jovi when you need them, I thought.

Eager to enter the fray myself, I went to draw my bow, but thought better of it and chose my daggers instead. For the same reasons for which I'd stopped Bell's fireball spell, my bow would likely cause more damage to the ship than it could take.

No Soul Shot for me, I grumbled internally, *let's see what my Newly Qualified Apex Skirmisher skill can do.*

I smiled to myself and dashed towards the second tentacle, stabbing my right-hand dagger into its soft flesh and dragging it through the skin as I bolted up the stairs.

The skin smouldered and bubbled as the acid began to take effect, it would have smelled quite nice if it wasn't for the overpowering sent of rotted fish that stung my nostrils, threatening to burn the nose hair within.

I paid it no mind and dived onto the thickest part of the tentacle, straddling it like a jockey as I stabbed at it over and over, alternating between each dagger. The putrid smell of burning, melting flesh only aided my vigour as I mercilessly attacked the strange creature.

"GWAAAAH!"

An unrecognisable roar of pain came from below the ship and the tentacle retracted, but not before squirming under my acidic onslaught.

I held on tight as it thrashed like a bucking bronco, continually stabbing at its slimy skin.

That was a mistake.

As the tentacle fought to free itself from me and the ship, I realised that it was a pure slab of muscle. Even with my strength stat as high as it currently was, I was no match for it.

The tentacle wriggled and pulled away from the ship, smashing the railing and dragging me overboard. I jumped up, ready to leap back to the ship as the tentacle crested the vessel, but I was too slow.

Just as I leaped, I was slapped by the underside of the monstrosity which wrapped around my torso like a boa constrictor. I felt a gross sucking sensation as I noticed my stamina bar begin to drain at an alarming rate.

The underside of the tentacle was filled to the brim with suckers and I was helpless to remove them. I stabbed at the outside of the appendage with my free arm and another monstrous cry threatened to burst my ear drums.

Still, the tentacle's grip never faltered and I found myself held aloft, in mid-air, too far from the ship to return even if I did break free.

"Kaleb!" I heard Panda shout from somewhere behind me, "It's a Kraken, you have to go for the main body, the tentacles will just grow back."

"Thanks for the info mate," I replied absently as I continued stabbing at my captor, "but I'm a little tied up at the moment."

A blaze of searing heat brushed past my free arm and I felt the tentacle shrivel around me. Using that distraction, I pulled myself out of the monster's grip and found myself free falling towards the main body.

Focusing, a notification popped up in my HUD, slowing down time momentarily and allowing me a precious few second to come up with a plan.

You have discovered a new monster:
Kraken

There are many legends about the *Kraken* throughout the world of Celestia, but none are so well known as the story of *Kra-Karen* who, legend says, attacked over five thousand fishing vessels demanding to speak to their managers.

Sadly, she was eventually murdered by a team of adventurers in Athenile 275. By the time they were finished, all that was left of her remains was a bottle-dyed, blonde inverted bob.

R.I.P

"This is not the time to be *Kraken* jokes!" I yelled, as time resumed and my stomach somersaulted as I fell towards the creature's ugly face.

Despite the system's nonsense, the notification had provided me with a few precious seconds with which to formulate a plan.

Kaleb: *Everyone, fire off everything you've got at the main body.*
Bell: *Will do!*
Sally: *Don't order me around, Gonads.*
Panda: *I don't have any attack magic...*
Kaleb: *I wasn't talking to you.*

Dismissing the chat function, I summoned my bow and immediately loaded one of my new arrows and pulled the draw string back.

After weeks of practicing with Sally, I knew exactly how much energy I could force into a single *Soul Shot* before the arrow would shatter. Thankfully, these new arrows could hold a lot more power than the previous ones.

I focused on pouring my soul power into the arrow. It was a similar technique to my meditation, but much more lucid, and fast.

I imagined the power in my core circulating throughout my body and draining from the tips of my fingers into the arrow. It was a tiring process as I was quite literally forcing my stamina coil to deplete.

Previously, I'd only managed a sickly, green glow from this process. My old arrows couldn't handle much power. The new arrows, however, hummed with a living hue the colour of an evergreen forest.

The green glow was brighter than I'd ever seen it, even leaking into the bow itself. It would have been pretty if it wasn't for the burning acid power that caused *Soul Shot* to take on that particular colour.

I faced down the giant creature, which stared back at me through beady, yellow eyes. Its skin was slimy, black and covered in barnacles and other ocean dwelling things.

Most notably though, was the sheer size of the beast. It was an absolute kaiju of a thing, stretching to the height of a small mountain with tentacles that could reach the clouds.

As my arrow reached the familiar capacity for soul infusion, I fired.

It rocketed away from me, shooting downwards towards my foe. There was a crack and then smoke as it tore through the kraken's face, leaving a medium sized hole in the front and blasting chunks of flesh out of the rear.

"GWAAAH!"

The kraken screamed again, its atonal voice blasting outwards in an omnidirectional shockwave that threatened to burst my eardrums.

I'd been to plenty of metal concerts in my life, and I'd never worn ear protection, but the sheer power behind the kraken's shout was like nothing I'd experienced before. It was debilitating.

The back blast from my arrow had the intended effect.

I was fired high into the air, away from the kraken and the deadly freefall that had threatened my life.

I rose up past the ship, just in time to see Bell launching a humungous fireball at the creature.

I guess her training paid off too.

She strained to keep her hands held out over the side of the vessel, as if she was actually holding the fire which spun and compacted in front of her.

It was huge and I felt my arm hair singe as I sailed past it, high into the air.

When she couldn't take the strain anymore, our fireball mage released her gigantic flame which fell slowly towards the kraken.

"Well that's a little anticlimactic," I heard Panda say, a statement which he followed up with a yelp as I crash landed onto the deck behind him, cracking the boards as a plume of dust and wood filings covered me.

I consumed a health potion and a stamina potion from my inventory screen and groggily got to my feet. Despite the magic of alchemy, I was still pretty dazed from…everything.

"Where's Sally?" I asked as I staggered to the railing.

"Following your orders…I guess," Bell replied.

Furrowing my brow, I looked over the side of the railing just in time to see the fireball slam into the screaming monster. Its flesh began to melt away, green tinged skin receding as the acid from my arrow melted skin from the inside, Bell's fireball melted it from the outside and the ocean was filling with a thick, black ink worthy of an environmental disaster.

"I didn't know *BP* operated in Celestia," I chuckled.

"How old *are* you?" Bell replied, eyes glued to the scene below, "that happened when I was a kid."

I didn't reply.

Instead, I watched, mouth agape, as I realised where Sally was. Following in the wake of the fireball was a huge sword attached to a, comparatively, tiny catonid.

Sally dove towards the kraken which was now burning and had a large hole through its face. Her oversized sword was lifted above her head, glowing with a red hue that bordered the blade's edge.

As she reached the kraken she slammed down, like she was wielding a war hammer, and cleaved the beast in two.

Tentacles flailed wildly in the air as the monster fought to the very last breath, but Sally was no slouch and she pressed even harder into the centre mass of the beast.

In less than a second, the body...head? It doesn't matter...of the monster was fully separated as jet black ink gushed out of its carcass, turning the local ocean into a gothic swimming pool.

Bell and Panda cheered, raising fist and paw alike as I grinned to myself and breathed out a sigh of relief.

I was rather pleased with how my new powers had performed. That being said, Sally's level of power was my current goal. I wanted to be able to do *that*. Her level of formidability was a sight to behold and I wanted it.

CRASH.

I flew to the side, crashing into the ship's mast as a flailing tentacle smashed into the deck of the ship once more.

"I thought it was dead?" Bell yelled in a panic as the boat groaned under the pressure.

There was a loud crack as the deck's wooden boards, which had taken quite the beating already, finally gave way and snapped. The mast I was laid against creaked and started falling to the side, just as the ship ripped in two and the stray tentacle fell through the wood and back down to its owner with a hearty splash.

The magic wind bubble that surrounded the ship and prevented us from being blown off the side popped. The ship stopped flying forwards and began to lose altitude, a fact I only realised so quickly because of the sudden feeling of somersaulting in my stomach. It felt like I was on *The Tower of Terror* ride…but ramped up a fair few notches.

I felt weightless for a moment as wind rushed around me, blowing my cheeks back and threatening to give me an unwanted botox.

We were falling, and the ship was about to crash.

Chapter 46
Shipwrecked

My stomach flopped as the sudden feeling of weightlessness enveloped me.

I tried to get to my feet, but the crushing pressure of the wind kept me stuck to the cracked decking of the ship. I needed to do something fast or we were all going to need scraping off the ocean floor.

You'd think that falling from great height into a body of water wouldn't be too bad, but at the velocity with which we were descending, the crash would be akin to hitting solid concrete.

Nope, I definitely don't want to end up as a Kaleb flavoured pancake.

A kill notification popped up in my HUD and I mentally waved it away, it could wait.

Looking around frantically, my eyes levelled on the pirate-style steering wheel above the cabins. It was worth a shot.

I crawled, or rather climbed, in that direction.

The ship had fallen into a nosedive and the ascent was no easy feat. Luckily for me, gravity almost aided my climb as the lose items on the ship's deck fell at roughly the same speed as the ship itself.

If this were a platform game I'd have had to dodge falling boxes and debris, but most of that stuff appeared to float around me as we all fell towards the ground.

My arms burned as I focused on sending the energy from my metaphorical stamina coil into my muscles. I'd always heard that you should climb with your legs, but there were barely any footholds on the ship's deck to help me.

Instead I had to force my bleeding fingers into small cracks in the wood and hoist myself up on strength alone.

Thank God for my strength stat, I thought as I pushed a little further and managed to grab onto the wrong side of the wheel.

I hoisted myself over the frame and planted my feet on the railing below me. Leaning back and pulling with all of my strength, I grabbed onto the wheel's handles and yanked.

The wheel was designed to work in a similar way to a joystick and pulling backwards on it should, theoretically, cause the ship to fly upwards.

Of course, that design relies heavily on the ship actually being intact, not to mention the need for a mana source to fuel the damned thing and keep it airborne.

Why is the only guy on the ship with zero mana the one doing this? I thought scathingly as I narrowed my eyes against the harrying wind and scanned the deck.

Bell was holding Panda under one arm and grabbing onto the railing for dear life with the other. Her body flapped around in the wind like a flag on a high pole.

I guess they're a little too tied up to help.

I continued wrestling with the ship's wheel, pulling hard and hoping against all odds that it would eventually level out.

Meanwhile, we were approaching the sea fast.

I couldn't even see the remains of the kraken anymore, instead my vision was filled with what looked like a resort on a sandy beach.

Is that Asquith Town?

I hoped not. It wouldn't look very professional for the very adventurers they'd hired to kill their kraken to crash their ship slap bang in the middle of the town.

Turning the wheel slightly, I attempted to control the direction of our descent. I wouldn't have the deaths of a town full of people on my hands.

Still yanking on the wheel, I threw it as far to the right as I could. The main mast was gone, so we had no large sail to catch the wind for quick, evasive manoeuvres. We did, however, still have the two smaller sails at the front and back of the ship.

They weren't much, but slowly the ship began to turn as it levelled out to a gentler descent.

I had no way of levelling the ship off completely, but I did manage to mitigate the nosedive and turn the vessel away from the resort town…kind of.

CRASH.

The underside of the ship hit the water with a thump and I was thrown violently into the air as wooden planks smashed beneath me.

I dropped back down with a smack and, ignoring the pain as best as I could, focused on grabbing the wheel and yanking it fully to the right once more.

The vessel began to turn in a way that reminded me of a race car drifting. It was almost as if I had performed a handbrake turn with a damned flying pirate ship.

I barely had time to contemplate how awesome that was before the side of the ship marooned itself on the beach and I was thrown from the vessel once more.

I flew through the air, over the side of the ship, and landed face first in the sand.

I felt like a chicken, and I probably looked like one too – or at least like a human who was pretending to be a chicken…which was infinitely worse.

Bracing my hands against the soft grains of warm sand, I pushed myself free, falling backwards as my head popped out of the hole it'd made.

Gasping for breath, I looked around to see a gathering crowd of worried onlookers. They kept their distance and many had mouths which hung agape as they took in the wreckage of our flying ship.

Following their gazes, I turned around to see Sally's prize possession snapped almost entirely in two. There was a large, gaping crack in the middle of the ship's hull, held together only by a thin strand of iron at the very bottom.

Bell's body hung limply over the side of the railing, her newly acquired, scarlet robes ripped and tattered as they caught on the breeze.

"I'm…alive," I heard a small, bewildered voice say to itself.

Looking in that direction I saw Panda sat on the beach a mere few meters from me. He was gawping at something he clutched in his paws.

With a pained grunt, I forced myself to my feet and stumbled towards him.

"Kaleb…" he began slowly, looking up at me with large, glistening eyes, "I broke my pipe."

I looked down to see his bamboo pipe was snapped at the middle, a piece held firmly in each paw.

"We can get you a new one buddy," I said gently, stroking the top of his head.

"You don't get it…" he sobbed, "*she* gave it to me."

I was a quite dazed from the fall but I knew enough about my familiar to understand who *she* was. In a previous life he had been summoned by a female adventurer who had died. That was about the extent of what I knew about her as he'd never really spoken about her before.

I *did* know that she meant a lot to him though, a wound that was still relatively fresh.

I sat next to him silently, rubbing the soft fur on his back whilst we gazed at the broken ship that very nearly spelled our doom.

"Do you think Bell is alright?" He asked slowly.

"The party function hasn't told me she's dead so I'm sure she's fine," I replied quietly, "probably just taking a nap."

He laughed softly as we both looked towards the unconscious fireball mage hanging limply over the side of Sally's broken ship.

I leant backwards, stretching my hand out when I felt something slimy caress my fingers.

Jumping slightly, I looked behind me to see part of a tentacle resting idly on the golden sand. It must have been the part Sally had cleaved in two when we were first attacked.

Hovering above it was a welcoming message.

Do you want to loot *Kraken*?
Y/N

Damned right I do! I thought with a grin, *Sally's not getting all the spoils for this one.*

You have received new items:
10,000 gold
X1 bottle of refined kraken ink
X1 kraken eye

"They're used in crafting," Panda said as he looked through the loot notification with me.

"I have quite a few crafting items now, but I've never met anyone who could actually use them," I replied half-heartedly.

During our week off in Havar after saving Bell, I had visited the blacksmith, a few weapons dealers and spoken to Taylor about getting something made with my crafting spoils, but none of them had the expertise to use the items I had.

"You'll be able to find a gold ranked artisan on the continent," Panda reassured me, "looted crafting components take a lot of skill to work into items."

At least that was something.

In the corner of my vision was a blinking symbol which I knew meant I had unopened notifications. It had to be the kill notification from the kraken, so I opened it.

You have assisted in the defeat of *Kraken lvl 96*

Experience has been split as you did not strike the killing blow.

Bonus experience due to level disparity.

Congratulations! You have advanced to level 46

The surprise level was certainly a welcome sight. I hadn't advanced even once during our two-week voyage; despite all the rigorous training I was doing. I quickly allocated two of my five points into perception and the rest into intelligence before the second notification popped up.

Quest Complete:
Kraken Skulls and Taking Names

The Adventure Society in Havar has received an urgent request from a smaller branch located in Asquith Town. The local fishermen have been unable to ply their trade for weeks due to an unknown threat in the nearby waters. They've requested aid to deal with this. Society intelligence suggests that the monster in question is both large and at least as powerful as a high-level silver ranked guild member.

Objectives:
Investigate the waters near Asquith Town 1/1
Kill the monster 1/1

Rewards: *Adventurer Sally has set the terms of this quest as [subcontracted]. As such your reward will be the terms agreed upon by your party [Dissident Flame] and Adventurer Sally.*

That was quick, I thought idly.

Usually a society quest could only be completed once you handed it in at the society building. This had to be different because it was subcontracted.

"*I* wonder where Sally is?" Panda asked, gazing out towards the turquoise sea.

"I wonder how long the locals are going to gawk at us before someone says something," I replied quietly, glancing over my shoulder at the growing crowd of terrified, swimsuit clad, onlookers.

With a hefty sigh, I pulled myself up from the sand and, together with Panda, we wandered back towards the wreckage that had been our home for the past few weeks.

Using the rigging, or what was left of it, I climbed aboard and approached Bell. Her body was still limp and draped over the side.

Maybe I should have checked on her sooner, I thought as I placed a hand on her back.

Her skin was warm and it trembled slightly at the touch of my cold palm. Her body rose and fell in time with her breathing and there was no sign it was laboured. Still, just to be on the safe side, I tipped her head back and carefully poured a healing potion down her gullet.

After that, I picked her up in a princess carry and, with great difficulty, climbed back down the rigging and onto the sand.

As I reached the golden, warm beach, some of the onlookers had grown backbones and were tentatively approaching our ship.

"A-are you alright?" A nervous catonid man asked, his reddish-brown tail tucked firmly between his legs.

"I think so," I replied, "our ship has seen better days though."

"Indeed," he replied, stroking his chin thoughtfully. "What exactly happened to have you arrive in such a sorry state?"

"Oh, nothing much," I said with a lazy shake of my chin, "we were just getting rid of that kraken that's been terrorising the area."

The man took a step back, narrowing his eyes. Audible gasps could be heard from among the growing group of beach goers as they listened into our conversation.

"Might I take it you're the Havarian adventurers we sent for th...AHH!" He screamed, stepping backwards and tripping over his feet as he fell to the ground with a soft thump. His arm was outstretched, pointing towards something behind me. "I-it's a m-monster!"

I turned quickly, preparing to give Bell to the man so that I could fight. Wading out of the sea was a muscular...thing, covered in black ink which dripped from its hair, clothes and the tip of the oversized blade with rested loosely over its shoulder.

"GONADS!" It roared, "WHAT THE HELL HAVE YOU DONE TO MY SHIP!"

Chapter 47
The Prophet

Sally advanced towards me; a stern expression etched onto her face. Her battle junkie eyes gleamed with murderous intent.

My dragon's eye allowed me to see a glowing red aura that covered her blackened, ink-stained body. She looked like an anime character mid power up.

That was not a good sign.

"I did everything I could Sally," I pleaded, raising my hands in surrender and taking a few tentative steps backwards. "It was the kraken!"

"Yeah Sal, it *krak-end* the ship in two," Panda laughed from my side.

Bad move.

Sally lurched forward with terrifying speed and booted Panda like a football. My fury familiar flew into the air and I half expected to see a little glimmer in the sky and hear words to effect of "blasting of again."

In lieu of that, he flew a few meters backwards and landed hard in the middle of the large group of onlookers and in the back of my mind I imagined Bell's gleeful voice yelling "goal!"

"What was that?"

"An angel?"

"Angels don't fall from the sky you berk."

"He looks like…"

"A prophet?"

"*The* prophet."

Various members of the group spoke in awe, as if Panda was some magical being that had been delivered to them from the heavens. Hadn't they just watched Sally kick him at them like a furry, screaming beach ball?

Taking any excuse to flee the ink covered catonid, I jogged towards Panda and attempted to pick him up. However, a line of swimsuit wearing locals blocked my path.

"Hold up stranger, this is *our* prophet, not yours," a muscly human man said in that typical peasant accent from literally every high fantasy movie ever made.

"Actually," I replied calmly, "I think you'll find he's my familiar. Now if you'll excuse me."

I forced my way through the crowd who were either too powerless or too taken aback to stop me.

Score one for investing in my strength stat.

In the middle of the group Panda was in the lap of a beautiful catonid woman in a golden bikini. Her hair was tied up in two perfect circles on each side of her head.

"Look Kaleb, I'm *Panda The Hut*," he said dazedly, gesturing towards the poor girl as his pupils danced in and out of focus.

"I can see that," I replied, placing my hands on my hips and shaking my head. "Are you alright?"

"Of course he's alright!" The same, obnoxious man from before said from behind me. "He's *the prophet*, and we'd be happy to see to his every need whilst you stay here. Assuming you *do* plan to stay for a while." He raised his eyebrows, gesturing to our broken ship.

"Well, it doesn't seem like we have much choice in that," I sighed.

"Perfect!" He replied clasping his hands together.

"My dear adventurers," the catonid man from earlier said as he approached from behind me with a furious Sally in tow, "perhaps I could show you to the local inn? Your friend looks in dire need of some rest and, of course, we can look after the prophet for you whilst you get settled in. I believe he would like *this* fixing?" He held out the fractured pieces of Panda's bamboo pipe and my familiar looked up at him in awe.

"You can fix it?" He said, sounding just a little bit concussed.

"Of course Prophet, we are yours to command."

"Kaleb, I'm going with these guys for a bit," Panda said, looking around the group of his adoring fans, "Miss Golden Bikini, please carry me to the closest bookstore whilst my new friend fixes my most treasured possession."

Well that was quick concussion.

"Of course Prophet, as you wish," the woman said softly.

I wasn't sold on the idea of Panda wandering off with these over-zealous idiots, but they seemed harmless enough.

Bell stirred in my arms, reminding me that she was still unconscious. I'd almost forgotten I was carrying her. She needed a place to rest and we needed to find someone who could fix Sally's ship, before she murdered me.

"Who do you worship to believe that the furball is a prophet?" Sally asked the catonid man, seemingly regaining some of her composure.

"Why, The System of course," the man replied with a wide smile, "who else?"

The System? I thought, glancing up.

***

Shortly after our arrival, Panda was whisked away as the odd locals fell over themselves to languish upon his every need and desire.

Meanwhile, the catonid man, who seemed to be a local leader of sorts, guided us through the small resort town to an inn.

Asquith Town was an odd-looking place.

The small island in which it was located was supposedly known for its golden, sandy beaches, and as such the entire town was set up as a resort for tourists.

Their entire economy was based around providing services and, to that effect, there were shops and stalls everywhere.

On the beachfront stood a magnificent, modern-looking hotel that could easily have been pulled from a holiday brochure back on Earth. Its whitewashed walls and myriad of apartments and balconies gazed out over the beautiful turquoise sea in picturesque tranquillity worthy of a postcard.

Sadly, that view was a little tarnished currently as our broken ship lay marooned on the sands. Then again, considering the blackish hue tinging the sea from the corpse of the dead kraken, perhaps the ship was a blessing in disguise.

It was behind the hotel where the town really started though. Colourful stone buildings lined the cobbled streets in perfect blocks which all led out from the local religious site.

It was a magnificent cathedral whose spires added a certain gothic flare to the otherwise cartoonish town. Stained glass windows projected a purple tranquillity to the natural light that passed through it and at the very tip was a symbol that reminded me of computer coding.

Ones and zeros combined together to create an S that took pride of place over the system worshipping residents.

The local inn reminded me of a quaint bed and breakfast, the kind found in any English seaside town. It was simple and homely with a few amenities and basic rooms.

I placed Bell delicately in a bed and left her to her slumber as Sally talked with the catonid man. We discovered his name was Clive, it suited him...though for some reason I had a sudden urge to joke about his wife, despite being pretty sure he didn't have one.

His clergyman robes of golden thread didn't project that of a married man. Though perhaps that was my Earthen bias showing through since men of the cloth often didn't wed where I came from.

"How is she?" Sally asked as I returned to the foyer.

"Sleeping," I replied, "I don't think she's injured, probably just used too much mana sending that massive fireball at the kraken."

"Probably," Sally said half-heartedly.

As the day began to wane, and with no sign of Panda, Sally retired to her room to shower off the ink which plastered her skin, and I decided to have a drink with Clive.

He led me down the cobbled streets of the quiet town to a little rooftop bar which sat in the purple-orange glow of the cathedral.

"So, tell me about why you worship the system," I said, curiosity finally getting the better of me as we sat at a small, round table on the edge of the bar.

"I'd be glad to," Clive said with a smile. "The System is the one true god of this world. That is a simple fact that many seem to overlook when choosing their patron.

"You see my boy, there are many false gods in this world. Gods such as Athena, who take the name in vain. They are powerful of course, much more so than you and I, but there can only ever be one god.

"The false gods gained their power through the benevolence of The System, as do we all to some extent. The System guides us through the holy interface and the quests which it so lovingly imparts onto us.

"If the false gods can only gain their power from another, more powerful being, then they are really no gods at all. Thus, we here in Asquith Town have chosen the righteous path of following The System, the one, true, God."

His speech sounded practiced as if he'd given it thousands of times before. I struggled to find fault with his argument, though of course the entire debate hinged entirely on semantics.

The idea of worshipping The System was amusing to me. The same system that made terrible jokes, gave uninformative notifications about the world around us and, who was unironically nicknamed, by yours truly, the passive aggressive *Pokedex*.

It was just comical.

"I see your point," I began measuredly, "I'm an atheist myself though."

Clive balked at that, furrowing his brow. His eyes seemed to flash with a strange…anger, for just a moment.

"An atheist?" He said incredulously, "how can you deny the existence of God? Do you not have a holy interface? Do you not commune with The System though his most blessed notifications?"

"Of course I do," I replied lightly, "I'm not denying the existence of the system, I mean it's right there in my head twenty-four-seven. I just don't believe there is a such thing as gods."

"Blasphemy!" He cried suddenly, causing me to jump back a little, "please, have some respect for our lord young adventurer."

He caught himself and coughed politely, covering his mouth with his fist.

"I think you've confused respect with subservience," I replied casually, "the entire concept of blasphemy is based on the idea of placing someone, or *something*, else above you in some kind of divine pecking order. Respect should be mutual, and I believe we are all born equal. Gaining power over others might make us stronger, but it doesn't make us better or more worthy of respect."

Clive scoffed, shaking his head as he considered his glass of green, glittering liquid. The juice they served here was truly divine, forgiving the pun and I was enjoying having an intellectual chat about faith and religion.

I usually tried to stay out of such things, especially politics, though I seemed to keep getting dragged into it anyway, but talks like this were harmless. No *god* was going to smite me down or anything, so what was the harm?

"If we are all born equal," Clive began in a, once again, measured and practiced tone, "then why are we so different from one another? To deny that difference in favour of forcing an agenda of equality is rather ignorant, wouldn't you say?

"For example, in a crowd at mass where the flock gather to watch the priest deliver his sermon, can you really say that the dwarf, who cannot see past the taller humans blocking his path, is equal to them? In that regard, I would say he is rather unequal by mere right of birth."

I considered his argument; I'd heard something similar before.

"I think that comes down to your definition of the word," I began, a slight smile appearing on my lips, "you're thinking in literal terms like rich versus poor, tall versus small etcetera. However, I believe that equality is simply a mutual respect and acknowledgement that no man is better than someone else, regardless of stature or luck of birth."

"And thus you have handed me victory in this battle of wits young man," Clive began triumphantly, "for The System is *no man.*"

There he goes with his fallacies again, I thought, suppressing the urge to laugh.

"That's just semantics," I replied, "but maybe we should call it there, it's getting late and I'd like to explore the town tomorrow."

"Of course," he said, bowing slightly and still wearing a triumphant smile on his face, "I think you'll find our humble town to your tastes Kaleb, and should you need anything at all, please don't hesitate to ask. I am certain that by the end of your stay here you *will* believe in The System as I do."

There was something oddly malicious in his eyes as he spoke those words, but only for a second. My dragon's eye ached slightly as a light purple hue glistened on Clive's skin during that moment and then faded away like dying embers.

Chapter 48
Those Are The Rules

I still hadn't received any word from Panda by the next morning. I woke up, caught Bell up on the previous evening's events, ate a hearty breakfast, and with literally nothing else to do, the two of us headed out.

Sally had disappeared early on, leaving me a system message to say she was handing in the quest and then spending the day patching up her broken ship.

I had no need to visit the local society branch so I left her too it.

Kaleb: *I had no idea you had crafting skills.*
Sally: *Do you really think I'd sail the high seas without the ability to fix my own vessel?*
Kaleb: *You mean high skies.*

Sally has muted the chat.

It was a beautiful, sunny day as Bell and I wandered the cobbled streets in the picturesque little town. Not long after leaving the inn we decided to stop at a small juice stand.

After the drinks I'd shared with Clive the previous night, I was craving some more of the delectable island juice they served.

"I'll take two green juices please," I said, approaching a well-dressed man wearing sunglasses and a bowler hat.

"Right away sir!" He replied chirpily, "if you'll just fill out this form, I'll get your beverages lickety-split."

"Why does he need to fill in a form to buy juice?" Bell asked, placing her hand on the cart.

"He doesn't *need* to fill out the form," the man replied, "but if he doesn't he'll be charged the blasphemer's tax and it's a hefty sum indeed. I wouldn't wish that on any man."

"How much tax are we talking here?" I asked.

"These juices cost one gold a piece," he replied as his eyes unfocused and he began counting on his fingers, "…carry the two, plus forty-eight…the total would come to a little over 2,000 gold pieces."

"2,000?!" I gasped. Snatching the piece of parchment from his hand and I reading it over quickly.

I [insert name here] do hereby declare my unwavering faith and loyalty to The System and the holy church who profess its will.

Signature:.............

"Is this a religious sign-up sheet?" I asked incredulously as Bell snatched the parchment from my hands and scanned it herself.

"Why of course," the man said happily.

Shaking my head, I dropped the sheet back onto his cart and walked away. What a farce, having to pledge to a religion just to buy a damned drink. They were starting to seem more like a cult.

One gold per drink was already a rip off, the so-called *blasphemer's tax* was just taking the piss. I hadn't even said anything blasphemous…yet.

"I bet if you had signed that form," Bell began, "they'd be trying to convince you to give away all of your worldly possessions to the church. That happened to my uncle once. The family wasn't very happy when he tried to sign over the company. Luckily, my father was the managing director at the time though so there was no legal ground for the cult to stand on."

"Yeah that…" I began absently, "wait…your family owned a company?"

"Ooh, a spell shop!" She said, completely ignoring my question, "let's browse their wares."

Taking me by the hand, she led me into a small shop filled with stacks of scrolls. I didn't even know you could buy spells; I thought all magic was skill based.

I wondered if you could use any of them without having any mana.

"Good morning!" Bell chimed as she approached the counter with a devilish grin. "What kind of fireball spells do you have."

Resisting the urge to facepalm, I moved next to her and nodded at the shopkeeper. She was a svartalf with midnight purple skin and a surprisingly friendly smile. Nothing like Wendy back in Havar.

"Blessed greetings young ones," she said, bowing slightly, "we have all kinds of fireball magic here. There are acidic fireballs, noxious fireballs and a few types of fireball enhancements, as well as the basic stuff. What exactly are you in the market for?"

"Kaleb!" Bell squealed, "they have *noxious* fireballs. I can burn people *and* poison them…all at the same time."

"That would certainly be…something," I replied dryly, "do you need to have mana to use these scrolls?" I asked the shopkeeper.

"Yes, but not very much," she replied casually, "these are single use items gifted by the system. The mana requirement is so low that even a child could cast at least one of them."

Shame I don't even have the mana pools of a child, I thought, glancing down at the shopfloor and shuffling my feet slightly.

Bell patted my back, likely in consolidation. Though it came across as a little patronising and I felt myself glaring at her. She was too busy to notice.

"I'll take all of them," Bell stated, slapping the table for effect.

"All of them?" The svartalf replied incredulously, her eyes lighting at the prospect.

"*All* of them," Bell affirmed confidently.

"That…that's great!" The woman said, "if you'll just sign here I'll start gathering them all up for you. Gavin! We're going to eat like royalty this winter!" She called happily into the back of the shop.

"Really sweetheart? That's incredible, I was worried we'd have to brave the weather to hunt again. System's blessings, what a miracle."

"I know!" She replied in a shrill, excited voice, "we might even have enough left over to pay the healer to fix Timmy's chronic mana sickness." She turned her head towards us and explained, "our boy has this terrible condition that makes him turn practically paraplegic when he casts spells. It's no way to live, but thanks to this generous purchase I can pay the healer to perform mana conversion therapy on him."

I had no idea who Gavin was, but I guessed it was the shop-keeper's husband. They both seemed ecstatic at the prospect of such a large sale, I guessed that spell scrolls weren't in high demand in such a quaint little seaside town. I wondered how Bell had saved enough gold to afford so much.

The svartalf woman passed Bell a piece of parchment and a pen and began excitedly gathering scrolls by the armful. Without looking, Bell picked up the pen and began writing her name.

Then I slapped it out of her hand.

"What was that for?" She asked in a hurt voice, rubbing her wrist.

"Read it."

"Oh for god's sake!" She exclaimed as she scanned the paper, "not again."

"Is there a problem miss?" The svartalf asked, looking worriedly up from her scroll gathering.

"She doesn't want to join your cult," I replied dryly, "she just wants to buy some scrolls."

"Cult?!" The woman replied in an unnaturally high-pitched voice. "The religion of the one true god is not a *cult* young man and I'll thank you not to persecute our religion again. Besides…it's law in this town that magic scrolls cannot be purchased by non-believers." She looked a little disheartened as she spoke.

"Why not?" Bell said, her eyes glistening.

"I'm sorry deary, but those are the rules," the shopkeeper replied sadly, refusing to look her in the eyes, "I can't sell these to you if you don't sign the form."

"Kaleb, I *really* want those scrolls." Bell said pleadingly, as if I was her keeper or something.

"I won't stop you if that's what you want," I began, "but my dragon's eye is showing some pretty weird colours around that thing so I'd be careful if I was you."

It wasn't a lie. The parchment lit up with a strange purple hue. I didn't know what that meant exactly, but I had a funny feeling that it wouldn't be anything good.

"Fine," Bell said sadly as she turned to leave the shop.

I promptly followed her, hearing the woman's downtrodden words as we left.

"Sorry Gavin, they're non-believers. I guess we'll have to go hungry again."

"Poor Timmy," he replied with a sniffle.

The rest of the day passed the same way. Everywhere we went people shoved signup sheets in our faces demanding we join their church or be subject to outrageous taxes or outright refusal of sale.

With slumped shoulders, as the sun began to set, the two of us walked drearily back towards the inn. At least *there* we could eat and sleep without selling our souls.

As we trapsed down the cobbled street, a small catonid girl skipped towards us holding a basket of glass bottles. She looked pretty chipper in her ratty pink sundress and straw hat. Her clothes looked old and well-worn but from her intoxicating smile, I barely noticed.

I wondered if my child had been a girl. I'd always kind of wanted a daughter. Of course, I'd have just been happy with any healthy kid, but secretly, all prospective parents tend to lean one way or the other.

As we passed the happy girl, I noticed her shoelace was undone. I'd been levelling my perception skill recently and was beginning to spot little things like that.

Breaking me from my reverie, the girl tripped. I instinctually activated *perception of the apex predator* and halted time for about a second to catch her.

I knelt down, looking into her adorable, wide-eyed face as she stared up at me with a trembling lip.

"Thanks mister," she said shyly, "I don't know what I'd have done if I'd have broken these bottles. I've been collecting them all day from the tourists. I should get a warm meal tonight if I sell these to the bottle bank."

My heart could have melted.

"Aren't you cute," Bell said sweetly, standing above me. "Here, this should see you fed for a few days." She flicked the girl a gold coin which she caught clumsily, holding it tightly with both hands.

"Wow, thank you so much!" She said, tail wagging behind her. "This will mean me and big brother can have a full meal each, normally we have to share."

"Don't mention it," Bell replied with a warm smile of her own.

"Please, could you tell me your names?" She asked, grasping my hand, "I want to be able to tell my brother of the kind strangers who helped me today."

"...Sure," I began, "I'm Kaleb and this is Bell."

"Ka-lib...and Bell," She sounded my name out phonetically, it must have been one she hadn't heard before. "Thank you, could you write them out for me? I'm still new to reading and writing and I'm trying to learn more words."

"Why not?" I replied lightly with a shrug.

"Yay!" She sang, summoning a piece of parchment and a pen from her inventory, "you can use this."

I took the scrunched up, off-white parchment and began writing my name.

"Kaleb no!" Bell shouted, kicking me in the ribs.

I fell sideways and looked back at her, grimacing, and then to the parchment.

I [insert name here] do hereby declare my unwavering faith and loyalty to The System and the holy church who profess its will.

Signature:..............

"God damn it!" I screamed, standing up and ripping the parchment in two, "I hate this fucking island!"

"Y-y-you tore my paper," the girl sobbed, staring up at me in terror. "You're not a kind stranger at all, you're a meany. Y-y-you...blaspheming infidel!"

With that she barged past me, covering her eyes in the crook of her elbow as she sobbed.

This time I hoped she really did trip over.

"This place is weird Kaleb," Bell said with a light shake of her head, "I hope Sally fixes the ship soon."

"So do I."

We continued our walk back to the inn feeling even more downcast than before. That was, until we both got pinged by a new message in the group chat.

Panda: *Kaleb help! S.O.S! They're trying to sacrifice me!*

"You know, I'm not even surprised at this point," I said absently to Bell before thinking out my reply.

Kaleb: *Where are you?*
Panda: *The big church thingy. These people are crazy.*
HELP!!!!!
Bell: *We're on our way, try not to die before we get there.*

Chapter 49
The Dangers of Being Worshipped

Panda had enjoyed a wonderful evening in Asquith Town. After a rocky start due to all that kraken business, he had finally met a group of people who truly appreciated him.

The system worshippers were a little odd, but they treated him so well that he hardly noticed…or cared.

After leaving the beach they had bestowed gifts upon him, mostly in the form of books. His personal storage was overflowing with every kind of literature imaginable.

From popcorn fiction to magical theory and even a few rare tomes about the history of their island. He wanted for nothing.

Having the beautiful catonid woman in the golden bikini tend to his every want was just the icing on the cake. He wasn't one for inter species relations, but he still had functioning eyes, and the prestige that came with being accompanied by a beautiful woman was certainly not something he was going to pass up.

In the evening, he was bathed by the woman and finally got to wash the stink of travel from his fur. She lathered him in a shampoo that smelled like lavender and then coated his fur in smelling oils that left a lovely sheen to his coat.

That night he slept in a king sized, four poster bed that he got all to himself. It sure beat the hell out of sharing a bed with Kaleb and his incessant snoring.

Seriously, the guy could shake the entire room with his blocked nasal passages. Panda had never heard anything like it in his life, and he'd lived for centuries.

The following day was more of the same. He was treated to a luxurious meal of freshly harvested crops and sea plants finished with the finest bamboo. Then he had been paraded around the town and people bowed wherever he went.

I could get used to this, he thought smugly as his entourage carried him on a cushioned seat fit for a king.

That all changed when he was brought to the cathedral.

The building, which had pride of place in the centre of the town, was an architectural marvel. Its large stone walls and stained-glass windows were really something to behold.

Sitting on his pillow throne in the main room, he was surrounded by bowing locals in golden robes. It was a little odd, but no more than he deserved. He was finally being recognised for his sagely wisdom.

His retinue brought him into the centre of the room and placed his throne on the ground. Miss Golden Bikini lifted him delicately under the arms and placed him on a large stone circle in the middle of the room.

It was sat on a raised platform which lifted him high above the crowd. He wasn't used to being above other people.

I could get used to this, he thought.

A catonid man stepped up from the crowd and Panda's entourage all bowed like the rest of the locals in the room.

Panda recongised him, though he didn't know his name. It was the same man who had approached Kaleb and himself just before Sally had kicked him.

That damned cat, not a respectful bone in her body, he thought, moodily remembering the indignity he'd suffered at her hands…or rather, feet.

It was like he couldn't even make jokes anymore without suffering her wrath. What was the world coming to?

The catonid man stepped in front of him and bowed deeply. He was wearing a fancy golden robe and a tall golden hat with a weird S symbol embroidered on it. The symbol seemed to be made up of ones and zeros and despite all of Panda's sagely wisdom, he did not recognise it.

"We are gathered here today to give thanks to the system for sending us one of his treasured prophets," the man said, opening his arms out as he addressed his people. "The legends tell of the one, created by the most venerable and holy system, who would come to deliver us from evil and into the guiding light of our lord.

"I do believe that Panda here is that very same prophet who we have waited for so long to meet. On this, the second eve of his blessed coming, we shall carry out the system's will and commit this great sacrifice in the name of the lord…"

Sacrifice? Panda thought, his ears perking up.

"Excuse me," he said hurriedly, interrupting the man's sermon. He stopped abruptly and turned towards Panda, bowing his head graciously. "When you say sacrifice, what do you mean exactly?"

"Why, you, of course dear prophet," the man replied quietly, "the scriptures told us of your fated coming: *and we shall lavish him with gifts upon the first day of his coming and on the second eve, his blood shall fill the holy alter so that we might partake of the system's holiest of wines.*"

"Oh ok, because when you said sacrifice I assumed...WHAT?!" Panda shouted, causing the man to take a startled step backwards, "you're going to kill me and drink my blood. Who does that?"

"Fear not dear prophet," the man replied calmly, taking a step closer, "you shall finally be allowed to fulfil your destiny, your most honourable sacrifice shall not be in vain."

At that point, Panda did the first thing he could think of and mentally messaged Kaleb and Bell. Luckily, they'd had a private group chat function since they'd formed the *Dissident Flame* party.

He just hoped they would arrive in time.

***

Bell and I sprinted through the cobbled streets of Asquith Town after receiving Panda's message. After the day we'd had I wasn't even surprised by this strange turn of events.

Oddly, the town seemed deserted.

Were they all at the cathedral? Were we going to have to fight an entire town of religious zealots?

Thinking as I ran, I opened my chat with Sally in the hopes of getting some assistance.

Kaleb: *Sally where are you? Panda is in trouble. He's at the cathedral. Meet us there.*

Sally had muted the chat earlier, I just had to hope that somehow it would get through.

"Where is everyone?" Bell puffed as she ran next to me, "this place is even creepier now, I almost miss being asked to join the church."

"If my instincts are right," I began, "we'll be joining them soon enough."

We approached the cathedral in the centre of town. An ominous, orange and purple glow shone through its stained-glass windows. The previous night I had thought that same glow to be beautiful.

"What's the plan?" Bell asked.

Without answering, I bolted for the front door and booted it open. Luckily my increased strength made it easy work.

"Oh…" Bell said as I dived through.

The door flew off its hinges and we entered the large, central room.

I might have fucked up, I thought as I gazed at the hundreds of heads which turned to look at us.

The central room was filled to the brim with zealots. The entire town was in attendance. They all wore golden robes and every eye was on us.

Clive stood in the middle of the room, ornamental knife in hand, as Panda sat on…*is that a pillow throne?*

"Sorry we're so late to the party," I said, drawing my daggers from my inventory, "and we didn't even bring a gift, where are my manners."

"Kaleb!" Panda shouted, "they want to kill me and drink my blood."

"Who does that?" Bell asked in an appalled sounding voice.

"That's what I said," he replied.

"Good evening adventurers," Clive said with a wide smile. "Please accept my most sincere apology, but this is a private gathering for followers of the system only," his eyes took on a steely glint as he added: "no atheists allowed."

"Technically I'm agnostic," Bell replied, "does that mean I can stay?"

"Oh really?" I replied calmly, "I'm so sorry for the intrusion, let me just grab my familiar and we'll gladly get out of your way."

"I'm afraid I can't allow that," Clive replied politely, despite setting his jaw as he spoke.

"Are you certain?" I asked, "because I really don't want to slaughter an entire town, but it has been a frustrating day and if you insist on forcing my hand…" I shrugged.

"I do!" Bell chimed, holding out both of her hands, a fireball forming on the tips of her fingers as a wide grin split her face.

"Kill them," Clive said almost exasperatedly as the townsfolk began to rise from their bowed positions on the floor.

"And this," I said, slashing the throat of the person closest to me, "is why I'm an atheist."

Bell unleashed her growing fireball into the right side of the cathedral with a glint in her eyes and a toothy grin on her battle junkie face.

Who hurt you? I thought as I slashed at the next attacker.

The fireball exploded in the middle of the crowd. Screams erupted from the area as the smell of burning flesh filled the room.

Concentrating on my own battle, I channelled all of my energy into my agility stat, ducking and weaving as I slashed at the zealots.

One man threw himself at me and I stabbed him in the eye. It popped, covering me with gross eyeball fluid as he screamed and threw his hands to the zone on his face which was bubbling and oozing a thick green acid.

With my upgraded *Acid Dhampir Weapons* skill I was able to steal a portion of HP from whomever I attacked. Unfortunately though, I couldn't go beyond my max. Not that I was likely to need to against these people, it was like shooting fish in a barrel.

I almost felt bad for the townsfolk. They didn't seem to have any weapons and their martial skills left much to be desired.

It felt too easy.

To my left, Bell was obviously not feeling the same way. She giggled like a schoolgirl as she threw fireball after fireball at the advancing zealots.

"Die, die, die," she chanted maniacally. They didn't even get close to her. It was an unequivocal slaughter.

My arms burned as I tore through people like butter. Their skin practically fell from their bodies as it bubbled with rotten acid burns. Despite their screams, the people kept pressing on as a forlorn hope. Did they not value their lives? It was like they had no fear of death at all.

It was unnatural and I felt like something was definitely off, but despite the ease of the fight, I still didn't have time to dwell on the niggling in the back of my head.

I didn't exactly feel bad for the people I was indiscriminately tearing through, after all, they had made their beds when they decided to kill my familiar. That being said, slaughtering an entire room of people wasn't exactly my idea of a good time.

Prior to my arrival in Celestia, the thought of killing a person was no more than a road rage daydream. Yet here I was, whimsically slicing and dicing the local clergy.

There must have been at least two hundred people inside the cathedral, but in less than a few minutes, we had slaughtered them all easily. Was this what being powerful felt like?

I felt icky and bile rose into my throat as I saw the slashed belly of the little girl who we'd ran into earlier. I didn't even realise she'd been here as I slashed my attackers indiscriminately in a battle frenzy.

I'd long gotten over my qualms with killing people in self-defence, but the ease of this battle felt…wrong. It was never this easy. Usually, I'd have nearly died at least twice by now.

And you murdered a child, my critical inner voice chastised.

Slicing through the final zealot, I reached Clive and placed my dagger against his throat.

Checkmate, I thought.

He didn't seem fearful in the slightest, staring at me with a gaze full of hatred.

"Come on Panda, we're leaving," I spat as my furry familiar hopped from his pillow throne and ran to my side.

"What about him?" He asked.

"Death is more than he deserves, let him stew in his-"

"They're not dead," Clive said matter-of-factly.

"Are you on crack?" I replied, grabbing him by the scruff of his neck with my other hand, "they're in pieces, burned alive and there's blood everywhere. In what possible way could they be alive?"

"Allow me to show you," he said with a malicious grin as he gripped my wrist and threw me backwards.

His strength was insane.

I flew across the room, landing in a pool of blood which I skidded through, crashing into the back wall. Just who was this guy?

As I looked up from my position from the floor I was blinded by a sickly purple glow which pulsed out of him. My dragon's eye must have allowed me to see it, but before it had barely been a sliver of a hue. How had he hidden such radiant power from me?

He raised his hands and his face darkened and wrinkled. Before my very eyes he seemed to turn into a grey mummy.

The purple light shot from his hands into streams which hit every corpse in the room at once.

"Rise my flock and be...*REBORN,*" he proclaimed as one by one the corpses reanimated and began to rise from their places on the floor.

"Well, shit," I said, looking on in horror, "he's a god damned necromancer."

Chapter 50
Son Of A Litch

Slowly, and with a lot of groaning, the hundreds of slaughtered townsfolk rose from the floor: a procession of the undead.

I gazed in horrified bewilderment at Clive as his grey, mummified skin shrank before my eyes, hugging his bones like it was a size too small. In contrast, his golden robes hung off him and, thanks to my dragon's eye, I could see the vibrant, sickly, purple glow which surrounded his visage.

The power radiated from him.

Focusing on his undead face, a system notification popped up in my HUD.

You have discovered a new monster:
Elder Litch

Have you ever wondered what happens when a necromancer casts a resurrection spell on himself with his dying breath?
This...this is what happens.
When a powerful caster has reached the level cap, his soul transforms, taking on the properties of his most prominent spell casting ability.
In the case of the necromancer, this can have *deadly* consequences.

**There are few known ways to permanently kill an
Elder Litch. The first is to destroy them so thoroughly
that there is no vessel to harbour the revived soul. The
second is to completely drain their mana pool before
killing them.
Neither are easy, especially at your level.
Oh and watch out, if you die your corpse will likely be
defiled...*necro*-style.**

"Well shit," I muttered as I finished reading the unusually helpful description.

Perhaps the system was feeling bad about the whole situation
considering it was all its fault. I mean, who lets their underlings get
to *this* level of unhinged?

"Kaleb!" Panda screamed as Clive moved to grab him with a
bony, grey hand. "Help!"

Without thinking I launched my dagger from across the room,
knocking the hand away. Clive shot me a deadpan glare as he wiped
a slither of blood from his grazed skin.

The shallow cut bubbled momentarily but he shrugged it off like
it was nothing. I guess the system wasn't lying about the Elder Litch
reaching the level cap.

More worryingly, my HP didn't increase as it should have from
my *acid dhampir weapons* skill. Maybe undead didn't have HP. That
was a chilling prospect.

"Go forth my flock," he began, gesticulating wildly with his skel-
etal arms, "and rid our town of these disgusting infidel."

With accenting groans, the zombie hoard began to shuffle towards us. The man closest to me, who had tried to sell me juice
earlier today, picked up his severed arm from the floor and swung
wildly at me.

I rolled to the side, narrowly avoiding the impromptu club as it
smacked the floor with a wet squelch that turned my stomach.

A fireball shot through the air, impacting the zombie and throwing him backwards. His skin alighted and the smell of burning flesh and hair stung my nostrils.

"Come on Kaleb," Bell shouted from across the room as she shot two smaller fireballs at the undead closing in on her, "get your head in the game, that one was *'armless.'*"

"Sorry dad," I muttered as I stumbled to my feet, slashing at the knee tendons of a nearby zombie as I went.

The skin fell off like rotted meat and the knee joint clinked to the floor as the undead in the golden bikini toppled over.

Meanwhile, Panda waddled and staggered through the legs of the undead as he made his way towards me. They completely ignored him, but Clive did not.

The angry son of a litch barged his way through his undead minions, launching them like a bull in a china shop as he chased after the screaming familiar.

"Get back here!" he yelled, "the sacrifice must be made tonight, so it has been written, so it shall be done."

Clive was getting worryingly close to Panda, though the little bear was doing well to avoid his bony clutches. I slashed at two more undead, one of them lost his head to my blade…literally.

My attacks didn't stop them for long though. The decapitated undead dropped to his knees searching for his head in the way that Velma might search for her glasses in a *Scooby Doo* episode. It would have been comical if we weren't fighting for our lives.

I forced my way through the zombies who were thankfully rather weak and found myself face to face with Clive. Panda ran through my legs and stepped behind me, using me as a shield to block his pursuer.

"Kaleb, what do I do?" He yelled in a panicked voice.

"Get to Bell and get the hell out of here, I'll hold them off," I replied without looking away from the cold, dead eyes of Clive the Elder Litch.

"So boy," Clive spat at me as our eyes remained locked, "do you still deny the power of the almighty?"

"I never denied the system's power," I replied as we began slowly circling each other, the undead hoard crowding in all around to form a circle of rotting, charred or acid burned flesh. "I just don't think it's a god."

"You close your eyes to the divine," he yelled, lifting his arms dramatically. "I have been gifted eternal life, I am a master of death, able to pass on my blessing to my flock. If that is not divine then I don't know what is."

"You look like my Grandad's ball sack, and he's been dead for twenty years," I replied calmly, still keeping my eyes glued to him. "Not to mention that these moving cadavers are not alive, they're just flesh puppets you control with your magic. There's nothing living within them anymore, they can't even speak."

"Speech is not indicative of life you closed minded fool!" Clive shouted, seemingly ignoring my insult, "animals do not speak yet they are undoubtably alive."

"Animals can't pick up their own severed heads and reattach them to their rotted neck flesh!" I shouted, dashing forward and swiping with my dagger.

Clive dodged nimbly and swatted my hand away with ease as I stumbled forward into the front row of the hoard. I was shoved hard and found myself back in the ring, still facing Clive.

"So what if they lack beauty?" Clive responded, "those with leprosy are still alive and their flesh too, rots and looks unpleasant. Your bigotry is showing my dear boy."

"Why are you even trying to convince me of any of this?" I asked incredulously.

Of course, I knew why *I* was humouring *him*. Whilst this ridiculous conversation was going on, Panda and Bell would have time to escape. I just needed to think of a way to get out of here myself.

"I'm a theologist, it's what we do," the litch shrugged matter-of-factly, "but if you'd rather get this over with, I can just as easily kill you."

My dragon's eye burned in my eye socket as Clive released a powerful wave of energy. Bright, violet light fired out of his body, covering him in a deep purple hue as it settled. He grinned a toothy smile and raised his fists like a boxer.

Looking at me through his raised hands, he winked and held out of a single finger, motioning me to come hither.

I guess it's go time, I thought.

Dismissing my dagger, I summoned my bow and nocked an arrow. I had gotten pretty quick at channelling a *soul shot* and hoped to catch him off guard with a powerful attack.

If he truly was a gold ranker then I had no chance of beating him one on one. The best I could hope for was a good distraction so I could escape and regroup with the others.

As I pulled back the drawstring and began adding green soul energy into the arrow, Clive disappeared.

"Too slow," he said jovially as I felt a powerful gust of wind followed by a pain in my abdomen so sudden that it caused my eyes to black out for a moment.

I flew up towards the ceiling and Clive jumped up with me.

"Just so you know, I'm a mage, and hand to hand combat isn't even my strong suit," he said before swatting at my upper back like a one might bounce a basketball.

I was hurled back to the ground, smashing into the stone floor as chunks of grey pieces broke from the ground below me and covered me in a thin film of dust.

The wind was knocked from my lungs and my health bar dropped to less than a quarter. I barely had time to slam on a HP potion before I was launched through the air once again by a devastating kick.

How was he so fast? I didn't even have time to think between his pummelling. Was this the power of a gold ranker? I didn't stand a chance. I needed to get out of the cathedral, and fast, before he killed me.

"How is it that one so weak dares to question the divine?" Clive called out, spittle flying from his tight lips.

His aura pulsed out and somehow I knew that his next attack would be the end of me if I didn't act fast. Jumping up from the floor I ran as fast as I could towards the entrance of the cathedral and resummoned my one remaining dagger.

Clive's eyes locked onto me and the purple hue emanating from his body shone brighter and brighter. I had an idea, but I wasn't sure it was something I wanted to do.

Either way, as Clive dropped into a sprinter's pose, I knew that it was the only chance I had to survive this blow.

Dipping into my inventory, I withdrew an item I'd received a little while ago and shoved it into my mouth.

Cursed Mystery Seed:
This seed is a consumable item with a one-time use. You probably shouldn't use it unless you're in a dire straits. It *might* save your life, but there *will* be a cost.

The taste was revolting.

Mango…watermelon and the smell of a week-old corpse all filled my mouth in a circling, fragrant taste that had me swallowing hard and trying not to vomit.

Clive charged, and the world slowed down before me as a notification popped up in my HUD.

You have consumed an item:
Cursed Mystery Seed.

For the next ten seconds your health pool will double
and you will be nearly impervious to mana-based
attacks.
In return, you will be unable to heal yourself in any
way for an hour after the effects wear off.

Oh fuck, I thought as I read the description.

Ten seconds was not a very long time, but an hour of no healing, mid battle, well that could be deadly.

Mid thought, time resumed, Clive struck me and before I even had the chance to gasp I was flying through the air.

You have been struck by a Jade level magical attack
Magical damage negated

My health dropped significantly, but thanks to the seed's abilities I was still breathing and still had more than my usual maximum HP.

I didn't know what a jade level magical attack was, but as I saw the cathedral explode behind me as I continued to soar through the open doors and into the street, I was pretty damn relieved that I'd been able to negate it.

I landed like a skipping stone, bouncing three times along the rough cobbled street before coming to an abrupt halt.

Rolling onto my front, I coughed so hard I thought I was about to lose a lung, before looking up at a bewildered Panda.

"How in the world did you escape?" He asked, "we were just about to come back to get you."

"It's a good job you didn't," I coughed, rising shakily to my feet, "that litch is pissed."

"We managed to get through to Sally," Panda cut in urgently, "she's almost got the ship in sailing condition but we'll have to hurry."

"She hates sailing," I replied dumbly.

BOOM.

Panda and I both turned in the direction of the cathedral. Its beautiful stone walls crumbled inwards as fire and purple aura exploded outwards.

Zombies poured out, running frantically in our general direction. Floating ominously above them was Clive.

"You won't leave this island alive!" He screamed, "the prophet will be sacrificed...tonight!"

Undead groaned avidly as they ran with reckless abandon through the cobbled streets.

WARNING
Cursed Mystery Seed effects have ended. You will be unable to heal for one hour.

Chapter 51
Escape From Zombie Island

"I take it this is the part where we run?" Panda asked, raising his arms like a toddler wanting a piggyback ride.

"It is," I replied, lifting him up and placing him on my back.

His furry arms wrapped around my neck and, with one last glance in the direction of the swarming hoard, I ran for my life.

Cobbles were not the easiest surface to run on and, if not for my stats taking the strain, I'd likely have twisted my ankle after a few sprinting steps.

As luck would have it, my agility and strength skills seemed to kick in. My running speed would have been world record breaking back on Earth as my legs pounded the floor in a practiced rhythm. My strides were long and I was incredibly sure footed.

All of that was extremely helpful, but the zombies had the advantage.

With no brain power to tell them they were tired, or in pain, or, in the case of one undead, severely leg disabled, they sprinted with wild and reckless abandon.

The sound of hundreds of decrepit, but speedy, zombies chasing after me was horrifying. The incessant groaning did not help.

Yet still, I ran as fast as my legs would carry me in the direction of the beach.

Without warning, a new notification filled my vision:

New Quest:
Escape From Zombie Island

No this is not a *Scooby Doo* **episode; this is real life. So
you can either run or die.**

Objectives:
Escape Asquith Town 0/1
Reward: *Continuing to live.*

Thankful that it was a short quest message, I mentally swatted it
off screen and dove into the chat function.

Kaleb: *Sally, how long until the ship can sail?*
This chat has been muted by: *Sally.*

"God damn it!" I yelled, pumping my arms as I deftly turned a
corner.

SPLAT.

The first wave of undead on my tail didn't react in time and
smashed into the brick walls of the pub whose alley I'd just taken.

"How is that one still running?" Panda shouted in my ear, "its
foot is facing backwards."

I couldn't risk looking behind me, but from what I'd seen in the
cathedral, I was not surprised by this.

"Panda, get Sally to unmute me," I huffed as my lungs fought
against me with every step.

Maybe I should add some more cardio training into my regimen. I
thought for a short moment before remembering how much I hated
cardio. Leg day? No thanks.

"Done," Panda said as I rounded yet another corner and made a
beeline for the large hotel which marked the start of the beach.

Sally: *anchors up in five, how close are you?*
Kaleb: *Coming up on the hotel now, we should just make it. Is Bell with you? Also, never mute me again.*
Sally: *No?*

Where the hell was she? I had assumed that she'd gone on ahead when I ran into Panda alone outside the cathedral, but now I was worried that we'd somehow left her behind.

"Where's Bell?" I asked Panda through heavy breaths as the stomping zombies continued to chase me like a dog with a tennis ball.

Before he could reply, a volley of fireballs lit up the evening sky above me, crashing behind me and causing a deafening sound like a howitzer.

"Never mind," I said.

The heat seared my back as I was pelted with bits of flesh and viscera from the chasing zombies. Looking around wildly, I managed to spot a tiny silhouette on top of the large hotel complex.

"Fire in the hole!" She shouted, raising her palms as a dozen little fireballs manifested in the air.

Throwing her hands down in a mockery of prayer, the fireballs released and catapulted through the air throwing dust, cobbles and...*was that a ribcage?* Over my head and into the street in front of me.

Whatever her plan had been, it seemed to be working at buying me a precious few seconds to get ahead of the closing hoard.

"When did she learn to do that?" I asked as I rounded the hotel's outer wall and headed onto the beach.

If I thought running on cobbles was difficult, the beach was hell mode. With every movement my feet sunk into the sand. It was slippery, it was slow, and mostly, it caused my quads to burn like they'd just received a heavy dose of Bell's fireballs.

398

Kaleb: *Thanks for the covering fire, now get down from there and meet us at the ship. It's about to leave and I for one don't wanna be stranded on zombie island when we miss it.*

Bell: *As luck would have it, I just unlocked the perfect skill for that. See you on board.*

Kaleb: *Unlocked? Where are all these new skills coming from?*

Bell: *Remember the shop with all the magic scrolls?*

Kaleb: *Yes...*

Bell: *I may have looted them all.*

Why didn't I think of that? I thought, *damn how I wish I had mana!*

My thoughts were sadly cut short.

Seconds after closing the chat, a brilliant fire erupted from the roof of the building and something with the visage of a phoenix glided over my head and towards the ship.

"Was that Bell?" I asked incredulously as I enviously watched the beautiful display of gliding fire.

"Huh," Panda said from my back, "she kinda reminds me of that *Molotov Cockatiel* we saw that time."

I didn't have time to contemplate that as a loud groaning started to tickle my left ear.

Turning slightly, I saw the culprit.

It was the reanimated corpse of the little girl I'd tried to help earlier on in the day. Her guts were hanging out and she was covered with thick, golden sand that clung to congealed blood covering her tiny torso.

"Ew, sand zombie!" Panda screamed, patting me on the top of my head urgently. "Kill it! Kill it now!"

Had I stopped to contemplate the fuckery that was slaughtering a child only to desecrate her corpse with my acid knife, I might have hesitated.

However, when one sees a sand zombie, one does not question. They slash.

With barely a thought, I summoned my dagger into my left hand and slashed out at the undead child. The dagger sliced through her small frame like butter as it fell in two. The pair of legs continued chasing me and the torso began to crawl after them, though at a much slower pace.

Clive's powers are messed up, I thought, wanting to shake my head but preventing myself from doing so for fear of forcing myself off balance.

The ship lay ahead, no longer on its side.

It sat in the water just offshore; its sails were up and the large crack that had almost split the vessel in two was now a patchwork of mismatched woods and hurriedly welded metal.

It wasn't the nicest looking ship I'd ever seen. Hell, it didn't even look fit to sail, but, in that moment, it may as well have been a *Ferrari.*

I *needed* to get on that ship.

Mustering the last of the power I had left, I sprinted into the water, splashing like a child at a holiday camp. For a split second I'd wondered if I could run across the water like some kind of ninja, sadly I couldn't.

However, I could wade through it faster than a normal human.

Salty water sprayed my face, half choking me as I forced myself to breathe through it.

"Come on Gonads!" Sally shouted from up on the deck, "if you don't hurry up I'm leaving without you."

"Hoist the anchor!" I screamed back.

"Ay, matey!" Panda growled from my back.

I jumped out of the water and grabbed the rigging. My stamina was running low and I hammered on a potion to fix that.

Luckily, I hadn't sustained any damage during the chase. After eating the seed I was unable to heal for an hour, though that was now more like fifty minutes.

Thankfully, stamina potions were not blocked. Though I wouldn't be able to take another for at least an hour anyway due to the restrictions on effective potion consumption in this screwed up world.

The potion rejuvenated my muscles. I felt fresh all of a sudden and began climbing with renewed vigour as the ship began to move with the wind.

Something grabbed my leg and I looked down to see a fat zombie trying to drag me down.

How had it kept up during the chase? Surely a fat zombie would be slower than an athletic zombie?

Either way, I kicked it in the face and its head fell off. I was fortunate that most of the zombies had suffered either acid or fire damage when they originally died, otherwise, fighting a fresh cadaver would likely have been much more challenging.

As I reached the top, Sally grabbed my forearm with her meaty hand and hoisted me on board.

We had made it!

"Hey Kaleb," Bell said, nudging me in the ribs as I turned to watch the hoard of zombies diving into the sea in a vain attempt to follow us. "what's a pirate's favourite letter?"

"R?" I asked absent mindedly as I finally got to catch my breath from our mad sprint through the town.

"No," she replied with a terrible pirate accent, "you would think it'd be the R, but a pirates first love will always be the C."

Zoning out her chattering, as I often found myself doing these days, I reopened the quest I'd received.

There was no way the undead could catch us now, the ship was picking up a head wind and soon we'd be way too far out to sea for them to reach us.

The quest hadn't changed at all.

Objectives:
Escape Asquith Town 0/1

"That's odd," I mumbled to myself, "usually there's no lag with quest completion."

That was when a sickeningly bright green star rose from behind the hotel, casting an eerie light on the dark night.

Clive.

"You will not escape me!" He said, his voice blasting out over the cold night air like he was using a megaphone.

That has to be a skill, I thought.

"Be...REBORN!" He shouted and the green light blasted from him, disappearing into the ocean ahead of us.

"What's he planning to do?" Bell asked, folding her arms, "attack us with fish?"

A huge wave crashed from the front of the ship, causing me to lose my footing as our vessel bobbed and swayed violently in the choppy ocean.

As the waves died down, a huge, beat-up monster appeared blocking our escape.

"Not again," I groaned, as a kraken with a missing tentacle and rotted flesh bore down on us.

Chapter 52
Puny Litch

"This is so unfair," Bell grumbled as she pushed her arms out to steady herself against the violent waves. "We already killed this thing once, why should we have to do it again?"

"Kraken sighted off the forward bow cap'in," Panda shouted as he hung off the railing.

"Enough with the goddamned pirate jokes already!" Sally shouted from her position behind the wheel.

She spun it wildly and I braced myself as the ship turned at a sharp angle, narrowly avoiding the kraken's lashing tentacles.

"Sink the ship!" Clive's voice rang out across the air, "but don't kill the prophet, we need him alive!"

"This guy is seriously starting to piss me off!" I shouted to be heard above the roaring waves and the obnoxious zealot.

Summoning my bow I nocked and arrow and charged a full powered *soul shot*. Thanks to my upgraded arrows, I could add even more soul power into each shot now, though it would badly drain my stamina bar.

With a crack, the arrow loosed from my bow, splitting an oncoming wave in two. It sliced through one, two, three tentacles before impacting the front of the kraken with a shockwave that forced the ship backwards at an alarming angle.

GWAAAG.

The kraken screamed a high-pitched cry as the arrow blasted a nasty-looking hole through its partially rotted skin.

Acid dripped from the wound in thick green globs of congealed blood and viscera as the skin began to melt from the inside…*again*.

"Why did it scream?" Bell asked, "I didn't think zombies felt pain."

"They don't," replied Panda calmly, "but they do feel frustration."

Despite the gaping wound and severed tentacles, the kraken did not tarry. It still had four remaining limbs with which to attack us and it used all of them to slap the deck of the ship simultaneously.

I dived to the side, taking Bell with me, as slimy, rotting flesh began to wrap around our newly repaired ship.

Sally is not going to be happy.

"Motherfucker!" She growled from her position at the wheel.

I knew it.

The catonid jumped from her position above the rest of us, flipping as she unsheathed her huge, black sword. With a double handed grip she came crashing down on the main body of the kraken, slicing it almost entirely in two.

"At least she had enough sense not to do that on the deck tentacles," Panda said as the ship rocked with the force of vicious waves.

Almost out of stamina, I did the best I could and summoned my one remaining dagger. With as much strength as I could muster, I stabbed the acidic weapon into the closest tentacle and ran to the other side of the ship, dragging the blade through the partially rotted skin.

The bubbling acid left in my wake made short work of the few remaining muscle fibres and the tentacle involuntarily unwound itself from the hull.

One down, three to go, I thought.

My stamina was almost completely drained, but we were slowly forcing the kraken back into the ocean. It might not have been killable, but it couldn't heal either. The only way to get rid of it was through dismemberment.

Bell sprang into action, pulling out one of her newly pilfered scrolls.

"Fire touch," she said as she began dancing around the two remaining tentacles and...*is she high fiving them?*

Each place she patted left a burning handprint emblazoned on the peeling, putrid flesh. Within moments the skin began to burn away like cigarette paper until there was nothing but large piles of ash littering the ship.

With the ship's hull secured, I turned to watch as Sally began a speedy flash of constant sword strokes which shredded the main body.

She'd slice it from one angle, then jump off the body to come down at another angle for a second cut. It was like a special move in a *Final Fantasy* game. It was epic. She repeated that many times in quick succession as black and red aura emanated from her muscular body.

It wasn't as strong or blindingly bright as Clive's aura, but she was certainly a force to be reckoned with in her own right.

With a final slash, the catonid landed deftly back on the ship covered in black ink and smelling like a fish market as she cooly sheathed her sword. Pieces of the kraken pebble dashed into the water behind her as the guts and viscera that clung to her violet hair dripped onto the deck with a gross wet sound.

"Are we safe now?" Panda asked, appearing from behind a wooden crate and drenched from head to toe, "are we safe?"

"There is only one path to salvation for you, dear prophet," Clive's voice echoed all around us.

"This guy just doesn't know when to quit does he?" Bell said exasperatedly.

"Be careful guys," I warned, looking around for signs of the necromancer's location. "He's hit the level cap."

"And here we are, all warn down from fighting his monstrosities," Sally groaned, unsheathing up her sword once more with a weary look to her reddened face.

I felt something in the air and looked up in time to see the decrepit, grey elder litch land gracefully on the deck of our ship. His skin wrapped tightly around his skeleton and his golden robes looked freshly laundered as they hung loosely from his body.

"I told you that you wouldn't escape from me," he said, his voice filling the back of my mind as he spoke. "The sacrifice must be made. The prophet will deliver us from evil and into the arms of our lord."

"You are certifiably insane," I replied, but in the back of my mind I knew we had no chance of beating this guy. He was just too powerful and we were all low on...everything.

"Into the arms of your lord?" Bell repeated slowly, "I think this guy just wants a hug, who hurt you?"

"He has a face even a mother wouldn't love," Sally added, "no wonder he's so starved of human contact, he's probably never had any."

"ENOUGH!" Clive shouted, throwing his left arm out to the side regally. "I shall listen to this folly no longer."

My dragon's eye reacted quicker than my mind, forcing my body to automatically dive to the ground. I pulled out my trump card *scales of the apex predator* which summoned dragon scale armour across my body, but I was too slow.

An ephemeral line of pure, purple aura cut through the air like a sharpened blade. The skin on my stomach ripped open and my scales dropped to the ground like little pellets as my health dropped instantly into the red.

He must have been toying with me earlier, I thought as my body crumpled to the ground.

With no way to heal, I'd be a goner if he attacked again. Hell, I might be a goner anyway. Without meditation or potions, it was very possible that I was going to bleed out.

With great effort, I managed to move my head to the side where I saw Bell lying face down in a pool of blood. Sally crouched next to her, her sword had been sliced in two and she bore a deep cut across her chest.

Her cat-like reflexes must have allowed her to attempt to block, but even with her strength it was no use.

We were all going to die.

Son of a litch.

I had to think of something. In my weakened state I doubted that even my soul power could kill this guy, at least not without ending me in the process.

There had to be another way. I was not going to die like this. Not here, not at the hands of…*that.*

"See?" Clive said, spreading his arms out wide. "I have power gifted to me by the system. All shall prostate themselves before our mighty lord…"

That was when it came to me. I did have one more ace up my sleeve, though its effects could be catastrophic.

It's not like I have much of a choice, I thought.

Jumping into my inventory, I equipped the chaos seed.

Chaos Seed
Summon a chaos demon for 60 seconds.

Results may vary.

It happened instantly.

The moment the seed left my inventory a solid beam of blackness, darker than the abyss, shot upwards in a cylinder just in front of me, cutting off Clive's sermon.

"What did you do?" Sally gasped, her dark blue eyes casting a horrified look at me.

The cylinder of darkness expanded until the entire ship was shaded. With the ability granted to me from my dragon's eye, I was almost blinded from the sheer power that radiated from the beam.

"You cut him off mid villain monologue," Bell said and then coughed as something, probably blood, splattered my leg.

"I skipped the cutscene," I replied with a shrug, not that she'd be able to see it in the darkness.

With a flash, the black cylinder disappeared leaving a hole in the dark grey clouds that had covered the sky. The night was dark, lit only by the stars above. All the wind from the sea had vanished and the waters were eerily calm.

I looked around, but there didn't seem to be anything there. Clive stared upwards at something, *the sky?* All I saw was darkness and stars.

Wasn't the seed supposed to summon a demon?

"H-how?" Clive stuttered, stumbling backwards and falling onto the deck. "How are *you* here?"

I looked around, still failing to see anything other than the pitch-black night. Was my demon invisible?

"Necromancer!" A deep, rumbling voice declared, shaking the ship as pieces of wood chipped from the decking due to the sheer power of the voice. "How dare you steal from me!"

"I don't get it," I said, shaking my head.

"Look…up," Sally replied, the terror in her voice apparent. I'd never heard her speak so shakily before.

I cast my gaze upwards once again but there was only darkness, and stars. Why couldn't I see it?

"There's nothing there, it's just the sky," I said.

"That's not the sky…" Sally breathed.

I focused on the starry sky and, to my surprise, a notification appeared.

You have discovered a demon lord:
Asmodeus

Asmodeus **is the demon of lust, and no that doesn't**
mean he spends his night scouring *Pornhub*.
His lust is far more unquenchable than that. He desires
all things. In his eyes, everything that ever was, is or
will be belongs to him.
He's a bit of a prick to be honest.
Best not piss him off though, he's pretty strong.

I read through the notification and that was when it dawned on me.

I wasn't staring at the starry sky.

No, I was staring at a demon's massive caboose.

"The souls of the dead are rightfully mine!" Asmodeus proclaimed, causing the mast to crack as his powerful voice boomed.

He's going to destroy the ship…with his voice.

"I-I'm sorry," Clive stuttered feebly, "I was using the power the system gifted me-"

"Fuck the system!" He said and Clive rolled backwards as if caught in a strong gale, "there are none more powerful than I. None!"

"You dare to blaspheme against our mighty lord!" Clive shouted, forgetting his stutter as his zealous tendencies took over, "he who grants life, power and the abilities which we all-"

Before he could finish, a hand the size of a building reached down and the *sky* above me flexed. It seemed the stars were just a feature of the demon's skin as his hand was also littered with tiny glowing lights.

Asmodeus plucked Clive from the ship's deck, by his head, with his thumb and forefinger. Then he moved his middle finger back and flicked the necromancer far away. All that could be heard was a thin scream in the distance as specks of grey blood splashed the demon's massive hand.

"Puny litch," he said in a satisfied boom before reaching across to wipe his hand on the main sail. It looked like a tissue next to his meaty palm.

I stared at his gargantuan figure.

Unable to move, I absently wondered what would happen next. The notification on the chaos seed said that he would only manifest for sixty seconds, but it was hard to get a good grasp of time, all things considered.

To the side of me Bell groaned lightly, seemingly flickering in and out of consciousness, and Sally stared dumbstruck at the behemoth I'd unwittingly unleashed upon us.

"Now then," Asmodeus said, though I still couldn't see his face, "which one of you had the audacity to summon me?"

I stared blankly at the demon's behind as, almost in unison, Panda, Sally and even the semi-conscious Bell pointed at me.

Thanks guys, great teamwork, I thought, *so loyal...*

"You?" Asmodeus bellowed, "a mere phase three, have the audacity to summon one such as I?"

"We needed help with the litch," I answered, unsure of what else to say.

"Well I suppose you got it," he replied, seeming to consider his words for a moment before continuing. "I guess that means your soul is mine now."

My blood ran cold.

The sheer flippancy of his words sent a shiver down my spine. I'd just seen him flick Clive god knows how far away. It was easy for him. I didn't know power that vast even existed in this world. He must have been stronger than the self-proclaimed gods, and those guys were insanely strong from what I'd heard.

If he wanted my soul, there was nothing I could do to stop him.

His building sized palm moved towards me at an odd angle and the same thumb and forefinger that had vanquished our enemy, reached for my tiny, mortal body.

POOF.

Just like that, he disappeared and the grey clouds that had covered our ship reappeared over them as if nothing had happened.

The timer must have run out.

I breathed out as sweat dripped from the tip of my nose.

"Well that was a close one," Panda said flippantly, "might wanna read the terms and conditions before summoning a demon lord next time though, those guys can be real asshats."

I tried to stand but was forced back down as my gut wound began to reopen. The blood must have congealed.

I guess I'm staying put for a while.

That was when I noticed something sitting off to the side of me.

A small, glimmering egg. It was jet black with tiny little lights twinkling around it.

Reaching out unsteadily, I picked it up.

Chapter 53
Casing Castalor (Feat. Jack The Reaper)

I picked up the egg that laid next to my limp body. It felt warm to the touch, though its scales were sharp and oddly uncomfortable to hold.

Where had it come from?

I focused on it, but no notification came to me. It was as if it was some kind of anomaly that even the system wasn't aware of. Either that or the system was just being an asshole and refusing to tell me about it.

Something about the egg seemed to draw me in, I wanted it and I felt like, somehow, it wanted me as well.

"That was a close one," Sally said through staggered breaths. "Is everyone alive?"

"I'm fine," Panda said with an air of disbelief, "I don't have a scratch on me."

"I can't heal," I said feebly, my dry throat croaking out the words.

"Why?" Sally and Panda asked in unison.

"I used an item to temporarily increase my HP back at the cathedral," I replied, "the backlash from it is that I can't heal for an hour after using it. My health is in the red and I took a pretty nasty hit from Clive's purple force slash thing."

"A minor setback," Sally said nonchalantly, "we're safe now, so as long as you don't die before that timer runs out you can heal as normal then. Bell, how are you doing?"

The fire mage replied with a snore.

I guess she's alright then, I thought.

Somehow, we'd all survived Asquith Town. It felt like a Christmas Miracle.

I longed to know what would hatch from the egg, but first I'd need to rest.

***

Jack sat idly at a small café in Castalor, the largest trade city on the central continent.

He had been ordered to meet with an important man there on behalf of his god, Diako, who naturally, popped in and out of his mind to keep tabs on him.

…He is one of our most valued clients Jack, the god whispered into The Reaper's mind, *I cannot stress how important it is to keep up appearances around him.*

"Which is why I can't understand why you're sending me," Jack complained, whispering into his drink so as not to draw attention. "I'm great at killing people through a scope, I can do CQB in a pinch, but all this sneaky beaky stuff isn't really my strong suit."

Missions like these are what your class was made for and you know it. You ned to stop dwelling on your past life and start embracing your new one. Now go and fulfil your mission.

With a sigh, Jack rose from his seat at the outdoor table, dropping a single gold piece for his drink, and walked the busy streets of Castalor.

The city was quite the culture shock for the Earthen man as so much of it seemed mismatched to him. Amidst the glass skyscrapers which dominated the skyline, there were also boardwalks and clay buildings.

In the centre of town was a middle eastern bazar, which certainly was bizarre in that it was located in an otherwise western setting. He'd also heard that it rained blood here, though he hadn't seen a single drop so far.

Off to the side of the bazar was Jack's target.

It was a large palace compound with multiple roofs made of ostentatious golden plated domes that reminded him of the Taj Mahal. Sitting in the centre of the domed palace building was a tower which seemed to crest even the clouds.

It was shaped like a sail from one of those windsurfing boards that attractive assholes rode through the waters of small island nations. That conjured some bad memories for Jack as he remembered catching his second wife in bed with one of those exact same assholes.

He'd spent nearly three weeks in a foreign prison for what he'd done to that ponytail having asshole before the agency had him released. Naturally, his leave privileges were revoked for quite some time after *that* fiasco.

His objective lay at the very top of the tower, the penthouse suite of some rich dude who held power over the city.

Supposedly this guy had far surpassed the level cap, but thankfully, this wasn't an assassination mission.

Jack had chosen his café wisely as it gave him a clear line of sight to the palace gate and the guards who controlled it.

Having memorised their patrol patterns and mannerisms already, what came next should have been child's play.

The Reaper activated one of his skills.

Faceless Man:

With this ability you can change your face, voice and clothing to an exact copy of someone you have seen before.
This is an illusion skill and the glamour will fail should someone grow too suspicious of you whilst the skill is active.
This is a high-cost mana skill.

Jack had tested this skill numerous times before and had learnt that he needed to copy his victim's mannerisms and way of talking if he wanted to blend in.

Thankfully, the glamour also changed his voice to match theirs as long as he had heard it. Though it did not change *how* he spoke. Copying a person's speech was harder than he had expected, though through diligent practice, he was getting quite good at it.

The guard he had studied was about to change shifts with the next guard on the rotation and, as expected, when he did, he walked happily into town to grab a drink.

Jack had been staking out the palace for a few days now and had memorised the guards schedule, so he was confident that his plan would go smoothly.

Stepping out from the crowd he was hidden in; he activated *faceless man* and strode towards the new guard who had taken over the watch.

In an instant he'd traded his trench coat for a silver breast plate, a red headband and a red wrap which hung nicely around his waist.

It was an odd mix of medieval European soldier's attire and middle eastern robes.

"Jiriyah," the bearded guard who had taken over from Jack's mark said. "What are you doing, your shift is over?"

"Apologies, I left my coin purse in the guard house," Jack replied in Jiriyah's voice, "I'll only be a minute."

"Well hurry up," the guard said moodily, "the lieutenant will have both of our heads if he finds us breaking protocol like this. You know you're not allowed inside the premises when you're off duty."

"I'll only be a minute," Jack smiled, "thanks Mark."

He brushed passed his pretend colleague quickly and made a beeline towards the guard house. As soon as Mark turned back to watch the civilians outside the gate, Jack changed directions and headed through the central courtyard.

A few nights ago he had taken up a vantage point on the roof of the nearby church of Athena. It gave him brilliant sight lines into the interior of the palace compound and, thanks to his rifle's scope, he'd been able to see and then memorise the layout.

Jiriyah walked towards the base of the tower, knowing that confidence was key. His uniform was that of a guard and not of a *body*-guard, but it was close enough that he hoped no one would notice.

All he had to do was act as if he belonged.

It was easier said than done, he was an assassin, a fighter, a long-range sniper, not a sneak thief – despite what Diako would have him believe.

Soldiers in similar, but not identical, uniforms to his passed by on all sides. They seemed pretty casual, but Jack knew that they were patrolling.

The guy Diako had called a *most valued client* was one of the most powerful men on the continent and, despite his personal power, he had one of the tightest security details Jack had seen since arriving in Celestia.

Thankfully, they paid him no attention as he slipped through the sliding glass doors at the bottom of the tower.

He breathed out.

Now he could begin phase two: reaching the penthouse.

The foyer seemed to be open to soldiers and guards, but men in black suits guarded the mana-lift to the next floor. Thankfully, with a little help from his contacts, he had prepared for that too.

With purpose, Jack marched down the corridor to the right and, when no one was looking, ducked into the maintenance tunnels.

A friend of Jack's at the organisation had provided him with blueprints of the tower which had helped him formulate this part of his plan. The tunnels acted as little rat runs for the help to use to fix problems without cluttering up the place.

Apparently this was commonplace on the continent.

Despite his own misgivings about the attitudes of the rich and powerful, these tunnels were the linchpin to his plan's overall success.

He squeezed down them, barely able to fit his wide shoulders between the closed in walls, until he reached his target: the back of the mana-lift.

There were multiple mana-lifts in the building which all gave access to the many floors which the tower had. However, there was only one lift which gave access to the penthouse.

The golden one.

Which, in Jack's humble opinion, told him everything he needed to know about the asshole who lived there.

Thankfully though, it made his job easier.

From the back of the golden elevator, Jack hoisted himself on top and waited.

He meditated as he waited for his mark to return, a skill he hadn't yet mastered but was certain he would with practice. By the time the elevator finally moved, he'd been able to completely restore his stamina.

It was a long ride to the top and Jack had to time his movements just right.

Mana-lifts do not work like Earthen elevators, they don't need cables. That means that when you reach the top, if you're stood on top of one like Jack was, you get crushed.

Taking a deep breath, Jack channelled his stamina into his legs and as the lift closed in on the penthouse, he jumped.

He grabbed onto the doors and pried them open, slipping inside just as the lift whooshed past him.

"That was a close one," he said casually as he dropped the persona granted to him by his *faceless man* skill.

Calmly, Jack strolled into the penthouse office and took a seat behind the desk of the most powerful man in Castalor, if not the entire continent.

With a ding, the elevator opened its doors and a good-looking black man in a very expensive suit waltzed in, stopping suddenly as he noticed the trench coat wearing assassin sitting in his chair.

"Mr Regina," Jack said, spinning the chair around to face his target, "Diako sends his regards."

Chapter 54
Soul Bonded

A few days passed whilst we all recovered from the battle with Clive.

Sally kept the ship on track towards the continent but spent most of her time relentlessly attempting to fix its flight capability.

The catonid really hated sailing, but honestly, I was happy to have a few days to relax.

Having waited out my mandatory hour of no healing in relative agony, I had then spent an entire day meditating to fix all of my wounds and regain some stamina.

According to Sally, if I hadn't activated my scales when I did, that force blade would have sliced me clean in two. The only reason it didn't kill Bell is because she had the sense to activate a fireball shield scroll she'd pilfered.

Sadly, despite killing plenty of zealots and hacking my way through countless zombies, I didn't gain a single level. I guessed they were all just weaker than me and in the end decided that was probably a good thing.

I nearly died as it was.

Worryingly, I also didn't receive a notification for Clive's death meaning either, I'd not managed to cause enough damage to him to merit me getting in on the death experience points, or he was still out there somewhere. A notion which sent a chill down my spine.

The rest of my time was spent trying to hatch my mystery egg. Most of my efforts resulted in keeping it with me. I had just enough room to tuck it into my armour, keeping it next to my heart and hopefully warm.

Though of course, that logic may apply to birds back home, but I had no idea if it would work on *whatever* this thing was.

For some, unexplained, reason I couldn't place it in my inventory and no matter how much I focused on it I couldn't get a system notification to appear.

It was almost as if it existed outside of the system entirely.

Yet, something drew me to it. I wanted to hatch it, but more than that, I felt a bond with the glimmering, black egg like it belonged to me, or was part of me.

"I've never seen anything like it," Panda said amazedly when I pulled it out during breakfast one day. "It's almost hard to look at, it kinda hurts my eyes."

"Do you think?" I replied quizzically, "I think it's hard to look away from it."

"I can crack it open if you want?" Sally called from the kitchen counter, "we didn't get a chance to resupply in Asquith Town and an egg that size would make a mean omelette."

"NO!" Panda and I shouted back in unison, though likely for entirely different reasons.

"I want to study it," he said adamantly, "a discovery like this is sure to increase my sagely wisdom after all."

"I hope it's a dragon," Bell said casually whilst flicking through a book she seemed oddly engrossed in. I didn't think I'd ever seen her read anything before. I didn't even know she *could* read.

She had slept for about twelve hours after the battle but woke up in perfect condition. However, she was a bit upset at having missed the demon flicking Clive to God-knows where like a crumb.

I tried to tell her that she must have been awake because when it had asked who'd summoned it, she'd pointed at me. Something I wasn't planning to forget anytime soon, but she insisted that she had no memory of any of it.

"Why would a dragon egg randomly appear on the ship?" Panda replied, shaking his head at the fireball mage, "if anything, it's probably a kraken egg. At least that would make some kind of logical sense."

"I hope not," I said, curling my lip at the thought. "I've seen enough krakens to last a lifetime."

"Must be all that hentai you've been watching," Bell said nonchalantly.

"There's no internet here," I replied dryly.

"I know," she said, flipping a page in her book, "and that makes it *so* much worse."

The days passed in an almost splendid reverie as I read books, slept in, trained and meditated the time away. Sailing was a lot slower than flying, but thankfully we didn't run into any storms or more sea kaiju.

In fact, I was almost sad when we finally spotted a land mass in the distance.

From out at sea the continent looked like a long green lump stretching across the entire horizon. Though from the map on my HUD, I knew it was a near exact replica of the land masses back on Earth.

The continent we were headed to was North America back home. More specifically, we were going to land somewhere on the Florida coast.

"We should be there soon," Sally crooned as she joined me and Panda on the bow of the ship. "Hopefully there will be some skilled craftsmen at the port so we can get the ship sky worthy again."

"Where are we landing exactly?" I asked.

"Cali Port," she replied, "it's the biggest trade port in the south of the continent. It's no Castalor of course, but I bet there will be all sorts of exotic items for you to buy. That should be your number one priority if you want to survive this place. Havar was like kiddie camp compared to the continent."

"What's wrong with my gear?" I asked incredulously.

"Nothing...per say, it just needs some upgrades," she replied patting me firmly on the shoulder with her massive hand. "For example, do any of your enchantments add 100% to your stats?"

"You can do that?" I replied dumbstruck.

"You can," she nodded, "100% is the maximum you can increase each stat through enhancements and basically every adventurer on the continent has at least one stat buff that has a 100% buff. If you don't, then you're already massively behind the curve."

"Sounds a bit pay to win," I muttered, but she ignored me and continued.

"Not to mention that there are a lot of level cappers on the continent," she took a breath, wrapping her arm around me and pointing out at the closing land mass. "You were a respectable level in Havar, here you're not. On the continent, you're a lower level than most blacksmiths. Of course, you'll gain levels much faster here, but you won't get any special treatment..."

As she spoke I felt something wriggling beneath my cloak. I ducked out of her grip swiftly and pulled the egg from its place under my torso armour.

It shook.

"Hey, don't ignore me when I'm trying to help...oh, it's moving." Sally said, gazing at my egg with wide eyes.

I pretended not to notice her hand twitch as if she wanted to unsheathe her sword.

"I'm telling you it's going to be a dragon," Bell said as she looked over the rim of her book at us. "Try channelling some mana into it."

She had been lounging on a deck chair for most of the day reading that same book.

"I don't have any mana," I replied.

"Oh yeah," she said absently, "well the book says that you need to channel mana into it, that's what mother dragon's do to hatch their eggs."

"Wait, that book is about egg hatching?" I asked, turning towards her, "where did you even get something like that?"

"Panda let me borrow it," she said with a shrug.

"Whatever it is," Panda said, "I'm sure it's going to be a great find. Maybe it'll be a creature we've never seen before. How great would that be? I can see the award ceremony now."

As the egg shook in my hand a small piece of the shell chipped away and my dragon's eye took over. Suddenly, the black, glimmering shell which had previously shown no sign of mana, was overflowing with a gentle, dark glow.

I felt a sudden urge to pour my own mana into the egg, just like Bell had suggested, but I didn't have any to use.

There was *something* I could channel into it, though it could be dangerous. Before I could let that thought linger, I began channelling a small amount of my soul energy into my fingertips.

Another piece cracked off and before my very eyes the glow darkened and began to tinge with a forest green that swirled within its natural black energy.

Was that my doing?

I almost lost my grip as the gentle shaking turned into violent thrashing I put the egg down and backed away. Whatever was inside the shell was ready to get out.

I couldn't help but feel like introducing my own soul power had pushed the hatchling into hatching faster, just like Bell's book had suggested...kinda.

"You did something didn't you?" Bell said with a satisfied smile.

Sally's hand was fully on the hilt of her sword as she took a tentative step backwards and Bell put down her book, leaning forward eagerly.

"This thing better not destroy my ship, Gonads," Sally hissed.

"It's a hatchling, what could it possibly do?" I replied with an irritated shake of my head.

"Can you not see that aura?" She demanded, "whatever it is, it's not normal."

I *could* see the aura leaking through the cracks, I was pretty sure I'd helped to form it. I wasn't going to tell Sally that though.

"Green and black is not a good mixture," she said, eyes glued to the vibrating egg.

A few more pieces of shell came off and then...CRACK.

"Oh thank the gods, I'm finally free of that retched place," a deep, booming voice said loudly. "I'll tell you; it was terribly claustrophobic in there."

Standing before us, with a tiny piece of shell stuck to its head like a little hat, was a baby dragon.

"I told you it'd be a dragon!" Bell yelled, jumping out of her lounger.

The dragon was about the size of a small chihuahua and its scales were jet black with a slight green tinge to the tips. Hidden within the blackness was small, glimmering dots of white light which looked like stars. The dragon had two, tiny wings that didn't look fully formed yet and deep, forest green eyes.

"Oh Kaleb, it's so cute!" Bell squealed, clenching her fists as she seemed to struggle to control her urges, "what are you going to call it? How about…"

Before she had a chance to offer up a suggestion, the baby dragon dived at my chest, knocking me to the floor.

"Try to soul bond with me will you?" It yelled. It was surprisingly strong for such a tiny creature. "Your soul is *mine* human; I claim it in the name of Asmodeus!"

At that we all went silent.

Sally reached for her sword once again, Panda took a step back and Bell's eyes went wide.

"Asmodeus?" I asked, speaking to my hatchling for the first time as it wriggled against my chest like it was trying to burrow through my rib cage.

"Ow, stop!" I shouted as it nibbled at my clothes. Grabbing it by the scruff of the neck I ripped it off of me and held it at arm's length.

"Unhand me this instant!" It protested, kicking its underdeveloped legs helplessly in midair. "This is not how one treats a demon lord."

"Listen buddy," I began, shooting the baby dragon a disapproving look. "I've met Asmodeus, and you're not him."

"How dare you assume to know me," the dragon hissed, "we've only just met, Kaleb Akabane."

I paused for a moment as he continued to wriggle and fight against my iron grip.

"How do you know my name?" I said quickly.

"We are soul bonded," he replied with a slight flutter of his wings, "how else?"

"*You're* soul bonded?" Sally asked incredulously, shooting me a wide-eyed stare as her grip tightened on the hilt of her oversized sword, "to the demon of lust?"

"He's not the demon of lust-" I began but was cut off.

"I can't believe you didn't tell me," Panda said sulkily, "*I'm* your familiar, we're supposed to discuss things like this, kid."

"I don't even know what soul bonding is!" I yelled, throwing my hands up in the air in frustration and further upsetting the aggressive baby dragon who swung in my grip like an empty shopping bag.

"Wait," Bell said, putting herself between me and the others and scratching her chin. "When I told you to channel mana into the egg, what did you do?"

"I don't have any mana," I began, "…so I channelled soul energy in there instead."

"Why would you do that?" Sally said exasperatedly as she pulled her hand slowly down her face.

"I don't know…" I replied, "it just felt…right."

"To think that one such as you would believe your soul to be of high enough quality to merge with me," the baby dragon scoffed. He had stopped wriggling around now and instead hung from my hand with his front legs crossed like arms. "Do you have any idea of the power I possess as a demon lord?"

Was my new pet scolding me like a child?

I scowled at him for a moment when a notification popped up in my HUD.

You have unlocked a bonded familiar:
Asmodeus (Soul Bonded)

Due to your use of the *Chaos Seed*, a small fragment of the demon lord *Asmodeus* has remained in the mortal plane.
Possessing a miniscule amount of his powers and personality, he has hatched as a demon familiar, taking on a shape imposed on him by the imprinted soul to which he is bound.
As a soul bonded familiar, *Asmodeus* cannot directly disobey your commands.
Make sure you house train him.

I guess it did say "results may vary" when I pulled the seed out, I thought.

I wondered why I couldn't conjure a notification when he was still an egg? Moreover, why would my soul imprint make him take on the shape of a chihuahua sized dragon?

I did have a few dragon related skills, and a dragon's eye. Still though, was that really all it took for my soul to take on that shape? Did that mean *I* was part dragon now?

I had so many questions and literally no answers. One important part of the message stuck with me though: Asmodeus couldn't disobey my commands. So, surely, he wouldn't be dangerous as long as I ordered him not to be.

"Asmodeus," I said and the little dragon glared up at me. "I'm going to put you down now, but I forbid you from attacking me, or anyone else on this ship. Understood?"

"How dare you presume to order *me* around," he began, "do you know who I am!"

Despite his bravado, when I placed him on the ground he made no attempt to go after any of us.

"Good boy," I said patting him softly on the head.

"One day I am going to devour your soul, human," he muttered and a little snort of black fire poofed out of his nostrils.

"I think the demon lord needs a nap," Bell said, scooping him up before I could stop her.

"How dare you!" He roared, his unnaturally deep voice carrying loudly across the ocean air. "Unhand me *this* instant, you insolent cur I will...actually, I am kind of sleepy," he yawned, "After some consideration, your offer of nap time is agreeable to me, human, show me to your finest lair."

"We are going to talk about this when she gets back," Sally said in low, dangerous voice as Bell cradled the baby dragon in her arms lovingly.

Chapter 55
My Trusty Soul Devouring Steed

Whilst Bell put the demon lord down for a nap, Sally, Panda and I sat in a tense silence at the kitchen table. The catonid glared at me, her muscular arms crossed in a way that showed off the tone of her forearm's musculature.

She had the kind of muscle development that would make any man jealous, myself included. Meanwhile, though I had a rather athletic body now, thanks to my raised stats, I was in no way large.

Bodybuilders are all for show anyway, I thought moodily, *meanwhile, I have functionality.*

With the light tap of a closing door, Bell entered the kitchen with a finger to her lips.

"He's down for the count," she whispered, "better keep it down though, I don't have any bottled milk."

"It's a dragon," I replied dryly, "I'm pretty sure they eat live goats and dwarves, I doubt he wants to suckle at a plastic teat whilst you rock him and sing lullabies."

"It's not *just* a dragon," Sally snarled, making a concerted effort to keep her voice down to a respectable level. "It's the demon lord of lust, do you have any idea the kind of shit show you've caused by bonding with it? Asmodeus is a dangerous name, feared across the world for good reason. Adventure Society loses hundreds of people every year preventing zealots and cultists from completing rituals to allow him to cross into this realm.

"And, in a matter of days, you've not only allowed him to enter the mortal plane in his full form, but now he has a permanent fragment of himself here. THAT YOU SOUL BONDED!" Forgetting her inside voice for a moment, she shouted the last part, slamming her fist down so hard on the table that it broke in two.

"I guess we'll be eating off the floor for the remainder of this voyage then?" I said monotonously.

"I don't think you understand just how dangerous this thing is Kaleb," she said, turning away from me and rubbing her fingers through her hair so forcefully that little clumps came out.

"She used your real name," Panda whispered to me from behind his paw, "that's how you know she's serious."

Shooting my familiar a harsh glare that silenced him, Sally continued: "he may only be a hatchling at the moment, but what happens when his powers grow stronger? Do you think your soul bond will be enough to prevent the *real* Asmodeus from stepping into the mortal plane permanently and exterminating us all?"

"I get that you're upset," I said diplomatically, "but you can't blame me for doing something by accident. Not to mention that if I hadn't used the chaos seed against Clive we'd be too dead to even have this conversation."

"Well I'm sure that will be of great comfort to the billions of people inhabiting this world when your new pet murders them all and eats their souls," she said flippantly.

"What do you suggest we do then?" I replied, crossing my arms and feeling more than a little annoyed. None of this was my fault, I was doing everything I could not to die at the hands of some creepy, skeleton-looking necromancer. How was I supposed to know my survival would bring forth such a calamity. *If* my dragon was even as dangerous as she was suggesting.

"We should kill it," she said sternly.

My heart skipped a beat. I didn't know why, but the idea of killing Asmodeus felt wrong. It hurt, like physically hurt me deep down in my...stomach?

"You can't kill it," Panda said, jumping up onto his stool and pointing fiercely at Sally. "Its soul bonded to Kaleb. He hasn't even reached the level cap yet, the strain on his core will be too much."

"Will he die too?" Bell asked, looking at me with a concerned expression.

"Worse," Panda began, "his soul will rupture."

We all stared at each other in a harsh silence for a moment. Sally paced aggressively around the room, throwing her hands onto her head, clenching her fists and moving to kick furniture, but then stopping herself. She was a mess to look at. I'd never seen her act this way before.

"What's a soul rupture?" I asked quietly, though I feared I already knew what it meant. "Would it kill me?"

"It's more than death," Panda replied in a hoarse whisper, "a soul rupture is...it's like being tortured for eternity. When a person's soul breaks like that, they're said to be trapped within a single second of agonising pain...forever.

"It's bad for the world too, a powerful soul rupture can cause a person to explode with the power of a nuclear bomb. If your soul was to rupture with that power of yours...I dread to think what would happen."

"Is that why you told me not to use that power again?" I asked, thinking back to Panda's warning after I'd first discovered I could use soul attacks on a quest that had us trapped inside a little girl's memory.

"It's part of it," he said, a little squeamishly.

"Look," Sally said with a sigh, "obviously I don't want Gonads to explode all over the place, but we still need to deal with this issue. That dragon is a danger to the entire world."

"But he's soul bonded," Bell said in a small voice, the rest of us all turned towards her. "In the book I was reading, it said that soul bonded familiars can't grow more powerful than their masters. If Kaleb is his master, then won't he always be able to control him?"

"That's how it would work with a *normal* soul bond, yes." Sally replied, taking her seat at the table once more. "But as far as I'm aware, no one has ever bonded with a demon lord before-"

"Fragment," Bell interrupted, "a demon lord's fragment. He hasn't bonded with the whole thing, just a tiny part of it."

"Well…" Sally said tentatively, "I guess…we just don't have enough to go off."

"Is there anyone who might know more?" Bell asked.

"Possibly," Sally relented, stroking the back of her head awkwardly. "I'm friendly with the director of the Adventure Society at Cali Port, we could ask her for help. At the very least I'm sure she knows a guy."

"Great," Bell smiled, "and in the meantime we just need to keep Asmodeus alive so Kaleb doesn't blow his load or whatever."

I rolled my eyes at that, still, she was right. That seemed to be the best course of action to me as well. I didn't want to die any time soon and who knew, maybe my new dragon would come in useful. If he got a bit bigger he could become my trusty, soul devouring steed.

We passed the rest of the evening in a tense silence, each doing our own thing. Sally retired to the wheel above the cabins, presumably guiding us into port, or doing push-ups or…something.

Bell went back to reading her book and Panda shot me the occasional concerned glance as he delved into a pile of his own, which he'd been gifted by the zealots.

Overall, it wasn't a very pleasant evening.

After a little while of no sleep and feeling bad about putting my team in such an awkward position, I decided to meditate.

Exploring the inner workings of my body always helped to calm me down. At the end of the day, what was done was done and we'd found the best solution for the time being.

We couldn't kill Asmodeus without risking my soul exploding like a bomb. I didn't want to kill him anyway, he was mine. Something deep within me wanted to protect him, like some kind of subconscious, knee jerk reaction.

As I wandered my soul view I decided to delve into my core to see if it might hold any answers to my new, weird feelings.

I gazed for a long time at the swirling mass of energy which settled deep within the pit of my stomach. It was mesmerising, calming.

It had changed colours many times over the course of my time in Celestia. Now, it was a deep, royal green speckled with tiny dots of lighter, acidic green and shadowed in a deep black.

It reminded me of Asmodeus' scales, but the colours were inverted.

Eventually I came out of soul view to find Bell snoring and slumped over the table with her face planted firmly in her book. Panda would not be happy when he saw the drool stains on the page.

Speaking of my sagely familiar, he was nowhere to be found.

I thought about venturing outside to see how Sally was doing but decided against it. Her temper had run unusually hot that evening and I figured she needed some space to cool down.

Instead, I found myself absently wandering towards my little room at the back of the ship. As I opened the door from the kitchen to the cabins, I saw Panda leaning idly against an open door.

Silently, I moved next to him and saw that he was gazing at the sleeping dragon who was starfished across my bunk.

Great, someone else I have to share my bed with, I thought with a sigh.

Back home my wife had insisted on letting the dog sleep on the bed with us. He was a big, bear of a hound though and when he stretched out I was left with no cover and barely a corner to curl up in. Naturally I kicked him down every night once she'd fallen asleep.

I missed my wife. I hadn't thought about her much recently and that realisation stung a little bit. Still, she was my reason for going through all of this pain and effort. Levelling up, the life of an adventurer, none of it was easy.

Exciting, sure, but hard all the same.

It's difficult to fully describe the pain of being nearly killed countless times. The numbness that comes with battle fatigue and living in a world where death is ever present. I wondered if people back on Earth felt that way, those who were unfortunate enough to be born into a war torn or famine ravaged country.

What am I doing, I thought admonishingly, *I never get this deep. Where's Bell when you need her, I could really use a bad movie reference or a penis joke right about now.*

"What do you think?" Panda said softly, rousing me from my spiralling introspection.

"I think that for now, he's one of us," I said, nodding towards the slumbering dragon.

"He's going to be a handful you know," Panda said, gazing at me out of the corner of his deep eyes, "just having him will paint a target on your back."

"Like I don't already have one…literally," I snorted, thinking of the map pieces that were permanently tattooed on my skin.

"Also," Panda continued, "he seems like a real piece of work."

"So did you," I whispered. "Remember when we first met and I mistakenly thought you were a demon summon."

"How could I forget," Panda replied, "it was in that moment that I knew you desperately needed a sage."

"Well, now I guess I finally have one," I winked at him and scratched behind his fluffy ear.

"You know he wants to eat your soul, right?" Panda said pointedly, "he's a real asshole."

"I know," I replied softly, "but something inside me wants to protect him. I can't quite put my finger on why, but I just can't help it. It's the same feeling I got when I thought you'd died. It's like a piece of me is…"

"That's what a soul bond is," Panda said, resting his paw on top of my quivering hand, "familiars are a strange thing in Celestia. We're connected to you, and you to us. It's more than just a friendship or a comradery. The soul forms a powerful connection. It's like the blood ties you share with family, but…more."

"Is that how it was with your last summoner?" I asked, thinking on the girl he'd been summoned by in a previous life. She had died young and recently, at least by his perception of life.

"Yeah…" he shuddered, "I won't make the same mistake again. You'll survive, kid. I can't go through that again."

"Don't worry buddy, I don't plan on dying any time soon."

Chapter 56
That's What *She* Said

I spent most of the night watching the dragon sleep whilst whispering conspiratorially with Panda. It was pleasant. Peaceful moments were getting harder and harder to come by these days. I had to enjoy them when I could.

Since embarking on the membership exam for the society, it felt like my life had been one mad rush after another. If I wasn't fighting for my life or rescuing a comrade from the depths of a secret gang base, I was training like a mad man to make those things easier in the future.

I didn't regret my choice to prioritise those things, but it was relaxing to take a break from it every now and then.

Of course, that break only lasted until sunrise.

Asmodeus awoke with a start, springing up onto his feet with widened eyes and flapping wings. His body hadn't formed to a point where he could actually fly yet, it was more like a momentary hover before a slow descent.

He wasn't very happy when Panda laughed at him because of it.

"Why are you watching me slumber?" he shouted accusatorily in his unnaturally deep voice. "Where are the servants? Have them prepare my breakfast. I'll take a partially boiled dwarf with a side of goat's milk, hold the pasteurisation."

"We don't have any servants," I replied dryly, "...or partially boiled dwarves."

"Hmm," he said, considering my words for a moment as he brought his claws to rest under his chin. "Well, what partially boiled creatures do you have?"

"We could probably boil some fish?" Panda suggested. "We have lots of those."

"Never!" Asmodeus roared indignantly, "I am a dragon, not a bear. I dine only on the finest quality red meats...if you don't have anything else then I guess this panda will have to do, though it looks a little fatty for my tastes," he said, turning to me as if his request was entirely reasonable.

"Did he just call me fat?" Panda asked in a higher pitch than normal.

"How do you feel about *fried* meat?" I asked.

"I am a dragon, we do not lower ourselves to such debased forms of cooking" he replied, lifting his head.

"I'll tell you what," I began, "let me give you one of Sally's famous breakfasts and we'll see if that'll satisfy you."

"The catonid can cook?" he asked, an air of genuine surprise in his voice, "when I was still but a freshly hatched lower demon their kind still licked their genitals as a form of grooming."

"Just try it," I said, trying hard to get the image of Sally doing just that out of my mind.

Fortunately for me, she was already hard at work on the breakfast preparations when we entered the kitchen. I thought I'd smelled the familiar wafting of bacon when I'd offered it to Asmodeus.

Bell was snoring, head resting on the same book she'd been reading the previous night, though now she was using it as a pillow at the kitchen table.

"My tomes!" Panda cried as he saw the crusted gleam of dried drool staining the pages. "That's the last time I let you borrow my books, your membership at the sagely library is revoked, hand me your card so I can rip it in two." He held out his paw expectantly as Bell was roused from her sleep by the racket.

She sat up lazily, her bee's hive of hair sticking out at odd angles, a few stray strands stuck to her plump lips.

"I don't have a card," she said with a yawn, then she looked down and saw the residue of spittle on the book she'd been reading about dragons. "Oh no Panda, someone's gotten your book all wet."

"Why you little…" he growled but didn't get to finish his sentence before Sally began placing dishes around the table.

I glanced at Asmodeus, who had demanded to ride on my shoulder so that he could "*look down on the mortals*", and his twinkling, green eyes were locked onto the food.

"Smells good doesn't it?" I said quietly to him.

"We shall see, human," he replied aloofly, "we shall see."

Placing him down on the table I watched as he hesitantly picked up the cutlery and began dissecting the fat from the edges of the bacon.

His precision was masterful, and when he finally deigned to put a piece of the sizzling, pink meat into his mouth, I thought his eyes might pop out of their sockets like a surprised cartoon character.

"Well?" I asked.

"What is this miracle meat?" He replied, looking at me with hungry, glinting eyes.

"It's called bacon and it comes from pigs," I said.

"Actually," Sally corrected, "this bacon comes from Havarian jungle boars. It's pretty hard to get since the locals almost hunted them to extinction a few decades ago, but I know a guy."

"I demand that we capture this bacon merchant at once," Asmodeus replied animatedly, "this is a delicacy too rare to be sold to any common rabble. It must all be mine."

"Um, yeah," I said, trying to keep the amusement from my voice, "I'll get right on that once we dock."

"Speaking of docking," Bell said, "are we nearly there yet?"

"We'll be arriving within the hour," Sally replied, despite being civil, she kept a cautious eye on Asmodeus the entire time we were eating.

"Is nobody going to ask why he can use cutlery?" Panda asked.

***

As the ship pulled into the docks amidst the beautiful, turquoise sea, I was awestruck.

Cali Port was huge, much bigger than Havar had been. Glass skyscrapers dotted the coastal skyline contrasted with medieval stone walls which bordered the sea itself.

From what little I could see from the bow of the ship, the city seemed to be set out in an old-fashioned ring formation of varying sections of wall.

Naturally, the docks were located immediately outside the outer ring and were a bustling hive of trade activity. We pulled up to a wooden moor and Sally tossed some rope over the side to a group of lycanids who began tying it off.

The dock was massive and I counted at least fifty vessels in the immediate vicinity, ours was among the smallest.

As we stepped off onto dry land, Sally tossed a bag of coins to the worker who had caught her rope.

"Anything happens to my ship and I'll come back for that," she said, flashing him a fangy smile.

He grimaced back at her, that was until he looked inside the bag and began grinning instead.

We followed her hurried march through the docks, twisting and turning as busy workers rushed around completing their business.

I didn't have a lot of experience with sailing, so I was a little caught off guard at how still the ground felt beneath my feet.

After a while at sea I'd gotten used to the feeling of waving movement below me and my muscles had adapted to counter it as I walked around the ship. I'd barely even noticed it at the time, but that sudden absence was weird and I felt slightly off balance. The ground was too still.

"Where are we going to in such a hurry?" Bell asked as we marched behind the hurrying catonid.

"To the society building," she replied, "we need to report this *new development* at once," she glanced over at Asmodeus who was obliviously taking in the sights from his position on my shoulder.

Surprisingly, his weight didn't tip me off balance or hurt much at all. He was only the size of a chihuahua, but I had still expected some kind of trade off from carrying him like that.

I guess my improved strength stat must have been compensating, or perhaps it was my agility? It was hard to know for certain but either way, I was sure it had something to do with the way the system altered my physiology.

We made quick work of traversing the docks and soon found ourselves staring up at the huge stone wall that bordered the town. It was even bigger in person and I found myself wondering if I'd be able to climb it *Assassin's Creed* style.

Joining a queue, we stood before a large, iron portcullis that barred entry into the city itself. A group of lycanids led by a heavily armoured svartalf stood guard, processing people as they came to them.

"They sure run a tight ship around here," I said absently.

"This is the continent," Sally replied with a shrug, "they have to prioritise security procedures when so much money is at stake, not to mention the average level is much higher here than it was on the islands."

"Their levels are laughable," Asmodeus said with a tut, "it took me less than one hundred years to become a demon lord, yet these *people* spent twice as long just to reach jade. It's pathetic."

"Maybe keep the demon lord stuff to yourself buddy," I said, patting his head, "we don't want to freak people out, they might try to take you away."

"Let them try!" He roared, earning us some worried looks from the others in the line. "No one here is more powerful than I."

"That may have been true when you were the big scary giant dude," Bell said, "but now you're a baby dragon with barely a fraction of that power."

"A fraction is all it takes," he replied indignantly, lifting his head to the side.

"That's what *she* said," Panda sniggered.

We stood bickering idly for a short while as the queue whittled down. It was surprisingly fast; Cali Port must have much more streamlined processes than we did back on Earth.

Upon reaching the front of the queue, Sally flashed her silver rank ID card at the guards who peered back at her, seemingly unimpressed.

"Remember to walk on the left newbie...and watch out for the protestors, they're violent," the svartalf said in a bored voice before allowing her through.

I practically willed Sally to ask about these violent protesters but she simply scowled and nodded grimly. Did she know something about this already?

The svartalf said the same thing to Bell, then it was my turn.

I showed her my card as the others did and she seemed to be moments away from waving me through, until she looked up.

"Is that a dragon?" She asked.

"He's my familiar," I replied.

"And the Panda?"

"Him too."

"You're listed as a skirmisher on your ID but you seem more like a beast tamer," she said contemplatively, "have you changed classes recently?"

"No?" I asked, "I didn't even know you *could* change classes."

"Make sure you get this updated," she sighed, "go on through and keep to the left."

I rejoined the others and we wandered through the busy portcullis entrance. I wondered what she meant by keep to the left, she'd said it to all of us.

More importantly, I'd had no idea that you could change classes. I was certain that when I'd made my initial selection it had said it would be permanent.

"Panda?" I asked, "can you really change classes?"

"That was the first I'd heard of it," he replied with a scowl, "but I can look into it for you. Maybe there are some local books with knowledge on the subject."

We continued onwards as I thought about the implications of class changes. There was still so much I didn't know about this world.

Dropping off the pavement, I stepped out into the road idly...and almost got flattened by invisible oncoming traffic. Something passed me at such a ferocious speed that I felt my skin ripple.

Chapter 57
Watch Out For The Protestors

"Watch out!" Sally shouted, grabbing the back of my collar and yanking me out of harm's way.

Something zipped past me so quickly I felt my skin ripple and I was certain that if I was hit by whatever force that was, it would have turned me into paste.

"Thanks," I replied breathlessly.

"Be more careful, human," Asmodeus admonished me, "I cannot have my transportation being damaged by carelessness."

I gave him a deadpan look which he didn't seem to understand.

"You need to listen to instructions, Gonads," Sally said, "the guard at the gate told you to keep left. She told all of us to."

"Well she could have told me that not doing so would result in death," I replied grumpily. "Seems like the sort of thing one might mention."

"Keeping left is universal in high level locations," Panda said matter-of-factly, "I thought you knew that?"

"You're my sage," I said through gritted teeth, "making sure I know things is literally your job."

"Sorry, kid," he replied sheepishly.

"Why *do* we have to keep left anyway," Bell asked, "besides the obvious…"

"Well technically you can keep left or right, it's just that we're on the left-hand side of the street. This walkway is reserved for anyone below the level cap," Sally explained as we continued walking, this time making sure to keep firmly to the left, "the middle is reserved for jade souls and above."

As I followed her meaty hand gesture, I saw that the street was indeed laid out this way. It was almost familiar, a middle section bordered by two walkways on either side. Just like how roads and pavements were laid out back home, just with a less obvious dividing line between the pedestrian walkways and the road itself.

"Why?" I asked after a long moment of staring at the road in the middle. It seemed deserted with the exception of the vibrant flashes of colour my dragon's eye was detecting, and the displacement of air.

"Because those above the level cap can move at extreme speeds and have extreme strength," she replied patiently, "they're not like you and I, their abilities far surpass those of a normal person."

"It's like when you're driving a car," Panda took over, dipping into his limited knowledge of Earthen culture, "when a bug hits your windscreen do you pullover? Do you even notice right away."

"So you're saying we're like bugs to them?" I asked.

"Exactly."

Well that's a terrifying thought.

With the exception of the segregated walkways, Cali Port was visually wonderous. As we journeyed through the outer level of the city, I certainly wasn't starved of things to look at.

We passed by typical stores and stalls just like there had been in Havar, but this place also had multi-floored department stores, some of which were dedicated to armour and weapons.

There were smaller crafting supply stores, there were bars lit with neon signs, rooftop cafes and plenty of magic shops.

It was a fantasy world metropolis, ripe for the picking.

I decided right then and there that as soon as we were done checking in at Adventure Society, I was going shopping.

In the meantime, we headed towards the centre of the circular city. Well, not the exact centre, but we headed in that general direction.

The closer we got to the middle of town; the stranger things got. People watching was amusing, if a little concerning.

All kinds of different races cluttered the streets, there were even ones I hadn't seen before.

We passed a small stall that said "courthouse" on it in crude writing. A man with the legs and face of a kangaroo and the torso of a hairy human manned it. He was dressed in dark robes and wearing one of those silly barrister wigs found in the British courts back home.

I never understood why they wore those.

Stood opposite him and, flanked on either side by two lycanids with barred teeth, with hands gripped around his arms, was a crow person.

The strange creature looked like a failed science experiment. For all intents and purposes he was a human, just with a crow's head and feathers where the body hair should be.

I couldn't help but focus on him for the notification.

You have discovered a new race:
Garuda

Though once a proud race of powerful humanoid-avian hybrid warriors, the *Garuda* have since evolved to be almost identical to humans.
They have racial skills related to sight and thievery due to their naturally eclectic nature. Though they cannot

fly in their infancy, upon reaching the level cap many have been known to grow wings.
The origins of the *Garuda* are unknown, but if you think about it long enough, I'm sure you'll come to the same gross conclusion that I did.
Human's will fuck anything.

"Ew," I said as I finished reading the description. "I half expected them to be called *crowanids*, considering how the naming scheme for the other races has worked so far," I muttered to myself as Panda laughed at my side.

Just as I was about to focus on the kangaroo person he banged his mallet on his shabby wooden stall and began talking loudly, though no one stopped to listen to him. It must have been a regular occurrence in Cali Port.

"Order in the court," he said in a loud, pompous voice. "Sir, you stand here today because you have been accused of being involved with a murder."

"Well, I always try to be social," the Garuda replied, jolting its crow-like head around nervously.

Shaking my head, I began to focus on the judge once more when Sally growled the words "it's worse than I thought," under her breath.

I turned to her, but before I could ask what she meant my thoughts were drowned out by unintelligible shouting coming from the direction we were heading in.

We turned a corner and the familiar sight of a large glass sky-scraper with neon, vertical writing running the length of it filled my vision.

Worryingly, a large group stood outside it. They were a strong mixture of all the races I knew about, and some I didn't, and they were so loud I couldn't actually make out what any individual was saying.

Were these the protestors the guard at the gate had mentioned? If so they weren't very organised. What happened to picket signs and call and response phrases?

There seemed to be a distinct absence of humans from the large crowd. A thought that compounded inside me as I caught angry faces glaring at me and Bell.

Sally pushed her way through and we stayed close behind in her slipstream. It was nerve wrecking. We had just arrived in this new place, a city whose residents were much stronger than the people of Havar, and now we were forcing our way through a crowd that was seemingly hostile towards adventure society.

I felt the hairs on the back of my neck stand to attention as we moved through the crowd. Every time we took a step forward, our exit path was closed in behind us. It was as if we were being swallowed by a sea of unbridled outrage.

I honestly wouldn't have been surprised if they smashed the glass and stormed the building at any minute. If that happened would I be expected to defend it as an adventurer? I hoped not.

"Why aren't they bowing?" Asmodeus asked in a loud, deep whisper. "They should be bowing as I pass them, and why is the catonid having to carve us a path?"

I shushed him with a stern glare but not before he earned some angry stares from the closest protestors who'd heard him.

Eventually Sally broke through the crowd and we followed, popping out of the mass protest and hurrying straight through the open door that was held tentatively by a burly lycanid in heavy plate armour.

BANG.

447

A piece of rotten fruit hit the guards armour with enough force to leave a small dent in the heavy metal.

Without looking back, I dived through the door with Panda and Bell hot on my heels.

"What the hell was that?" She shouted as we made it into the foyer.

"Looked like a rotten apple to me," I replied breathlessly.

"Fucking scum," the lycanid guard half breathed, half growled as he wrestled to slam the door shut behind us. "The director is waiting for you upstairs," he said to Sally, who nodded her thanks.

The foyer was laid out just like the one I was used to; however, it was completely deserted. There was no attractive catonid receptionist manning the front desk and not a single adventurer milling about.

Beckoning for us to follow her, Sally strode up to a magic elevator, just like the one back in the adventure society building in Havar.

I felt sorry for the single guard manning the door, it must have been a lonely job and he had no chance against the gathered protestors if fighting broke out.

We entered the elevator in silence as it took us to the top floor.

The director's office stood in stark contrast to Lucas' office in Havar. Director Lucas was a minimalist of refined taste. With the exception of a large desk and constantly filled decanters of amber, and likely expensive, alcohol, his office was bare.

The Cali Port director had a different approach.

Fancy swords in glass cases lined the lower half of the walls whilst glimmering, golden framed pictures sat above them. Fancy oil paintings depicting battles and, what I had to assume were, famous ships.

A large, oak-coloured desk took up the final quarter of the room with comfortable looking chairs lining it. There was one for each of us, was that on purpose or a happy coincidence?

The director stood with her back towards us, gazing out over Cali Port from, what was probably, the best view in the city.

Her dark purple skin was scarred and tattooed with deep black lines, crosses and other artwork which seemed spiritual in nature.

"Welcome," the director said, "please take a seat, I've been expecting you."

Her voice was warm and soothing. It matched her deep scarlet hair perfectly. As she turned towards us, a long, black formal coat swayed elegantly. It hung from her shoulders like a cape, she hadn't put her arms through the sleeves.

Underneath the massive coat, she wore a black corset and tight, leather pants. Her body cut a much more feminine shape than Sally's, it was captivating.

The delicate features of her face only added to the fantasy.

"Why is a svartalf in charge of this branch?" Asmodeus scoffed as I took a seat. I immediately gasped and moved to cover his mouth with my hand.

Sally shot me a wide-eyed look and began apologising.

"I'm sorry director, I-"

"Don't worry," she replied, cutting the catonid off with a casual wave of her hand, "I'm well aware of the demon lord's *way with words*."

Her ruby eyes washed over me in a calculating gaze that, coupled with a knowing half smile, told me that she was a very well informed and intelligent woman. A dangerous combination.

The fact that she not only knew that I had Asmodeus, but she knew his real identity as well must have meant she had spies in the city. Possibly the city guard? No, the guard at the gate didn't seem to recognise him. Her spies must be elsewhere, or maybe she had a skill.

Either way, I'd have to be careful around her.

"Mmmmmm mm mmmmm!" Asmodeus tried to shout as my hand muffled his words.

I glared at him, before lifting my palm from his muzzle.

"Unhand me human!" He roared, "…oh, you have. Well, don't attempt to silence me again."

"I know why you've come to see me but I'm afraid the discussion about what to do with our little flying demon will have to wait," the director said grimly, "I have an urgent problem that I need you to deal with."

"*Gliding,*" Panda corrected with a smug grin.

"We weren't really looking to stay here for very long," I said.

"I'm sorry Mr Akabane," she replied cordially, "but until this problem is solved, no one can travel further inland anyway, including your party."

"Why not?" Asmodeus erupted, "this is an outrage. No one prevents my freedom of movement and gets away with it!"

"I agree," she replied in a low voice which shut him up straight away. "You've seen the civil unrest plaguing Cali Port I presume?"

"How could we not?" I replied, "we had to fight through an angry crowd just to get inside this building."

"Well, that isn't the only protest hotspot I'm afraid," she continued. "There are protests all across the city, the biggest of which is barricading the inland gate, which is why no one can leave. I need every adventurer I can get my hands on to look into the matter and find a way to resolve it."

"What do you expect us to do?" Bell said, "we're probably lower ranks than most of the normal citizens here. We're not exactly in a position to go marching up to a group of powerful protestors and beat them into submission."

"Have you heard of a little thing called diplomacy?" The director replied with a half-smile, "that would be my suggestion at least."

"What is this civil unrest about?" I asked, trying to cut through the pleasantries.

"We have two main factions in this city," she explained, "the capitalists and the communists."

Oh here we go, I thought with a roll of my eyes. The director furrowed her brow at me but continued anyway.

"The continent is a capitalist federation," she said, "that relies heavily on industry and a free market. Naturally, that means that some people are in charge of the businesses they create and others have to work for them for the good of the economy.

"However, recently there have been growing concerns over workplace discrimination and monetary compensation, particularly among the minor races within our population.

"You see, Cali Port is a minor race dominated city which means there are a lot of minority species living and working here. These are creatures who tend to be less humanoid such as the Garuda, gnomes and the like.

"In Cali Port, there are growing concerns that the humanoid workers are treating the minor races unfairly: paying them badly, giving them poor working conditions, refusing to promote them into positions of power and the like.

"As such, some of the most unhappy workers have formed a new kind of workers union which they have called *communism*, supposedly it has something to do with everyone being treated and paid the same regardless of skill. It sounds like nonsense to me, but these people are very serious and have begun blockading key infrastructure across the city. I need you to solve this problem for me."

I took a moment to consider what she'd said before replying. Her explanation was more in depth than I was used to, though from her tone I could tell that what she really wanted was for me to get rid of the communist protestors.

"When you say *solve the problem*," Bell said, running a finger across her throat and winking.

"If that is what it takes then it is permitted," the director sighed, "however, I would prefer a diplomatic solution if you can find one."

"You want us to convince the protestors to come to heel?" I asked.

"Either that or convince the business owners to bring them to the table for a peaceful resolution," she replied, "I don't really understand these strikers but I don't want my city turning into a warzone. If you can prevent that from happening then I don't really care how you do it."

Chapter 58
Put Down That Pickaxe

"Ok," I replied with a sigh, send me the quest.

"Hold on," Panda said, holding up his paw, "why ask us?"

"Actually," the director replied, "I've offered this quest to every adventurer in town. It's an emergency, guild-wide quest. Sadly, a lot of my adventurers are currently out of town on contracts, but all those still here have been assigned the same quest."

"Lay it on me," I said with a reluctant sigh.

Emergency Quest:
Put Down That Pickaxe

Civil unrest has erupted across Cali Port between the capitalist and communist factions. Find a way to stop the madness before someone gets hurt.

Objectives:
Stop the protests: 0/1
Reward: A mobile base for your team.

"A mobile base?" Bell squealed, "that sounds awesome! I wonder what it'll be? Ooh, maybe it'll be a flying aircraft carrier like in *Avengers*."

"I hope it's a mobile tree house," Panda added, "stocked with natural bamboo and with a hot spring included."

"Don't be ridiculous," Asmodeus said, "the only mobile base fit for one such as I would be a flying fortress with stealth capabilities and a legendary-grade weapons attached."

I couldn't help but smile at their excitement, though knowing my luck it'd be a tent and not even a magic one, just a bog-standard festival style tent that would blow away with the slightest breeze.

Regardless of the reward, if we wanted to be able to leave Cali Port to continue on our way to Castalor we were going to have to complete this quest.

My stomach sank as I thought about meeting the communists. Knowing this stupid world they would be utterly ridiculous and they'd probably call me comrade and think I was one of them thanks to that stupid torch I had stuck in my inventory.

"Ok director, we accept," I said begrudgingly. "Do you have any places for us to start in?"

"Please, call me Freja," she replied with a calculated smile, "and yes actually, there are two main locations that I need you to start with. The first is the gate itself, I need eyes on the crowd there. If all hell breaks loose, it'll start there. The second place is outside a government building not far from here, one of the leaders of this communist movement is conducting a protest there."

"I'll check out the gate, Gonads," Sally said, piping up for the first time since the meeting began, "the rest of you can check out the government building."

"Of course," Freja replied, "thank you for your assistance in this. Please feel free to pop round any time if you need anything. I will help as much as I can."

With that we bid her goodbye and took our leave. Once we reached the foyer the guard pointed us towards the back exit, which meant that thankfully we wouldn't have to push through the angry mob outside a second time.

Sally left with barely a word and I made her promise to keep in contact. Then the rest of us headed back in the direction we'd originally come from.

"I wonder what these communists are going to be like?" Bell asked, an air of whimsy to her tone as if this entire quest was simply a game to her. She seemed oddly excited; it would have been infectious if not for the sinking feeling in my gut.

We walked for a short while back in the direction of the kangaroo court when I spotted our likely objective.

On the opposite side of the street from us stood a group of extremely small humanoids holding picket signs. I couldn't quite hear what they were saying, but they stood in front of a government building.

"This has got to be the place," I declared to Bell and Panda's nodding agreement.

"Human," Asmodeus declared, "take me over there, I wish to see the little people."

"You can't call them that anymore, Azzy," Bell began, "it's offensive."

"Azzy?" He roared, turning his small head to glare at the fireball mage, "...I like it! I shall permit you to address me by this nickname and I shall call you...Ifrit, after my brother, the fire demon."

"How about you just call her, Bell...*Azzy*," I interjected, "it's only one syllable, she doesn't need a nickname."

"Aww," she protested quietly as we carefully attempted to cross to the other side.

The city was structured with underpasses for those of us below the level cap to move across the road without risking death.

It was essentially treating those above the level cap like vehicles would be treated back home. I guess it wasn't too much of a leap, getting hit by a truck would probably do *less* damage than getting hit by a jade soul.

"Do not call me Azzy, Human," Asmodeus grumbled from my shoulder, "that is *our* thing," he said, glancing at Bell who smiled pridefully back at him.

"Great," I sighed, "my new familiar likes you more than me."

"I am not your familiar, human," he spat, "we may be soul bonded, but know your place. You are my transportation, a future soul for me to devour and, in the case of an emergency, food."

"Don't worry kid," Panda said patting my upper thigh reassuringly, "*I* would never eat you."

"You're a herbivore," I replied dourly.

As we trapsed up the other side of the underpass the shouting got louder. The tiny people were chanting and raising their picket signs which had a plethora of pictures scrawled across them. I focused on them and the notification popped up.

The one closest to me bore a crudely drawn picture of a gold coin with a large cross over it. I was about to wonder why they would be protesting money and not the conditions of the working class as were described by director Freja, but then I realised what they were chanting.

"Down with the bourgeoisie!" A little guy on a soapbox shouted in a squeaky, high-pitched voice.

"The proletariat will rise again!" The rest called back, equally high pitched.

"Oh no," I said as my stomach did a somersault, "this is not going to be pleasant."

I didn't even need to read the description that popped up in my HUD when I focused on them to know what that sinking feeling was.

You have discovered a new race:
Gnome

The *gnomes* are a subspecies of *dwarves* who have evolved to be even smaller due to the lack of sunlight in the mines.
Do they photosynthesise? Who knows.
Whereas *dwarves* have natural abilities for working with rocks and minerals, metal working, smithing and basically anything that involves intense physical labour and skill for low pay, *gnomes* evolved into something else entirely.
They are the antithesis of their *dwarven* ancestors, preferring to spend their time on political protests, attempting to sway the other races towards their way of thinking, rather than honing their craft.
Put down that pickaxe and pick up a hammer and sickle.
After generations of being used as a cheap labour force, the *gnomes* decided it was about time that they saw the fruits of their labour, instead of working to make the rich, richer.
Gnomes are a hive mind species, an echo chamber who are hell bent on taking down the rich and elevating the poor.
I hope you still have *The Torch of Eternal Communist Supremacy*, because these little firecrackers are going to love you.

Before I had a chance to turn around and run in the opposite direction, the entire group turned towards me all at once.

They had wide, happy grins on their faces as they looked up at me expectantly.

Damn that system and its stupid passive aggrieve gifts!

"Comrade!" The leader shouted happily.

"Comrade!" The rest repeated.

"Have you come to aid us in our revolution comrade?" The leader said.

"Aid us!" The others repeated.

"What the hell is going on," Bell asked me, "do you know these guys?"

"Explain human," Asmodeus added, "what is the nature of your relationship with these little people?"

"I've never met them in my life," I replied, holding up my hands in surrender, "but I think it might have something to do with that damned torch the system lumped me with."

At least we were in the right place, even if it was going to be painful.

Chapter 59
The Proletariat Will Rise Again

"Listen," I said, backing away slowly with my hands held up, "I'm not one of you-"

"You must aid us on our quest comrade adventurer!" The leader interjected.

"Aid us!" The rest echoed once more.

I knew what was going to happen. I had been in Celestia long enough to understand how this damned system worked and there was absolutely no way I would be accepting it.

No, no, no, no, no...

New Quest:
The Proletariat Will Rise Again

"God damn it!"

The *gnomes* need your help comrade!
Aid them!

Objectives:
Help the gnomes: 0/1
Reward: *Unlock a powerful skill for Asmodeus.*

I knew this was going to happen. I just knew it.

That being said, I was rather interested in what giving Asmodeus a new skill would do and I guess this *did* qualify as a sub-quest for the director. Would this reward mean that Asmodeus could help me in combat?

Or use it to eat my soul… I shivered.

"Human!" The dragon whispered in my ear, at least he seemed to intend it to be a whisper, but I was certain that everyone in the immediate vicinity could hear him. "You must aid these little people. My skills are locked away as I am only a fragment of a demon lord in this current body."

"Will you try to eat my soul if you get more powerful?" I asked.

"*…nooo…*" he replied, quite unconvincingly. "I can help you fight with my skills unlocked. They are quite powerful you know."

"Aid us!" The gnomes said in optimistic unison.

"…But I'm not a communist," I protested as they moved in closer, looking up at me with happy, heart wrenching smiles.

"But you smell like a communist," one of the little fellows said after making an exaggerated sniffing noise in my general direction.

"Please comrade, you hold the eternal flame, I can sense it," the gnome leader said, dropping off his soap box and approaching me with his hands clasped firmly behind his back.

He was an aging man with a trimmed white beard and big, round eyes. Perched on top of his head was one of those furry hats with the ear flaps, a hammer and sickle insignia was sewn onto the front.

The hat reminded me of those that the Russian soldiers wore in *Call of Duty: World at War*, a game I had fond memories of from my high school years. That wouldn't be enough to sway me though.

I wasn't sure that helping the gnomes would qualify as completing the quest Freja had given me. I wasn't even sure if I should be taking sides at all.

"Kaleb," Bell said, tugging on the sleeve of my armour like a child attempting to emotionally manipulate their parents into buying them a new toy, "you can't say no to that face. Just look how cute he is."

"That's not the word I'd use," I moaned. "This damned torch has been a pain in my arse since the day I got stuck with it. If I help out a group of commie gnomes in the middle of the aggressively capitalist continent we're on, you just know that it's going to spell trouble for me later down the line."

"The director *told* us to resolve the situation," Bell replied hopefully.

"She didn't say to join the protestors though, did she?" I replied, rolling my eyes as I spoke.

"Kid," Panda said, clasping his own hands behind his back and mimicking the gnome. "Do you even know what the gnomes believe in? Back in Havar, your definition of socialism was quite different to the king's. It might be worth talking to them before you brush them off. Besides, we don't even know what they *want*."

"The back-up snack speaks truthfully, human," Asmodeus agreed, "…and I want one of my powers unlocked. I demand that you speak with them."

Panda glared back at the dragon but didn't retort.

Looking around at the group, I eventually gave in. Panda made a good point and the thrill of completing quests was always a nice dopamine hit. Hell, maybe it would be a quick and easy one for once.

"Fine," I sighed, looking at the gnome leader. "Let's talk, then I can decide."

"Thank you comrade," he replied in his squeaky voice, with a little bow, "if you'll follow me, I know a place where we can discuss this in private."

461

"What about your protest?" I asked.

"The others will remain here, it is only this body that will accompany you," he replied and I shrugged back at him.

With his hands still clasped firmly behind his back, he led us off to the side and down an alleyway that snaked behind the building we had just been in front of.

Contrary to the clean and well-maintained streets we had previously been on, the alleyway was dirty and it smelled of urine. It reminded me of home.

"Where are you taking us?" Bell asked as we walked, very slowly, behind the tiny gnome.

"To the Under-Slums," he replied in an almost mechanical voice. "That is where the undesirables of this city live. Those chased out of regular Cali Port society for one reason or another."

"They must really hate communism here," I replied.

"It reminds me of home," Bell said, almost sadly, "my parents grew up during the cold war and the anti-communist sentiment was so driven into them that the mere mention of red made my dad...well...*see red*. I still remember the lecture he gave me when he found me reading Russian fantasy books."

"Well in his defence," I replied casually, "their way of thinking doesn't exactly have the best track record. It might sound nice in theory, I grew up poor as muck so I get the appeal, but in reality it always ends with one psychopath having too much control and everyone under him living in squalor."

"Maybe where you're from," the gnome said, "but we gnomes are of a hive mind, we are not individuals, we are one consciousness spread across multiple bodies. It is different for us."

"Sure, but you're only one of many species who live here," I replied, opening my palms as we followed him, "something that works for you might be to the detriment of everyone else."

"Perhaps," he responded absently, "we're here."

Pointing to a rusted manhole cover, he turned towards us with a wide grin and bowed once more.

"Your people live in the sewer?" Bell asked.

"He *did* call it the Under-Slums," Panda said with a shrug before taking a drag from his bamboo pipe.

I had a sudden flashback to my last trip into a sewer where I'd massacred a bunch of slimes and nearly died inside a slime queen.

Was this going to happen in every city I visited from now on? The obligatory sewer trip. I hoped not.

The gnome lifted the grate and a foisty smell of stale air and earth leaked out. It didn't smell even half as bad as the Havarian sewer, I'd needed a mask in that place. No, this smelled more like unwashed people and a lack of fresh air.

Grabbing the ladder with his stubby hands, the gnome began climbing down and an echoing thunk rang out with each of his steps.

I followed with my team.

"I know I requested the retrieval of my power, human," Asmodeus began, trying to pinch his nose shut with his claws, "however I did not realise that would require me to accompany you into a peasant hole. Perhaps you should make the retrieval without me?"

"No way," I replied sternly, "*you* wanted me to speak to the gnomes, *you* want your power back so *you're* coming with me...*Azzy*."

He huffed loudly and a small puff of flame erupted from his nostrils, lighting the sewer hole for a moment. It was made of damp, moss covered stones.

I reached the bottom with a light splash as my boots hit a shallow puddle which had gathered there. It was pitch black, but only for a moment. The gnome pulled a lit torch from his inventory.

The flames danced and flickered among the receding shadows and I saw that we were in a cramped drainage tunnel covered with moss and made of the same damp stones that I'd seen on the descent.

"Comrade," the gnome said, looking up at me through the orange flames, "add your flame to mine, I want to see it."

I rolled my eyes and did as he asked, equipping the *Torch of Eternal Communist Supremacy* from my inventory. The makeshift item I had made with the system gift of *Stalin's Stylish Socks* still burned brightly, the faint logo of a hammer and sickle dancing beneath the reddish, orange glow.

"Wow," the gnome said, clearly awestruck, "it is magnificent, comrade. Thank you for allowing us the privilege to gaze upon such a wonderous flame."

"Just get walking and take us to this private place of yours," I muttered back as Panda and Bell exchange whispered snickering behind me.

We were barely walking for more than a few minutes before the sewer opened up into a massive, sprawling favella.

"*Under-Slums* is right," Bell gasped, "it looks like the beginning of *Fast Five* down here."

She wasn't wrong.

The Under-Slums was a huge underground shanty town. Small structures were dotted about everywhere, seemingly made of corrugated iron, bits of wood and old tyres. It was a marvel that any of them stayed upright.

People littered the streets as we passed through the makeshift town. There were hundreds of them, possibly more. Noticeably, I didn't spot a single human or svartalf.

There were plenty of gnomes, lycanids, catonids and an array of different creatures I'd never seen before. I even spotted an unhappy looking garuda sat on a mouldy rocking chair and gazing up at the roof of the sewer system. I wondered if he was thinking about the sky outside. If I could fly, I'd hate to be holed up underground too.

I placed my torch back into my inventory, the slums was lit by glowing moss on the roof and an array of fires which burned in metal barrels.

The sewer dwellers were dirty and many had missing limbs and bruises. All of them were armed to the teeth like some kind of militia and in their eyes burned a searing hatred. I didn't like that look.

"Through here comrade," the gnome leader said chirpily as he ducked under a piece of corrugated iron, holding it back like a tent flap for the rest of us to follow.

I ducked inside, the others hot on my heels.

The interior was dark and the air felt moist, and kind of rancid.

"Hey, Mr Gnome," Bell called out, "it's a little dark in here, do you have a light?"

We waited a few moments but there was no reply. With a heavy sigh, I pulled the torch from my inventory once again and the room lit up in bright orange as the flames danced around the room casting shadow puppetry on the walls.

Stood directly in front of us was the gnome leader, his hands placed ceremoniously behind his back. Flanking him were two others: the biggest lycanid I'd ever seen, and a catonid wearing a beret.

Both of them held crossbows aimed squarely at mine and Bell's chests.

Well shit.

Chapter 60
What The Hell Are We Negotiating?

It barely took me a moment to survey the enemies before I reacted.

Stood in front of me was the gnome leader, he was unarmed and therefore not a threat. Next to him on the right-hand side was a small catonid woman wearing a green beret and army fatigues. She pointed a crossbow squarely at my chest, though she looked uncertain.

On the other side of the gnome was the biggest lycanid I had ever seen. His head nearly touched the roof and his back was wider than a car.

He'd give Sally a run for her money with his bloated, vein covered muscles. He also pointed a crossbow, though this one was aimed at Bell.

I decided that he was definitely the most dangerous of the two, his steely gaze told me that he wouldn't hesitate to fire. He was a born killer.

I acted, mostly on instinct.

Activating *perception of the apex predator*, I dropped my torch and dashed towards the large lycanid. It was a risky move. Stopping time severely drained my stamina which meant that if I didn't time it perfectly I'd be unable to attack once the skill wore off.

I drew my dagger as time stood still, reaching the lycanid just in time to perform a precise slash along the tendons of his wrist.

It was an odd thing to watch, I saw his skin split and I knew his wrist would go limp enough to drop the crossbow, but because time had been stopped, no blood gushed out when my dagger made contact with his skin. It was an eerie sight.

I wished I still had my second dagger; I had much more practice dual wielding them than I did using one at a time. Though I guess you can't cry over spilled milk. I made a mental note to buy a second one as soon as I could.

I resumed time after approximately two seconds and my stamina bar was down to less than a quarter.

Not wanting to waste time, I wrenched the crossbow out of the surprised lycanid's limp hand and jumped backwards as blood finally began to gush from his wound.

I expected him to howl in pain but he barely released more than a surprised grunt as his limp wrist dripped blood onto the ground.

As I moved backwards I swung the bow around and placed the tip of the bolt firmly into the side of the gnome's head. I was certain that he was the leader of this ragtag militia and hopefully that would make the catonid think twice about using her own crossbow.

"Drop your weapons!" I shouted, "or the little guy gets it."

The catonid swung around to face me, visibly much more startled than her growling counterpart. She looked between me and the gnome and then with a sigh, placed her weapon on the ground.

Bell hurriedly kicked it out of her reach and pointed a hand at both her and the lycanid, little flames sparked threateningly from her palms.

"Well done human," Asmodeus said with a little nod, "that was exhilarating…can we do it again?"

I'd almost forgotten that he'd been perched on my shoulder the entire time. I wondered how he'd experienced my skill. Maybe it felt like teleportation to him? I'd have to ask him later.

"Well, gnome," the lycanid growled in a deep huff that was quite typical for his people, "it seems this human of yours has spunk. I like him."

"Yes," the gnome nodded, seemingly unphased by the crossbow bolt prodding his podgy little temple. "He is quite unique...for a human. I think he could prove most useful to the cause."

"Hold on a god damned second," I said, feeling the temperature rise in my chest. "I haven't agreed to anything, why would I even *consider* helping you out after you led us into an ambush?"

The lycanid laughed dangerously, his eyes watched me intensely. It was unnerving.

"Apologies human, it was but a test," the gnome replied nonchalantly.

"Testing for what exactly?" I growled, "you're lucky I didn't kill you."

"A test," he explained, "to determine how you would react under unknown, threatening situations. We wanted to see what choices you would make. Would you try to talk your way out of it? Would you attack us in a fit of rage and get shot? Or would you use your personal power to turn the tide? Suffice to say, we are most impressed."

"Oh goodie, I'm so glad I've won your respect," I replied, shaking my head.

"You speak facetiously," the gnome continued, "but you *should* be glad to have won our respect. Without it you would never have made it out of here alive."

He shot me a devilish grin and then clicked his fingers. The room lit up suddenly with blinding florescent lights and I realised that we were surrounded by at least fifteen militia members all pointing crossbows at us.

Well shit, the little guy's got game.

"It seems we are outgunned, human," Asmodeus said loudly, "would you like me to devour their souls for you?"

"I can fireball them to death?" Bell suggested, "it's been a while since I got to enjoy the pleasures of burning flesh." She shot an evil grin at the group of guards closest to her and a few of them grimaced and squirmed where they stood. I couldn't blame them.

"You literally burned half the population of an entire island to death barely three days ago," Panda said, shaking his head and pulling out his pipe as if he hadn't a care in the world.

I smiled to myself. My little team was becoming pretty awesome.

"I like *her* too," the lycanid growled, gesturing towards Bell with his limp wrist, "the little dragon…not so much."

"How dare you?" Asmodeus said, glaring at the behemoth from my shoulder, "I am not *little*…I'm fun sized."

"Alright then gnome," I said, trying to put steel into my voice, "what do you want from us? You said we should talk in private, so talk."

"Perhaps you would like to remove that weapon from my head first?" he asked.

"No thanks, I think it's fine just here for now," I replied cooly.

"Very well then," he sighed, "this little community you see before you is called the Under-Slums, it is a place for outcasts, minor races and those who are mistreated and abused by the current capitalist system of Cali Port and indeed, the rest of the continent.

"Down here we follow a simple yet fair rule, 'all for one and one for all'. We have a hierarchy of course, which is run by an elected representative. Our council meets once a week to discuss the best ways in which to enrich our citizen's lives and we try to keep things fair and equal for all of our people.

"In order to do this we formed a worker's union above ground, the idea being to campaign for fairer wages and working conditions for the lower classes. As things stand, many can't afford to feed their young on the meagre wages forced on us by the bourgeoisie who own all the businesses and land."

"And that's why you blockaded the gates, to protest these unfair wages?" I asked.

"Exactly," the gnome replied, "when the upper classes decided to laugh at our demands we realised a show of force was necessary. Sadly, they only seem to understand violence and power, but they forget that there are many more of us than there are of them.

"All we want is equality among all the people of Cali Port, a fairer share of the wages, less discrimination, a peaceful and moral life. A communist utopia."

"This doesn't sound very communist to me," Bell pointed out, "it's definitely left wing, but I'd barely even call it soft socialism."

"Good point," I replied, furrowing my brow, "where we're from communism is about the government owning everything and dis-tributing it evenly among people. All jobs pay the same, it's true equality. Everyone works together for the good of the community. Well, that is, unless you're an artist, musician, writer or philoso-pher...and unless a maniac takes power and corrupts the entire idea, which literally always happens."

"That is very interesting," the gnome replied, his eyes twinkling slightly, "it sounds very similar to the gnomish hives we come from."

"Like I said before," Panda interjected, "your definitions are dif-ferent to theirs."

"Then why do they use the same words?" Bell asked, "How is it that two completely separate places have developed the same words for their politics but they don't have the same meaning?"

Panda shrugged and then a message notification popped up in our group chat.

Panda: *My best guess is that they aren't using the same words as you. They speak an entirely different language to you outworlders, remember? The language you hear is being translated by your skills, the political factions of this world use words that would be alien to you, so I think the system is translating them by using words that are close in meaning, but that you are also familiar with.*

Kaleb: *Then what about the race names? I've never heard of a lycanid before back on Earth.*

Panda: *No, but you have heard the word lycanthrope and the word cat, and a garuda is a mythical creature from Earthen culture. The words you're being given by the system all mean something to you, even if they're spliced together with another word.*

Bell: *Why didn't you tell us this before? It could have saved us a lot of confusion.*

Panda: *Honestly, I didn't really consider it until recently. As a sage I can speak the languages of this world and the language of my summoner automatically. All of those languages get jumbled up in my head, they make sense to me, but it's as natural as breathing. It's part of being a daeomon.*

Kaleb: *I guess that makes sense. So we need to abandon everything we know about Earthen politics and assume that our faction words don't match up with those of this world.*

Panda: I would say so, yes. It seems that the factions of this world have similar ideas to that of yours, but they're not identical.

Asmodeus: Cease this idiocy, the three of you have been standing in silence for almost a minute. The gnome looks quite worried.

Bell: HI AZZY!

Panda: Who added him to the chat?

Bell: I did, we're besties now.

"Ok gnome," I said, pulling out of the chat and seeing the puzzled expression on his face. "I understand what you're saying, so how about you call off your guards and we can chat about it over a nice drink?"

"…ok…" the gnome replied warily, lifting his hand which in turn signalled the guards to lower their weapons and leave the room. "Would you mind explaining why you were silent for so long?"

"I just needed a minute to think things through that's all," I replied with faux confidence. "You threw a lot of information at me there and I needed to sort through it."

"Like a loading screen," Bell added unhelpfully.

"Well then, shall we move to a more comfortable room and begin negotiations?" He asked.

"Yes, of course," I replied courteously.

Negotiations? What the hell are we negotiating?

"This is going to be fun," the lycanid said in a deep, hoarse voice, "he he he."

Chapter 61
Oh, What Big Eyes You Have

Still carrying my stolen crossbow, I followed the little gnome out of the dark trap room and into a moderately furnished sitting room nearby.

It had two large, if a little worn, sofas and a coffee table in the middle. The gnome sat on one side and I sat directly opposite him. As my butt touched the cushions I sank deeply into the soft, well used, upholstery.

It was comfortable, but not exactly the best position to initiate combat if the worst happened. I still wasn't willing to let my guard down, at least not yet.

Bell sat on one side of me and the giant lycanid sat on the other side. I shot him a worried glance as his huge posterior lifted my side of the sofa upwards. It protested with a threatening creak as his full weight sank into the cushions.

The catonid sat next to the gnome, looking quite dismayed at having been so easily beaten. By contrast, the lycanid didn't seem to care at all. He stared at me with challenging eyes, but it wasn't a look of contempt.

"You're fast, human," he said in a deep, gruff voice. "We should spar for real some time. I wanna see *exactly* how tough you are."

"Thanks…" I replied awkwardly, "but how about we have this conversation first. I wouldn't want to keep our host waiting."

"Have it your way," he replied with a disappointed sigh.

Bell looked across me at the lycanid, staring intently at his ripped, furry body. She had that fiery look in her eyes and I knew what she was thinking before she even opened her mouth.

"Not now, Bell," I said before she had the chance to challenge him to a duel. She frowned at me before forcing herself to look away from him.

Seriously, what's with all the battle junkies in this place.

"Shall we begin?" I asked, gesticulating towards the gnome who had watched my exchange with his friend quietly.

"Of course," he replied cordially.

"Sweet," I said, "before we get into the details of what exactly it is that you want us to do for you, I want to ask you a little bit more about your beliefs. From what you said before, you seem like the good guys in all of this. However, we haven't met the capitalists yet and I'm pretty certain that even most villains believe themselves to be righteous."

"There isn't much more to tell," he began, looking between his two companions. "As I said before, we strive to create a utopia where all are equal and there is peace and morality. The first step towards achieving that future is to secure fair wages for our people and to fight back against the discrimination they receive."

"Ok," I said thoughtfully, "but what is morality to you? Your ideas surely differ from the capitalists and their ideas differ from the Havarian socialists I met before. How can you be sure of who is right or wrong?"

He looked at me with beady, black eyes, squinting slightly as if he misunderstood the question. In all honesty, I just wanted to check that he wasn't secretly a terrorist or something before I helped him.

Director Freja gave me free reign to solve this conflict however I wanted and I needed to make sure that I made the right choices. I doubted she'd be happy if I helped the gnome overthrow the current government and created Stalin 2.0.

"Morality is simple," he said after a long moment, "it is a code of hard rules that must never be broken. The contents of them usually differ slightly from person to person, but in general if you use empathy as your guiding principle I don't think you can go far wrong."

"Ok then," I said, taking a moment to think before continuing. It was a pretty good response in my opinion, but it seemed to lack depth. Not that my own thoughts on morality were any deeper, the most thought I'd ever put into the subject was when discussing philosophy with my mate Luke over a few pints at our local pub and that hardly made me an authority on the matter.

Still though, I'd been intrusted with this quest and I had to try and make the right choice, so I probed further, "let me ask you a question. What if you had to choose between two strangers dying or someone you loved dying. Who would you choose? This is a question often asked by ancient philosophers from my worl- country," I hastily added, correcting myself before I let even more people in on my biggest and worst kept secret.

"Your silly mortal problems bore me," Asmodeus announced, "I am declaring nap time, please wake me when this tedium is over."

He jumped from my shoulder to Bell's lap and curled up. From the gormless expression on her face, I could tell she thought that was adorable.

"The person you love," the lycanid answered in place of the gnome, furrowing his brow. "What kind of question is that, human? I thought your kind were supposed to be smart."

"What about you?" I asked the gnome.

"Gnomes are a hive mind species, so this concept is a little alien to us," he began slowly, "however, I would have to agree with comrade Rex."

Rex? I thought, *I wonder if he gets why that's so funny.*

"Wait!" Bell shouted, "your name is Rex and you're a dog person? That's hilarious."

Before I could stop myself I felt my palm slap against my forehead. I removed it slowly by rubbing it downwards as if trying to rub away the headache my teammate had caused.

"Rex is an honourable name!" he declared, half standing, fury burning in his yellow eyes. "In my culture, names with too many syllables are weak names. There has never been a strong Geraldine or Joshua. Besides, I am a lycanid not a *dog person.*"

"Ok…" I jumped in before the big scary wolf man decided to challenge my fire mage to single combat, "back to the matter at hand. Of course you would choose your loved one, everyone would, but that in itself shows the flaw in using empathy as your guiding principle. One life isn't worth two when you look at it objectively."

"That is mere fallacy," the gnome countered, "would you rather we lived with no morals? No code? Are you an anarchist human?"

"Huh," Panda muttered, "I guess that word means the same thing no matter where you're from."

"Not at all," I replied with a shrug, in fact, I knew that I would make the same choice myself. The entire reason I was levelling up and trying to gain power was for the sake of seeing my family again. "The point I'm trying to make is that I don't think there are any hard-set rules when it comes to right or wrong. Good people don't need rules to do the right thing and bad people will always find a way to break them.

"The hard-line view of morality as you see it can only be kept by threat of force and where I'm from, that has always created a breeding ground for dictatorship. From what you've said, I don't disagree with your views, but the idea of a perfect and harmonious utopia is just that…an idea. It won't work because people have the capacity to be different, especially here where there are so many different races with their own ideas and perception. You already said you're a hive mind species, surely you must agree that a lycanid or catonid will view the world, and morality differently to you?

"So, if I do help you out, I need to know that you're not going to try and turn this continent into a massive gnome hive. I can't help a side that opposes freedom."

I took a deep breath.

My HUD buzzed and I opened the group chat.

Panda: *Since when did you care about politics, kid?*

Kaleb: *Freja gave me the power to choose in this quest. I just don't want to pick the wrong side. I'm trying to be responsible for once.*

Bell: *FREEDOM!*

Kaleb: *Look, I just want to know that these guys are as good as they think they are. Whatever choices I make in the coming days could affect thousands of people.*

Panda: *People you don't know. Just pick a side, complete the quest and let's leave this town in the dust in our new mobile treehouse. We have to get to Castalor remember?*

Kaleb: *I need to be able to look myself in the mirror once all this is done. If a job is worth doing, it's worth doing right. Besides, it definitely won't be a treehouse.*

Panda: *Fine, but if it's not a treehouse you owe me a lifetime supply of bamboo.*

Bell: '*MURICA! FUCK YEAH!*

Perhaps I was being a little too preachy with the gnome, but something about his hard-line way of thinking just rubbed me up the wrong way. I'd seen enough shows on the history channel to know that it never worked out, and yes, I used to watch the history channel, sue me.

The gnome had already mentioned that his species was a hive mind. When segregated from the other races I was sure it was a perfect, communist utopia…if such a thing exists. However, his Under-Slums militia seemed to be an equal mix of races and I just hated the idea of them losing their agency if this guy went off the rails.

Fighting for equality and fair wages was a noble goal, but he'd already alluded to it only being the *beginning* of his plans.

"You think too much human," Rex said, slapping me on the back with his uninjured hand. "The little gnome is ok in my books, don't get your panties in a twist. Besides, all he wants you to do is help him to arrange a meeting with some prissy rich guys. He's not asking you to lead the revolution."

"Rex speaks true comrade," the gnome added, "we merely wish to be able to speak with our adversaries on equal ground. There is no diplomacy without dialogue."

I looked towards Bell and she shrugged back at me. Panda nodded at me once, I think that was his way of saying that we should take them up on their offer.

What could possibly go wrong if all they wanted was to set up peace negotiations. Surely that was better than a killing spree. Besides, Asmodeus would probably devour my soul if I didn't accept this quest. He really wanted that power back.

"Ok," I eventually said, "if that's all you want then we can certainly try. Though I have to warn you, I haven't actually met the capitalist faction yet. I can't guarantee that they'll speak to me at all."

"You speak with the authority of Adventure Society, of course they'll listen," he replied with a smile. "We do have one more condition though…"

I narrowed my eyes at him.

Who was *he* to give *me* conditions? We'd just met and I was helping him free of charge. A meaty palm clapped my shoulder once more, pulling me from my thoughts.

I turned towards Rex; his large, yellow eyes boring into me with a passionate fire lit beneath them.

All I could think was, *oh, what big eyes you have*, as the massive wolf-man stared directly into my soul. I'd just have to hope I wouldn't end up like *Little Red Riding Hood*'s grandma.

"Now that you've seen our home we can't risk you selling us out to the capitalists," the gnome continued in a calm and confident manner. "As such, Rex will be accompanying you on this quest."

The wolf grinned at me and my stomach churned as his dripping canines glinted right in front of my face.

"This is gonna be fun, human!" He said in that horse, guttural voice of his.

Chapter 62
We Have A Lycanid In Sector Three!

We left the Under-Slums shortly after our meeting and I found myself breathing fresh air again. Well, mostly fresh. The city had a thin smog which seemed to cover most of the area. I hadn't noticed it before but I was pretty certain it was factory smoke, not that I'd ever seen a factory in Celestia so who could know for sure?

Asmodeus was still sleeping and Bell carried him dutifully as we walked through the back alley towards the centre of town.

"The capitalists have a poncy council," Rex said as we walked, "it is made up of a bunch of rich guys who own the biggest corporations in town. You'll need to meet with one of them to get them to agree to talks."

"Who would you suggest?" I asked.

"Fredrick Millicent should be the easiest to convince," he said, absently scratching at his facial fur, "that guy is a weasel. Easily intimidated. Give me five minutes alone with him and I'll get us that meeting."

"Somehow I don't think that's what the gnome wanted," I sighed, "...wait, did you say Millicent?"

"I guess his family was a big deal after all," Bell said, "and here I was thinking he was just some low rent noble's son...maybe I should have slept with him after all."

We all looked towards her.

"When were you going to sleep with him?" Panda asked.

"Oh, at the king's ball," she replied lightly, "he propositioned me whilst Kaleb was talking to the big guy. Naturally I said no, I have more class than that."

"Do you?" Panda asked, raising an eyebrow.

Bell looked at him with a fake shocked expression and then laughed.

"Where can we find Mr Millicent," I asked Rex.

"In the financial district, I'll show you the way."

With that we followed the huge lycanid through crowded and twisted streets that were nothing like the parts of town I'd seen on the way in.

In lieu of the wide main streets that made room for those who had reached the level cap to be able to zoom around like the *Flash*, these streets were made of broken cobles and looked more like something out of a Victorian period drama.

We passed rows of closed down shops with boarded up windows. People littered the streets and the smog above them seemed thicker somehow, darker.

Groups of catonids, lycanids, garuda and even a smattering of leprechauns huddled together beneath large, mouldy blankets as they warmed themselves on trash can fires.

It was a horrific sight, but the smell was worse. Unwashed bodies, urine and the all too familiar stench of depression hung heavy in the stale air. It reminded me of the day my first stepfather left.

I'd come home from school to find the house in tatters. Furniture upended, glass broken, the stench of spilled beer and mascara tears. Of course that happened every time my mum broke up with someone. After a while I stopped caring so much. But the first time, well that was something to remember.

She took me out for pizza and a movie and by the time I'd woken up the next morning it was as if nothing had ever happened. There was no trace of him having ever been part of our lives.

I hated reliving that moment. It's amazing how something as inconsequential as a smell can bring it all flooding back.

"Who are all these people?" I asked.

"Most of them used to run the stores around here," Rex answered, "but they were put out of business by the corporations. They've been making bids recently inside the local government, buying up land for their factories."

So there are factories in Celestia.

"If they're buying the stores shouldn't the owners be rich now?" Bell asked flippantly.

"No, the land and buildings were all owned by the council," Rex replied sombrely. "The small business owners leased them. No normal person can afford to own property in this town, sweet cheeks."

"And the government just sold off all its land to these rich guys?" I asked.

"It's hard to say no when they offer you billions of gold coins, besides the council basically is the government around here." he shrugged.

"That sounds about as corrupt as where I'm from," Bell murmured with a smirk. I got the impression that she didn't really care too much about bigger issues, still, she seemed to know more about it than she let on.

The sceptical part of me had to wonder if Rex had taken us this way on purpose, part of the gnome's plan to garner our sympathy for his cause. Either way though, it was a difficult sight to look at.

Even if it had been engineered and this was just a small part of Cali Port, no one should have to live like that.

"I guess Havarian Socialism is looking *pretty* good right now, ay kid?" Panda asked smugly.

We turned a corner and it was like walking through the wardrobe to *Narnia*. I swear that even the sky was brighter as we stepped onto a high street full of well dressed, happy looking people.

Wind distorted through the large centre road from the superhero-like level cappers as people went about their day without a care in the world: shopping, eating out, buying adventuring gear. Happy families barely a stone's throw away from the desolate area just behind us.

I wondered if they knew.

"These idiots bury their heads in the sand," Rex growled, mostly to himself.

"Who are they?" Bell asked.

"Factory workers, middle management mostly from the looks of them," he replied, his voice was ragged as if he was suppressing violent urges. "You can find Millicent in there," he said, pointing a large, hairy finger towards a huge, glass skyscraper.

It looked remarkably similar to the Adventure Society building, it even came with loud protestors outside the sliding glass doors.

"How are we going to get through the crowd?" I asked.

"They're *my* protestors," Rex said, opening his arms, "hey, human, watch this."

He took a few steps forward and cleared his throat loudly. A few people from the back of the crowd turned around and then the mumbling started. Like a game of whispers, within barely a minute the entire crowd had turned around to look at the massive lycanid with his smug grin.

"I'm here on urgent business," he said in a voice loud enough to put Asmodeus to shame, "these adventurers are acting as a delegation for us, let them through."

Like Moses parting the red sea, he spread his arms out and people moved aside clapping and cheering as we walked through the gap like movie stars attending a premier.

"This looks suspiciously like a wall of death," Bell commented, "we're gonna go so hard when that breakdown drops."

I chuckled as we passed through the crowd towards the main doors.

"See human," Rex whispered in my ear, his breath warm and foisty, "you're not the only *unique* one around here."

"I didn't realise it was a competition," I replied light heartedly.

"It's not," he said hastily, "but if it was I'd win."

We reached the front of the crowd and I found myself staring directly at a wall of armed men. It was like a police barricade minus the riot shields.

They all wore black suits underneath their thick, metal armour. It was an odd combination. The man in the centre, who seemed to be in charge, held up his hand as I approached.

"Sorry sir but this site is on lockdown at the moment," he said formally, "I'm afraid you'll have to come back later."

"I need to speak with Fredrick Millicent, it's urgent," I replied.

"Mr Millicent is unavailable at this time," the guard said, "if you'd like to schedule an appointment I can look at his itinerary for you? Though I doubt he'll be able to see anyone until this mess is dealt with."

I opened my mouth to speak but was harshly knocked to the side by the large lycanid before I could say anything.

"Get out of my way you puny little capitalist worm," Rex said, literally picking the man up by the scruff of his neck and throwing him to the side.

The rest of the guards didn't like that.

"We have a lycanid in sector three, send reinforcements!"

484

"The commander is down, I repeat, the commander is down!"

"The line has been compromised! Johnson, get in there and sure up our centre."

"Yes sir!"

They sprang into action, presumably talking through some kind of verbal voice chat function.

"Hurry up, human," Rex said as he battered a nearby guard with his shoulder, "get in there and get us that meeting! I'll hold them off."

Though this wasn't exactly the *diplomacy* I'd had in mind, I didn't need telling twice. Quickly, I ran through the gap Rex had created and dived through the automatic sliding door.

Inside the foyer was a contingent of surprised people dressed in formal shirts with strange patterns and embroidery on them.

One of them dropped his steaming beverage as I walked past him, fixing the collar of my armour as if this was just like any other day.

They layout was pretty similar to the Adventure Society buildings apart from the water fountain in the middle which said *Millicent Industries* in large, bold letters.

Behind the fountain was what looked like duelling escalators with a small elevator tucked into a corner to the side.

There was a receptionist desk in the other corner and an array of coffee tables and seating scattered about, that was where most of the employees were sat, steaming cups of...*something* in hand.

"Which way to Millicent's office?" I asked the crowd of startled employees.

No one spoke, but all of their eyes were on me.

"Why even bother asking?" Bell said as she waltzed up behind me like she owned the place. "It's obviously going to be on the top floor, that's where they always are."

"Good point," I replied before jogging towards the elevator.

Panda looked up at me and sighed before lifting his arms, I picked him up and pressed his paw onto the nearby control panel.

The lift door opened with a ding.

The elevator was mana controlled so, as possibly the only person in Celestia with no mana for himself, I couldn't activate it.

"You know, *I* could have just done that for you," Bell said over my shoulder.

We entered the elevator and this time Bell pushed *her* mana into the switch, instructing it to take us to the top floor.

The doors shut and our little tin box began moving upwards when a jingle began to play. It was a hearty tune, very happy.

"I hate elevator music," I mumbled.

"Really?" Bell asked, "I always think it's so peppy." She bobbed her head to the lacklustre tune and her turquoise hair bounced around her shoulders.

"Right guys," I said, changing into my formal suit through the quick equip function in my HUD. "I think it's time for a meeting with the big guy."

Chapter 63
Who Needs Personal Power When You Have Money?

The elevator doors opened with a ding and I stepped out into a familiar office suite.

"Do you think there's a company who build all of these glass skyscrapers?" Bell asked, "I mean they're all pretty identical, sounds like lazy writing to me."

"Probably," I replied, "either that or it's one guy with a very specific skill."

"*Liam Neeson?*" Bell asked.

I ignored her.

Looking around the room it was plain to see that the only real difference between it and the director's office back at Adventure Society was the style choices.

It seemed that Fredrick Millicent was a man of extravagant tastes.

The walls were painted a mixture of gold and royal purple and large oil paintings hung on them. The one closest to his fur coated desk seemed to be a portrait: a man sat astride a large red dragon, his bare chest rippling with sculpted pectoral muscles and a sceptre was held firmly in his grip.

It in no way represented the very average looking man who turned to greet us as we entered the room.

Fredrick Millicent wore a suit that looked a few sizes too big for him. His thinning hair was poorly covered by a combover and his massive pecs…were non-existent.

I walked towards him brashly and stood at the edge of his desk as he stared up at me with a furrowed brow and eyes that suppressed a hint of fear. I wondered if he thought we were protestors who had managed to breach the gates.

"Mr Millicent I presume?" I asked.

"I might be," he replied shakily, "who's asking?"

"Kaleb Akabane," I said curtly, "I'm an adventurer and I've been tasked with putting an end to this civil war you've got going on here."

He looked at me through narrowed eyes and then glanced around at my team. Though he didn't seem perturbed by the sight of a smoking panda in the room, he frowned deeply when he laid eyes on the sleeping dragon in Bell's arms.

Seriously, how had Asmodeus managed to nap through all of the ruckus outside. My wife had always been a heavy sleeper, but even she would have been roused by *that* racket. I was a little envious.

"I wouldn't go as far as to call it a civil war Mr Akabane, not yet at least," Millicent replied, "however, I would be grateful for your help. This riff raff has been causing us no end of grief these last few days. We're losing millions of gold per day and the shareholders are one more mess away from lynching me."

Frederick looked extremely gaunt in the face. It was hard to imagine someone as successful as him going without, but I had the distinct impression that he hadn't eaten in days.

"Well Mr Millicent," I said taking a seat in front of his desk, "I might have a solution to your problems, but first let's talk a little shall we?"

"You do?" He replied hopefully before regaining his composure and fumbling for a decanter of amber liquid and a few glasses. "Any help you could offer would be most appreciated. Can I offer you a drink?"

I nodded and he began shakily pouring glasses of the unnamed alcohol. They sparkled with refracted light; small curling patterns had been sculpted into the glasses causing them to glint like diamonds.

Glassware this fine must be expensive, I thought darkly, thinking back to the homeless people we'd passed earlier.

I took a sip of the harsh amber liquid once Fredrick had poured it; it tasted like smoky motor oil and reminded me of *Jack Daniels.*

"So, back to business Mr Akabane," Fredrick said, "what is it you would like to discuss with me?"

"Well," I began, taking a moment to compile my thoughts, "mostly I'd like to know about the events leading up to these protests from your perspective."

He gulped and loosened his tie slightly before draining his glass. There were bags under his eyes. Considering that *I* barely needed sleep anymore and he was no doubt levels above me, he must have been deeply stressed by the situation.

"It's those ungrateful gnomes' fault," he sighed, "we've had a good thing going in Cali Port for generations. This city has been a cornerstone of industry, supplying wares across the continent and beyond.

"The populace has worked together like a well-oiled machine since well before my time. My father started this company after settling down from being a famous adventurer and people were happy to work for him. He was a true visionary that man. No one has ever complained about the hours or the pay rate before now."

"How much do you pay them exactly?" Bell interrupted.

"I don't know," he shrugged, "that's payroll's job to manage. I *do* know that it's at least one gold per week which is far more than they'd get in other places."

"*One* gold per week?" I asked, struggling to stop my eyes from blinking rapidly in disbelief.

"*I know!*" he replied, gesticulating wildly, "how can they complain about it? It's very generous if you ask me."

"Just out of interest," Panda said, "how much do *you* make per week as the owner?"

Fredrick sat back for a moment, crossing his arms and rubbing a wrinkled hand across his bare face.

"I'm not quite sure to be honest," he said thoughtfully, "but whatever it is, I deserve to make it. I'm the owner, this is my company and I've worked damn hard to make it the international corporation that it is today. You have to understand, there's a lot of risk in running a company. I could go bankrupt. So naturally, I deserve the biggest slice of the pie."

"I thought you said your father started the company?" I asked, folding my arms.

"He did," Fredrick replied nonchalantly, "but *I* run it *now*."

"Ok," I sighed, "well we're not here to open that particular can of worms. The solution we have is pretty simple. All I need is for you and the council to agree to meet with the communists for a discussion. That's all they want."

"A *discussion?*" He asked in a high pitched and offended voice, "why on Celestia would I agree to that? Why would any of us? We've all worked hard to get to the positions we're in now and suddenly these damned gnomes think they deserve a seat at our table? It's an outrage…it's a scandal…it's…"

"It's the only way you're going to be able to stop them from dragging you out into the streets hanging you in a public execution," I interrupted, folding my arms and giving him a poignant look.

He took a step back, locking eyes with me. He looked tired, yet still, somehow, prideful. His features were haggard and after a moment his shoulders sagged and he dropped into his lavish chair with an overly dramatic sigh.

Pouring himself a large glass of the motor oil booze, he downed it in a single go and then reached into his draw and pulled out a long cigar. He lit that and began puffing on it like a chain smoker would with a cigarette.

I was pretty certain that wasn't the correct way to enjoy a cigar, but I kept my mouth closed.

"Fine," he said defeatedly. "I'll convince the council, but I have one condition."

I raised my eyebrows to get him to continue.

"I want you and your party to attend as well," he said, refusing to meet my eyes. "If you back our agenda in the talks I'll make it worth your while and if not…well, we could always use extra security. You can't trust those wretched commie gnomes."

"You *do* know that gnomes are only one of the races that'll be attending right?" Panda asked, taking a cue from the businessman and puffing on his own bamboo pipe.

"Of course I do!" He spat, "but before *they* showed up the others were happy to fall in line and do what they've always done. Mark my words, you can't trust the gnomes, this is all their fault."

"Oh definitely," Bell agreed sardonically, which seemed to go right over Fredrick's head. "It's got nothing to do with the wealthy fat cats like yourself exploiting poor workers for cheap labour, this is *entirely* the gnomes' fault for putting ideas in their heads.

"My family's company wasn't exactly renowned for giving their employees benevolent wages, but it was at least enough to live on."

That was the second time she'd mentioned her family owning a business. Was Bell rich back home? She certainly didn't act like she had been…most of the time.

"I'm glad you agree," Fredrick said curtly, "it's nice to see that Adventure Society, at least, has reasonable employees. What was your name miss? I have a son who is of marrying age and-"

"Yeah…" I said, cutting him off and rolling my eyes. "Anyway, we need to report back to the director, so can I trust you to set up the meeting?"

He frowned at me for a moment and then nodded and we left his lavish office as fast as we could. I didn't want to spend another moment in his presence.

***

Fredrick slumped back in his chair as the adventuring party left, letting out a long sigh and loosening his tie further.

Staring into the bottom of his empty glass, he saw a much older gentleman looking back at him. His frown lines had stretched and his forehead held a sheen that was unbecoming of a man in his position.

Had this whole debacle really hit him *this* hard?

"Are you sure that was the right move sir?" He asked, though there was nobody present in the room.

It was, an eerie, serpentine voice said directly into his mind.

He would never get used to communicating with Chrysus this way. Fredrick still remembered the day his father had inducted him into the capitalist cabal of Cali Port.

It has been a cold winter's evening as he rode silently in the elevator with his father. He'd always been a hard man, but Fredrick looked up to him with gleaming eyes.

A group of the wealthiest people in the Port stood in a circle wearing cloaks and hoods. It was terrifying. His father had taken out a small snake and Fredrick had been ordered to let it bite him on the collar bone. The fang marks had blackened and were still there to this day, then the voice spoke to him and he was inducted.

All he'd ever wanted was to take over the family business. He'd fought endlessly with his brothers to be the one to inherit the role. Though these days he wondered if he'd really been the winner.

He hadn't spoken to his siblings in years, but last he'd heard his elder brother, the man who would have taken over the company if not for him, was living a peaceful life on some island to the south.

Apparently he even had a kid now. Fredrick had fought tooth and nail to usurp his brother and become the heir. Now though, he wasn't sure it was worth it.

I need that boy, Chrysus continued, *and for him to come to me he needs to be able to leave Cali Port. You will crush the opposition at this meeting and open the gates for him to leave.*

"If that's what you wish sir," Fredrick replied monotonously. "I'll speak to the council and see if we can arrange for something tragic to happen to the gnome and his envoy."

Perfect, Chrysus replied, *just make sure that the boy is not harmed.*

Then the god vacated Fredrick Millicent's mind and he sighed, dropping his shoulders as his body felt like it physically deflated.

He knew that he'd need to scheme carefully with the council. The god of wealth was their most important patron, without his protection his father never could have made the business what it was today and Fredrick couldn't have continued to keep it afloat the way he did.

Luckily for him, his close friend and confidant ran a local mercenary company. All he had to do was invite the gnome in and then set his hired muscle loose. Who needed physical strength when he had money?

Chapter 64
Every Dog Is A Puppy At Heart

I left the building with a sour taste in my mouth. Something about the gnomish leader didn't sit right with me, but Fredrick Millicent was an out and out parasite.

People like him were the reason I'd chosen to become self employed back on Earth. Pompous, self-satisfied idiots who'd inherited their fortune and yet still deluded themselves into believing that they were somehow above everyone else.

I wouldn't have minded so much if he was at least honest about the real reason he had so much money and power. You can't choose the circumstances in which you're born. But somehow, people like Fredrick Millicent could never seem to grasp that they were painfully average and it was their parent's wealth that allowed them to delude themselves into thinking they were above the rest of humanity.

"Do you think his son's good looking?" Bell asked wistfully, breaking me out of my spiralling thoughts as we slipped back into the crowd of protestors.

The ruckus Rex had caused seemed to have died down a bit whilst we were inside. The guard's line was reenforced and the protesters were back to shouting recycled call and response lines.

"What?" I asked irritably.

"His son," Bell repeated, "he offered to marry me to him. Do you think he's attractive?"

"Judging by the look of his father, probably not," I sighed, moving like a snake through the grass as I led my party out of the crowd.

"That's a shame," she said happily, "I might have considered it."

"You'd give up this great adventuring lifestyle for a bit of money?" Panda scoffed, though it seemed a little sarcastic.

"Of course not!" She protested, "but having a wealthy husband at home couldn't hurt could it? I could winter in his fancy home and adventure during the summer. It'd be great."

I shook my head as I finally broke through the growing crowd and found myself face to muzzle with Rex. The huge lycanid towered over me, his eyes glimmering in the evening twinkle.

"How'd it go?" He asked in his gruff, dog-like voice.

"They've agreed to meet with you," I replied, "or at least, Millicent said he'd convince the council to."

"Perfect!" He yelled, almost loud enough to startle the rambunctious crowd behind us once more. "In that case, I'd better go and let the others know. I assume you're coming to our *negotiation*."

I nodded, feeling suddenly very tired.

"Good," he said, slapping me on the shoulder, "in that case I'll see that our leader sends word of the time and place. Where are you staying?"

"I don't know yet," I replied wearily, "we'd only just arrived in town when we got sent on this fool's errand."

"It's not a fool errand human, this mission you've been given will help us to make great changes," he said, "you'll see. Anyway, in that case I'll have him contact your director with the details."

Without another word he turned and ran up the street. As Rex turned the corner and disappeared from view I could have sworn I heard him howl in delight. It was hard not to smile at that. Even if he was a massive killing machine I guess every dog is a puppy at heart.

That was when a system message lit up my HUD.

Quest Completed:
The Proletariat Will Rise Again

The *gnomes* need your help comrade!
Aid them!

Objectives:
Help the gnomes: 1/1

Reward: *Unlock a powerful skill for Asmodeus.*

Well at least Asmodeus will be happy, I thought tiredly, glancing over at my sleeping dragon as he breathed heavily in Bell's arms.

I exchanged a look with Panda who seemed as surprised as I was that the notification hadn't woken him up. I decided to let sleeping dragon's lie for the time being, we'd find out what *amazing* power he'd unlocked once he woke up.

"We should find Sally," I eventually said to the others wearily.

I wanted to update her on the day's events. She had told us that she'd head towards the gate leading out of town. Supposedly that was where the largest and most unruly protest was taking place.

Hopefully she'd still be there.

"Then can we get a drink?" Bell asked, "I could use one after today. We've been trapsing round all day playing gofer for these idiots and that's not what I signed up for when I decided to become an adventurer."

"Agreed," I replied as we began walking in, what I hoped was, the right direction. "The sooner we put this to bed, the sooner we can leave Cali Port in the dust and head towards our real objective."

"And we can do it in style," Panda said with a grin, "don't forget the reward for this mission, Castalor is a long way from here and I for one don't want to walk there."

I smiled at him and nodded. He was right of course, as bothersome as it was, completing this quest should help to cut our travel time down significantly. Besides, who wants to walk thousands of miles when you can ride?

As we reached the high street I noticed a large number of people hurrying in the opposite direction to us. It must have been a sign that we were going the right way, though why they were fleeing was anyone's guess.

I hoped Sally was alright.

"What's going on?" Bell said, grabbing a running man by his sleeve and nearly toppling him to the ground.

"There's monsters fighting," he said breathlessly, "barely got out with my life."

Then he shrugged her off and continued to run away.

"Well, there's that excitement you were looking for," I sighed, glancing at Bell. "We should hurry."

Breaking into a run, I deftly avoided the oncoming crowd as I made my way towards the epicentre. The closer we got, the louder it was.

"Seize the means of production!"

"Down with the bourgeoisie!"

"The proletariat will rise again!"

The air was thick with the sounds of protestors chanting their communist catch phrases. I didn't see any sign of a monster though. Surely they wouldn't continue to protest if some beast had appeared to cause havoc would they?

I pushed my legs harder and arrived at the scene.

Located in a large square that was bordered by town houses and stone buildings, was a huge crowd. There must have been thousands of them. Gnomes seemed to make up the bulk but there were other minor races there as well, and an entire garrison of guards surrounding them.

The protestors were blocking the gate out of town just as Freja had warned us. To their backs was a lowered portcullis, they even had people on the walls themselves. It was a straight up hostile take-over.

The guards were penning them in and though there was no fighting, they had their weapons drawn and huge shields covering their fronts.

That's when I saw it, a huge, fireball of aura permeated the sky above. It seemed to be coming from somewhere within the guard's ranks.

"That looks…tasty," a sleepy Asmodeus said as he roused from his slumber.

Before she could stop him, he launched himself from Bell's arms and buzzed towards the powerful aura at full speed.

Shit! He's going to get himself killed.

"Since when could he fly?" Panda asked, "he was barely gliding last time I checked."

With an aggravated grunt I dashed after him, Bell and Panda following panickily in my wake.

"Oi, who are you?" A burly guard asked, but I'd flipped over his shield landed and behind him before I could reply.

Hell yeah, I can do flips now! Must be the stat increases.

Dodging confused guards like a cat, I swerved through their ranks as my dragon's eye showed me the way towards the power source.

As I got closer I saw a few guards squirming and looking uncomfortable. I slipped passed them and found myself in the middle of a ring of guards. Two people were going at it in the middle.

One of them was Sally, but surprisingly, her aura wasn't the strong one I'd sensed.

She was bleeding heavily and her oversized sword laid abandoned on the ground as she panted on her knees. Her chest was soaked with blood and sweat covered her body.

When did she get that fixed? I wondered. It had been snapped clean in two during our fight with Clive the elder litch. Did the craftsmen in Cali Port work *that* fast?

Standing over Sally was an athletic-looking man with tied back, black hair and a rapier in his hand. He looked like some kind of Middle Ages duellist with one hand behind his straight back.

"Do you surrender Adventurer?" He said in a strange, almost French, accent.

The tip of his sword was pressed firmly against Sally's neck. It looked like a needle next to her thick muscularity, but the red and black aura that enveloped it made it glow even larger than Sally's oversized broad sword.

As I stood, staring at the scene, Bell crashed into me from behind and I stumbled forwards.

"Why'd you stop?" She asked.

The man turned towards me with a surprised expression on his face, though his sword remained firmly at Sally's throat.

"And who might you be?" He asked, ignoring Bell, raising his eyebrows and tilting his nose up at me.

What a bellend, I thought, but before I had time to answer I heard a familiar buzzing from above.

"Your soul shall be mine!" Asmodeus yelled as he dive-bombed the man and sank his fangs into his neck.

Chapter 65
Scarlet Mascara Tears

"Ahh!" The startled rapier wielding man screamed as Asmodeus sank his fangs into his neck.

My dragon's eye burned as I watched the red and black aura get sucked out of the black-haired man. It looked as if my little dragon was leeching the life force from him.

"Get off me you cur!" The man shouted as he thrashed about and tried to slap Asmodeus away as if he was an annoying, deadly fly. "Guards! Help me!"

His pleas fell on deaf ears as the terrified guardsmen watched in horror, eyes wide and mouths agape. To a man, they appeared to be terrified.

"That's the power of a demon lord!"

"It can't be."

"By the gods, is it the end of days?"

"Don't be foolish, it must be a monster, perhaps a tiny succubus?"

Asmodeus suddenly stopped his feasting for a moment to glare at the last man to speak, who fell to his knees as he, presumably, saw the little dragon's aura burst out in a furious black fire which surrounded his tiny body.

Instinctively I moved my hand to my dragon's eye as it burned in my eye socket. However, despite the warmth, there seemed to be no pain.

The same couldn't be said for the unfortunate guard who had earned Asmodeus' ire though. He clutched at his eyes and fell to the ground as smoke rose from between his fingertips.

"I AM NOT A TINY SUCCUBUS!" Asmodeus roared in a voice that was so loud it drowned out even the chanting from the nearby protestors.

"Azzy, stop!" Bell pleaded, clutching her own eyes as steam began to emanate from them and thin trails of blood leaked from them like scarlet mascara tears.

It seemed to fall on death ears and the dragon turned his attention back to the man whose neck he bit into once more. The guard on the floor sighed for a moment and then looked up, removing his hands to reveal charred sockets where his eyes should have been.

Blood and viscera flowed down his face, but from the grim smile upon it, you'd wouldn't have guessed.

"Thank you oh merciful one for sparing my life!" He said in a grateful and awestruck voice.

Who was this idiot to thank a dragon for scorching his eyes out? That didn't matter now though. All of the other guards in the area were clutching their faces and for some reason I was the only one who wasn't properly affected. I needed to act.

I ran towards my dragon and grabbed him, tugging hard, yet as I staggered backwards, so did the black-haired man. Asmodeus' jaw strength must have been incredibly strong to be able to latch on so tightly to a man.

Damn it! I thought, *it's like playing tug of war with a Pitbull,* but then I recalled the system message I'd gotten when he'd first appeared.

502

Asmodeus (Soul Bonded)

Due to your use of the *Chaos Seed*, a small fragment of
the demon lord *Asmodeus* had remained in the mortal
plane.
Possessing a miniscule amount of his powers and
personality, he has hatched as a demon familiar, taking
on a shape imposed on him by the imprinted soul to
which he is bonded.
As a soul bonded familiar, *Asmodeus* cannot directly
disobey your commands.
Make sure you house train him.

Presumably, if I commanded him to stop he would have to listen, if the message was accurate. It was worth a try.

"Asmodeus!" I bellowed as loudly as I could to make sure he could hear me above the riotous noises coming from all around us. "I command you to release this man and stop burning people's eyes out, you're hurting Bell."

He gave me a defiant, sideways glance and continued his life sucking as red and black aura left the man's new neck holes and was adsorbed by the dragon.

Then, suddenly, he stopped.

"Arrg!" He exclaimed, dropping to the floor and covering his head with his wings. "Damn you human, let me feast!"

"I said no," I replied sternly, like a trainer scolding a dog.

"F-fine," he relented, "just make this infernal pain in my head cease."

I didn't really know what he meant, but if I had to guess, it must have been physically painful for him to disobey me. That had to have been what the system message meant when it said that he couldn't.

What a barbaric form of control, I thought with a grimace. Then again, the system could have easily messed with me and given me a squirt bottle or a clicker or something. At least *this* worked.

I didn't like seeing him in pain though, something inside me felt oddly empathetic towards him. Perhaps it was a biproduct of the soul bond? Either way, at least my command had worked.

"Wow," Bell panted as she trotted up next to me, that was really...something. Are you a dragon or a vampire?" She asked Asmodeus who looked at her bleeding eyes and lowered his head, looking away.

"This is why you don't bond with a..." Sally said, shooting a look at the dragon. I was thankful she didn't outright call him a demon lord in front of the guards.

Her top was bloodied, bisected by a deep gash which scarred her from shoulder to naval. I wasn't sure why she'd been duelling the man with the rapier, but if he'd managed to land a hit on her that badly, he must have been good. Possibly even beyond the level cap.

"G-guards," he said breathlessly, as if on cue, "arrest them, arrest all of them. That dragon needs to be put down immediately."

I turned towards him to see his bleeding eyes shooting daggers at me as he lifted his rapier with an unsteady hand and cupped his neck wound with the other. Scarlet blood dripped from his formally pristine black uniform and the tips of his hair were matted with it, giving him the look of a noughties emo with dip dyed hair.

"I just saved your life," I growled, feeling something primal rouse within me, "and I can just as easily *sic* my dragon back on you."

I was seething and I didn't even know why. I hadn't had the best day, true, but under normal circumstances I considered myself to be a pretty reasonable fellow. Not today, however.

Asmodeus looked up at me with greedy eyes as I mentioned letting him suck the life force from the man, and I realised that the eyes of every other person in the circle were on me too.

There was a tense atmosphere as I looked around at the injured guards. Fear, scorn, loathing, I saw all of that and more in there bleeding eyes.

Bell's expression told me that she was ready to back me up at a moment's notice, Sally, however, seemed unsure. Had she not just been fighting this man herself? What was that look for?

Her dark blue eyes were piercing as she gazed at me from the floor, a meaty palm pushing into her chest wound as she attempted to stem the bleeding.

"I am the captain of the guard," the rapier wielding man replied after a moment, "threatening me is the same as threatening all of Cali Port, do you really think you are strong enough to best an entire city?"

"I don't need to," I said coldly, "I just need to let my dragon kill you. Which of your men would dare to face me after watching that? You saw his power, just look at their faces, they're terrified."

Murmurs escaped the crowd of guards who looked at each other uncertainly and I knew I was right.

"What were you even fighting about?" I asked Sally, making a point of turning my back on the captain.

"Nothing important," she muttered, "we used to know each other a long time ago, wanted to settle an old score."

I looked at her face for a moment as it twitched and she looked away from me. I wanted to know more but now wasn't the time to pry.

"We need to report back to the director…remember?" Panda said, tugging lightly on my trouser leg.

I nodded.

505

"Sally, can you walk?" I asked.

She nodded at me and struggled to her feet, a shallow pool of blood began to gather beneath her and I passed her a healing potion from my inventory.

"That won't work," she said, "or I'd have already taken one myself. His blade is magic, normal potions can't stop the bleeding."

"Are you ignoring me?" The captain asked incredulously, "guards, do as I order and arrest these scoundrels!"

A few men took steps towards us but were halted as Bell summoned fireballs into her palms.

"Sorry boys," she said with a smirk, "but I can't let you do that."

"Are you deaf?" The captain erupted, "fine then, I guess I'll have to do it myself and the lot of you will be on half rations for the rest of your pitiful careers!"

He took a step forward, pointing his blade directly at Bell's chest. She glanced up at him and rolled her eyes.

"You'll never take me alive copper!" She yelled, casting both fireballs at the man's face from close range.

The captain made to dodge but he wasn't fast enough and his clothes erupted in a sea of flames. Fortunately for him, he still managed to slice through the fireballs and save his face.

Summoning my dagger, I performed a pirouette and was on him before he had time to recover. I slashed downwards at the nape of his neck and he flicked his rapier over his head with a flash, blocking my attack.

"You are resisting lawful arrest!" He called at us as Bell blasted another fireball his way, which he successfully dodged.

Using her attack as a distraction, I dropped into a crouch and sliced at his Achilles tendon but he must have been a mind reader because halfway through my attempted slash he threw his leg out in a powerful back kick, disarming me as my dagger sailed through the sky.

I rolled backwards with the force of his blow and withdrew my bow as Bell began blasting him with a quick chain of fireballs.

Panda dived to the side and Sally summoned her oversized sword, getting it in front of her body just in time to save herself from the excess flame which exploded out of the area attack.

The captain dashed towards Bell in a zig zag motion, slicing through each of her attacks with ease before shoulder barging her backwards.

With a grunt, she staggered back into the waiting arms of two burly guardsmen who grabbed her from behind and held her still as they struggled to close manacles on her wrists.

As this was happening I pulled back the drawstring on my bow and channelled my *Soul Shot*, lining up the strike for the dead centre of the rapier wielder.

Even if he tries to block this it'll still do some damage, I thought as I loosed my arrow.

The arrow exploded from my bow string with a deafening crack as it broke the sound barrier. The backdraft from the shot blew a devastating force of air behind me which knocked three advancing guards off their feet, they hit the ground with a thud.

The captain spun masterfully and batted my arrow with the flat of his blade, causing it to go off course and head directly for the crowd of protestors.

Oh shit, I thought, *if that hits them there will be God knows how many civilian deaths on my hands. That bastard.*

Just as the arrow whizzed past Sally's head, shortening one side of her hair by a few inches, a powerful crack emanated across the battlefield.

"THAT IS ENOUGH!" Freja shouted as she appeared in front of the protestors as if out of nowhere, catching my arrow with her bare hand and snapping it in two with a clenched fist.

Veins popped in her forehead, her scarlet hair seemed to defy gravity as it floated around her beautiful, if contorted, face.

She strode towards us like a furious runway model, her heeled boots clacking against the ground menacingly with each step.

"Does someone want to explain to me just what in Athena's name is going on here?" She asked, her eyes bulging and her jaw clenching with every word she forced from her lips.

The captain was the first to speak.

"T-these miscreants attacked me," he whined like a little bitch.

"Are you telling the teacher on us?" Bell asked, still struggling with her guards, "snitches get stiches!"

Freja shot her an icy look and she went quiet.

"Right," she said, "I want to see all of you in my office immediately. Bickering in the streets like children is unbecoming of Adventure Society professionals."

The captain, showing either extreme bravery, or extreme stupidity, stepped towards the director, pointing his rapier at her throat.

"They are in my custody," he began, "you might be the queen of your little rag tag group of misfits, but in Cali Port, I am the law."

She backhanded him in the face and he flew across the circle, crashing into a group of his men.

"Holy fuck," I breathed.

"My office," she said once more, taking the time to look between each of us. "Now!"

Chapter 66
Pompous Prick

I gazed at Freja with a slack jaw as she waved her arms in a circle and a glowing purple gateway appeared in front of us.

Looking like a mirror, it showed the calm, decorated interior of her office back in the Adventure Society building.

She was a portal user.

I wasn't even aware that they existed.

"Ooh, fancy," Bell crooned, "*Yennefer of Vengerberg* would be proud."

Now was not the time to be making pop culture references, but I was too shocked by the director's awesome display of power to chastise my companion.

She had just batted away a man who had beaten Sally in a duel, literally! I knew that Sally was below the level cap and therefore wasn't a big fish here in Cali Port like she was in Havar, but still.

"Shut up and go through," Freja commanded and without hesitation I obeyed her.

Stepping into the portal felt like jumping into an ice bath, my blood felt chilled and my bones creaked as I was sucked into the venerable whirlpool of icy cold and motion sickness.

It wasn't too dissimilar to the time I'd used a portal to enter The Morningstar Hotel and Spa, but it *was* much rougher.

Falling through space, I was ejected onto the other side with flailing arms and legs. I shot across the room, sliding on my belly, and crashed headlong into the far wall.

Ouch.

"Wow," Panda said groggily as he calmy stepped through the portal without a crash landing. "Personal portals sure are rough on the old equilibrium."

"First time using one?" I asked, struggling to form the words as my head span like it did after a night of too many beers.

"Yup, and hopefully it'll be my last." He replied, "that was awful."

Despite his claims, he didn't seem to have been affected nearly as badly as I was. Though when Bell came flying through the portal next, I felt like I'd gotten off lightly.

The teal haired fireball mage seemed to fall through the portal as if she had been launched by a trebuchet. Her scarlet red robes moving at such a speed made her look a bit like the fireball magic she was so fond of.

Somehow she hit the ceiling when she reached our side of it and then landed on her back with a nasty thud as the wind was knocked from her.

Sally followed behind, stepping through as if it was nothing new to her.

Show off.

Still clutching her wound, she staggered to the nearest chair and collapsed into it with a groan.

"How can we help you?" I asked, putting my dizziness aside and stumbling over to her.

"I'm sure the director will patch me up in a moment, Gonads," she wheezed, grimacing at every other word as if it was painful to speak.

A loud crack came from behind me and I turned just in time to see the purple rimmed portal snap shut as Freja strode through gracefully, her long, open trench coat fluttering magnificently behind her, Asmodeus struggled under her arms as she trapped him there.

"Unhand me this instant," he protested, "I am a demon lord, not a handbag."

Freja slapped the dragon on the tip of his nose, shutting him up, and without sparing the rest of us a glance, she strutted up to Sally and placed her palm directly onto the catonid's wound. Muttering something under her breath, a bright, golden light sparkled around her hand like a glove made of sunshine, and Sally's face visibly relaxed.

"I've dispelled the magic but you'll still need to heal the wound normally," Freja said clinically, "there's a chance it may scar, I'm sorry."

Sally nodded thoughtfully as the svartalf removed her hand. Closing her dark blue eyes a bright red potion appeared in her hand and she guzzled it like booze. The catonid's wound healed before our eyes, leaving a deep crimson line in its wake.

"That'll have to do for now," she grunted, "I'll finish the healing process later. Thank you director," she said, turning towards the purple skinned powerhouse and nodding once.

Without replying, Freja moved behind her desk, placing the subdued dragon on it. His stomach was bloated to twice its normal size and his tiny wings seemed to have grown a bit. He laid out like a starfish on the desk, sulking and refusing to take his eyes off the director.

She reached into a draw and produced a finely crafted decanter which sparkled in the setting sun's orange glow as it shone through the floor to ceiling window. Freja poured herself a full glass and swallowed it in a single gulp before sitting down and leaning back in her chair.

"Well that was a political disaster," she eventually said with a long sigh as the fierce demeaner she had shown to the rapier wielder vanished entirely. "Care to explain what happened?"

All eyes turned towards Sally who visibly seemed to suppress the urge to squirm beneath our inquisitive gazes.

"It was an old dispute," she said, closing her eyes hard for a moment before reopening them with a determined and resigned look. "We trained at the same academy when we were young. He always made a point of flexing his superiority to the entire class...I didn't like that. When I ran into him earlier today he challenged me to a *friendly* duel for old time's sake...It didn't stay friendly for long."

"You trained at an academy?" Bell asked, still laying in place on the floor where she'd fallen through the portal, her hands placed as a cushion behind her head.

"All those who wish to serve royalty do," she replied and I guessed that she had no intention of explaining any further.

Thinking back on our time in Havar, Sally had seemed to have a history with Raphael as well. He was the king's guard who had escorted us to our award ceremony shortly before the assassination.

Did they train together too? I wondered.

Keeping my inquiring thoughts to myself, I looked towards the director who was staring into the bottom of a second emptied glass.

"What about him?" She asked, glancing at Asmodeus who snorted loudly in response.

Taking the initiative, I explained what had happened when we arrived. My tale barely instigated a response from Freja, even the part about Asmodeus going dragon vampire on that dude's neck.

"That tracks," she eventually said, "I won't shed a tear for the commander, that man is a pompous prick, though it seems that I made a mistake in ignoring your demon lord to focus on political affairs. I'm interested to know the details of this new *power* he has unlocked.

"That being said, now that we know you can control him, I am placing responsibility on you to do so. If he attacks someone like that again, it'll be your neck on the chopping block. Do you understand?"

I nodded solemnly. Controlling the dragon was easier said than done but he had obeyed me in the end. Hopefully I'd be able to keep that leash on him, at least until we could leave Cali Port. I also wanted to know more about his power and I was pretty certain the information would be ready and waiting in my HUD, but that could wait for later. I liked Freja, but I didn't know her well enough to expose too many of my secrets to her and Asmodeus was an unknown factor.

"Good," she continued, "you said your destination was Castalor? The director there is more versed in these matters than I, seek him out and see if he has any further insight into your unlikely familiar. In the meantime, what of the quest I assigned you?"

"We've managed to get both sides to agree to a meeting tomorrow," I said, placing my hands behind my back as if I was reporting to my commanding officer, which in a way, I guess I was. "Hopefully they'll be diplomatic about it. Both sides have asked me and my party to attend though I don't trust either of them to play nice if I'm being honest."

Freja looked up from her glass finally, her sternly beautiful eyes seemingly gazing straight into my very soul.

"Good job," she said as a smile twitched in the corner of her lips, "you've managed in a single day what no one else had managed in weeks. I'm impressed."

"It was probably because of that torch that system gave him," Bell sniggered on the floor and I shot her a deadpan glare.

Freja ignored her outburst and continued. "I shall accompany your party to this meeting as well, it'll look good for the society as a whole if we can get them to come to some kind of amicable arrangement. The quest boards have been pretty light lately since no one can leave the city right now and we need that to change."

"Then will we get our magic transport?" Bell asked sweetly, throwing her hands forward to propel herself into a sitting position on the floor.

"Mobile base," Freja corrected, "and yes, assuming it puts a stop to the protests. That was the wording in the quest, after all." She smiled slightly before taking another drink from her ornate glass. "Now, you'd better get some rest before tomorrow, politics is exhausting and we might be there for a while. The last time I had to attend a negotiation it lasted for three days and nights and that one wasn't nearly as standoffish as this one has been."

The svartalf director sighed loudly and slumped back into her chair, spinning it away from us as she gazed contemplatively out of the window. I took that as a clear sign to leave.

Scooping my sulking dragon up off the desk, I led my team and Sally back into the elevator.

"Where are we going to sleep tonight then?" Panda asked, looking up at me with his large eyes.

"There's an inn just down the street," Sally replied hoarsely, "I know the owner, we'll meet back here at first light and make our way to the negotiation together."

Chapter 67
The Things I Do For Questing

That night, once arriving at the inn, we gathered around a small, private booth in the corner and ordered some drinks. I was dog tired, but I needed to know about Asmodeus' new power.

"So," I said, looking at him expectantly as the rest of the group followed my lead, gazing at him eagerly. Sally was the only one who didn't seem excited, even so, she hadn't turned in for the night just yet.

"So?" He replied.

"It looks like you got that new power," I said, trying to hide the smile that was forcing its way to my lips.

"It isn't new," he muttered, "it's ancient, and it is no where near as powerful as it should be. It's quite the disappointment really."

"It seemed pretty powerful to me," Bell grinned, "you made my eyes bleed when you sucked off that captain."

Panda snorted and I shook my head, talk about poor phrasing. Unable to take the suspense any more, I delved into my HUD and found the familiar tab. Under it was Asmodeus' section and under that, a brief explanation of his new power.

Leech Life – Adsorb another creature's power and use it as your own by draining their life force. Only one skill

can be stored at a time. Excess power will be used as nourishment to enhance the overall stats of the wielder.

"Ok that sounds super OP," I said aloud as I read through the unlocked power. "He can copy people's skills and enhance his stats by sucking out their life force."

"So you *are* a vampire!" Bell proclaimed. Sally's eyes went wide with horror as the prospect of what I'd said began to sink in.

"I am not a vampire!" Asmodeus protested, "besides, this weak rendition of my power is just that. In my full form I could steal an unlimited amount of skills and keep them indefinitely. Now I can only keep one at a time. It's utterly useless."

"I'm sure it'll get better as you get stronger," Panda said, placing a comforting paw on the little dragon's wing which he shoved away.

"It will get better as *he* gets stronger," he said, glaring at me, "and who knows how many centuries it could take for him to reach my former level."

"Thanks for the vote of confidence there," I replied dryly, "in the meantime why don't you tell us what skill you stole from the wanky captain?"

"It was nothing special," the dragon huffed, "merely a basic bubble shield. Hardly worth the effort. His life energy was rather tasty though," he grinned showing us his little fangs.

Sally grimaced.

***

I felt groggy the next morning as we wandered hazily through the streets towards the Adventure Society building.

Bell's groaning and Panda's plodding reflected my own feelings as my head swayed like a balloon filled with clouds. Sally had left a message in the group chat a few hours earlier saying she was going to meet with Freja early.

It seemed that despite my stats allowing my body to heal and recover in a superhuman manner, my mind was still subject to fatigue.

Of course, I didn't need as much sleep as I did back on Earth, but it seemed my abilities hadn't eliminated the need entirely.

Though I was happy with the results I'd achieved the previous day, navigating the world of politics wasn't really my thing and my brain power could only stretch so far. They say fake it until you make it but I doubted I'd ever become a politician, no matter how much our current quest needed me to pretend I was one.

Asmodeus sat animatedly on my shoulder, gazing at the sights like a puppy fresh from the tit. He seemed to have perked up again. Freja's scolding and his disappointment at his new unlocked power had put him in a foul mood the previous night, I was thankful that some rest had sorted him out. His stomach bloating had shrunken considerably overnight but he still looked like an overweight chihuahua.

"Human," he shouted in my ear, "those little people are making fluffy pink clouds on sticks. We must obtain one for ourselves!"

"They're called dwarfs and the pink clouds are called candy floss," I replied monotonously, "It's literally just sugar."

"Human, look!" he called once more as we passed a group of street performers, "that dirty elf is attempting to swallow fire. Ha! Foolish elf, you can't hope to match the power of dragons, for only we can…oh, she did it. Most impressive."

"They're called svartalfs," I replied, "and I think the director would snap your neck if she heard you calling her people *dirty* elves."

He shrunk back slightly at the mention of Freja, even one as overly proud as he, was frightened by her – especially after last night. At least there was some sense in his noggin.

It continued like that for the thirty minutes or so of walking we had to endure to meet up with Sally and the director at the society building.

We were up at the crack of dawn, the golden rays of the sun had barely begun to sneak through the clouds and the sky was still lit with the orange glow of sunrise, yet we were awake, and ready to endure these ridiculous political talks.

The things I do for questing.

As we approached the sliding glass doors that marked the entrance to the society foyer, Sally and Freja walked out to greet us. They were chatting like old friends.

Sally's wound seemed to have healed nicely. She was dressed for battle, that is to say she was dressed how she always did, with her oversized sword slung over her back and her piercing dark blue eyes shining like sapphires in her eye sockets.

Director Freja's attire didn't leave much to the imagination, her dark purple skin wrapping tightly around her exposed and toned core as her signature trench coat hung loosely over her shoulders like a cape.

She was honestly one of the most beautiful women I'd ever laid eyes on, her tight corset helped with that of course. Though, sadly, as a married man I had to abstain from her charms. Or at least, that's what I kept telling myself, I knew deep down that I wouldn't have stood a chance with her even if I was single.

"You're late," Sally huffed as our group huddled together.

"I am always on time," Asmodeus said haughtily, "it is you that are early."

"Yeah, what he said," Bell added with a grin.

"I want to make sure that we arrive before the discussions start so I'm going to open a portal," Freja said, forgoing all pleasantries.

"Where exactly are we going?" Panda asked.

"To the city's central circle," she explained, "the noble district is well fortified and it is not easy to get far into it. They have guard patrols, high walls and magic barriers. As it is, I can only penetrate far enough through their enchantments to get us in front of the tower, we'll have to walk from there."

"The tower?" I asked, raising a single eyebrow.

"You set up the meeting without even knowing where it would be held?" She asked incredulously, "The Ivory Tower is our destination. It is home to the council that governs Cali Port and is the most well protected place in the entire city."

"It's called the *Ivory Tower*?" Bell asked with an amused expression on her face.

"Of course it is," I sighed sarcastically, "why wouldn't it be?"

Without answering, Freja lifted her hands and made a show of straining her face as she swirled them like an actor before the CGI was added in the postproduction edits.

It looked ridiculous, or at least it did until an impressive, purple rimmed portal opened up in the centre of our group huddle.

It looked like a watery surface that reflected a golden building that shimmered as the portal jiggled like a spilled jelly shot.

"Let's be off then," Freja began, "I can't hold this for long so hurry."

I stepped through the portal and once again found myself overwhelmed with nausea, this time however, I at least managed to remain on my feet.

Looking up as I gasped for air, a tower made of gold stood before me reflecting with a magnificently overstated orange glow from the sunrise.

"What happened to ivory?" Panda sneered as he stepped out behind me.

"They should have called it the golden tower," Bell chirped, though she bent over, placing her hands on her knees and looked as if she was going to vomit. Thankfully she didn't.

"It's a little small," Asmodeus remarked.

"Yes, yes it's quite marvellous," Freja said impatiently as she barged through our group, Sally trotting awkwardly at her heel. "Now follow me, and don't go wandering off. I have limited influence in this part of the city so I won't be able to bail you out if you go challenging guard captains to duels." She glanced meaningfully at Sally who looked away, refusing to engage with her superior.

We followed the director through the front door which was at least four times the height of a lycanid and thrice as wide.

Well-dressed guardsmen blocked the entrance, though they doubled as door openers once Freja spoke to them.

"She sure has a way with people," Bell muttered happily as Freja berated the guards until they succumbed to her whims.

Inside, the foyer was extravagant. There was marble flooring, roman columns, a masterpiece painted on the ceiling and beautiful human women, painted golden and carrying glasses of bubbling wine serving all who entered.

"I'm starting to understand why the gnome was so upset with these guys," Panda said, shaking his head.

"Nonsense," Asmodeus replied, "this poorhouse has nothing on my underworld palace, why, the women don't even have tails."

"Are there people starving in the streets where you're from?" Panda bit back.

"Almost exclusively," he said evenly, "why do you ask?"

Panda shook his head and Bell bit her lip to suppress a laugh.

We continued to follow Freja through the extravagant entry way to a glass elevator which took pride of place in the centre of the room. Small waterways surrounded it like a miniature moat and we had to cross a tiny bridge to get to the entrance. Water shot up from the mini moat as we crossed, spelling out the words Cali Port, before tumbling back down into the moat with a splash.

"I need one of these in my front room," Bell gushed.

"You don't *have* a front room," I replied with a smile, tapping her shoulder lightly with my own.

"I will one day," she said, gesticulating by tapping the air in front of her eyes and punctuating her words, "and when I do it'll have a water feature that shoots up into the air and spells out the words *no cold callers*. It'll be magical."

I couldn't help but laugh at that as we followed Freja into the glass elevator. Sally seemed oddly nervous, and quiet. As I thought about it I realised that she had been acting a little strange ever since we'd arrived in Cali Port.

"I think those two have a…*history*," Bell said in a loud whisper she attempted to hide behind her hand.

Both Sally and Freja shot daggers at her and I honestly wondered for a minute if one of them might have the power to kill with a glance.

"Have you only just noticed?" Asmodeus said pompously from my shoulder, "can you not smell the sexual tension of human pheromones and shame in here? I've frequented underworld brothels with less-"

He stopped suddenly as Freja barred her teeth at him. Sally went bright red but the dragon, at least, stopped talking.

Well, that makes sense. I thought, thinking back on how oddly the catonid had acted since we'd arrived here.

The director turned around promptly and brushed the control panel with her slender fingers, it slowly rose into the air, turning as it went and giving us a full 360 view of the foyer before we disappeared into blackness.

Standing in awkward and tense silence, we waited for the doors to open and release us from the thick quiet that clung to the interior of the elevator.

Bell began humming elevator music. It did nothing to alleviate the tension.

Finally, the doors opened and I stepped out into a large room with a long conference table taking pride of place in the middle, and floor to ceiling windows covering three of the four walls.

"Who has an elevator come out in the middle of a conference room?" Bell scoffed, shaking her head as she followed behind me. "It's so…tacky."

"Ah, you've made it," Fredrick Millicent said, walking towards me and offering out his hand.

I did not take it.

"Well," he continued as if nothing had happened, "allow me to extend my most sincere gratitude for your attendance of this negotiation. Let me introduce you to my colleagues…oh, director, I wasn't aware you would also be in attendance?"

Dropping the fake politeness immediately, Fredrick walked around me and straight up to Freja who gave him the same expression one might give a persistent fly in their living room.

Ignoring them, Bell grabbed my arm and led me to the table.

"Networking is the most important part of any event," she said in a deep voice, "or at least that's what my father used to say. Not that I was ever healthy enough to attend events…still, let's say hi."

I made a mental note to ask Bell about her life back on Earth sometime. I knew next to nothing about her childhood, but it sounded…interesting.

She walked towards a slender, middle eastern-looking man in a robe adorned with thick golden pieces. He was dressed much more like how I'd expected people of a fantasy world to dress. Though, that made him the odd one out in a room full of suit wearing aristocrats.

"Look Kaleb, it's *Gandalf*," Bell said in a loud whisper.

The man *did* look like a wizard in those robes, I was just glad that there was no way that he knew who or what Bell was referring to.

"Ah, you must be the young adventurer who forced us to be here today," he said, offering out his hand, "Callum Govetchkz, at your service…though I'm sure you already know who I am."

"Kaleb Akabane," I said, taking his hand firmly, "and actually, I've never heard of you."

"Really?" Callum smiled, seemingly amused by the prospect, "well then let me educate you, young adventurer. My family owns the largest fishing conglomerate on the east coast. Every single fish you've eaten in Cali Port came from my company."

"We haven't eaten any fish in Cali Port," Bell began but was promptly interrupted.

"Oh give it a rest, you old trout," a dark-skinned man with a thick black beard said, "I doubt the boy has any interest in your fish. He's an adventurer, his entire team are only here to complete their quest and get paid. Am I right?"

"Pretty much," I said, looking up at the tall man, "we're just here to make sure this whole thing goes off without a hitch. We'll leave the politicking up to you."

"Excellent, just as I thought," he replied jovially, holding out his hand which I took, "Ernest Regina, at your service."

"Regina?" Bell and I both said at the same time.

He raised an eyebrow and I began to explain.

"We're good friends of Lucas Regina, the director of the Havarian Adventure Society," I said. "Are you his brother? We're actually on the continent helping him with a quest."

I chose not to say anymore. Lucas had mentioned that he believed his father was going to be assassinated, but surely if *this* Regina could have been of any help he would have sought his aid already.

"Well, I guess it truly is a small world," he replied dryly, all of his previous charm disappearing suddenly. "How audacious of my brother, sending low ranked adventurers to fulfil a continental quest. I guess he truly has gone native if he can't handle his own affairs anymore...Not that he was ever any use to family on this side of the pond anyway."

"I like this human," Asmodeus said from my shoulder, "can I devour his soul?"

"Talk about pulling a 180," Bell said with shock in her voice.

"Definitely," I agreed, then hurriedly placed a hand on my shoulder dragon who beat his wings excitedly. "Not you!" I said to him before turning back to the confused looking aristocrat. "You do know he's the strongest person in Havar right?"

"That's like saying the hobgoblin is the strongest subspecies, it's still no dragon is it?" Ernest spat on the floor and looked as if he was about to continue with his derivative drivel when he was interrupted by the clinking of glasses.

We turned towards the noise to see the communists had arrived and Rex had already grabbed Fredrick by the scruff of the neck.

524

Chapter 68
Hive Mind

"Milicent you odious coward!" Rex roared as he grabbed the squirming noble by the scruff of his neck, lifting him off the ground. "Your fucking guards tried to arrest us on the way in. What kind of bullshit are you trying to pull here?"

"Now, now Rex," the gnome leader said in a calm and squeaky voice, "we're here now, no harm no foul. Let him go."

Rex turned towards the tiny gnome, his muzzle looked tense as he snarled and hot steams of breath left his mouth. He looked tentatively back at Fredrick Milicent before dropping him and marching towards me, grunting under his breath.

"What a brute!" Milicent cried, "this is an outrage, Director, surely you can see why we refused negotiations until now. These...these rapscallions know no bounds!"

Rex turned back and growled at the man who let out a short squeal before hurriedly moving behind Freja who clasped her face in her hands, looking like she was nursing a migraine.

"Kaleb!" Rex said, grasping my entire arm with his paw as he pulled me in for a hug. It was surprisingly warm and fluffy being wrapped in his fur, like being held by an animated teddy bear. "Thank you for coming, it's good to have you here. We need all the help we can get if we're to deal with these backstabbing sissies," he said, muttering the last part in my ear.

"It's good to see you too mate," I replied, failing to recall when we had become such good friends, not that I minded. "Just to be clear though, my team and I aren't here to support a side, we're just here to make sure no one dies."

"And to ensure that there is no foul play," Freja said, striding towards me with the gnome on one side of her and a trembling Milicent on the other. "Well, no *more* foul play," she added, shooting a poignant look at Fredrick.

"Quite so," Ernest Regina said, stepping in front of the chair at the head of the table. "As chairman of the council I believe it is my duty to lead this *negotiation* today on behalf of-"

"Actually," Freja interrupted, appearing behind him suddenly and placing a firm hand on his shoulder. "I came here today expressly so that *I*, a neutral party, could chair these talks for you. I assume no one opposes this?"

Ernest looked deeply offended as frown lines cut his lower mouth like trenches, but he didn't speak against the formidable director, instead choosing to move to the seat next to her.

"Good," she continued, taking the seat and leaning back in it like she owned the room, placing her feet up on the table and crossing them. "In that case, if you'll all please take your seats, we shall begin."

The conference table was long enough to accommodate the entire council on a single side. There were twelve of them overall, though I'd only had the chance to meet three of them.

That meant that Sally, Bell, Panda, Asmodeus and I had to sit on the same side as the communists, since there were only the three of them in attendance: the gnome, Rex and the small catonid woman complete with the same green beret and army fatigues she'd worn the last time I'd seen her. I still didn't know her name.

"Alright gnome," Regina said with an air of hostility, "spit it out, what is it that you dirty slum dwellers want from us?"

"Mr Regina," Freja sighed, "might I ask that you at least try to show a modicum of respect to the participants of this discussion. You could at least call the man by his name...what is your name?"

"We are all gnomes," the gnome leader replied with a shrug, "we do not have individual names, this vessel has been chosen to represent the species in political matters but we are all of one mind, a shared consciousness."

Freja rolled her eyes and lifted her palms in defeat as Ernest gave a satisfied smile. A small victory for a small man.

"Well then gnome-" Fredrick began again but was promptly cut off by a growl from Rex.

"That's Mr Gnome to you, Trust Fund."

"Mr Gnome," he corrected, "what is it that you want from us?"

"It is quite simple," the gnome replied curtly, "we represent the people working across Cali Port in your factories. The people who are underpaid, underappreciated and many of whom can't even afford to feed their families whilst you sit in your...well, ivory towers, if you'll excuse the pun, hording more wealth than you could possibly ever need.

"All that we ask is for fairer wages for the workers, a recognised union system so that we may renegotiate these terms as the economy fluctuates, and shares for employees in the businesses that they work for so that they might one day sell them back to you for a small retirement sum."

"Absolutely not!" Callum said, slamming his fist on the table and standing up abruptly. "Hell will freeze over before I give away shares in *my* company to peasants. They should be thanking me for the opportunity to work for such a well-loved and trusted business!"

"That's right," another council member joined in.

"Paupers are workers, not owners," someone else said, "they fronted none of the risk to create the businesses they work for and now they wish to reap the rewards?"

"Greedy," a man in a green blazer added, "the whole lot of them."

"Ahem," Freja coughed into her hand loudly and the buzz quieted down. She nodded at Ernest Regina and he leaned forward, placing his hands under his chin as he considered the gnome.

"I told you," Rex said flippantly, "they were never going to listen. These silly nobles look at the stars reflected on the sea at night and mistake it for the stars. They will never understand the plight of the working man."

"I'm pretty sure he stole that line for *The Witcher*," Bell said, leaning in and whispering in my ear.

"I am a reasonable man," Ernest said, completely ignoring Rex's comments, "*we* are reasonable people. I'm sure we can come to some kind of agreement that doesn't spit in the faces of the hard-working entrepreneurs sitting before you. Perhaps a wage increase, say…one gold more per month?"

"One gold?" Rex yelled. It was now his turn to slam his fist on the table in outrage, except he was much stronger than the council members and he broke off a chunk of the table in his rage, causing a few of them to go wide eyed and lean back in a startled manner.

The gnome put a calming hand on the lycanids arm and he sat back down, mumbling to himself.

"I'm glad to see that the council is in fact willing to negotiate," the gnome said calmly, "however, you must understand that a single gold will make little difference in the workers lives. Why, rent alone is five gold a month for a single room. Even with the increase you'd need three workers to a room for them to be able to afford that, when you factor in utilities and food. Why Mr Millicent's workers only earn one gold per week at the moment. Surely you can see why we have such an issue with this treatment?

"I believe the only way to live in a truly fair society is to share the wealth. Public ownership of business is the pinnacle of social development. There's no room for greed if we are all sharing, all working for the greater good. Though of course, currently we're only asking that you give your employees shares so that they might use them to retire one day. Doing so would align your interests with theirs as they'd have stakes in the company and so wish to see it do well."

"So you wish to take what's ours?" Milicent said in an icy tone, "you demand shared ownership in the businesses that we built from the ground up? In a civilised society, gnome, we call that theft."

"Didn't his dad do the building and he just inherited it?" Bell said in a purposefully loud whisper which earned her a slight laugh from Rex, a smile from the catonid in the beret, and a scathing glance from every member of the council.

"No," Milicent said, standing up and pacing behind his colleagues. "I simply won't stand for it. You can't seriously expect to come in here and bend us over a barrel like this. What do you take us for, common trollops?"

"You've got a big enough mouth for one," Rex sneered, "you could fit at least three cock-"

"Rex!" The gnome hissed, cutting off the lycanid who shrank down in his chair slightly.

"If you're not willing to make any concessions Mr Millicent," Freja interjected, "then why agree to these talks at all?"

"So that we can finally put an end to this silly public dissonance," he replied, a half-smile appearing on his face. "In fact, Adventure Society has done us a huge favour in bringing the communist leadership here, all in one room…Arrest them!"

On command the elevator appeared in the centre of the room and a group of mean-looking mercenaries in fancy armour stormed in.

"Coward!" Rex roared as the sell swords swooped towards him.

However, before Rex could act, the catonid in the green beret, who had been silent so far, leaped across the table dagger in hand.

Fredrick screamed as she drove the point of her blade through his solar plexus and the room turned to chaos as council members dived from their chairs and moved back to the wall.

I jumped from my own chair, drawing my bow from my inventory and turning it towards the advancing mercenaries. However, before I could nock an arrow I felt something hard punch me in the face.

I flew across the room, landing besides Freja as a smiling, scarred sell sword looked at me, licking his lips. Another one held a long sabre to Bell's throat and began frog marching her and Panda towards us.

I felt rumbling in my shoulder as Asmodeus tensed up and growled. I considered letting him lose on the mercenaries but thought better of it as I saw my other companions' actions.

Sally didn't make any attempt to draw her oversized blade, which sat on her back and joined, us without resistance. I felt my insides boil as I watched her compliance. I knew we were supposed to be neutral but this farce was anything but that.

The air besides me felt heavy and I turned in time to see Freja conjure a portal around the dagger wielding catonid's neck. Her head disappeared as the magic dispersed and her body dropped to the floor with a wet clunk as blood gushed from her neck.

"No!" Rex growled, throwing a guard off him as three more piled onto his back, successfully forcing his hands into huge metal cuffs.

The gnome sat silently in his seat the entire time. Watching the debacle with sad eyes.

I stood up, raising my bow but Freja put a steady hand out in front of me, preventing me from aiming at anyone.

"Kaleb don't," she said, looking at me with tired eyes. "This isn't our fight."

Like hell it's not! You got involved. I thought, but the words wouldn't come.

As I looked into her beautiful face I could see the hidden rage. Yet she controlled it so gracefully. Surely she must have something else up her sleeve, or was she just as corrupt as the rest? I honestly didn't know, but if there was one thing above all else that I could read in her expression, it was the knowledge that to defy her would mean my death.

"That is quite right director," Fredrick said, standing up, downing a healing potion and brushing off his suit as the fighting subsided. "And I'll see to it that your guild is amply compensated for maintaining its neutrality in all this. As for you gnome, it seems that you have been well and truly bested."

He took his seat back at the table and a few other council members joined him. Ernest Regina had gone as pale as a ghost, but he recovered quickly, if silently.

Rex was dragged into the elevator by a group of burly mercenaries, he fought them all the way but even he was no match for their strength.

Two more stood behind the gnome threateningly and my team, Sally and Freja were left standing near the window, well and truly out of the fight.

"You see gnome," Fredrick continued, "money is power and I used my power to hire the famous Everett Company. No doubt you've heard of them?"

I looked around blankly, and the gnome stayed silent.

"They're a famous group of mercenaries, jade soul and above only. We'd have never beaten them." Sally said through gritted teeth and I felt my anger at her dissipate as I saw her contorted face.

"Exactly," Millicent said gleefully, "so now, gnome, you're going to tell your people to get back to work and then you're going to rot in a jail cell until we decide what to do with you."

The gnome looked deeply into Fredrick's eyes for a long moment and then began to smile.

His demeanour changed drastically as he tipped his head back and belly laughed in a high pitched, squeaky voice. Millicent's face reddened as he stared at the hysterical little man.

"How foolish you are to think that you've won, why, because you hired a few famous mercs?" The gnome began, regaining his composure as the nasty smile split his face. "We have an army of workers that vastly outnumber you and your sell swords. Though, I must admit Kaleb," he turned towards me and I saw his eyes had turned completely black. "You have done me a service as well, by placing the entire council in one room. Like *fish* in a barrel."

He shot a meaningful look at Callum who frowned.

"Cease this nonsense," Ernest said, speaking up for the first time since the fighting began. "Your threats are cheap gnome; how do you plan to hurt us when you're flanked by armed men with no allies anywhere near here?"

"How easily you all forget," he said in a chuckle, "I've said it plenty of times. Gnomes are a hive mind species, losing one vessel is akin to shedding some hair. Deadly…explosive…hair."

Jumping up onto his seat the gnome's body began to glow with a bright orange light which only intensified with the voracity of his mad cackling.

"What the hell is going on?" Fredrick shouted, "kill him, kill him now!"

The mercenaries flanking the gnome raised their swords, and then he exploded.

BOOM!

The End

Achievement Unlocked:
In A While, Bibliophile

Congratulations, you have reached the end of this book.
I guess it was bound to happen eventually.
Now is the perfect time to leave a rating or review
(pretty please?) In all seriousness it really helps trick the
algorithm into showing this book to other people,
which is a really novel idea.

All hail the algorithm.
Reward: -2 Intelligence Points

Acknowledgements

Thank you to my wife, Leah, for putting up with me during my hyperfocus days when all I want to talk about is books, writing and numbers going up. I love you and I'm thankful that you never get *too* annoyed with me for this. Big thanks to my mum who is always the first person to read these books and help me correct the copious typos that I always make. And, of course, a shout out to my friends and other family members who have always supported me in my creative endeavours. Lastly, this publication would not have been possible without the help and support from the team at Level Up Publishing. Cheers for taking a chance on this novel, hopefully it was worth it.

Cullen Spurr (known as Panda Sage on Royal Road) is a British novelist and web serial writer of series you've probably never heard of, such as: ODINSALL, The Crimson Cage and The Celestial Map.

(Side effects of Cullen Spurr novels may include but are not limited to: sudden dizziness, loss of reflection, an unexplainable aversion to garlic, craving bacon in the middle of the night when you don't have any in the fridge, and insomnia.)

If you find that you are experiencing any of the above then please do not hesitate to contact him in one of the following ways:

Facebook: @cullenspurrauthor

Instagram: @cullenspurr

Patreon: @PandaSageWebNovels

Join the Discord server

Or, you could attempt to summon him by chanting his name three times into a mirror, downing a shot of flaming tequila and shedding a single tear—no more, no less.

The Part Where I Shout Out Facebook Groups So They'll Let Me Spam Their Members:

LitRPG Books – This is the perfect group to get recommendations and talk to other, likeminded people about the genre. I comment on a lot of posts here, so feel free to say hello some time.

GameLitRPG Society – Another awesome group for likeminded people to chat about their favourite books and Royal Road fictions.

LitRPG Legends – A hangout spot for all things LitRPG and Gamelit related, they also have a discord server.

For more Level Up books, please visit:
https://www.levelup.pub/books

From there you can sign up to be an ARC reader for our books, find out about new releases, apply to join in the WhatsApp group and read dozens of features about LitRPG.